JAMES MIT

Lucia

CHAPTER 1

Looking back I guess I've always been lucky, a condition, which must include being born with all my physical faculties intact, and a reasonably agile mind, something, that none of us can, or indeed should, take for granted, although most of us do of course. So no setbacks at all really and then, from an unexpected source, I was suddenly presented with a bit of additional good fortune, quite a substantial windfall in fact.
Yes, there most certainly was. It consisted of a nice bit of cash together with some property that was left to me when I was in my early twenties, an unexpected gift that would eventually make a huge difference to my life.

My parents had provided me with a good enough education at a half decent public school, at the end of which the headmaster made a somewhat revealing written comment on my final report.
"Bright, but despite our efforts remains disinterested and seemingly uninspired!"
Well, fair enough I thought at the time, couldn't argue with that and could hardy make a protest about what was probably a quite reasonable observation.
I suppose I was very much like a clean slate waiting to be written on by some life experience or another.

Anyway, after leaving school I never had a proper job because I never needed one.
When I say 'proper job' what I mean really is one that even remotely interested me or required anything other than minimal exertion on my part.
"Only fools and horses work!"
I wonder who came up with that little gemstone of erudition?
My father had attempted, quite strongly in fact, to encourage me to follow him into the local council where he had a fairly high level job. However, the prospect of turning up at the same office every day for the foreseeable future was less than appealing.
The expectation of eventually participating in interminable departmental meetings, at which very little I suspect was ever accomplished, apart perhaps from proposing further and even longer meetings, so it all seemed fairly pointless. To me it did anyway.
And then the prospect of churning out reports that fostered even more reports that in themselves almost certainly achieved no real change in the lives of ordinary folk, which by definition surely is the whole point of having local council services in the first place.

Or was it?
Initially I suppose it was a good idea, but now it seemed that this particular institution for public administration was nothing more than a self-perpetuating aberration. An inefficient money gobbling monster if you like, that has very little to do with the original and perhaps fair minded concept that had first been devised no doubt countless eon's ago.
Sound in principal, unworkable in practice!
How do I know all this? I don't, I'm just guessing, an educated guess that is, divined after long one-sided discussions initiated by my father, who as I have said had made great efforts to bring about my induction into the large county council of a wealthy borough just north of London.
The rewards of security, a good salary and an obscenely fat pension, which he assured me (although not in so many words of course.) would be mine on retirement, might I suppose have been tempting, although not to me!
The long sentence of public service that was required to achieve it was I knew, more than I would be able to withstand.
Bureaucracy and boredom as far as the time-orientated eye could see.
So no! I think you need a special mind-set to be a civil servant and I was quite sure that I didn't have it!

This was a few years ago now, when I was in my late teens. I had left public school with a few inconsequential low grade 'A' levels and was literally twiddling my thumbs.
University? __No thanks, not interested! Not in anything at all requiring further formal education.
After a year of resisting my fathers continuing overtures to join the paper shuffling brigade at the local town-hall, I decided that I must find a job of some sort if only to avoid his increasingly reproving eye!
Following a brief search I managed to land an undemanding position with a medium sized company that produced cooking utensils.
Not on the shop floor of course as my practical skills were non-existent and would hopefully remain that way.
It was a desk-bound job in marketing, where my public school accent was deemed useful on the telephone and my acceptable appearance and amicable manner equally so during occasional meetings with clients.

So in fact the job fitted like a glove and allowed me to float along happily enough for a number of years.
A pretty girl in the accounting department soon made it known to me that I suited her requirements and my sexual needs were thereafter adequately satisfied.

Fortunately no mention was ever made of a permanent relationship and I presumed that she was as content as I was with our purely physical association.

So that was that!
But then came the pre-mentioned windfall.
It was an inheritance, which included a very decent sum of money together with a number of small houses, left to me by an aunt on my mother's side when she died quite suddenly of a heart attack. Not a young woman obviously, but not that old either, in her late sixties perhaps.
There were no other relatives except for her sister and myself, in addition to a few distant cousins, who for whatever reason didn't qualify for my aunt's generosity.
Although I barely knew her I was the only one named in the will.
I think the legacy was more out of spite to my mother really because they had never got on too well, or perhaps more to the point they hated each other.
I offered of course to pass the cash and property directly to my mother as it seemed the right thing to do, but she would have none of it. Her abject refusal implied almost that my aunt's DNA was all over the proceeds of her estate and as such couldn't be touched by human hand, not my mother's hand anyway.
Not that she needed or really wanted the legacy, she was well provided for and in any event she had very simple tastes in life, very much like myself I suppose.
I never discovered what the cause of the animosity was between them and to be honest I didn't much care, but here was an opportunity for me now to expand the limited parameters of my life and I began to consider the matter in great depth.
Start a business perhaps, but what kind of business?
I had no particular attributes apart from those previously mentioned (See above!) and very little ambition really to do anything productive.
No real interest in sport, no natural talents that I might have been able to exploit, so it was really quite a dilemma that I was faced with. Eventually I made the only possible choice left to me.
I decided to travel the world in the hope that I would discover a stimulus of some sort and to that end I have to admit that I was successful.
Not in travelling the world I should say because I never got further than the Caribbean. It wasn't that I knew anything about that particular location, as the extent of my geographical knowledge acquired at school was pretty dire.

However the Caribbean was where I ended up, and after that I never looked back.

I boarded a cruise liner in Southampton destined for the string of islands grouped around the eastern edge of the Gulf of Mexico.
First stop Cuba.
Best way to travel if you can spare the time and could afford it, so for me of course there was no problem!
The ship arrived on the large island in the Caribbean three days after my twenty-seventh birthday. Didn't bother mentioning that to anyone on the boat because they make a big thing of it on these cruises, birthdays, anniversaries, anything for a party, and the thing is I was probably the youngest on board, another good reason for keeping quiet.
In fact I kept a very low profile during the whole of the voyage. The prospect of being mothered, or perhaps something even worse, by rich elderly widows was not in the least desirable!
Average age; about sixty odd I would say, the passengers.
Mostly retired and eating their way happily to the grave, not a bad way to go I suppose because the cuisine on these luxurious ships is superb.
Combine this with the turquoise seas of the Caribbean, the balmy ocean breeze and the spectacular scenery of the Latin Hispanic islands and you have all you need for the perfect inactive vacation, together with the un-needed calories.

So yes, Cuba, Havana, a beautiful old city that was literally falling to pieces.
But what a town, the ambience, the sheer feel of it, the tropical climate, the completely alien smells, the constant noise of people and traffic, in fact everything about the place.
Abject poverty for most I suppose, but maybe that's the way it's always been, even before Castro and his dreadful predecessor.
The thing I noticed at once is that everyone; well most anyway, always seemed cheerful and certainly not under-nourished.
And boy, do they know how to enjoy themselves!
I think it's the music, the rhythmic unrelenting Afro-Caribbean sounds that are just everywhere! Seeping out of cafes and bars, constantly permeating your ears. But wonderful, that's what I really mean, instead of walking along the street you want to dance!
Music! Salsa! The life-blood of Latin America!

So you can presume correctly that I fell in love with the place almost at first sight.
Ever had that instant feeling that this was a place where you were always meant to be, well it felt exactly like that.
It was the sheer differentness of the country. After dull old England with its dull weather and dull everything else, the contrast was extraordinary.
And the women, God, the women!
I had known a couple of girls in the UK. At my age that was hardly unusual, but in Cuba, well, it was explosive! I couldn't keep my eyes to myself. Black hair, smooth honey coloured skin, clear deep brown eyes that you just wanted to plunge into.
And voluptuous, Christ they were certainly that!
One seductive smile from full lips, peeling back to reveal perfectly white teeth, was enough to vapourize any man, including most certainly me!
So I expect you've got the idea by now.
After a week I never wanted to be anywhere else, certainly not back in dreary north London.
I only experienced the best of it I suppose, I had money, I had all the time in the world and I was of course young.

Purely on impulse I decided to stay for a while. A twenty-four hour stopover simply wasn't enough, not for me anyway, and to the initial consternation of the ship's purser I allowed the vast liner to sail on its way without me. I needed time to discover more about this fascinating place.

It wasn't very long, only a few weeks in fact before I fell in love!
I mean *really* fell in love!
Carnal at first I suppose if I'm to be completely honest, but no, it was so much more than that.
Besotted is the only word that fits, besotted to the exclusion of everything.
Lucia! Sensuous, beautiful almost beyond description, perfect in every way.
'Love is blind', so it's said, and I was certainly that, blind to everything except her.

I met her in a bar just after midday less than a month after arriving on the island. It was in Calle de Galiano, a run-down part of the town, and there were certainly plenty of those in Havana after countless decades of non-investment had allowed the grand old colonial buildings to slide gradually into decay.
I was having a cup of coffee while I watched an unfamiliar world go by when she plonked her lovely bottom on a chair opposite, dropping a bag of

groceries between her feet and calling out to a waiter for a glass of water in that staccato Spanish tone that they all seem to use.

I didn't know one word of the language of course, which didn't seem to matter very much as so many of them seemed to speak English. From the days of senor Batista no doubt when the American Mafia owned the bloody place, lock, stock and roulette wheel.
She didn't notice me. In fact the only reason that she was sitting opposite on the same table was because it was one of only a few available seats in the busy, crowded cafe.
But I noticed her all right and could certainly be forgiven for that because she was everything and more that I have earlier described about Cuban women.
The waiter brought her a glass of water and she sipped at it thirstily.
It was hot, well nothing unusual about that, not in Cuba, and I could see tiny beads of sweat on her smooth forehead and semi-circles of damp beneath her armpits on the short sleeved white shirt she was wearing, under which the prominent outline of firm breasts were clearly evident.
Her long hair sort of flowed outwards, tightly waved and as black as night, the African heritage clearly apparent, then, overtaken by gravity it tumbled in an even cascade around her beautiful face, which unlike her hair, had the even features of Spanish ancestry mixed with those of the natives of South America.
I had nothing to lose and had certainly never been shy so I spoke up while I had the chance.
'Pretty hot again!'
Was the only stupid comment I think of on the spur of the moment.
To my surprise she turned and gave me a devastating smile, details of which also described previously.
'Dis is Cuba senor, you shouldn' be surprised!'
She replied at once.
There was a distinct Americano accent laced with the Spanish.
'You on holiday mister? You look a bit young, the tourists here usually carry walkin' sticks!'
'Yes I'm on holiday!'
I replied.
'Not quite that I guess, just travelling around really.'
'You are lucky you can afford to do that.'
'You're probably right. __My name's Harry!'
I held out my hand, which she took at once with her's, slim and and smooth and with long light brown fingers.
'Lucia.'

She said simply.
We began an animated conversation that was as natural as breathing.
She was a hooker of course, even I guessed that at my tender young age, not that I cared one bit.
After an hour we went back to her apartment, a couple of run-down rented rooms on an upper floor of a crumbly old Hispanic-colonial building that in that part of town was like so many other brightly painted, falling-apart tenements in central Havana.
Then, in a tiny bedroom with the window opened onto the street, she stripped off her clothes unashamedly and perhaps with justifiable pride, because her naked body was as close to perfect as made no difference.
No need for detail, but the next hour was probably the best and the closest to heaven that I had ever experienced in the whole of my short existence.

Yes, Lucia Jose Martinez, the woman who captured my heart and changed my life forever!

She moved into the hotel I was staying at for the next month or so.
Then she suggested a plan, which to many, ok then most, might seem bizarre, although I think quite frankly that I would have gone along with any plan she came up with.
I suppose at the time it was the idea of living for the moment, the 'Sartre' experience, to exist on the knife-edge of the present,
very popular in those days during the early-nineties.
Free living and free love, as long as you could afford it!
The point I should make here was that Lucia was not only beautiful, but an innately intelligent woman. Never went to school beyond secondary level, even though the Castro regime encouraged education and made it available to all.
Her reason for this, so she said, was the increasing doctrinal influence of the communist state, supported and influenced of course by the Soviets, which inhibited a broader educational view of the world in general.
Lucia's parents had both been killed fighting for the revolution and she had been cared for by her grandmother who had looked after her earthly requirements, leaving Lucia to her more academic needs and to virtually educate herself, which she did with admirable dedication, seeking out books that had been banned as corrupt by the worker state.
There was still an older element of the population in Cuba at that time that had hidden away degenerate literature, books by the great American and European authors thought to be politically subversive and as such unacceptable in Fidel's brave new totalitarian world.

Lucia had, at some risk to both the lender and the borrower, sought out these forbidden volumes and became an avid reader.

So why had she become a prostitute, a woman of the streets?
I asked her this and her answer was surprising.
Apart from the money, she had said, as it was no easy matter making a living on the economically as well as politically isolated island, she had told me quite openly that she enjoyed what she did, choosing her clients rather than them choosing her.
In truth I could find no fault with her reasoning.
But back now to Lucia's suggestion.

It was in fact that we should get married!
This was for practical purposes she told me, more than anything else. Did she love me I pondered? I wasn't sure at the time or though I had certainly fallen in love with her. Her free spirited manner, her quick mind, her small kindnesses to most of the people she came into contact with and of course the truly wonderful uninhibited sex. We certainly mustn't forget that!
So, as to the more practical reasons for her idea!
She hoped to get away from Cuba eventually, from the politics anyway, which she said were stifling her and I believed her.
So one evening in a bar she proposed to me.
She knew that I was by no means poor, I had already made that clear to her, so I suppose it was an added attraction, which again she was quite open about. In return she promised, quite solemnly, that she would be good to me as long as I was good to her. Not a bad deal when you think about it!
It also meant she could eventually get a passport, a British passport.

So, I didn't even think twice about it, God no!
This beautiful woman was like a gift from heaven. That was how I saw it then, that's how I still see it. And so that's what we did.
It was a civil wedding with just a few invited guests, including the owner of the bar where we had met, a man who she knew well, both as a friend and also on a business level, because that was the place where she had usually found her previous clients.
In fact the proprietor acted as the best man.
Her closest and dearest relative had been her grandmother, but she was absent from the celebration having passed on some years previously through an untreated illness. However an elderly aunt on her mothers side, turned up for the wedding.

It could have been a Catholic ceremony I suppose because in spite of the revolution, religious faith in Cuba was still immensely strong, however Lucia would have no truck with religion of any kind.

So it was a joyful occasion, for both of us, and also I was quite certain, for all those that attended.

A big party was held afterwards in the bar where I had first met her and in addition to invited guests, many people just simply turned up, neighbours and people that she knew locally, with the proprietor footing the whole bill on his own firm insistence.

There was plenty of drinking, music and dancing late into the night. I wasn't able to participate in the last activity, simply because I didn't know how, but it didn't matter because it was sheer pleasure to watch Lucia and her friends enjoying the insistent rhythms of the small live band that had turned up for the occasion and played until the early hours.

And afterwards there was a honeymoon, a trip to Cienfuegos, which is a small town on the coast on the other side of the island, a torturous trip made by bus through the mountains, which took many hours.

Why there? Because another younger aunt with her husband lived just outside of the town in a house that was little more than a rough shack, built close to the sea, and with scenery so spectacular it literally took my breath away.

For eight days we did little more than swim and make love and sleep for long hours during the day. In the evening we assisted in making food together with the middle-aged couple who occupied the house, a couple who's lifestyle seemed idyllic and far removed from the intense political climate of Havana.

They spoke no English and I felt slightly left out as Lucia and her two relatives chattered away constantly in a language of which I knew only half a dozen words.

A nudge, or with the slight touch of Lucia's hand on my arm, accompanied with a lovely smile reassured me that I wasn't totally excluded.

'They like you Harry! If they didn' I would have walked us both out of here the day we arrived.'

I couldn't understand how these two people managed to make a living and the subject never came up.

I asked Lucia at one point if they had children, but a very brief 'No!' put an end to that conversation.

None of that mattered, not the language barrier or anything else, as our brief stay in Cienfuegos was a wonderful form of escapism, for me at least because I had never experienced anything like it before in my life. The

simplest of simple pleasures enhanced by an environment that was unbelievably beautiful.
So in that period of two weeks or so I got to know Lucia even more, and the revelation was by no means disappointing.
Eventually of course we had to leave this little isolated haven of peace, life moves on, except that I wasn't sure exactly where to at that point.

'So what now Lucia?'
We were on the ramshackle bus as it fought its way up through the mountains towards the town of Colon, lurching around hairpin bends, the engine revving at full throttle, the gears crunching noisily as the driver changed from one to another in a constant battle with the gradients,
With the permanent roar of the engine and the bus continually lurching from one side to the other on the poorly maintained road, it was impossible to sleep or even to doze for ten minutes or so in the unrelenting heat.
For me at least, because half of the passengers seemed to have no problem at all.
An old man in the seat opposite was leaning against his wife, his eyes closed and his mouth hanging open. At least I presumed she was his wife because she was leaning against him and was also sound asleep.
The constant jerking and swaying of the old vehicle didn't appear to bother Lucia much either. She was sitting next to the window gazing out at the hills and the dense undulating forests of Pine trees stretching away into the distance.
I had rested my hand on a firmly rounded thigh and she turned to me with another of her lovely smiles.

'What did you say Harry?'
'Nothing important. I was just wondering what we should do when we get back to Havana.'
'The firs' thing we do carino,'
She whispered.
'__ is go to bed and fuck, that's what I would really like to do.'
Moving her head towards me she kissed me firmly on the mouth.
As well as feeling an instant surge of desire, I couldn't help but smile at her frank and unaffected manner.
Lucia's openness in all things was actually refreshing, __ once you got used to it of course.
'Well I can't disagree with that particular idea sweetheart.'
I replied.

'Although that's not quite what I meant, we have to decide what we are going to do. We can't stay in a hotel in Havana forever!'
'Then we shall move back into my apartment!'
'Well we can, but__'
'Don' you like my apartment Harry?'
She was in a teasing mood now, grinning as she spoke.
'The apartment is er, fine. A bit small, but, __well I was actually thinking beyond that Lucia. __The future I mean. __Would you like to go to England?'
'It rains a lot, is that true carino? An' i's also cold so I've heard.'
'Both correct I'm afraid, I have to admit to you love!'
'Would I like it in England Harry?'
She was gazing at me with that uninhibited expression that I was now almost getting accustomed to. It was a look that demanded a truthful response.
'Would you like England?'
I considered for a moment, glancing out at the distant tree covered mountains and the deep blue sunlit sky beyond them.
'Mmm. __Well we could always go for a short visit I suppose.'
I remarked hopefully.
'Give you a flavour of the place!'
'Do you wanna' go back to England Harry?'
'Well I'm not sure anymore, but we could always visit I suppose!'
'Vale carino, we will visit, but in the summer, yes?'
I smiled at her, at that lovely face framed by the wild abundance of dark hair. She was irresistible, and I was once again completely overwhelmed by her.
I still found it difficult to believe that only a month or so before, I had just arrived in what, for me at least, was a magical place.
Even with the poverty and the crazy political system that couldn't possibly survive now that the USSR had recently abandoned the island as a result of its own radical political changes.
Because of this, the economic hardships were already becoming apparent in Cuban society.
But in spite of it all, the country with its easy pace of everyday life, the cheerfulness and good humour of the Cuban people and their irrepressible zest for living, which seemed somehow to be an innate part of their character, was something I had never before encountered.

Apart from the occasional, uninspiring visit to Northern France with my parents, this was after all, the first time I had ever left my homeland in the UK and this new experience was beyond anything I could ever possibly have imagined, but then I had a great deal more to learn, as I would soon discover.

'We will be at Colon in one hour Harry. Then we can get something to eat and talk about what we shall do when we reach Havana. Vale?'
I smiled at her.
'Sure Lucia. Vale! __Anyway there's no hurry, I still feel as though we're on holiday.'
'It's true carino!'
She linked her arm with mine.
'But you mus' get a job soon, because now you have a wife who you must attend to!'
'I don't need to work sweetheart.'
'So I married a rich man then?'
'Not rich exactly, but I have a good income. I told you this.'
'Yes you did. I am joking with you Harry.'
She leaned her head on my shoulder and we were both silent for a while, swaying together from side to side, lulled by the constant motion of the bus.
The smell of her hair was intoxicating, the smoothness of her skin against my arm, utterly sensual. I rested my hand on her thigh again and she sighed, moving even closer, pressing her leg against mine.
Suddenly Havana and our room in the hotel were too far away.

We stopped for an hour in Colon and got something to eat, while the old bus got its breath back with the driver sound asleep behind the wheel.
Then, together with the dozen or so passengers, we climbed back on board and started off again, now on an easy downhill gradient towards Havana, reaching the city at dusk.

In the hotel room we virtually tore each other's clothes off and were quickly sprawled on the bed making love with a joy and a passion that was impossible to describe.
Too tired even to wash after the long tedious journey we lay close together, the window open to the warm night air.
With the low sound and the rhythmic beat of Cuban music drifting upwards from a bar on the opposite side of the street, I drifted into a deep slumber.

Chap. 2

I woke at around eight after a long dreamless sleep. Lucia lay with her face towards me, the single white sheet that partially covered her, a perfect contrast to her naked light brown body. Her eyes were closed, her dense black hair splayed across a pillow.

With sublime pleasure I stared at her for several moments wondering, not for the first time, how a woman with such astonishing beauty could ever have been created.

At that moment it was easy to believe in a God of some kind.

Then I got out of bed, carefully, so as not to wake her.

The noise of a new day in the capital floated up from a street that was already buzzing with the sounds of traffic and people.

I got myself a glass of water, closed the window and slipped back into bed again.

Staring up at the ceiling I tried to think about exactly what lay ahead. We couldn't stay here forever, although the idea was certainly tempting. I had to make a plan of some sort and I knew that. The difficulty was deciding what! A solution seemed elusive.

'What are you thinkin' about Harry!'

Her voice startled me and I turned to look at her.

'Thought you were asleep.'

'I was carino, now I'm awake, so tell me?'

I yawned widely, thought for a moment longer and then told her what was on my mind.

'The same as yesterday really, what do you want to do? __I mean, you don't want to go and live in England__'

'Did I say that?'

She stretched and then reaching her arm across, pulled me towards her.

'Not in so many words.'

'Do you wanna go back to England carino?'

I turned to her again and smiled.

'I'm not sure anymore. I know I'm seeing the best of Cuba, the best meaning you really!'

'No' jus' me Harry.'

'Mostly you sweetheart if we hadn't met in that bar, I would probably have left Cuba by now and be off on my odyssey again. It's funny the way things happen.'

'Wha' does odyssey mean?'

'Journey. Trip around the world.'

'So because of me, you__'

'Are the luckiest man alive!'

I interrupted.
She laughed this time at my impromptu compliment.
'That was nice Harry.'
'Also completely true.'
'Vale, so why not stay here carino?'
'And do what Lucia?'
She turned on her back and stretched both arms out, the sheet slipping down to reveal her perfect breasts.
'I don' know harry, __buy a boat maybe, what about that? Take the Yankee's on fishing trips. They have all the money.'
'Could do I suppose, but I suspect you'll get bored with that pretty quickly. And anyway what do I know about fishing?'
'You're wrong about that carino. When I was very small I used to go fishing with my padre and I loved it.
That was before he died fighting for Castro of course.
Have you ever been deep sea fishing Harry?'

She had me there because I'd never done anything remotely like it, not even in a river in England. My old man wasn't up for that kind of activity. For any kind of remotely adventurous pastime come to that! Civil servants have a particular approach to leisure activities; at least my father did, so maybe I shouldn't generalize.
If the outcome was unpredictable then he wasn't interested.
Visits to museums, walks in Hyde Park and the occasional trip to the seaside were the closest we ever got to adventure of any kind.

'No sweetheart, never!'
I responded.
'__And I'm not sure if I'm up to it because I've never tried.'
'Then 'ow can you say until you do?'
I smiled, giving way to her unassailable logic.
'You got me Lucia. The most exciting thing I ever did in my life was to get on a passenger boat and sail to Cuba.
Best thing I ever did in fact because I met you!'
'That was also a lovely thing to say carino, but I will probably drive you crazy eventually.'
'I'll take my chances. You've changed the way I see things entirely Lucia, and I can never look back now. __In fact I don't want to look back.'
'More compliments.'
She looked at me with an expression of affection, as though for a child rather than a man, a husband, or a lover.
'You deserve them.'

I replied simply.

'I hope I do Harry.'

She continued looking at me with that direct gaze she had, as though she could almost see what I was thinking, and who knows perhaps she could.

'You're a good man and I want you to love me.'

'Well I do love you and you should believe that!'

'Yeah, but maybe it's jus' the sex?'

'Making love to you is __wonderful Lucia, I don't have to tell you that, __but that's not the reason I married you.'

I meant what I said and because of that, because I was completely sincere, I think she believed me.

She put her hand on the back of my neck.

'Kiss me Harry. I think tha' you mean what you say, so now is a good time to kiss me.'

Which is what I did, needing no further encouragement from this beautiful woman who had changed my life completely.

An hour later we were having breakfast in a café outside the capital building, a brilliant white edifice that looked almost identical, albeit a smaller version of the government building in Washington.

Lucia looked wonderful, even simply clothed in a light green dress and with her jet-black hair, which I had brushed for her before we left the room in the hotel, bursting outwards in a glorious cascade.

'Ok, so do you wanna talk about my idea Harry?'

'Why not? __ You mean about getting a boat.'

'Sure. __Look, Fidel is realizin' that we have to get along with the Americans if we are to survive.'

'Yes he does, I mean he will, __like it or not!'

'Oh he don' like it carino believe me, but 'e has no choice. We don' want a regime similar to Batista again, but times have gotta change.'

'So your idea is to attract American tourists and separate them from their Dollars, is that correct?'

I smiled at her as I spoke.

'No that isn't fair Harry. __We take them fishing, get them drunk and *then* we separate them from their cash.'

'Sounds good to me sweetheart!'

'Do you mean it carino?'

She looked at me wide eyed and I could see now that she really was serious about the plan.

'Yes of course love!'

'So can you afford to buy a boat carino?'

'Depends how big it is.'

'Well it has to be quite big, __no muy grande, pero__!'
In her enthusiasm she had slipped into her native tongue.
'I's easy to get a bargain now in Cuba Harry. __Are you really sure tha' you want to do this?'
She looked at me with clear, unveiled excitement.
'Yes of course, why not! As a matter of fact it's not such a bad idea really. Problem is I know nothing about boats or fishing for that matter. I led a sheltered life before I met you.'
'Sheltered life?'
She wrinkled her smooth forehead.
'It means I never did anything exciting.'
'Well I change' all that for you Harry, ain't that right!'
'You certainly did honey. I don't think I realized what being alive actually meant until quite recently.'
She leaned across and kissed my cheek.
'You're a nice man Harry! __A good fellow, __is tha' what you English say?'
'Yeah. __It is if it's true!'
I looked into those deep brown eyes and fell in love all over again.

'Ok, so when do you want to do this Lucia? __Buy this fishing boat I mean, assuming you've got one in mind that is.'
'We can go today carino!'
'Are you serious! Go where?'
'The other side of the bay, that's where the boat is tied up.'
I laughed at that point. Lucia had obviously thought about this in some detail.
'Sounds like you've got this all organized.'
'So, shall we go?'
'What *now* you mean?'
'Sure. The guy who owns the boat lives on board.'
'So if we do buy it he'll be homeless, is that right?'
'I guess so. I didn' ask him!'

To get to the ferry terminal we caught a taxi, a splendid old Chevrolet convertible that must have been built thirty years before, but looked as though it had just left the assembly line in Detroit.
The journey across the bay was short enough and we wandered ashore with the other passengers into the rundown, impoverished district of Regla.
'Do we get a taxi Lucia?'
I asked.

'We can walk, I's not so far.'

We set off along the road that ran along the side of the bay with dilapidated warehouses on one side and the usual groups of run down tenement buildings and a few cafes with the omnipresent sound of music drifting out into the street.

There were merchant ships tied alongside the docks with men unloading cargoes by crane, the modern container ports not yet having made an appearance on the unindustrialized Caribbean island.

The jetties leading out into the clear water gradually became smaller, with a few aging pleasure boats tied alongside, then an area used by fishing vessels with plastic crates piled up along the dockside.

At the last of these a solitary boat was moored.

It needed a coat of paint. That was the first thing that I noticed. Apart from that it seemed, to my inexperienced eye, to be quite a strong looking vessel.

Built from timber rather than plastic, about forty foot in length and broad beamed. There was a large cabin at the front with a covered bridge on top, which was open at the back, revealing the steering wheel and a couple of high backed chairs that were screwed to the roof of the cabin below.

At the stern there was a large open area of planked decking with a strong looking single chair, very much it seemed like that used by dentists or barbers. It faced backwards, or aft as they say, and was also firmly bolted down.

On the rear deck, a man in an unbuttoned flowery shirt, and grubby shorts, was sitting in a fold-up canvas chair reading a newspaper and drinking beer from a bottle.

Lucia called out to him.

'Alberto ola! Buenos tardes, como esta?'

Without waiting for a response she was already trotting confidently down the makeshift gangway, jumping down onto the deck.

I followed gingerly along the narrow plank, glancing down at the clear water on each side, blemished with streaks of oil that reflected the full spectrum of the rainbow.

The man looked old, with a weathered face that was adorned with a magnificent white mustache the colour of which was matched by the thick unruly hair that burst out from beneath a panama hat.

When he smiled his teeth were equally brilliant white, with the exception of a single sparkling gold tooth that replaced an incisor.

'Lucia! Que tal chica?'

'Muy bien!'

She replied, leaning over and planting a kiss on a wrinkled cheek.

'No Spanish Alberto, vale! This man wants to buy your boat, so serious talk, ok!'
'The boat is not for sale guapa!'
'It *was* last week hombre!'
She turned to me with a smile as I stepped down onto the stern of the boat.
'This is how they negotiate in Cuba carino! They are, __how you say?'
She slapped a hand against her perfect derriere.
'A pain in the backside!'
I translated.
The man pushed himself up out of his chair, his ample belly leading the way and forcing apart the two halves of the 'Palm beach' shirt to reveal a barrel chest covered in curling hair that in contrast was dark grey in colour.
'You wanna beer Senor?'
Another broad smile, the gold tooth twinkling.
'Sure Alberto!'
Lucia answered for me.
'One for me as well! __Then we talk about this boat!'

The man disappeared below deck. I heard the rattle of a fridge door and the clink of bottles, then he reappeared handing a beer to each of us. He took an opener from the pocket of his shorts and levered the caps off of each in turn.
'Salud!' He offered cheerfully and the three of us touched bottles together. The sun was hot now and we gathered under the wooden overhang of the fly-deck. The man Alberto sank into his chair again while Lucia grabbed a couple of beer crates and she and I both sat, tipping back cold beer into dry thirsty mouths.
'I can't sell you this boat senor, how will I make my living?'
With a bottle in one hand and a newly lit cigar in the other, the man spread his arms apart defensively, but Lucia was regarding him with scorn.
'When was the las' time you went fishing Alberto? Your brother died six months ago an' lef' you money! __God rest his soul!'
The man shrugged.
'It's true, he was a good man! __But when the money is spent, what then?'
'Well I guess you must go back to fishing again. __In your other boat!'
She added with a sly grin.
'What other boat chica?'
He lifted bushy eyebrows in surprise.
'That new one, tied up along the dock there!'
She pointed to a sleek new motor cruiser moored further along in the port.
'Madre mia! How you know this Lucia?'
'My spies tell me everythin'. That's how!'

He couldn't resist a deep belly laugh, drawing on the corona cigar and exhaling a cloud of white smoke.

'You don' miss much guapa!'

'So wha'd you say Alberto? Tell me your price!'

He glanced at her quizzically.

'What d'you wan' the boat for?'

'Wha' do you think hombre! For fishing!'

'*Feeshing!*'' He gave out another bellow of laughter.

'Sure why not? This man here is my business partner. Together we will separate the gringo's from their American Dollars. Help them catch swordfish maybe, get them drunk, maybe sell them some Cuban cigars!'

'Chica, wad' you know abou' *feeshing*?'

'Not too much, only what my padre showed me, but you can show us as well Alberto. All part of the deal, no?'

She gave him one of her irresistible smiles, a brief flash of white teeth against her deeply tanned skin.

He turned to me.

'Senor, theez woman, watch out for her amigo!'

'I am!' I responded.

'We were married a few weeks ago.'

His look of surprise was, I was sure, quite genuine as he leaned forward in the canvas 'directors seat'.

'Lucia I din' know this! I am so happy for you chica! It's won'erful news.'

He turned to me.

'But you are not American No?'

'English.'

I responded.

'And a good man Alberto!'

Lucia broke in at once, clutching my arm briefly.

His look of surprise still lingered and it didn't take a lot of thought to guess why, given Lucia's past occupation

'But you never invited me to the wedding chica. I am __muy triste__ como se dice?'

'Sad!' Lucia replied with another grin.

'Si, very sad.'

His comment was accompanied by another huge plume of cigar smoke.

'It was nothing fancy Alberto. Jus' a few friends, tha's all, No church, no Padre involved.'

He rocked his head from side to side.

'Who gets married in the church anymore chica? Not in Castro's godless society '

He paused.
'But I mus'n' call you "chica" anymore. __Now you are Senora!'
'Call me what you like Alberto!'
She commented with another devilish smile.
'As long as we get a deal about the boat.'

The elderly man finished his beer and tossed the bottle into an empty fish crate. Then he stubbed out the half smoked cigar on a leg of his chair.
'Ok Lucia! Now I show you the boat, an' we take a liddle trip around the bay so you can see that everythin' is workin' good.
Then Senora. we talk abou' money!'

Twenty thousand American. That was the figure arrived at during the haggling process, during which I took a back seat. From choice really as it was all held in Spanish and at times was, shall we say animated if not actually fractious.
I've no doubt I'd got the wrong end of the stick because Spanish speaking people generally are quite volatile and tend to use a higher decibel level when it comes to discussions of any kind. This was an aspect of their nature to which I quickly became accustomed.

It took a few days to get the money transferred to a Cuban bank and then withdrawn in cash in American dollars, with much serious debate among bank officials as to the legitimacy of the transaction, however with Lucia's almost natural diplomacy and a brown envelope, which she passed surreptitiously to the bank manager, all was eventually well.

It didn't seem like a bad deal to me. Although the boat was old and of timber construction it seemed pretty sound, at least to my inexperienced eye.
The engine of American make, still with the original yellow paint and the legend 'Caterpillar' molded into the metal casting, also seemed in good shape and thundered away quite happily on the hour long trip that we had made around the natural haven that formed the port of Havana.
Lucia took no chances however and insisted on a marine insurance certificate being issued before any money changed hands.
I had a married a smart, street-wise woman there was no doubt about that.

'So now I'm twenty thousand out of pocket and we have a fishing boat! What happens next Lucia?'
'Carino, with my plan we will get the money back in six months!'

We were lying in bed in Lucia's run down apartment having woken in late afternoon after our siesta, a Spanish tradition which was making increasing sense to me after the short months I had spent in the constant heat of the Caribbean island.

'Six months seems optimistic, and anyway you haven't told me what the plan is yet sweetheart, not in detail anyway.'

She turned on her side next to me with one hand supporting the side of her head, her lush dark hair cascading over her arm and with one smooth delicious breast suspended invitingly above crumpled sheets

'Harry, I tol' you all this before.'

She scolded gently.

'Now the boat is getting a __revision, __how d'you say?'

'I suppose you mean overhaul.'

I murmured, staring at her with a grin as I corrected her English.

'Ok wad'ever! __An' a nice paint job, then like I say we are in business! Vale.'

'I guess so, but__'

'Then we get the cash customers and take them fishing!'

'Just like that!'

'Yeah jus' like that!'

'And where do we find these people? We can't exactly sail across to Miami and put up a sign! __Or can we?'

'Miami is three hundred kilometers carino! An' we would be picked up by the U.S. coast guard long before we arrive there.'

'So?'

She slipped her arm around me.

'The Yanks get to Cuba via Mexico or maybe Jamaica or one of the other islands so there's no problem with visa's. Believe me there are people waiting Harry. Next week on Wednesday we have four Americans, our first customers.'

'Assuming the boat is ready of course, and seaworthy! The guys working on it seem to have, shall we say, a relaxed attitude when it comes to deadlines.'

'Don't worry carino. They will have me to deal with an' they know it! The boat will be ready.'

'Ok I leave it to you. __Anyway where did you find these Americans?'

'Simple. I went to the best hotels and talk' to the people on the desk. They will get a commission for every payin' customer. The cash incentive always works Harry.'

She raised her eyebrows, daring me with a 'next question' smile to which I responded.

'Right, __just one problem now, we don't know anything about fishing!'

'Maybe you don' Harry, but my father was a fisherman all his life. I tol' you before, I have been out at sea with him many times. __An' with my uncle as well, he is also in the fishing business.'
'Another uncle?' I raised an eyebrow.
'Sure. On my Mothers side.'
'So why couldn't we use his boat and pay him?'
'He doesn't own a boat carino. He works for a company.'
'A company! I though everything here was owned by the state.'
'Not anymore Harry! Times are changing.'
'Yeah I guess you're right.'
I glanced at her skeptically.
'Lucia, can we really make any money out of this?'
'Well let's see!'
She put on an exaggerated expression of seriousness.
'Two hundred American dollars for a whole day__'
'That doesn't sound much after expenses, fuel and whatever!'
'Each carino, *each*! __Tha's eight hun'red bucks for one day!'
'Oh right, well that's different. __And will they pay that?'
'If they want to catch a Marlin Harry, tha's what they will pay!'
'Ok! __Well __I suppose it doesn't sound like such a bad idea after all sweetheart.'
'No it's not a bad idea carino, it's a good idea. __Trus' me!'

I couldn't hold back a grin because I knew she wanted this little scheme to work. We didn't need the money and she knew that because I had been entirely open with her about my financial assets in England. I suppose within reason we could live a comfortable life and didn't need to earn a living, but she was determined right from the start that she would make a success of this venture and I certainly didn't want to discourage her in any way. It made her happy, so it made me happy.
With every day that passed I was becoming more attached to this woman. Yes she was beautiful, no question. The sex was wonderful, no question there either, but it was so much more than that. I think it was her disarming openness, about everything in fact. I had never met anyone else in my admittedly short existence who possessed such an unadorned, cheerful and optimistic view of life. It was more than refreshing it was a revelation! Years afterwards I still used to ask myself what the odds were of meeting someone like her in such an outlandish place as Cuba.
A person who's honesty and straightforward approach was almost disconcerting. Whose cheerfulness and love of life was an inspiration.

I kissed her briefly and jumped out of bed pulling on my trousers and a shirt.
'Come on Lucy, let's go for walk.'
It was just after five, the best part of the day as it was cooler and the sun would soon be dropping to the horizon. In two hours it would be getting dark.
'What's this 'Lucy' thing Harry?'
She asked. She was still in bed her arm still propping up her head the luscious mantle of dark hair overwhelming her slim naked shoulders.
'Not sure love really. It just, __I don't know, __came out! Is it ok if I call you that? Lucy's an English name.'
'I don't mind carino.' She shook her head and smiled.
'Do you love me Harry?'
I laughed at once
'What kind of question is that sweetheart!'
'My kind'a question!'
Her dark brown eyes stared up at me.
I finished fastening the buttons on my shirt as I spoke.
'Lucia I love you more than I can ever adequately describe. You are my life now. I don't need anything or anyone else as part of it! __That's the best answer I can give you on the spur of the moment, although I can probably improve on that.'
Her expression for once was serious, which was unusual for her.
'No Harry, you don' need to. Tha' was a good thing to say.'
She slipped out of bed.
'Now I gotta' pee, then we go for a walk!'
'Dressed like that!'
I remarked with contrived amazement.
'Sure! __Why not!'
She replied with a smile, closing the door to the bathroom before I could respond.

Oddly enough I never called her by the name Lucy ever again. It just didn't seem to fit somehow.
However we did find another use for the title.

We walked down to the sea wall at Malecon and took an easy stroll along the front towards the remains of the old castle of San Salvador.
Across the narrow inlet to the port the lighthouse stood out clearly against the deep blue, darkening sky. In an hour or so it would be sweeping its light across the entrance to the bay.

I sat next to her on the ancient but solid sea wall that acted as a breakwater in bad weather.
On the opposite side of the road that ran the length of the sea front, the decrepit rows of tenement buildings, dating from the early part of the last century and with the familiar covered arched walkways at street level, were badly in need of renovation after many years of neglect, not only by the communists, but by previous fascist dictators who had pocketed public money at every opportunity.
At least Fidel had made a valiant effort to improve the lot of the masses, no easy matter with the Americans doing everything they could to destroy the Cuban economy.
Now, reluctantly, the regime was beginning to embrace the capitalists, if for no other reason than merely to survive.
'Embrace!' __If ever there was an inappropriate word to use that was just about the most!
'Reluctantly accept!' 'Grimly acknowledge!'
Nope! That didn't do it either.
Castro I believe did his level best to improve the lot of his impoverished and underdeveloped country.
Supported by the Soviets, sure! But was he a rabid Marxist or a genuine freedom fighter?
When he was hiding out in the mountains, living rough with his rag-tag group of revolutionaries, it must have required enormous courage and will to carry the fight to the well-equipped army of Batista and to win against such formidable odds.
Afterwards maybe the picture got blurred and he certainly made mistakes in his alliances, foolishly offering a haven for soviet military bases.
But there it is.
Cuba is still a socialist country. For how long, who can tell? I've always been an apolitical bystander and I planned to stay that way.

'Wha'd are you thinkin' about carino?'
Lucia had taken my hand in both of hers and was resting her head against my shoulder.
'Oh different things. __About you, about Cuba, __this beautiful island. __I don't think I ever want to go back to England again.'
'Never Harry!'
'No.'
'Never is a long time.'
'I'm happy here. Why would I want to go back?'
'I don' know Harry, you're family maybe, your friend's.'

'I don't really have any. Family of course, people I know, sure, acquaintances, but friend's? __Well if I'm to be honest I can't think of any.'
'No brothers, no sisters?'
'Nope!' I turned and smiled at her.
'Just me! __I haven't even told my parents yet that I'm married.'
'You 'ave to tell them sometime carino.'
'I suppose so. At the moment it doesn't seem that important.'
She laughed suddenly and put a hand on my cheek.
'An' what will you tell them? __Oh by the way ma and pa, I met a hooker in a bar in Havana, an' we got hitched! That will, __how do you say, __ put the cat in with the chickens!'
'Amongst the pigeons!'
I corrected, smiling at her again, not for what she had said but the unaffected way she had said it. Her free-spirited view of life was as always, infinitely inspiring, even intoxicating.

'So next Wednesday is our first fishing trip.'
'Yeah, our first day as partners.'
'We're partners already aren't we?'
'You know whad' I mean Harry. This is business we talkin' about!'
'Have you met these four yanks yet?'
'Jus' once at the 'otel. I tol' them they must pay us in cash dollars before we cast off.'
'Ok that sounds like a good plan. And what is my role going to be in this little enterprise?'
'Keep them happy, fetch beer for them, drive the boat. __When I'm not driving that is.'
'Ok skipper, you're the boss.'
She didn't argue the point.
'The boat should be ready tomorrow Harry. So we go across to Regla in the morning and pick it up.'
'Not too early I hope. I'm used to lying in now!'
'You' gettin' lazy muchacho!'
She scolded.
'The sooner we get busy with the fishing trips the better it will be for you. You need somethin' to occupy you' mind.'
She poked my forehead gently, then she jumped down from the low sea wall where she had been sitting.
'Ok. Vayamos carino! Let's go! __Somethin' to eat, then bed!'
Lucia took my hand as we crossed over the road, almost devoid now of traffic, and began the short walk back to the centre of the old town, to

Lucia's somewhat primitive apartment, which we had moved back into two months before, and which in spite of its run-down condition she always kept immaculately clean and tidy.

We hardly spoke as we strolled arm in arm, enjoying the warm night air and the ozone smell of the sea breeze wafting inland from behind us.
'Why did you marry me carino?'
She remarked out of the blue.
'Because you asked me to honey!'
'No. __You know whad' I mean Harry.'
I thought about it for a moment or so.
'You know why. __Because I love you and because you're an exceptional woman. __Simple as that.'
I felt her hand tighten on my arm briefly.
'An' I gotta' nice ass as well!'
'Can't disagree with that sweetheart.'
We were silent again. Then after another few seconds.
'Do you want to have kids?'
She asked again.
'I haven't really thought about it, but sure, if that's what you want Lucia.'
'I'm serious Harry!'
'I never said you wasn't.'
I turned and grinned at her, but she persisted.
'S'pose I said I was pregnant!'
'Are you?'
'No.'
'Well then it's a hypothetical question.'
'Hypo__what!'
'A question that can't really be answered.'
'Ok I geddit!'
She fell silent again as we continued our stroll in what for me at least was total contentment.
'We gonna make a success of this fishin' business!'
'With you at the helm, literally, I'm sure we will Lucia.'
'I mean it Harry!'
She glanced at me with a solemn expression, gripping my arm again momentarily.
'I know you do love. It's quite an adventure, certainly for me, as I've never done a real day's work in my life. It feels very much like plunging into the deep end.'
She turned and looked at me.

'Don' worry carino, I will stop you from drowning.'

It was true enough. What I knew about fishing boats could be written on a pin-head, or about anything else for that matter, apart from sitting behind a desk all day.
The changes in my life over the previous months had indeed been remarkable and far beyond any of my wildest predictions.
I had no idea where it was all going and I didn't really care very much as long as I was with Lucia, this exceptional woman who I felt that somehow I had known for all of my short life.
Or perhaps even in some previous existence.

Chap. 3

The following Wednesday morning at eight o'clock we waited at the dockside for the four Americans to arrive.
The boat, which we had brought across from the small shipyard in Regla was tied up at a landing. Repaired, re-fitted out and with a new coat of paint, it looked immaculate and ready for sea.
On my whim we had named the vessel the 'Lucy', and the letters had been painted in bold white letters on the stern.
It was as good a name as any, and Lucia never objected for a moment, but after that day I never referred to Lucia by that shortened title ever again.
As it turned out it was perhaps in some way prophetic.
I had, I must admit, some misgivings about the final result of the overhaul, as the team of repairers she had employed seemed to have a rather casual approach to the job, but quite obviously I had not accounted for Lucia's role in overseeing the work.

'Vale! Not bad!' She had remarked a few days before, hands on hips as she surveyed the completed vessel, with the men who had carried out the repairs standing nearby, all of them with a distinctly nervous demeanour.
'Good job muchachos!'
Then she had turned to me,
'Ok Harry, now you can pay them!'
The men waited eagerly as I counted out twenty dollar US bills.

It was the start of another brilliant sunny day. Lucia stood next to me on the quay-side as we waited for our clients. She was dressed in shorts and a tee shirt with new white deck shoes on her feet. Her long thick hair was tied tightly at the back and a green cap, with the initials of a Cuban baseball team emblazoned on the front, pulled down firmly on her head. In spite of her casual attire she somehow presented a professional air of efficiency and authority. Maybe it was the baseball cap!
'Remember Harry, no one steps on the boat until they pay!'
She gave me with one of her no-nonsense looks.
'If they turn up love!'
I remarked.
'Oh they will turn up carino! I got two hundred off of them as deposit!'
She commented, with one of her wonderful smiles.
Sure enough a few minutes later a taxi drew up and four middle-aged men got out, all dressed for the part and carrying small travel cases.

'Senora Burgess!' one of the men said as he approached, his hand outstretched towards Lucia.
'It's good to see you again.'
He had a burgeoning midriff and wore a denim shirt draped over a pair of Bermuda shorts.
'An' you sir.'
Lucia responded taking his hand.
'This is my 'usband, Harry. __He is the boss!'
She added with firm emphasis.
'Oh ok, right.'
He turned to me.
'So you're the guy who gets paid.'
He had taken an envelope from his shirt pocket and handed it to me.
'Lets get *that* out of the way.'
He added with a grin.
The other three had now climbed on board, all of them I estimated roughly the same age, with pallid faces and with the comfortable overfed appearance of affluent middle Americans.
'I'm Mike Simmons by the way.'
The man in the denim shirt offered.
'This is Kevin, Tom, and this here is Harry.'
He gestured to each in turn, eliciting murmured greetings.
'Could be some confusion there!'
He added.
'We'll get round it I'm sure.'
I remarked as pleasantly as I could.

'You're English, right?'
'Yes I am. The accent's a big give-away I'm afraid.'
'Oh I got nuthin' against the Brit's. Hand's across the water, ain't that right! I'm a great believer in that long standing alliance.'
A brief silence followed which Lucia broke.
'Ok then gen'lemen, shall we get goin'?'
She jumped down onto the broad afterdeck, where mahogany decking gleamed under new varnish.
Climbing the flight of steps to the fly-bridge she started the engine. It turned over sluggishly a few times and then burst into life with a healthy roar.
With help from the man Simmons I handed down the men's luggage from the quay-side before joining the others on board.
'Boy your wife sure is pretty!'
The denim shirt remarked, pulling himself over the side of the boat with some effort.
'She certainly is!'
I responded, untying the stern mooring line.
'I hope you don't mind me sayin'!'
'Of course not! __ Could you catch hold of this for a moment?'
I handed him the end of the rope, which was still looped around the steel bollard on the quayside.
'If you could just heave on that while I get the bow!'
I untied the mooring at the prow of the boat and drew the line back on board before hurrying back to the aft end.
Taking the line from the American I dragged it back from around the bollard, feeling the vessel drift slowly away from the quayside. Then I glanced up at Lucia who was waiting with one hand on the wheel and the other on the throttle lever.
'That's it love!' I called out.
With the rudder hard over she pushed on the short lever and the boat surged forward away from the dock, quickly gathering speed as we headed towards the harbour entrance.

'Would you chaps like a beer?'
I offered.
'That sounds like a great idea Harry!'
Denim shirt responded.
The four men had seated themselves, sprawled out on the fixed wooden bench seats that ran along the port and starboard sides of the rear deck, while I man-handled their cases into the lower cabin.

I took four cans of American beer from the fridge and brought them topside just as the boat was passing the lighthouse and heading out to sea. Passing a cold can to each of the four men I glanced up to where Lucia was standing at the helm. She was gazing straight ahead, legs splayed to balance the slight rolling motion of the sturdy little vessel.
'D'you want a drink of something love?'
I called up to her.
'No I'm ok carino!'
She called back.
'Did you take care of the fenders Harry?'
'Er, no, __short answer. I'll pull them in now.'
Annoyed with myself for the oversight I jumped up onto the narrow gangway that led past the cabin space to the bow of the boat.
Leaning over the side I untied the inflated rubber fender and carried it back to the rear deck. Lifting one of the hinged bench seats I dropped it into the storage space, then I repeated the exercise with the single rear fender.
With the task finished I sank onto the seating, gazing for a moment over the stern at the wake churned up by the propeller as the boat surged through the clear blue water.
The lighthouse and the few high-rise buildings along the shoreline were soon receding slowly into the distance.

'So Harry! You gonna find us some Marlin?'
It was the man in the denim shirt again.
'That's the plan mister Simmons although I'm a novice here. It's my wife who knows where the fish are. She's the expert.'
'Ok.'
He took a pull on the beer can.
'How come you wound up here in Cuba?'
'Pure chance really. I was embarking on the grand tour. This was the first stop.'
It was easy to tell that the other three men, apparently preoccupied with their cans of Budweiser, were listening in.
'Pretty quaint kind'a place for an Englishman to end up!'
Denim shirt continued.
'I suppose so. __There are worse places.'
'Oh sure, I'll bet there are.'
He responded with a smile, glancing up momentarily to where Lucia was standing at the wheel.
'So how long you two young people been married? __If that ain't a rude question.'

Further probing to which I responded at once. No good reason not to even though it was none of his damn business.
'Three years, just over.'
I lied confidently
At that moment Lucia had eased back on the throttle and was glancing at a chart pinned to a board next to the control panel
'Is that right sweetheart!'
I called up to her.
'Is what right harry?'
'When we got married. __A little more than three years ago now isn't it?'
'You should know carino!'
She gave me a glorious smile and then addressed the four Americans.
'Ok guys, so we go west now for abou' ten kilometers then it's time to fish!'
She pushed the lever forward again turning the wheel as the boat surged onwards, quickly gathering speed.
The coast-line was now just a hazy blur on the horizon

In little more than half an hour the boat slowed again, and Lucia cut the engine, jumping down the few steps to the rear deck.
The boat gradually came to a stop, wallowing slightly in the gentle translucent waves.
Between us we brought up rods and fishing gear from the locker below deck and handed them out to the four men.
From a lift up refrigerator I pulled out a plastic bucket of fresh bait and took it up on deck.
The four men were strapping on back harnesses and pulling wide brimmed hats down over their heads.
The man named Kevin was slapping sun-tan lotion onto his fat white legs.
Denim shirt had fixed his rod into one of the holding sockets mounted on the edge of the boat. He had fixed a lure, a lifelike rubber squid onto the line and had begun to bait the hook.
'Any chance of another can Harry?'
He called out without looking up from his task.
'Sure! Anyone else?'
There was murmured assent from the other three.
Lucia gave me a rueful look, which escaped the other four.
'I'll get them Harry.'
She was already trotting down the few steps to the lower cabin.

'What happens to the Marlin when we catch it?'
It was the man Mike again.

'Well you can release it of course__'
I began.
'Hell no, I didn't mean that!'
'Well generally we take them back and sell them to a trader. There's always a market for Marlin.'
'That sounds more like it! __Who gets the proceeds?'
I presented him with a friendly grin.
'Fifty fifty!'
'Ok that's fair.'
'Of course you have to catch one first!'
I added, still with a smile.
'Oh we'll catch some Marlin, you can be sure of that!'
He responded in a manner that wasn't exactly arrogant but not exactly amiable either.
Lucia returned with four more Budweisers and handed them out.
Then she climbed the steps to the wheel-house and seated herself at the helm.
'You guys tell me when you are ready and we'll start draggin' those lures.'
She called down.
'About five knots is that ok?'
'Yeah that should be good.'
The man Mike again.

The four men cast their lines and Lucia re-started the engine, easing the throttle lever forward so that the vessel began to move at an easy pace through the water.
The men slowly began to let out more line from their reels until the lures disappeared into the deep.

After what could have been no more than ten minutes or so, one of the reels began to scream as the line was dragged off into the sea.
One of the four pulled the rod from the holder and dropped it into the pouch of his harness. With obvious expertise he gradually put a brake on the rapidly spinning reel, as he did so the rod began to bend under the increased pressure on the line, but with practiced skill he continued to let the line spin off into the water again until barely a third was left on the reel, then he began to brake gradually, bracing himself against the increasing load on the line as the rod curved downwards even further. The other three men sat back on the bench seats muttering words of encouragement to their companion.

The rod began to straighten slightly and at once the fisherman, now with rapt concentration, reeled in the line rapidly until the rod began to bend almost double again.
At that point he dropped into the heavy swivel seat that was bolted down to the deck.
'Whad'ya think Kev'?'
The man Mike asked quietly.
'Hard to say! Two__three hundred pounds maybe.
Strap me in Mike, he's strong and he's cute!'
The man obliged and took his seat again
There was dead silence as the fisherman released a little more line and then reeled in again keeping the rod now in a tight curve.
For the next half hour the man wrestled with the unseen adversary at the other end of the line.
Without my noticing, Lucia steered the boat so that the line was as central to the stern as made little difference.

This was my first experience of course of anything related to catching large fish in the waters of the Caribbean, a few short months before I had been discussing the benefits of non-stick frying pans to wholesale buyers with my feet on a desk, one eye on the clock and the other perusing the grey sky beyond the office window.
How could I have possibly imagined the extraordinary change in my life since that first day when I set foot in Cuba.
What's the expression? 'You couldn't write a book about it!'
And yes it was exciting, no question. Watching an overweight man with surprisingly expertise and strength slowly winching in a fish that was quite obviously very big and with an equally large determination to resist capture.
Slowly, inexorably, the man reeled in the line, fighting every step of the way with the invisible monster still concealed beneath the waves, the line slicing rapidly through the surface of the sea, creating a tiny wake as the fish ran impotently back and forth in a futile effort to free itself from the barbed hook.
Then suddenly, sixty feet of so from the stern a magnificent Marlin burst through the surface in a sparkling cascade of seawater. It seemed almost to hover for a second and then, in a perfect arc plunged into the depths again. It was a sight I would never forget, the glistening color the perfectly beautiful shape of this innocent seaborne creature that was struggling so bravely to escape from its alien predator.
In that moment my impulse was to leap forward and cut the line that would shortly end the life of this wonderful fish, and release it back into its under-

water environment, an environment, which, it suddenly occurred to me, was perhaps entirely beyond the understanding of mere humans.
Standing behind the four Americans I was entirely lost in my thoughts, then it seemed in that instant almost as though there was some subliminal connection between myself and Lucia, because suddenly she was standing next to me, gripping my arm reassuringly.
'Traquilo carino!'
She whispered.
'You ok Harry?'
'Yes, er yes of course Lucia, I'm ok.'
I remarked quietly.
At that moment I realized once again how much I cared about her.
I turned to her with a feeble grin.
'Who's steering the boat?'
She shrugged.
'It can steer itself now. The fish has had enough. The game is nearly over now. We will all need to help get it on board.'
She ran her fingers gently through my hair
'You' sure you ok carino?'
'Yes of course!' I answered her at once
'Quite a dramatic event really! First time I've ever seen anything even remotely like it.'
'You'll get used to it! __ So anyway now we help these guys. My guess is the fish is abou' three, four hundred pounds so I's gonna' take some work to get it over the side.'
With a direct look, Lucia handed me a long wooden shaft with curved spikes at the end. She was holding a similar tool, as were two of the other men.
'Take it Harry an' jus' watch!'
As the exhausted Marlin was gradually brought alongside the vessel, Lucia was the first one to gaff the huge body, swinging the pole downwards and sinking the spikes into the flesh of the creature, its blood instantly colouring the water. The other two swung their gaffs at almost the same moment and then with a distinct feeling of nausea I did the same.

It took all six of us, with enormous effort to gradually haul the magnificent glistening body of the Marlin over the side of the boat.
Perhaps eight feet in length it finally slammed down hard onto the wooden decking, thrashed for a second or so and then lay still.

Photos were taken of the giant fish, with the man who had caught it grinning broadly and with obvious satisfaction, posing in the background gripping the rod he had used to catch the Marlin that now lay stretched out in front of him.

I was unable to share the euphoria of the other men. It seemed to me an unequal contest. Unless the fish could have somehow slipped the hook it was inevitably doomed, the poor creature being no match for human ingenuity.

When we finally began to head back towards Havana at around six in late afternoon, there were three marlin lying next to each other on the after deck.

The four Americans sat on the bench seats celebrated their catch with more cans of beer. Three of them at least were celebrating because the un-official leader of the group, Mike, had failed to get a bite and had to endure some lighthearted banter from his companions.

I stood next to Lucia on the upper deck as she steered the boat back to port. A late breeze had come up, and as the strong little craft punched it's way through the waves we were both silent, for no other reason than there was nothing very much to say, the two us just enjoying the sight and sound of the sea, the pleasant warmth of the sun as is fell towards the horizon. In the distance the outline of Havana gradually came into sight.

As we approached the inlet to the harbour, with the distinct shape of the lighthouse silhouetted against the deep blue of the evening sky, Lucia took a hand from the wheel for a moment and grasped at mine.

'You ok now Harry?'

She asked again. I smiled at her.

'Sure.'

'You didn' enjoy that too much am I right?'

I smiled again, ruefully this time

'No, you're right as always sweetheart. It was just I don't know saddening I suppose to see those extraordinary creatures being dragged out of their natural environment just for the sport.'

Gutteral laughter drifted up from the rear deck, almost as though the men had heard what I had said.

'Well it will serve a good purpose carino. The fish will be sold and eaten, maybe by us. Blue Marlin are very popular in the restaurants. ＿You've eaten it yourself am I right?

She looked at me with those deep brown eyes and as always her frankness, her honesty, were impossible to dismiss.

I leaned forward and kissed her cheek

'Maybe I'll become a vegetarian after this.'

'No you won't honey. Tomorrow you will feel differently, trust me!'
'Well, maybe you're right. We'll see.'
I gazed through the windscreen as we approached the harbour entrance and Lucia began to ease back the throttle slightly.
'Hey Harry!'
The man Mike called up to me.
'D'you think you can you find us some more cans?
Lucia gave me a quick sidelong glance and a suppressed smile.
'Take care of the customers carino!'
She whispered. Touching my arm briefly she winked at me with a distinctly humorous expression.

I fetched some more beers from below deck and handed them out to each of the four.
'Did you enjoy the day gentlemen?'
There were murmurs of assent, all except for Mike Simmons.
'Well most of us did I guess Harry.'
He commented.
I gave him a reassuring smile.
'I'm sure you'll have better luck tomorrow mister Simmons.'
He cracked open the can.
'Lets hope so. __I gotta say your wife is pretty good at her job.'
'Yes she is. Her father was a fisherman I suppose that's where she learned her skill.'
He lifted the can to his mouth and took a long draught of beer.
'Yeah well like I say Harry, let's see how it goes tomorrow.'

We dropped the Americans off at the quayside and arranged to meet them again the next morning
To my surprise Mike offered his hand to me.
'Make it eight a.m. okay Harry. I got a good feeling about tomorrow.'
'Sure mister Simmons, we'll be here.'
The Americans strolled off to catch a taxi and I jumped back on board the boat.
Releasing the stern line I joined Lucia in the wheel-house again.
'Vale! Now we sell the fish then we get something to eat. Ok Carino!'
As she spoke she turned the wheel to port and accelerated the boat away, cutting cleanly through the flat oily surface of the water towards the far end of the bay.

'What did you make of the yanks Lucia?'

She shrugged indifferently.
'Just clientes honey! I don' think nuthin' abou' them.'
'No that's fair enough I guess.'
'An' you shouldn' either Harry. A couple of days more an' they're gone!'
She lifted her hand, making a fluttering motion with her fingers.
'No you're right sweetheart. __How much do you think we'll get for the fish?'
I glanced at the three shiny fresh carcasses lying side by side on the rear deck.
'It depends carina. Abou' four hundred maybe.'
'Who keeps that? It's half and half you told me.'
'Yeah, tha's the rule!'
Again she gave me a sly wink.
'But *we* decide which is the bigger half!
They got their photo shots to show their families, an' boast about it to their frien's when they get back home, an' tha's all they really want!'
She turned to me with a broad grin.
'I tol' you this was good business Harry!'

Chap. 4

Lucia's buoyant manner and irrepressible enthusiasm was contagious and right then I felt just as happy as she looked.
And indeed why not! Financially we didn't need this little enterprise that she had created, and I suppose talked me into and it was impossible to say where it would all lead, but at that moment I really didn't care.
It was a lovely evening, there was a cool breeze from the sea, and I was standing on an old rugged fishing boat next to a beautiful woman who I loved more than I could ever describe!
How can you improve on that!

If a fairground fortune teller had gazed into her crystal ball a mere four months before and had told me that I would soon be married to a beautiful Cuban ex-hooker and would be sailing into the Caribbean to catch large fish, I would have laughed her out of her tent!
How strange and unpredictable the future can be, providing, like me I suppose, you have the opportunity and the means to take a different direction in life.
For most it's going to be the dull routine with few surprises.

What is the point if, after being presented with this extraordinary gift of life, you don't make the most of it? That is of course if you're able to do so! Not a luxury everyone can afford.
And yes I was lucky, because without my financial windfall I might well, like most, have been condemned to a mundane future, although I suppose that even with my relative financial security I could, very much like my father, have quite easily settled for a predictable existence with all the familiar trappings of a 'normal' life.
So I had embarked on my odyssey of discovery, the caveat being of course that journeys into the unknown, __ok, so far no further than Cuba, but still unknown to me anyway, and as such, prone to unseen pitfalls!
Such adventures can quite easily end in disaster, and who knows that could still happen, I had no way of predicting.

The fish market, a large dilapidated shed with a corrugated roof was set back from the dockside where a number of commercial fishing boats were tied up, their work done for the day.
Despite this the front of the building was floodlit and still open for business for the late arrivals such as ourselves.
As soon as Lucia brought the boat alongside I jumped ashore and secured the lines.
Almost at once a bulky figure in dark blue work cloths strolled across to us. His cheerful weathered face deeply lined, presented a wide smile when he saw Lucia.
'Hola chica!' He bawled out.
'Pepe! __Que tal hombre?'
She called back at once.
'Don't tell me you know this man as well sweetheart. This town gets smaller by the day!'
'He was a frien' of my father carino. They used to fish together.'
The man was already swinging a primitive crane over the rear end of the boat and jumping down onto the deck he began to fix a line of rope around the body of a marlin just below the tail, his brawny arms covered with thick curling hair lifting the fish effortlessly.
The day's catch was winched onto the dockside at which point Lucia climbed ashore and almost at once a long animated debate commenced with much arm waving as the grizzled fish merchant lowered the Marlin onto a weighing machine one at a time.
The arguing continued in rapid garbled Spanish as Lucia and the merchant faced each other in what seemed an open conflict.

After a few moments wide smiles appeared on both faces and a final handshake sealed the deal.

They disappeared into the warehouse and a few moments later Lucia re-emerged still with a broad happy smile and carrying a fist full of money. She leapt easily down onto boat and giving me a generous kiss on the cheek, she trotted rapidly up the wooden steps to the wheelhouse.

'Venga! Lets go Harry!'

'Five hun'red dollars carino!'

Lucia remarked joyfully as we sat in a small restaurant in the centre of Havana.

She had taken the small bundle of notes from her bag and held it out to me, but I shook my head.

'You keep it sweetheart. You earned it! __If you hadn't navigated and steered the boat into the right places they might not have caught a bloody thing and there wouldn't have been anything to sell.'

'But we are partners Harry! Ain't that so?'

'We are I suppose. __I mean ok, I financed the deal, but you planned everything and you organized everything. I'm really just the deck hand.'

She looked at me seriously.

'Harry in two years I pay you back for everythin'.'

'Nonsense love! __Pay me back? We're married! What's mine is yours, isn't that right?'

She was still regarding me with the same, almost grave expression. Her eyes looking straight into mine.

'I love you Harry!'

'And I love you honey. __Look, I just want you to be happy Lucia. This little business idea of yours seems to have started off very well. You've obviously put a lot of thought into it and I think it's going to be successful. So lets drink to that!'

I lifted my glass of beer.

'But Harry__'

'No buts'! __You can pay the restaurant bill.'

Her lovely face broke into a broad joyful smile and now she lifted her glass as well.

'To us carino!'

We touched glasses.

'Yes, to us! __And to further fishing charters!'

I leaned back in my chair listening to the ever-present sounds of Latino music drifting in from the street, the talk and the laughter of the other customers echoing from the high ceiling of the restaurant where several fans rotated endlessly, the draught of air relieving only slightly the hot humid atmosphere of the evening.
At that moment I don't think I had ever felt so content and entirely at peace.
England suddenly seemed a thousand light years way.

The four yanks spent another two days fishing, with a respectable catch of more Marlin, although not nearly as good as the first.
Returning to Havana the fishermen left in high spirits, taking countless photos of themselves, with their trophies from the deep as a prominent feature.
There were more pictures of the boat, and with Lucia and I posing at the helm.
Then there were handshakes all round, a lot of sincere 'thanks' from the men and a kiss on the cheek for each of them from Lucia.
'Great trip Harry!'
This comment from Mike, the self appointed leader of the group.
'We'll do this again, __soon!'
'You have our number mister Simmons.' I replied with a wide smile.
Contrived of course because I didn't like the bloke very much, but business as always comes first.
'Call us any time, we'll be pleased to see you again.'
I sealed the offer with yet another handshake.

Then they piled ashore with their luggage, straight into a waiting taxi that pulled away at once.

'Well, __satisfied customers Lucia! __Thanks to you.'
'An' you as well carino.'
She smiled happily and planted a nice kiss on my mouth. Then she leapt nimbly up to the wheel-house, and starting the engine she steered the boat towards the old fish market at the far end of the bay.

We had an early night for a change, laying silently in bed next to each other in the dim interior of Lucia's apartment, the bedroom window wide open to the warm evening air and the sounds from the street below.
She turned slightly and rested her hand on my shoulder.

'Are you really happy carino?'
She whispered.
'What do you think! __ I've never been happier in my life!'
'We make good partners don' you think?'
'In more ways than one sweetheart!'
A short silence while I took her hand and kissed her fingers gently.
'We got more customers comin' on Saturday Harry!'
'Ok. It's Wednesday today so we have a couple of days off.'
'We have to clean up the boat carino!'
'We'll do it on Friday, ok.'
I turned over on my side.
'Right now all I want to do is sleep.'

The little business venture that we, or rather Lucia, had started up did very well and provided a modest income, income that we didn't really need, although I knew that the project gave her considerable satisfaction.
Perhaps for the first time in her life she was able to earn money and be able to stash it away in her own personal bank account.
In addition I found that I was actually enjoying the relatively undemanding life that now seemed almost routine.
I kept the boat tidy, touched up the paintwork, made any small repairs, my previously limited skills in that direction having rapidly improved, I suppose out of necessity.
I also learned how to look after the engine, having found a greasy and much thumbed 'Caterpillar' engine manual tucked away in a drawer in the main cabin.
During the fishing trips I supplied the customers with beer and small impromptu meals, cooked up on the tiny stove in the galley. The work was undemanding, but much to my surprise, satisfying and I never once became bored with what were essentially mundane tasks.
I was beginning to love the trips out to sea, with the small boat pounding its way through the waves, and the sun beating down from a clear blue sky.
I was also starting to participate in the excitement as the huge fish were caught, fought with for the best part of an hour, and then finally heaved over the side onto the timber afterdeck.
It was a wonderful period, for both of us I believe, and as I have already said, I had never felt happier or more contented in my life.

The two American clients turned up on a Tuesday morning early.

Early for me anyway, seven o'clock! The sun had just risen over a bank of dark clouds on the horizon, clouds that would soon evaporate as the morning rolled on.

They clambered on board wearing the standard attire of shorts and palm-beach shirts and carrying two small hold-alls, which I quickly stowed below deck.

They looked like businessmen, bankers perhaps of in advertising maybe, what did I know?

Not that it mattered one way or the other, they had paid up in advance, which was the usual deal anyway. So now we took them out to catch fish, We cast off, with Lucia at the helm.

I took my usual spot on the bench seating on one side of the after deck and the two guys sat opposite, as the boat cut through the flat oily surface of the bay towards the distant waves of the Caribbean.

With the somehow comforting sound of the engine, thundering away happily below deck, and the promise of yet another fine sunny day, I felt perfectly contented.

We passed through the narrow entrance to the port with the now familiar form of the lighthouse on one side and the long sea wall on the other.

When we hit the first waves the boat lifted and fell, gently at first, but as the waves grew stronger the bow end began to smash into them sending a fine warm spray over the prow, some of which continued over the rear deck laying a glistening carpet on the hardwood surface.

The boat began to roll slightly and the two men slightly nervous, or so it seemed, turned at the same moment to grip onto the sturdy timber bulwark that ran behind them.

'Is this your first fishing trip Gentlemen?'
I asked, in an attempt to relieve their apparent tension.
'We've been out a few times. __Off the Florida Keys!'
One of them said.
'Is it always this choppy?'
'It calms down as the sun comes up. You'll get used to it.
Do either of you get sea sick? __We've got some pills that will take care of that.'
'We're ok. __For now anyway. __Are you English?'
The same speaker again.
I smiled.
'Good guess, although I suppose it's obvious!'
'It sure is! __Can't be too many Englishmen in Havana!'
'No, probably not, at least I haven't met any yet.'
'Ok. So you're the boss, right?'
I shook my head and pointed to where Lucia stood at the wheel.

'She's the boss!'
I smiled again.
'I'm the crew!'
He looked from me to Lucia and then back again.
'Ok, I get it!'
He nodded slowly.
His companion remained silent and was staring out over the waves.
Can I get you get you both a beer?
I asked.
'Sure why not.'
The response was only just short of indifferent.

I brought them a can each from the galley and then mounted the steps to the wheelhouse where Lucia was preoccupied with navigating the vessel towards the fishing grounds.
'Hi Harry, you ok?'
'Yeah sure. A bit rough this morning, the sea I mean.'
'Not for long, in an hour it will calm down some! __How are the customers?'
I just gave them some beer. __Funny pair those two!'
'Funny?'
'Meaning strange. __I don't know, just something about them.'
'They've paid carino, we find some Marlin for them, an' everybody's happy.'
I grinned at her.
'Maybe you're right!'

Lucia eased back the throttle and then killed the engine.
The sea was calmer now, although the boat, now starved of its forward motion, rolled slightly in the gentle swell.
I started getting the rods and other equipment up from below deck while Lucia checked the huge reels and fixed them in place.
'I don' think we need live bait so we'll try the lures first, that usually gets the Marlin interested!'
Lucia said dropping a rod into one of the steel holders fixed to the transom.
'Sure, whatever you say.'
The man responded, the same speaker again.
'We're both novices here really, my friend and I!'
It was left to Lucia and me to fix the colourful lures to the nylon line, concealing the hooks just within the cover of the long rubber tentacles of the replica's that looked nothing at all like real squids, except perhaps to a Marlin. Then we tossed the ends of the lines over the stern.

'It's up to you now guys!'
Lucia remarked, watching skeptically as they struggled with some difficulty to fix rod harnesses around their waists.
'Where did you fish before?'
She asked with a doubtful expression.
'In the gulf, off the Florida coast.'
One of them murmured, as I helped him to buckle the cumbersome belt.
'What kind'a fish did you catch?'
'Well they were big, that's all I can tell ya'.'
'Mmm. Kingfish prob'ly.'
Lucia continued conversationally.
'Or Tripletails maybe, or Mahi. __Tha's all you can find along tha' stretch of coastline, apar' from Tuna.'
The man glanced at her with what could have been impatience.
'Well senora I guess you're the expert.'
Lucia gave me a quick sidelong look before turning and mounting the steps to the helm.
'Ok guys I'm gonna' start the boat up and cruise at about four knots. Let the line pay out about a hundred metres. My par'ner wiil help you out so don' worry.'
She started the engine again and the boat began moving forward slowly. At once the reels began to release the lines as the current snatched at the lures. I showed the two men how to partially apply the brakes on their reels when sufficient line had unwound, as they seemed to be fumbling with what was fairly standard fishing gear.
I was certainly no expert, having been involved in catching fish for no longer that three months or so, but I was getting the distinct feeling that these men had never fished before in their lives.

By the end of the day they had each caught a single Marlin, each of the fish just over a hundred pounds in weight.
I was surprised that they had caught anything at all in fact, as they seemed preoccupied somehow. With what I had no idea.

The next morning we picked them up at the quay-side early and began to make ready to head out to sea again.
Sitting in my usual place I tried deliberately to make conversation with the man who the previous day had said virtually nothing.
'Better luck today mister Peterson, lets hope! __Marlin fishing can be unpredictable.'
'Yeah, well we'll see!'

Came the curt response, but I pressed on.
'Usually Squid lures get their attention. If you don't get any joy this morning we'll try again with some live bait.
Like I say it's not an exact science, so if we__'
His companion interrupted.
'Can you ask your boss if she can head for these co-ordinates?'
He handed me a small piece of paper, which had hand written positions for latitude and longitude.
I took it from him and glanced briefly at the figures.
'Yes sure, I'll ask her now, but she has a lot of experience when it comes to locating Marlin.'
'I'm sure she does, but ask her anyway!'
It seemed more of a command than anything else, but, as they say, the customer is always right!
'Ok mister Levitt I'll pass it on.'

I walked up to the wheelhouse and gave the slip of paper to Lucia.
'Wha's this Harry?'
She looked at the note with a puzzled expression.
'Where they want to go today apparently!'
'Why they wanna' go there?'
'They didn't say.'
She continued to stare at the piece of paper and then unfolded a map and laid it out flat on the wide shelf beneath the windscreen, tracing her finger along the coastline towards the west.
'Are there any fish around that area Lucia?'
'Maybe, but I don' think so.'
I looked over her shoulder.
'So where is it exactly?'
'Jus' here carino, close to a place call' Varadero.'
'What, you mean this little spit of land sticking out into the sea?'
'Spit?'
'It means like a promontory, a piece of land that__'
'You mean like the Florida Keys!'
'Well I've never been to Florida, but you know what I mean.'
'Sure!'
'Ok, so what's special about it?'
'Nothin'! __Der's a golf course, coupl'a hotels tha's it!'
'But it's a good place to fish, yeah?'
She shrugged her shoulders.
'Who knows Harry! Not for Marlin tha's for sure!'
'Ok, but if that's where they want to go__'

I smiled and turned to walk back down the narrow flight of wooden steps, but Lucia caught my arm, holding me back.
'It's a hun'red kilometres carino! Maybe more. An' at least four hours at sea from here! __So it means more fuel. You better tell them that!'
'Yes love I certainly will.'
'We can take them, but they gotta pay, ok!'
She looked at me with that 'no nonsense' gaze that I knew well enough by now.
I smiled at her.
'Sure. Leave it to me honey!'

I explained the situation to the two men who listened without interruption and seemingly without much interest.
'Sure Harry no problem. How much extra do you want?'
The man Peterson responded quickly.
I made a quick calculation and then added a bit.
'A hundred and fifty U.S. should do it. It's about two hundred kilometers there and back, so quite a journey really. __It's just for the extra diesel fuel that's all.'
He had already taken out his wallet and was counting out the notes.
'The other thing is mister Peterson, the skipper thinks you won't find many Marlin in that area. It's too shallow for them she says.'
He presented a tight smile.
'Well who knows! __Hell, maybe we'll get lucky!'
I took the money from him and shoved it in my pocket.
'Anyway, as I said it's quite a good distance so the sooner we start the better.'
I smiled at them, taking on my other role as the on-board steward.
'Can I get you both a drink gentlemen?'
'Got any Whiskey Harry?'
'No problem mister Peterson. __We'll get under way and then I'll bring you both a glass, so make yourselves comfortable.'

I called up to Lucia and then hurrying to the front of the boat I released the bowline, as the boat slowly drifted away from the quay I let go of the stern. At that moment the engine roared into life and we headed away across the bay towards the harbour entrance with the lighthouse as the permanent sentinel.

The sea was a lot calmer that day, with just a light undulating swell and the vessel ploughed through the even blue water at a good eighteen knots.

'We should be there in abou' four hours at this rate Harry!'
Lucia said with a broad happy smile.
She was in her element now.
Out at sea, the draught through the open sides of the wheelhouse catching at her long dark hair and sending it dancing around her lovely radiant face, it was a joy just to look at her.
'Happy sweetheart?'
'Wha'd you think carino!'
She turned to me for a moment, her dark brown eyes regarding me with a look of sheer contentment.
'Can you ge' me a beer Harry?'
'Course I can!'

I made my way to the lower deck where the two Americans were lounging on the bench seats.
'More whisky gents?'
I asked them. It was Peterson who responded.
'No we're ok for now.'
'Good. Anything else you need?'
'No I guess not.'
He glanced up at the faultless blue sky.
'Great day for it eh Harry!'
'Yes it is. It should be a nice easy journey. __The problem is you won't have much time to fish. Two hours, maybe a little longer before we need to set back to Havana. And we won't be back until quite late'
'No problem! If we catch a fish, great! If we don't __well we don't! __Our fault not yours!'

I got a can of beer for Lucia and took it up to her.
'Everythin' ok chico?'
I popped the can and handed it to her.
'Sure. __I explained to the customers that they're not likely to find any Marlin, not where we're going! __And that they only have a couple of hours to do it.'
'An' they're ok with that, yeah?'
'Said they were! Didn't seem bothered to be honest love.'
'Maybe they got some other reason to go to Varadero.'
'Like what?'
'I don' know carino, maybe we fine' out when we get there.'

I made some lunch for all of us in the galley and by the time we had eaten it was just after midday.

'We shall arrive in one half hour at Varadero!'
Lucia announced to me and the two men.
It was a cue for me to start bringing out the fishing gear and fixing the rods in position. Lucia had said that we would need to catch some small fish for bait as lures wouldn't work in the shallow waters offshore.
The narrow strip of land soon came into view on the horizon, no more than what appeared to be a low sand bank with a few elevated white smudges against the blue sky. Smudges that slowly transformed into what looked very much like hotel buildings.
Lucia cut the engine and the boat drifted to a stop on perfectly calm water.
'Well guys this is it. Varadero! I don' think you fine' to many big fish here, but we try. Firs' we catch some bait.'
Using small rods Lucia and I attached spinners to the ends of the lines and cast them out into the sea, drawing them back slowly on the reels.
In less than ten minutes we had a small pile of fish squirming about in a barrel of water.
'Are you ready guys?'
Lucia spoke to the two men who hardly seemed to be paying any attention.
'Sure!' The man Peterson responded.
'Look do you think you could motor further east towards the far end of the strip?'
To my surprise he was holding a pair of binoculars, which he must have retrieved from his bag below deck. I had been too busy catching bait with Lucia to have noticed.
'Sure, if tha's what you want!'
Lucia gave a shrugged response.

She started the engine again and we cruised slowly along the coastline until we reached the end of the narrow promontory, which I guessed was about five kilometers away from our current position.

'Ok, you guys wanna' fish now?'
She shouted down from the helm above the noise of the engine.
'Just keep going!'
Peterson called back.
'There's an island further north-east. Head towards that.'
'Sure there's an island, bu' you won' fine' no fish there hombre! No' deep enough! _ The water I mean!

I looked in the direction he was pointing and sure enough a small green hump of land seemed almost to be floating on the calm blue sea.
'We'll take our chances skipper.'

Peterson responded.
'Ok, as long as you' happy with that.'
Lucia pushed the throttle forward and the boat gathered pace slightly.
I had joined Lucia again on the upper deck.
It couldn't have been more than six or seven kilometers to the tiny piece of land and I leaned over the side of the boat watching as we drew nearer.
It looked exactly like the archetypal desert island, a rocky outcrop in the sea with beaches of pure white sand surrounding it and a dense cluster of palm trees at the centre.
Peterson called up to us again when we were little more than two kilometers from the island.
'That's close enough, we can start fishing here.'
'FIshin' where?'
Lucia remarked softly.
'There's no Marlin here carino!'
'Who cares sweetheart, __humour them!'
I remarked with a grin.
'The customer is always__'
'Is always right! __Yeah I know that!'
She intervened, digging me in the ribs as she said it.

I trotted down to the rear deck again to assist the men in baiting their lines. Even with my limited experience. I was certain about one thing, and that was that neither of these two had ever fished before in their lives, so why now I wondered?
Peterson was preoccupied with gazing at the small island through his binoculars.
'Anyone live there d'you think Harry?'
He murmured.
'I've no idea mister Peterson, very unlikely I should imagine. __Lucia might know, shall I ask her?'
'No don't bother.'
I pulled a small live fish from the barrel and pushed a barbed hook through its mouth while it struggled relentlessly. Then I tossed in over the side and allowed the line to reel off as it swam away.
Then I did the same with his companions.
Levitt was seated in the heavy swivel chair in front of the transom. He too was staring over the starboard side of the boat, gazing in the direction of the island.
'Your line is ready now mister Levitt!'
His response was half-hearted, and he barely turned his head.
'Toss it over! __Who knows, maybe we'll a bite.'

I did as he asked, putting the brake on the reel after twenty meters or so of nylon line had spun off into the water.
These guys had absolutely no interest at all in catching fish! So why were they here?
I took the few steps down into the cabin and took a can of beer from the fridge, popping it open.
'So what!' I thought.
'It's their money, if they wanted to stare at uninhabited islands all day that was their business.'
I sat for a moment on the comfortable upholstered seating, threw my head back and took a long gulp of cold beer.

When I came back on deck five minutes later nothing had changed.
The boat was hardly moving in a perfectly calm sea and the two men were still watching the island. I turned my head to where Lucia was sitting in front of the helm. She was reading a book, her feet propped up on the shelf where the instruments were located.
'You ok Lucia?'
I called up.
'Sure!'
Do you need anything?'
'I'm ok Harry!'
She called back.
The two large fishing rods were still resting in the metal sockets fixed to the transom, pointing straight upwards toward the sky, the slack lines disappearing into the water.
'No luck yet?'
I enquired.
'Er, not yet.'
The man Peterson remarked distractedly.
I grabbed one of the rods and began reeling in the line.
Eventually the hook emerged with just the head of the bait-fish still attached.
'Well one of you had a bite! __The thing is as soon as you get any movement on the rod you have to take in some line. That way__'
That was as far as I got.
A small boat had appeared suddenly from behind the island some distance away and seemed to be travelling rapidly towards us.
At once Peterson threw the binoculars into his bag beneath the bench seat and took the fishing rod from my hands.
His companion grabbed at the other rod.
'What do I do now?' He growled.

'Well just reel it in. I suspect the same thing has happened.'
I was glancing now at the fast moving craft that was now approaching us directly. In the same moment I felt the familiar rumble of the engine under my feet. Lucia, alert as always had started it up and throttled back to leave it idling almost silently.
'Who are these people Lucia?'
I called out to her.
'No lo se carino!'
She spoke cautiously, reverting to her native language, but I knew enough words of Spanish now to understand what she meant.
Levitt had reeled in the line once again exposing just the head of the bait. As he swung it on board I grabbed at the body-less remains and pulled out the hook, tossing the fish head into the sea. I grabbed another live fish from the barrel and quickly fixed it to the hook.
'Ok, now cast it out as far as you can!'
I instructed him, still with one eye on the approaching craft.
Peterson had managed somehow to attach a small fish to his hook and had tossed it overboard.
The unknown craft was now no more than five hundred metres away and then in moments it was drawing alongside our boat.
The outboard motor was cut leaving the sleek vessel wallowing in its own bow wave.
Two men were on board one at the helm in the centre and the other standing in the bow.
'You guys having any luck?' The man at the front of the craft called out.
His spoke in English but with a strong Spanish accent.
'Not yet!'
It was Peterson who spoke. He had reeled in his line and was making another attempt at casting the bait over the stern.
'You won't find much fish aroun' this area Senor!'
The man in the other boat again.
'Well we're giving it a try, __who knows we may get lucky!'
Peterson responded nonchalantly.
'No senor! Your luck just ran out!'

What happened next was so quick that I had no time to react or even to think. The man had pulled a gun from behind his back and shot Peterson in the chest. The rod he was holding fell from his hands and dropped over the transom into the sea. He grunted and staggered backwards a look of sheer surprise on his face.

Then he seemed to be reaching for his bag stashed under the bench seating, but another shot stopped him dead and he dropped to the deck with blood pumping from a second hole in his chest.
Levitt meanwhile had made a desperate attempt to reach the same bag but was cut down by two further shots and without uttering a sound he fell on top of his companion.

There is a moment in life when you know with certainty that your number is finally up! The feeling is of total helplessness and the instant knowledge that there is nothing that you can do about it.
That was my feeling in that instant as the man in the other boat turned his gun on me. I was a dead man and I knew it!

Of course at that precise point I had completely forgotten about Lucia!
The engine below where I was standing instantly roared into life! The boat surged forward and the shot from the pistol missed me by God only knows how much.
The boat almost spun on its axis as Lucia turned the helm hard to starboard.
Then it seemed to rear upwards under the thrust of the powerful engine, heading directly towards the centre of the other vessel that lay stationary in the water.
There was nothing the man at the wheel could have done as our boat rammed it amidships.
The thing about older sea going vessels like ours was that they were heavy and extremely sturdy, built from solid hardwood.
The small fiberglass boat was no match, as we ploughed into it, forcing it sideways through the water and smashing the flimsy structure of the hull, ripping it apart as though it was made of paper.
The man at the centre helm had no chance as our boat surged onwards, the bow hammering down onto the smaller vessel with enormous force, crushing it and reducing it to fragments, and in the same moment smashing into the helmsman who managed a short scream before our boat hit him full on, forcing him beneath the water.
Lucia cut the throttle and began to race down the short flight of steps to the lower deck. With a massive effort I shook myself from my temporary stupor and threw myself to the starboard beam peering over the bulwark.
The two halves of the other boat were already disappearing beneath the surface with no sign of the man who was directly in front of the oncoming prow of our vessel. The other man who had fired the pistol was floundering amongst the floating debris.
He looked up at me with an imploring look.

'Senor, __please!'
His hand was outstretched towards me.
Then Lucia was standing next to me, appearing as though from nowhere. Only now she was carrying one of the long heavy gaff's that we used to bring Marlin on board after they were caught.
In one movement she had swung the instrument at the figure in the water. He screamed out as the large barbed spear pierced his neck, a sound that was instantly silenced as she forced him down beneath the waves. He struggled impotently for several moments as I had seen the Marlin struggle, unable to free their thrashing bodies from the steel spikes.
The water was coloured red, obscuring the body as she continued to hold the man beneath the surface.
Then with a final thrust she pulled the gaff free and tossed it on the planking next to the two corpses.
Lucia sank onto the bench seating and leaned forward resting her arms on her knees. Her tee shirt was sticking to her body, soaked with perspiration and I could see that her hands were shaking.
Without a word I dropped onto the bench next to her, unable to speak, and for a few moments even to move.

'Jesus *Christ* Lucia!'
I managed to stammer out at last, barely recognizing my own voice.
'What in God's name was that all about?'
'I don' know carino.'
Her voice, just above a whisper, was trembling.
'You saved my bloody life!'
'Tha' was the idea Harry, __an' prob'ly mine too!'

I looked over the side of the boat again. There were still swirls of blood in the water, but the body of the man who had tried to kill me had vanished.

'What the hell do we do now Lucia?'
'I don' know yet. We need to think! __Both of us!'

I stood up with some effort, my legs felt as though they were made of jelly and could barely support me. I gripped onto the handrail of the steps, glancing around in all directions towards the distant horizon.
There was nothing to be seen, just the island and the hazy coastal outline of Varadero. No other sign of life, no speedboats loaded with armed men speeding towards us, nothing but the open sea and total silence.
I stared down at the bodies of the two dead Americans both drenched now in their own blood.

Then I looked at Lucia. She was sitting upright now, staring at me. She looked on the point of tears and I sat next to her again, putting my arms around her shoulders and holding her close.

'Thank God you're ok love. If it wasn't for you and that quick mind of yours we'd both be dead!'
'There was nothing else I could do Harry!'
'Of course there wasn't.'
'I saw his face, __the man at the helm. He was starin' at me, his mouth was open. It was just for a second Harry, but He knew he was goin' to die__'
She covered her face with her hands.
'Listen honey! __He and his__mate, whoever they are, didn't care about you! We would be lying next to these poor buggers here if you hadn't done what you did. __I love you Lucia, you're a good woman, so don't waste one moment of your life worrying about those two bastards!'
I felt alert again, the strength was back in my legs and I stood up. 'First of all, we need to get out of here. We've got five hours more or less until we get back to Havana. Five hours to figure out exactly what we are going to do!'
I turned quickly and mounted the steps to the wheelhouse. Then I started the engine and pushed the throttle hard forward.
The boat surged away as though eager to leave behind the scene, and what few traces of the carnage still remained.

'Where to on the compass?'
Over the roar of the engine I yelled down to Lucia, who was still sitting in the same place.
'Just head west carino!'
She called back. Then at last she got to her feet and slowly mounted the steps to the upper deck.

Chap. 5

We stood next to each other in silence as I steered the boat westwards, back towards Havana.
It was little more than half an hour since the dramatic event that had very nearly cost us our lives.
I turned and glanced back briefly.
The island had disappeared from view completely now and only a faint outline of Varadero could be seen, just a faint blurred line on the horizon.

'Any ideas let love?'
I said quietly.
'I'm thinkin' about it!'
She remarked with surprising calmness.
I gave her a sidelong glance.
'Well I think we should call the police on the radio and tell them to meet us when we get back to port.'
'Yeah, maybe you're right Harry!'
She fell silent again.

After another five minutes or so of complete silence, apart that is from the constant noise of the engine she spoke again.
'You wanna' beer carino?'
'A *beer!* __What I want is a Whiskey Lucia! __A bloody *large* one!'

She went below deck into the large cabin space and reappeared perhaps fifteen minutes later.
'What happened, I'm dying of thirst here!'
She handed me a glass of Whisky and I took a good mouthful, swallowing hard.
'Uh! God that's better!'
Lucia opened her can of beer and sipped from it thoughtfully.
'I bin' goin' through their stuff Harry!'
She said quietly.
'Right, ok.'
'They each had a gun in their bags!'
'A *gun!*'
'Both of them! __Why would they need a gun Harry?'
'I'm buggered if I know!'
'Bugger? __Wha's bugger'?'
She repeated.
'Don't ask. __It's not a nice word!
__Guns! Jesus Christ! __Why guns?'
'Yeah tha's what I thought! Loaded pistols with spare cartridges!'
'Bloody hell! __What else?'
'Some clothes, no' much! __An' no pasaporte!'
'What! __They *must* have had passports Lucia!'
'Well I couldn' fine' them!'
'Maybe they were carrying them, __in their pockets maybe!'
'Why would dey do that?'
'Well, __I've no idea!'
'Who's gonna' check?'

I responded at once although my stomach was already turning over.
'I will! __You'd better steer.'
I ran down the steps to the rear deck staring at the two bodies, one lying on top of the other. Levitt was face down and I tapped at the back pockets of his denim shorts. __Nothing!
With some effort I rolled him off of the other man until he lay on the deck, sightless eyes staring up his mouth hanging open.
The front of his colourful shirt was completely soaked with blood that had ran down onto the decking and dried almost black in the heat of the sun. Gingerly I tapped the breast pocket and then the pockets of his shorts. Again there was nothing.
Peterson was also laying face down, the blood from the bullet wounds had spread in a wide circle beneath him, covering part of the rear deck.
I repeated the exercise and then with even greater difficulty managed to turn his large body over on its back. The blood from the two holes in his chest was considerable, having no doubt mingled with that of his companion.
A quick examination also revealed no passport.

Lucia had reduced speed almost to a walking pace and had joined me on the rear deck.
I had sunk down onto the bench seating and looked up at her, shaking my head.
'Nothing love!'
I stared out at the empty seas around us.
'What about wallets?'
I asked her.
'They must have had wallets!'
'Sure wallets, but no I.D.'s, no credit cards, only cash money.
'How much money?'
'About a thousand bucks between them, __I counted it.'
I leaned forward resting my hands on my knees, my eyes drawn towards the two corpses again.
What the hell was it all about. I couldn't even begin to imagine! More importantly, what the hell were we going to do now?

'*Harry!* __Your han's chico!'
'What! __Oh *shit!*'
I realized that my hands were covered with blood and now so were my knees.

Lucia found a plastic bucket and leaning over the side she filled it with sea water, splashing it over my bare legs. I plunged my hands in the warm water, washing away the blood with a feeling of profound disgust.
'Another bucket Lucia!'
I muttered, perhaps more curtly than I should have.
'Sure Carino!'
She dipped the container again, filling it to the brim.
'Over my head this time!'
She stood in front of me and tipped the contents slowly over my head and my body.
I scrubbed at my arms and legs feeling slightly better as the clean, clear seawater cascaded over me.
Then I sank back on the wooden seating again.
'What the bloody hell are we going to do here Lucia?'
She tossed the empty bucket on the deck and sat next to me.
'I bin' thinkin' about that Harry.'
'We call the police now, yes! There's no other way, is there love!'
'Harry if we call the police we are in big trouble!'
'Why, we just tell them the truth! __Tell them exactly what happened! Where's the problem?'
'You don' un'erstan' Harry. Dis is Cuba, not England! If we sail into Havana with two dead bodies on board, an' fill' with bullet holes, wha'd you think will happen? __One thing we know for sure, these guys are no fishermen! __Secon' thing we get thrown in the calaboose by the Guardia Nacional! That's for sure Harry!'
'Oh come on Lucia! __That isn't going to happen! __We're completely innocent here__'
'Sure we are! We know that! Bu' we have to convince the policia! __We don' know who this guys are, __maybe they work for Castro, maybe for the yanks, maybe dey're criminals, __gangsters or somethin'! Who knows carino?'
'But the men who shot them and nearly killed us! And the boat__'
'What boat? What Men? __They don' exis' anymore!'
She shook her head, tossing her lovely hair from one side to another.
'It's our word only Harry! __Don' you see!'

Oh I saw all right!
What she said made total sense and the same idea had already occurred to me. The difference was I suppose that I still had the English mind set. Tell the truth and all will be well!
Lucia was certainly correct about at least one thing, the two dead men were not interested in fishing, so what were they doing?

Why the interest in a small uninhabited island in the Caribbean?

'Ok, so what do you suggest Lucia?'
She looked at me steadily.
'We get rid of the bodies now!' '
'And their bags? __The money?'
'That too! Jus' get rid of everything!'
'And when we get back to Havana? If someone starts asking awkward questions, like where are the two men we picked up this morning?'
'We say that a boat came out from Varadero and picked them up as soon as we arrived. Thas' it! __End of story.'
'Picked them up where?'
'Anywhere! __It's a long stretch of beach there, a' leas' ten kilometers, __an' it's nearly deserted.
The guys got on board an' tha's the last we saw of them!'

She looked me with that direct gaze that she had, almost willing me to go along with her.
This was a new experience for me, the first time in my short life that I had to make a serious decision, and it wasn't easy.

'Lucia I have a nasty sense about all this!
These men were bad news right from the start.
We don't know what was going on, but my feeling is that somebody does! If we concoct a story and it doesn't fit, __or they think it doesn't fit, we could be in serious trouble. If we go straight to the police and tell them everything that occurred today then no one can argue with that, can they! We don't have to worry about keeping our stories straight, we just explain exactly what happened!'
She looked at me sheepishly.
'Maybe you' right Harry, but I think tha' we will still end up in the slammer! No matter what!'
'Well, 'detained' is probably what will happen, for a short time at least. But we'll come out of this Lucia, I'm sure of it. 'Tell the truth and shame the devil!' as my father used to say.'
With a curious expression she put her head on one side and wrinkled her nose.
'Wha' does that mean Harry?'
I smiled at once, relieving the tension. Or perhaps it was she who had relieved the tension.
'Er, I'm not really sure, it's just a daft English idiom.'
'An idiom? __Don' you mean idiot!'

I laughed at once at the naïve comment and putting my arm around her I held her close.

'Maybe sweetheart. It doesn't make a lot of sense so idiotic just might be the right word.

I squeezed her gently and kissed her forehead.

'I love you Lucia!'

'An' I love you chico!'

We sat holding each other for several moments, then I released my hold on her and stood up.

'Ok, so lets get going. __You ready for this?'

She looked up at me, her irresistible eyes looking directly into mine.

'Sure Harry, you' the boss!'

'Well I'm not sure about that, but let's just see how it goes!'

A little more than three hours later and we were motoring towards the now familiar lighthouse at the entrance to the harbour.

Lucia had already contacted the police in Havana by radio and said simply that we were returning with two bodies on board and explaining where they should meet us.

We had taken turns at the helm, and I had found a found an old tarpaulin from below deck and covered the grisly corpses of the two men.

There was nothing else to do as we approached the port with, for me at least, extreme trepidation. Perhaps Lucia felt the same way, although she looked completely calm and assured.

As we approached the quayside where we normally moored, half a dozen or more men in dark green uniform were standing waiting for us.

There were police cars and an ambulance with the blue lights on the roof rotating aimlessly.

'The welcoming committee love!'

Lucia turned and smiled, resting her hand on my arm for just a second.

'Don' worry Harry! Let me do the talking ok.'

I nodded and made a feeble attempt at returning her smile, although inside I was trembling like the proverbial leaf.

As soon as we drew along side I tossed the mooring lines ashore. One of the uniformed men grabbed them and made the boat fast, Then Lucia killed the engine.

In seconds the boat was inundated with policemen.

The tarpaulin was pulled back revealing the gruesome spectacle of blood soaked bodies.

One of the officers, perhaps younger than the others, proceeded promptly to the side of the vessel, leaned over and vomited into the water.
Two more uniformed men climbed onto the boat.
From the insignia on their epaulets they were obviously senior to the others. For a moment they surveyed the scene of the bloodied corpses. A man in jeans and an open necked shirt was already taking pictures of the two bodies from every conceivable angle.
Then one of the senior officers turned and spoke directly to me in what was quite reasonable English.
'Where can we speak in private Senor?'
He spoke quietly in a voice perhaps suited to the situation.
I gestured to the large cabin on the lower deck.
'Er, here is fine!'
I followed him down the short flight of steps with Lucia and the second officer following.
He took a seat at once at the far end of the cabin and removed a small notebook from the breast pocket of his immaculate uniform.
'Do you have your passport senor__'
'Burgess. Harry Burgess!'
I volunteered as calmly as I could.
'Yes sure! __Never go anywhere without it.'
I added needlessly, regretting the stupid remark at once.
I unlocked a small cupboard on the bulkhead where Lucia and I always kept our personal stuff and took out my passport, handing to the poker-faced officer.
He glanced through it carefully.
'You live in Cuba mister Burgess?'
'Well er, yeah. Temporarily, __or maybe permanently. Erm__'
'Which is it senor?'
I got a hostile look from the brown eyes.
He was young, carefully groomed with dark, short cut hair and a small neat mustache. One glance told you immediately that he was certainly nobody's fool!
Lucia interrupted at once, speaking to him in rapid Spanish of which I caught not even a word.
He turned to me again.
'You are, casado, __married!'
'Yes that's right.'
I glanced nervously at Lucia but she was staring at the cop.
'Siddown mister Burgess!'
He said quietly.

Both Lucia and I squeezed behind the long table and sat next to each other on the upholstered seating. The other officer, a much older man, took the seat at the other end of the table effectively blocking us in. Not deliberately I was sure, as it was the only other chair in the cabin.

The continued noise of the men on the deck floated down to us. It seemed that there were now in the process of transferring the two bodies onto the quay side.

The young officer spoke to his colleague.

'Raul, por favour, puede cerra la puerta!'

Without a word the older man stood and closed the small cabin door to the rear deck, reducing the noise to some degree at least. Then he took his seat again.

The young officer continued.

'So! You are Harold Thomas Burgess, yes!'

He stared at me expectantly, a pen poised above the notebook.

'Yeah. __ Yes that's me.'

He scribbled a few lines and then turned to Lucia.

'An' you are Lucia Jose Martinez!'

He began writing without waiting for her response.

'Lucia Jose Burgess!'

Lucia repeated in a deliberate tone.

'We know who you are Senora!'

The man said calmly, without looking up from his task.

Then he laid the pen on top of the notebook and leaned back in his chair.

'So! __ Now you can tell me what happened, hoy __ today, si?'

'Yes today!' Lucia repeated. She glanced at the heavy divers watch that she always wore.

'Abou' five hours ago, so yeah abou' midday, bit later maybe, __ media dia!'

In Spanish, but now more slowly, she began to relate the events of the last two days. Pausing occasionally as the officer, scribbling away rapidly in the notebook, held up a restraining hand.

She must have spoken for all of ten minutes, confidently and calmly.

'An' tha's it!' She said finally in her flawed English.

'Tha's the whole story!'

'And the man that shot at your husband!'

'As I tol' you, he went down with the other one in the boat.'

'They didn't try to, how do you say, __ nadada?'

'Swim! __ No, they did'n' get a chance after we, __ I cut their boat in half!'

Lucia had left out the detail of how the man with the gun had died and there was no way that I was going to intervene.
I know that it was anger that caused her to kill him and at that precise moment I had felt exactly as she had. The man was a cold-hearted bastard and was obviously quite ready to murder both of us for no good reason. He got exactly what he deserved.

The officer spoke again.
'So you didn't try to search for them?'
She shrugged at the question.
'We looked, but __no!'
'Carefully? __You searched the area?'
'No we did'n' search the area like you said! They went down with the boat! Tha' was it! __Who cares. They try to kill my husban', an' after maybe me as well!'
There was a sudden sharp rap on the cabin door, which then opened.
A policeman stuck his head through the opening and spoke rapidly to the older officer. Without a word he stood and climbed up to the rear deck closing the door again.

The man who had been asking all the questions released a deep sigh, laying his pen down on the table.
'This is a strange matter!'
He began.
'From what you have said I have the feeling that you are being truthful, however apart from yourselves there were no witnesses and the situation is very__bizarre? __Is that the correct word?'
He glanced at me as he spoke.
'Yes, that is the correct word and of course we have to agree with you, __my wife and I that is.'
He acknowledged with a brief movement of his head.
'In addition,'
He continued.
'__ it would have been possible for you to get rid of all the evidence and say nothing. Instead you came to us, in which case__'
At that point the door to the cabin opened again and the older man entered, closing the door. He trotted down the short flight of steps and took his seat again.
Before the younger of the two could continue, his companion spoke briefly in rapid Spanish.
Lucia turned to me at once with a broad smile, resting her hand on my arm.

'There is now some evidence that seems to support your statement!'
Our inquisitor continued in the same measured tone.
'Where were you exactly when you say that the man in the other boat took a shot at you?'
Again he was looking at me with the same unflinching gaze.
'I was sitting on the bench that runs along the port side of the boat.'
'You didn't try to stand when the two men were killed?'
'At the moment when the two men were shot I was incapable of movement of any kind.'
I responded ruefully.
He nodded.
'It seems a bullet has been found buried in the side of the boat, which would be close to where you say you were sitting.'
I raised my hands submissively.
'So there you are!'
I remarked with some sense of relief.
'You could of course have caused this yourself and then disposed of the weapon!'
I stared at the man with equal directness.
'Anything is possible!'
I responded.
At that point Lucia interrupted.
'Look, when we collided with the other boat d'ere was a hell of a crash. Why don' you look at the fron' of our boat an' see for yourself! __ There mus' be somethin' there, __ un rasguno, er, some danar of some kind!'
'Damage!'
I corrected her.
'Yes, we are doing that now!'
It was older of the two who now spoke. His English it seemed was as good as his colleague's.

There was a brief silence inside the cabin, in contrast to the constant activity that continued up on deck.
'Did you look through the bags that you say belonged to the two men?'
'I tol' you this!'
Lucia remarked with an edge to her voice.
'There were no passports!'
'No! __ We tol' you that as well!'
He nodded slowly. Lucia's impatient manner, so it seemed, had no effect on him at all. No apparent effect anyway.
He looked at the notebook again for a few moments.

'You also said that these men were not interested in catching fish. So why were they on your boat?'
I intervened this time, but in a more conciliatory manner.
Lucia was Lucia, and her level of tolerance wasn't particularly high when it came to what she believed at least, was a daft question, as I had discovered myself on a couple of occasions.

'Officer, if someone goes to a Beethoven concert, they are not stopped at the door to be asked if they're interested in music!'
'I raised my hands again.
'The thing is it was pretty obvious after the first day that they had no skill, or indeed interest in fishing for Marlin.
But the point is that they had paid for three days in advance and we are a commercial enterprise!'
I added a smile for good luck.
He raised his eyebrows, perhaps in agreement and nodded slowly.
After a moment or so he spoke again.

'These other men who appeared in the small boat, what did they say to your__clients?'
I shrugged.
'Not a lot really! __They asked if they'd caught anything and then said that it wasn't a good place to fish. __But Lucia had already told them that.'
'Nothing else?'
'No! It was a short conversation.'
'What happened then?'
'The guy in the front of boat pulled out a gun and started shooting.'
'He shot the two men, then he turned the gun on you. Is that correct.'
'Yes. At that point my wonderful, __'
I turned to look at Lucia.
'__not to say quick thinking wife, rammed them at full throttle.
She is the only reason I'm sitting here talking to you!'
'Yes, ok.'
He turned to Lucia.
'The engine of your boat must have been running surely.'
'Yeah it was running.'
'Why was that? You said these men were preoccupied with looking, for whatever reason, at this island, they weren't actively trying to catch fish!'
'Tha's right.'
Lucia's tone was level now.
'So why was the engine running. Fuel is expensive.'
'Because I started it up as soon as the other boat got closer to ours.'

'Why did you do that?'
'Instinct!'

The cabin was silent again and the noises from above deck had also decreased substantially.
At last the young officer released a deep sigh and leaned back in his chair again.
'I'm not sure wha' to make of this!
It seems you are telling the truth and I can't think of any motive you might have for killing these two men.
They carried no passports, no identification and there were guns in each of their bags, an' a large sum of money. We will check for prints of course, but it seems likely that the weapons belonged to them. But as I say, there are some things that__'
Once again he was interrupted by a rap on the cabin door.
The older man got up from his seat again and opened it.
A short whispered conversation was held on the upper deck and then the officer returned and sat down.
'There is clear evidence of a recent collision on the prow of your vessel! There are substantial marks and some slight damage to the bow.
Also some fragments of white plastic of some kind, __I'm not sure, como se dice?'
He turned to the junior of the two.
'Fibreglass!' I suggested.
'It was probably fiberglass!'
'Sure, fiberglass! __Pieces stuck in the wood, so that gives further strength to your story.'
He paused for a moment.
'So right now it seems that your account could be correct. We will wait for reports on the two bodies of course, but until then__'
'It's the hoosegow, yeah!'
Lucia interrupted, her anger rising like a volcano. Palpable, imminent!
'Now hold on love__'
I began.
'Hol' on! __Hol' on for what carino?'
Her eyes were blazing and her breasts were lifting and falling as her breathing rate increased. She had raised her arms straight, the fingers of her hands spread apart as she shook them back and forth, reminding me of how she would haggle over the price of a chicken in the market place.
'I *tol'* you this would happen Harry! I *say* this wo' happen!'
'Wait sweetheart__'
I tried again to restrain her outburst.

Then the elder of the two men spoke out in a strong but controlled voice that silenced both of us.
'*Senora*, por favour!'
He seemed almost amused and there was a slight smile on his broad lips.
'Tranquilo chica! We keep you' passports for now, an' please don' leave Havana without you tell us, ok. Otherwise__'
He shrugged his wide shoulders.
'Jus' get on with your business.__Bu' no more fishing trips, ok! __In any case we need this boat for more examination.'
I grinned at her and felt her collapse against me. If she *was* going to cry it wouldn't be here in front of the two men, her strong pride would never allow it.
'Ok then honey, lets get going. I could use a drink!'
I turned to the older of the policemen.
'It's been a long day. __For both of us!'
'Sure, we un'erstan' that!'
He stood up again to allow us to shuffle out from behind the table.
'We are staying at our apartment in__'
I began.
'We know where you are staying Senor!'
He looked at us both.
'Lucia was a frien' of my daughter, she don' remember!'
He gave a broad smile this time, and suddenly she did remember.
'Mari-Carmen!'
Lucia uttered in some surprise.
The man laughed.'
'You sho' contact her!'
'Yes, __we kind'a drifted apart.'
'Then drif' together again chica! __I get her to call you!'
Lucia embarrassed now by her brief outburst climbed the short flight of steps to the rear deck and pulled open the door.
I hesitated as she climbed out onto the deck, then I turned to both of the officers.
'This is a very odd business gentlemen. What worries me is that whoever these two men were associated with might well know where they were today and who they were with!'
I glanced at each of them again in turn.
It was the younger man who answered.
'Yes, we know this. __Call us at once senor if __well, for any reason.'
He paused.
'Tomorrow we will visit the island an' try to solve this mystery.'

He smiled for the first time and getting to his feet he offered his hand, which I took at once.
'You made a good choice by coming to us Senor Burgess.'
I nodded briefly and then turned and mounted the steps to the rear deck where Lucia was waiting.

Chap. 6

Exhausted, physically as well as mentally, we caught a Taxi to the town centre, to the bar where we had first met.
The owner greeted us both warmly and brought us two beers, which didn't last very long. I beckoned for two more and ordered some tapas for both of us.

Lucia was strangely silent, or perhaps it wasn't so strange, given what had happened earlier.
'You ok Lucia?'
I asked.
'Sure carino! __sorry I los' my temper Harry!'
'You can be excused for that. __At least we didn't get 'banged up' love!'
I grinned at her, trying to lift her mood, but it was obvious that the events of the day had affected her more deeply than I had thought.
'Lucia!'
She turned to me.
'Thanks for saving my life!'
She attempted a smile, which didn't quite work.
'Tha's ok! __You mean a lot to me Harry!'
'I know that sweetheart. __So now cheer up! Eat something, you'll feel better.'
She began picking half-heartedly at the small plates of dark cured ham and cheese and some fresh salad.
'I'm going to have a whisky, __what about you?' I said suddenly.
'Sure, __maybe tha's jus' wha'd I need.'

'Who was this friend of yours that the policeman mentioned earlier?'
I asked her, more as an effort to get her to say something.
'Mari-Carmen! __We were at junior school.
I didn' recognize her father today, he looked so much older than I remembered from before.

Yeah we were good friends. She was clever at school and went on to better things.'
'Like what?'
'I think she works for the government, I don' know exactly.'
Her mood was still flat and I tried again to get her to open up a little more.
'You're clever as well Lucia. You could have done whatever you wanted surely! Higher education is free here isn't it?'
'Sure, as long as you stick to the party line, Castro's line!
I hated school I jus' wanted to help my dad on his boat, but__'
Her voice tailed off.
I pressed her further for no other reason than to try and lift her out of her apparently low spirits.
'I'm quite sure that you could have been whatever you wanted to be Lucia__'
'But instead of that I became a whore!'
Her words were something of a shock. I knew of course about her past, she never tried to conceal it when I first met her and I wasn't bothered anyway. I suppose it was the way that she said it. Her whole manner it seemed had suddenly altered from the free spirited, lighthearted person that I had come to know so well, however briefly.
She now seemed to be a different person altogether and it was profoundly disconcerting.
'Honey that doesn't *matter* to me, it never *has*, you know that!'
I spoke quietly. Although there were only a few people in the small bar they were making enough noise for four times their number and it was unlikely that we would be overheard.
'Lucia, what's wrong sweetheart? This just isn't like you.'
I leaned towards her as I spoke and laid my hand over hers.
She gripped my fingers for a moment and then withdrew slowly. Laying her hand in her lap, she stared out into the street.
It was early, not quite eight o'clock, early for Cubans anyway as Havana never really came alive until after nine.
'Lucia?'
I said her name again, but she continued to stare listlessly towards the tree-lined avenue outside, where long shadows were being cast by the sun, low in the sky now after another sweltering day.
'Why did you want to marry me Harry?'
She remarked quietly, turning her face to me.
'What! __Well that's a bloody daft question love!'
I gave a brief laugh as I spoke.
'Is it Harry, __like you say, daft?'

'Of course it is! __Come on Lucia, you know very well why I wanted to marry you!'
'Why? Becos' I'm not bad lookin', __becos' I got a nice ass?'
I shook my head slowly. This just wasn't her and it was beginning to worry me.
'Lucia, 'not bad looking' is the wrong expression. You're very beautiful! __And you haven't got a nice bum, you've got a gorgeous bum! __But that's not the reason I asked you to marry me, __is it honey!'
I stared at her, wanting more than anything for her to believe me.
'I married you because you are the most honest and the nicest person I have ever met. Yes you are beautiful, no one could argue otherwise. Who can say why one person falls for another, but after half an hour just talking together, with you, in this same bar if you remember, I knew with certainty that I wanted to spend the rest of my life with you!'

She continued staring at me, looking perhaps for some indication or other, I didn't know what exactly, perhaps she didn't either.
Proving that you love someone is not easy when you think about it. I suppose it just comes down to a question of faith, something I didn't have very much of until I met Lucia.

I tried another smile.
'Come on honey, cheer up! I know it's been a bad day today, but none of it was our fault and I think the police know that.
We'll get our boat back in a few days or maybe a week and then we just carry on with what we were doing. Ok love!'
At last she gave me one of her irresistible smiles and it seemed that she was herself again.
'I'm sorry Harry.'
'I should think you would be! __Now eat your food!'
I grinned back at her.
'What about some wine for a change?'
'Sure why not. I leave it to you carino!'

I waved at the owner again and he strolled across to where we were sitting.
'Si Harry! Wha' would you like?'
'Some more jamon and some salad, and have you got any wine Diego?'
'Sure, __red or blanco?'
I took the decision before Lucia could say anything.
'Bottle of white would be great.'

'Have you come back to earth?'

I asked her.
'I never left Carino!'
'I know you didn't. It's my stupid British humour.'
She had brightened up now. 'Maybe it was the wine.'
I congratulated myself. More stupidity on my part!
'Harry!'
'Yes.'
'Can we go and live in England?'
'Bloody hell that's a bit sudden love!'
'I'm serious carino!'
'I'm sure you are, which makes it even more, __I don't know, scary I suppose.'
'What does scary mean?'
'Well er__'
I searched for the word in my limited vocabulary
'Erm, __miedo, de miedo I suppose. __Like when you see a ghost, __or some bastard is shooting at you'
'No I get it Harry.'
She paused, and she was smiling now.
'Can we Harry?'
'Can we what? Go to England?'
Maybe I was wrong. Maybe her mood, or whatever it was, was still in place.
But I answered her truthfully and almost without hesitation.
'Yes. Yes of course! __If that's what you want Lucia. Are you serious though, I mean is this a spur of the moment thing, have you really thought about this? Or is this just a reaction to what happened today?'
'Harry! Would you take me to England with you?'
I looked at her steadily.
'Yes. You know I would, I'm just not sure__'
'Would you?'
'Yes of course, I just bloody said so!'
I wasn't becoming impatient, or was I? __Yes I suppose I was.
She was stifling a laugh with a hand over her mouth.
'Honey! __Your face carino!'
I couldn't see the funny side however.
'Lucia, if you want to go to England tomorrow, then we can go. I'm absolutely serious! __But I'm not sure that you've thought about this properly.'
'An' if I have thought about it properly?'
Ignoring her expression I responded at once.
'Then we go! __As soon as we get our passports we're off!

Will you like it there?'
I frowned as I posed the rhetorical question
'Well I don't think you will, but__'
I raised my hands in acceptance.
'Who knows, and, like I say, if that's what you want!'
'Tha's the first time I see you angry chico.'
'You're wrong Lucia. I'm not angry, I'm not even annoyed.'
'You look like you are!'
'Well I'm not!'
I managed a semblance of a smile and considered for a moment before I spoke.
'Honey we can go to the U.K., sure we can. I've already said so! __Will you like it there, will you be happy? __I don't know, maybe you will! In which case we can leave as soon as we get our passports back from the police.'
'To London yes?'
'Absolutely!'
'You don' mind?'
'No I don't mind. __I'm happy here Lucia, you know that, but I'll be happy wherever you want to be! __Even if it's Timbuktu!'
'Where is,__that place you said?'
'It's not important!'
I refilled her glass with the very passable Chilean wine.
'Is that it, or do you want to torment me about something else!'
'No carino,__I don' want to tormen' you Harry. I love you.'
'I know that!'
I looked at her with genuine affection, and because it was genuine she must have seen that. There are some things that you simply can't fake.
'Like I said earlier, if you're happy, I'm happy!'
'Tha's good. __Ok, so maybe we go yeah!'
I attempted a smile.
'What did I just say to you!'
She shrugged her lovely, soft brown shoulders, draped by the mantel of dark, luscious, tightly curled hair. I looked into her face and once again I was entirely lost in her sheer beauty.
'You light up my life Lucia! __Before I met you I was only breathing!'
Her expression altered immediately and in a moment she was holding my hand in both of hers.

We finished our dinner, if you could call it that, and strolled back to our apartment, which was just a few streets away.

Did she really want to go to England? I wasn't sure. If she did then I supposed that we would go.
I wasn't going to press the point, I would let her do that.
Returning to the U.K. was not an attractive idea, not for me anyway. Perhaps a few weeks or months there would change her mind, especially with winter coming up.
I decided to leave it as it was, and not to mention it again.
If she brought the subject up then we would discuss it.
But not now! It *had* been a tough day and I think we were both exhausted. We barely spoke on the way back to the apartment and were quickly in bed. She had turned to put her arm around me as she usually did, her head resting against my shoulder.
'G'night Harry!'
'Good night sweetheart!'
It must have been only seconds before we both fell into a deep sleep.

It was ten o'clock the next morning when we finally woke up almost at the same moment.
With a long noisy sigh Lucia stretched her lovely naked body before turning to put her arm around me again.
'Wha' shall we do today carino?'
She asked sleepily.
'Nothing at all! That seems like a good idea!'
I responded, still tired and quite ready to go back to sleep again.
'I think we should go to the cops. __Fine out what's goin' on!'
'Oh come on love, that's a bit soon isn't it!'
'Yeah mebbe so.'
She paused, staring up at the ceiling.
'Wha' d'you think's goin' on Harry?'
'*Me!* __God, how should I know love! It's a total bloody mystery!'
'Yeah! __Somethin' to do with that island.'
'I think we can safely presume that honey.'
'Yeah but what? __There's nuthin' there.'
'Well there must have been something, quite obviously I suppose.'
I had the distinct feeling that she wasn't really listening to me.
'Mebbe it was drugs!'
'Maybe__'
'I's not far to the Florida Keys from there, only abou' three hundred kilometers!'
I released a short laugh, not derisory exactly, but not far short.
'Oh come on sweetheart! I don't know much about these things, but that would be the most obvious place surely. In which case the U.S. authorities

would pretty much have the area sewn up! Coastguard boats, radar, visual surveillance! __Not the best place in the world to deliver drugs Lucia!'
'You don' know Harry! Mebbe they fine' some new way, like a su'marine or somethin'!'
I smiled this time.
'Mmm, or a hot air balloon maybe.'
I threw back the sheet.
'I'm getting up! __I'll make you some breakfast.'
I pulled on a pair of trousers and strolled from the bedroom into the tiny kitchen that was no more than an annexe to the equally tiny living room. Then I filled a kettle and lit the calor-gas stove with a match.
'You don' know Harry!'
She called out.
'They' always findin' new ways!'
I shook my head.
'Perhaps love! __Like I said what do I know?' __What about egg on toast and some bacon?'
'An' some coffee carino! __Pronto!'

After a minute or so the phone rang, literally! A noisy bell from inside an old green plastic antique device with a chrome dialing wheel at the centre. I walked across and picked up the receiver.
'Ola!'
A woman's voice.
'Can I speak to Lucia Jose?'
It asked.
'One moment! __Honey it's for you!'
I called out to her.
I heard her mutter something and then leap out of bed.
Still naked and blissfully unconcerned about it, she walked into the room and took the phone from my outstretched hand.

'Ola? __Oh si, Mari-Carmen!'
Her face broke into a smile. She dropped onto one of the two straight backed chairs set in front of a miniscule dining table and proceeded to converse in rapid Spanish, which I didn't even try to catch.
After a minute or so and with several 'goodbyes' and 'see you later's' she replaced the receiver.

'Tha' was Mari-Carmen!'
'Oh right.'

I responded, juggling with a spoon, coffee bag and the two halves of a cafetierre on the single square foot of working space that the kitchen provided.
'The daughter of the policeman Harry!'
'Do we know a policeman called Harry?'
I remarked with a contrived frown.
'Uhhh! You *know what I mean* hombre!'
She retorted impatiently, bring the flat of her hand down sharply on the table.
I turned to her with another grin.
'Sweetheart! How I am I supposed to understand what you're saying? I'm making the coffee, and trying *not* to gaze at your beautiful body all at the same time! It simply isn't possible!'
She grinned wickedly, leaned back on the chair, stretched her legs out straight and held her arms over her head'
'Oh so tha's whad' it is carino! You' not use' to my lovely body yet!'
'You already know the answer to *that* one!
Now go and put something on, or there won't *be* any breakfast!'
She returned a moment later clad in a dressing gown and resumed her seat.
'You remem'er her Harry, the police man talk' about her yesterday. __We were at school!'
'Yes I remember. __So what did she have to say?'
'Oh nuthin' much. She wanna' meet with me, __an' I wanna show her my lovely husban'!'
'Oh right!'
I remarked lightly.
'Is she attractive?'
She lowered her voice.
'If I see you lookin' at her the way you look at me, I break you' arm mister! __Then I break her neck!'
I filled the caffetierre with hot water and wedged the filter in the top before setting it on the table in front of her.
Lifting my eyebrows I whispered to her.
'Plunge it in when you're ready!'
Then I took two cups and saucers from the single wall cupboard. Carrying them to the table I took the other chair opposite.
Now it was she who leaned forward seductively.
'Oh I will plunge it in chico!'
She whispered.
'You jus' tell me__*when!*'

The coffee had to wait as we rushed back into the bedroom.

There were other matters that suddenly needed some very urgent attention.

The coffee was still warm when we got back to the kitchen.
I pressed the filter to the bottom of the glass container and poured it out for both of us.
Leaning on her elbows, Lucia sipped at the dark strong liquid.
'Tha' was lovely carino!'
She murmured.
I raised my eyebrows again.
'The coffee you mean?'
'You *know* whad' I mean Harry!'
She prodded my shin with her toe.
The table was small enough for me to lean across and kiss her gently on her lips.
'Of course I do! __ It was the closest I'm ever likely to get to heaven Lucia.'

Nobody deserved to be this happy!
From a comfortable house in North London I was now living in what could only be described as a squalid dump, in a country that was permanently hot and with a language that I barely understood!
The extraordinary thing was that I had never before felt so content and so utterly at peace.
'The fools paradise'? Maybe, but I simply didn't care!
If Lucia was there when I woke every day, then nothing else mattered.

'Harry this is my frien' Mari-Carmen!'
'Hello, my Spanish is pretty lousy I'm afraid.'
I remarked to the young woman.
'It's getting' better carino!'
Lucia responded at once with an encouraging smile.
'Not fast enough, not for me anyway.'
I said ruefully.
I extended my hand to Lucia's friend who looked nothing at all as I had expected. She was slim, very slim. A nice face with light blue eyes and surprisingly light coloured hair, nothing at all what you might expect of a Cuban national, although given the cultural mix of races over God knows how many years , that shouldn't have been too surprising.
'Hello harry, I'm pleased to meet you.'
'Your English is good!'

My American you mean! __Thanks. In my job it's important.'
'Which is?'
'I work for a government department.'
'What kind of work, or is that secret!'
'No it isn't secret. Foreign trade!'
'Not much of that at the moment, is that right?'
'It's improving slowly.'
'I'm pleased to hear it. It can't have been easy after the failure of the Russian federation, __the collapse of the communist state I mean.'
'We don't see it in quite those terms.'
'No I suppose not!'
I retreated immediately, not wanting to create any premature waves, or indeed to talk about political matters.

The three of us were sitting in a smart café close to the Capital building, which was a short distance from the office where she said that she worked.

'To be truthful I've never been really interested in politics!
When I lived in England my father criticized me constantly about this.'
'He was a Politician?'
'No not really, he worked in local government, which I suppose is a variation on the same theme really.'
She shrugged but with a serious expression.
'You have to be political Harry! To make a stand on issues.'
'Well I'm not sure about that, given all the problems in the world! I'm quite happy being neutral!'
She turned and smiled at Lucia.
'Your husband is very diplomatic Lucia.'
'I guess so amiga. He don' get involved to much with tha' kinda stuff. __A bit like me Mari-Carmen!'
Her friend stared at her for a moment before turning to me again.
'Lucia was smart at school. She could have progressed to high school and even further if she had wanted. She could have got a good job and a good pension__'
'But I didn' *want* that chica!'
Lucia objected.
'Sure maybe I could have done these things you say, but you know you'self if you wanna' good job in the government, you got to be a 'socialista'!'
Her friend responded with complete calmness.
'Lucia, your mother and father died for the socialist cause!'

'No Mamen! They died to get rid of the criminal Batista an' the criminal yanks who back' him up. *Tha's* the reason they died!'
I could sense the increasing tension between them, or at least Lucia's increasing tension. Knowing very well what she was like when it came to political argument.
It was a good time to intervene.
'Hey come on you two!'
I laughed light heartedly.
'This is supposed to be a reunion isn't it!'
I raised my hands in protest.
'Forget politics for now! Lets talk about something more cheerful!'
Lucia's friend smiled at once.
'Harry's right! __ So tell me. When did you two first meet?'
'Five months ago, in a bar near the port.'
I offered before Lucia could say anything.
'Five months and already you're married! __ That was quick!'
'Quicker than you think!'
I added.
'We got married three weeks after we met.'
She looked genuinely shocked. Leaning back in her chair with her mouth open in surprise.
'Love at first sight then!'
'Virtually!' I responded with another smile.
'It was me who ask him!'
Lucia volunteered.
'Before he try to escape!'
Now we all laughed, and I at least was relieved.
The young woman seemed nice enough and with the current situation it seemed to me that we needed friends, particularly a friend with obvious connections.

'What about some more wine?'
I asked them both.
Without waiting for a reply I beckoned to a waiter.

We talked animatedly about a number of different subjects, including why had I ended up in Cuba, but there were no more controversial issues that emerged and the subject of politics was carefully avoided.
Lucia only mentioned the possibility of visiting England, but nothing very much more than had already been said, once again to my considerable relief.

However the previous day's episode near the isolated island was discussed in some detail.

It seemed that Mari-Carmen, generally referred to as 'Mamen', had been told of the events by her father, who it seemed had made no secret of it. Not to her anyway.

'Yes it all sounds very strange, but my father said that he believes your story.'

'Well I'm relieved to hear it, especially as it's the truth.'

'And you don't know who the two Americans are, __or were, perhaps I should say?'

'We know their names, or at least what they called themselves. But no, there was nothing in their bags, no identification of any kind. __All very strange.'

Her brow creased for a moment.

'Yes it certainly is Harry. I know that the police went to the island today, but of course that's all I know.'

'My wife thinks it might be drug related.'

I remarked, glancing briefly at Lucia.

'Not very likely! The drug route from South America is usually via Mexico.'

I nodded, but I didn't want to expand on Lucia's theories of how narcotics could be shipped across to Florida.

'If it wasn' drugs then whad' else could it be?'

Lucia said defensively.

'Yes you have a point!'

Her friend replied and perhaps Lucia did have a point. Drugs were now big business and I certainly couldn't think of any other reason why two men with Spanish accents could appear out of nowhere and shoot two men to death with the obvious intention of adding us to the list of bodies.

No, none of it made sense!

'We are goin' to the police station in the morning to ask them abou' this business! An to ask abou' our boat! __Like when can we get it back?'

Lucia remarked with obvious determination.

'Are we?'

I responded in some surprise.

'Er, I mean, yes we are! Why not in fact!'

'I doubt if they will tell you anything!'

Mamen replied with a frown.

'No harm in asking!'

'No, as you say Harry, no harm in asking!'

With a quick movement she finished her glass of wine.

It's getting late, I must get back home!'
'It's not even eleven yet!'
I protested.
'I have to be in the office by eight! __No excuses!'
She smiled at both of us.
'I'm so pleased we met Harry.'
Then we stood up together.
She and Lucia kissed and held each other tightly for several moments.
'We mustn't lose touch again Lucia. You have my number now.'
She turned to me and I offered my hand. Instead she held me close and kissed me on both cheeks.
'You are a nice guy Harry. Lucia is very lucky!'
'Not as lucky as me!'
I remarked with a grin.
'Perhaps not!'
For a moment there seemed to be an element of sadness in her face. Then she smiled again.
'Please keep in touch!'

She turned and hurried out of the café into the illuminated arched walkway, beyond which the blackness of the night sky was sharply etched by the continuous series of curves supported by the old stonework columns. Almost at once she hailed a cab and then with a final wave she was gone.

'Nice woman!'
I observed as we resumed our seats at the café table.
'Nother drink love?'
I asked Lucia who seemed deep in thought.
'Honey?'
I tried again.
'Yeah, er, sure Harry.'
Once more I waved a hand for the waiter.
'What'cha thinking about love?'
'Oh nuthin' really.'
'Your friend seems very pleasant!'
'Yeah, __you already said carino!'
'Is she married?'
'No.'
'Boyfriend then?'
'No!'
'Oh right. __Well that put's an end to that conversation.'

'She *had* a boyfrien'! __ She left him recen'ly. She explain' to me earlier. __He treated her badly so she left him.'
'Oh right, I see.' I shrugged.
'That's very sad.'
'He hit her apparen'ly!'
'*Hit* her! Then that's very sad indeed, not to say bloody awful! __There can be no excuse for that.'
'No, like you say! No excuse!'
The waiter brought us two more glasses of white wine and left us as quickly as he arrived.
'Anyway he got, how'd you say, __sorted out!'
'Good!'
'Yeah, she did'n tell her father, but he foun' out about it and the guy spent a few days in hospital.'
I pulled a non-committal face.
'Ok! So I guess he won't do *that* again in a hurry! __The bloke I mean!'
'*Bloke?* __Wha's this Harry?'
She wrinkled her smooth forehead.
'The guy, the __hombre!'
'Ok, __so tha's another word in your crazy language I learn today!'
'Well it's not a word really it's a sort of __colloquialism.'
A colo__*what?*'
'It means like er, an informal expression.'
'Listen hombre! __Tha's too many English words in one day for *this* chica!'
Lucia gave a deep cheerful laugh, throwing back her lovely head, her long, tightly curled hair moving en-masse in a dark cascade.
She looked to me, as always, irresistible!

'Give me a kiss Lucia.'
She glanced at me in surprise.
'Why?'
'Because you're beautiful and because I love you!'
She smiled at once and leaning across she planted a lovely kiss on my mouth.
'There! That better carino?'
'Infinitely!'
'I'm not goin' to as' what *tha'* word means!'
'It means much! __Mucho, but more than that!'

I sipped from the ice-cold glass that was beaded with moisture.
'Nice wine Lucia!'

'Yeah. Do you fancy her Harry? '
'What?'
'Mamen, my frien'!'
'You can't be serious!'
She shrugged her bare shoulders.
'Do you?'
'Lucia that would be a *no!* An unequivocal no!'
'Unequiv '
She struggled with the unfamiliar word.
'NO! It means NO in *very big letters!*'
She grinned wickedly.
'Well why didn' you jus' *say* that Harry!'

I smiled at her as I shook my head slowly.

'Your friend seems nice. You should keep in touch like she said.'
'Yeah I will. But I'm not leavin' you two alone together, tha's for sure!'
'Oh don't start that again sweetheart!'
I pleaded with a tortured expression.
'It's a broma carino! a joke!'
'Good! I should bloody well hope so!'
A brief silence.
'Shall we go home now?'
Lucia said quietly.
'I haven't finished my wine yet, and neither have you!'
She leaned towards me in her chair
'I want to make love to you Harry.'

I felt the sudden lurch in the pit of my stomach that signaled the anticipation and the sheer excitement of what I knew was coming.
In the tiny run-down tenement apartment, in the bed that was too small for us, we made love for what seemed like the first time ever.
Delicious, exquisitely satisfying, far beyond mere physical pleasure.
In Lucia's arms I was overwhelmed entirely, and for those few precious moments it was like flying through the stars in another universe!

The following morning we were up quite early. Not that we needed to be now that we no longer had a business to run.
I knew that Lucia was eager to get to the police station and to get our fishing boat returned, along with our passports.

However I was not in the least optimistic of achieving either result in such a short space of time. The investigative procedures of the police in Latin American countries moved, I was quite certain, at a more leisurely pace than one might expect in England or indeed in the U.S.!
Just a theory of course, but one which I had no doubt would soon be put to the test!
I didn't venture to voice my reservations to Lucia, deciding instead to go along with her plan and to console her afterwards.
In any event it didn't matter to me one way or the other, except that we would most likely have time on our hands.
Not a problem for me, but certainly a problem for Lucia however, as she soon became restless without something to occupy her extremely active mind.
But I had devised a solution to that particular problem.

At the station building we were led almost immediately to the office of the senior policeman, the older of the two men who had questioned us two days earlier on our boat.
He greeted us warmly and we were invited at once to sit.
'Mamen tol' me that you all got together yesterday evening for a drink.'
He was smiling broadly.
'I am very happy that you did.'
He looked at her across his desk with an expression that seemed close to affection.
'Mamen has always liked you Lucia and I believe that it's important that friends should keep together.'
Again he paused.
'You don't really remember me do you!'
'I'm not quite sure Senor. __Only a little I think.'
Lucia began.
'I used to pick you both up from elementary school when you were both young, maybe five, __six years old. You don' remember?'
Lucia looked slightly puzzled.
'I __I'm not sure. __I was a lot younger then!'
'Sure, but now you are only twenty eight, still a young woman, also very beautiful.'
'Thank you for sayin' so Senor.'
With a warm smile and a wave of his hand the compliment was dismissed. Although I could see that Lucia was pleased by his remark.
'I hope you will keep in touch with my daughter Lucia, she has had a bad experience recently and needs a good friend to talk to.'
'Yeah she tol' me!'

Lucia remarked openly.

'The thing was Senor that I finish' at twelfth grade, after that we jus'__'
She shrugged.

'I don' know, drifted apart I guess. She was clever at school. Tha's why she has a good job now.'

'No more than you were Lucia. She just studied hard!'

Maybe you' right, __anyway she choose one profession __an I choose another!'

She looked at the police chief directly with an unflinching gaze.

His eyes moved to me for a second and back to Lucia.

'Whatever we choose to do in life, the only thing that matters, in my opinion at least, is if you behave in a good way. And in spite of the er, __I mean the work that you chose, I have always believed that you were a good person Lucia!'

I intervened at once.

'I agree with you officer. My wife is a good woman, it's one of the reasons why I wanted to marry her.'

'I'm sure it was Senor Burgess!'

He smiled again, as a good friend might have.

My impression of the man initially and indeed now, was that he was a decent sort of guy.

'Anyway!'

I continued.

'I have to ask you now when it will be possible to return our passports?'

Without a word he opened the top drawer of his desk and taking out the two documents he pushed them across the desk.

'As I said to you a couple of days ago, you are under no suspicion, either of you.'

He lifted his shoulders briefly, almost apologetically.

'We will need your boat for another day or so I regret, but I will contact you when we have finished our, __well, when we have finished!'

'Any idea at all what it was all about? __The deaths of the two men, __the other vessel? The apparent mystery surrounding this island?'

I gazed at him enquiringly.

'We can't talk with you about that Mr Burgess, obviously!

Of the other boat I can say that no trace was found. The only evidence of its existence were the pieces of plastic and glass fibre embedded in the prow of your vessel. __Other than that?'

Again he lifted his shoulders.

'The two halves of the boat would still be on the sea bed surely?'

'Too deep!'

'But surely some divers with the right equipment__'

'It's too deep Mr Burgess. You must understand that we have limited facilities, financial and otherwise!'
I nodded in agreement because I felt sure he was right and also that he was being truthful, even though he was not telling us everything.
'I __we, are still concerned about our coincidental involvement in this business. The original innocent bystanders!
There may be others who know that we were perhaps the last to see these two Americans alive.'
'I can understand that.'
He pursed his lips, shifting his position in his chair.
'But I don't think that you are in any kind of danger, which is what I'm sure you mean. Whoever these men were, or whoever they were associated with is still unknown, but it seems unlikely that their employers will know of your incidental, and in fact innocent role in this matter. We shall assume for now that nobody knows anything.'
It may well be that the two Americans were acting independently and that the arrangement in hiring your boat was known only to them. __Was there any paperwork involved in the transaction?'
'No!'
Lucia intervened at once, too quickly perhaps, instantly qualifying the admission.
'Whad' I mean is, we didn' have a chance yet to give them the proper invoice for the fishing trip.'
The police chief raised his hands, dispelling the matter.
'Lucia we don' work for the tax authorities! God knows they would suck the blood from your body with haf' a chance!'
He grinned broadly.
'So the thing is there is no real connection here between you and them! I believe you got the job through the desk clerk at the Buen Vista Hotel, is that right?'
'Yeah. __I mean how did you know tha'?'
'There's not much we don' know chica!
We spoke to the guy, at the hotel. He will keep his mouth shut about this, believe me!'
Again he spread his arms apart.
'So tha's it! __We are gonna' keep a lid on this as the yanks would say. It's between you an' us ok?'
With another wide smile he stood up. A cue that the meeting was over.

Chap. 7

Outside in the street Lucia took my arm as we wandered back to the apartment.
'He seems ok love.'
'Maybe Harry. __I don' like the police, I don' trust them!'
'Why? He was very helpful, and we got our passports back didn't we!'
'I don't care carino. Before Castro the police were corrupt, sure, if you wanted somethin' you could pay them, but now? __Now the police are political an' tha' means you never know what's goin' on in their heads!'
'Well if you say so honey!'
'I do say so! __An' when are we gonna get our boat back? __We got customers waitin'!'
'Well that's ok love, we can take a bit of time off. As a matter of fact I've had a good idea. We'll get a cab and I'll show you.'
'Show me?__'
Before she could say anymore I had hailed a cab and pulled open the rear door.
'Come on, you'll be pleased!'

It was only a five-minute drive to where we were going.
I stopped the cab in a nice quiet shaded avenue near the city centre.
We got out and stood on the pavement as I paid the driver.
Lucia looked at me with a puzzled expression.
'What is this Harry?'
'A surprise!'
I took her hand and crossed the wide street.
There were buildings on each side, three or four story, old yes, but well cared for and well maintained and with rows of shops and a few cafes at street level. In the centre of the street with narrow lanes for traffic on each side, there was a broad walkway paved with marble and shaded with rows of trees on each side.
'Where we goin' Harry.'
'Like I said, it's a surprise!'
I led her towards large double doors set between a food store and a pharmacia, and framed with an elaborate carved stone portico.
Taking keys from my pocket I opened one of the doors.
'Come on!'
I led the way inside and then up a narrow stairway in a space that was well lit from windows in the stair well.
At the first floor level a suspended walkway led from the front of the building to the back with the staircase continuing upwards to other floors.

Using the same small bunch of keys I opened the first door that we came to and pushed it open.
'Whad' is this Harry
Lucia remarked with some reluctance.
'Come on, see what you think.'
I took her hand and drew her into a darkened hallway, with several doorways leading off.
At the end of the hall I pushed open one of the doors and we entered a large brightly lit room. With two tall windows that overlooked the street below.
'What do think Lucia? Our new home!'
There was no furniture, which made the large room look even larger, it also needed repainting, but that hardly seemed like a problem.
'Two bedrooms and a proper kitchen this time. __*And* a decent bathroom!'
Lucia was standing motionless in the centre of the room looking around in apparent disbelief.
'Carino__'
She started to say in a hushed voice.
I hurried on in case she needed more convincing.
'It was the guy who runs our favourite café. I told him we needed a bit more space and he put me on to a man in a government department who deals with this sort of thing. Had to give him a large envelope of cash, but that's how it works apparently.
So what do you think? Needs a bit of paint but__'
'What do I *think* Harry!'
She turned to me with an enormous smile, which said everything really.
Then she ran at me and flung her arms around my neck.
'Harry it's *fantastic!*''
Her joy was without bounds.
I *love* it Carino! It's perfect! __Oh Harry this is *such* a nice thing that you've done. I can't tell you!'
'Well as I said it needs decorating but__'
I might as well not have been speaking as she rushed from room to room, flinging open doors and windows and then, uttering excited squeals, she repeated the whole process.
'It's fantastic Harry! I can' believe you done this.
Then she rushed back to me again covering my face with kisses.
'Dis' is the bes' present *ever* carino!'
'Oh right, that means you like it does it sweetheart?'
'Like it!'
She flung her arms around me again.
'Tonight Harry, I'm gonna give you the *bes'* blow job you ever had!'

'So that means you like the place then?'
She looked at me for a moment and then she pressed her lips hard against mine.
'I love you Harry!'
She said simply.

For the next two weeks we were fully occupied. We bought furniture and a new bed, this time with more than enough room for both of us. Lucia bought curtains and a few rugs for the marble floors, she also bought pictures for the walls and some nice ornaments from the flea market. Whatever she wanted in fact.
I gave her a bundle of cash and let her get on with it.
With all her contacts there was no problem finding a decorator, who together with a second man had the whole apartment looking like new in just a week.
Our bedroom also had a balcony overlooking the street below, yet another embellishment that seemed to fill her with even more joy.
'Harry you can bring me coffee out here in the mornings, wouldn' that be nice!'
She remarked excitedly.
'Sure, why not. As long as you're properly dressed!'

The change from the seedy apartment to our new rented accommodation, from the noisy narrow street near the port to the sedate tree-lined avenue in the centre of the city was remarkable.
On the day that we moved in, Lucia, always buoyant and up-beat at the best of times, was happier than I had ever seen her.
We got our boat back a week after our meeting with the police chief, although all thoughts of fishing charters were temporarily shelved while we concentrated on getting the new apartment furnished and organized just as Lucia wanted it.
That short period of time was for both of us, the happiest that we had ever known. Lucia admitted as much to me and I didn't find it difficult to believe her.
It occurred to me then that my random decision to visit Cuba many months before was the best choice I had ever made in my life.

Lucia's expressed desire to travel to England was forgotten, at least for the present, as she relished the newfound relative luxury of our home in the Paseo de Marti.

It was just over a month before we decided to take new clients out into the Caribbean again to fish for the prized Marlin.

The slight damage to the bow of the boat was repaired and repainted and no evidence remained of the terrifying event that had occurred little less than two months before.

Yes business was good and so was life.

But of course nothing lasts forever.

We were I suppose relatively privileged as a result of the wealth that I had inherited in England.

For others the economic situation in Cuba at that time, with the loss of its only powerful patron and ally, was grim indeed.

Virtually overnight, the USSR, ruined by decades of communism, shrunk to a fraction of what that communist country had once been. The abundant supply of goods and cash to the small Cuban state ceased almost in an instant like a blocked spring that had run dry, and the result was little short of catastrophic.

Oddly enough our little charter business gradually increased as more visitors from the U.S. began to trickle in, perhaps in anticipation of the possible reduction in tension between the two countries.

But for the Cubans, for many people we knew, or at least people that Lucia knew, it was hard times in the extreme.

And so slowly, gradually, the burden of American trade sanctions and embargos began to ease as the Cuban regime had little option but to relent and to acknowledge the hated cancer of capitalism and to invite tourists to Cuba from around the world and to begin once more to export its goods.

It must have been a bitter pill to swallow for the dedicated socialists who had fought so hard to free their island from what was without doubt an obnoxious and corrupt regime, entirely supported of course by the U.S.

Never politically minded, I now found myself sympathizing with Castro and his government, for all its many faults.

But then with my scant knowledge of most things in this world, what did I know?

Lucia never said very much about her country and its recent struggles. I had tried a few times to talk with her about it but she seemed disinclined to discuss the matter. Maybe she was apolitical or simply didn't want to be reminded of the revolution in which both her parents had died.

There seemed little point in pressing the subject, because my own interest and knowledge was at best superficial.

'I have an excellent idea carino!'
Lucia had woken me early at eight o'clock on a cool morning in what passed for the beginning of winter in Cuba.
Early for me, as there never seemed much point in getting out of bed before nine, unless of course we had customers for a fishing trip, which on this day we didn't.

'Ok, so what's the idea this time?'
I grunted, emerging from the remnants of sleep, but in no particular hurry to do so.
'You' no' lis'nin' harry!'
'Probably not, I've just bloody woken up!'
I mumbled irritably.
'I's a brillian' idea carino!'
'Ok, if you say so.'
I turned my back to her with a groan and a distinct desire to slip back into sleep.
'Harry you still not lis'nin'!'
I yawned like a canyon.
'Oh come on love, give us a break here. __Look give me another ten minutes, make some coffee and we'll talk about it. __I mean whatever it is.'
She slipped out of the sheets and with one half-opened eye I gazed with sheer pleasure at her perfect figure as she pulled on a dressing gown, at the same time giving me a broad smile.
'Ok muchacho, I see you lookin'! __You got fifteen minutes before I tip you out of that bed!'
I could hear her rattling cups and spoons in the kitchen and closed my eyes again for a few minutes as random thoughts floated through my head.
It was impossible even to doze for a minute so longer, Lucia had seen to that!
With a sigh I sat up, swinging my legs over the side of the bed and ruffled my hair energetically with the fingers of both hands.
Then I pulled on some pants and wandered into the bathroom to throw some cold water on my face.
I was ready now to listen to Lucia's latest plan. __ Well almost!

'Ok, so lets hear it love, this grand scheme of yours. What's it going to cost me?'

I sipped gingerly at the hot strong coffee that Lucia had set in front of me on the kitchen table.

'No, no' you honey! Both of us, I got my own money now don' forget!'

'That's true!'

I couldn't help but smile at her eager expression, at her obvious spirited enthusiasm. It was a pleasure to see and I knew that whatever it was I would be unable to refuse her.

She leaned forward with her elbows resting on the table, her deep brown eyes staring into mine.

'Listen Harry, I think abou' this. I's a great idea!'

'Go on.'

She had raised both hands now, slim fingers splayed apart as she began her pitch.

'We open a café!'

'We *what!*'

'No, listen carino!'

'I am listening.'

'Be serious Harry!'

'I am being serious!'

'Ok. We open a café, but not jus' any old café, I mean really *smart* you know, with a long bar cover' with er, marmoles, como se dice?'

'Marble!'

Marble, sure black marble, an' stools in like shiny metal.'

'Chrome you mean.'

'Sure an' black leather seats and glass shelves with all the bottles set out behin' the bar, an' tables like in the same shiny metal, but really smart you know Harry?'

'I think so, but where? I don't know if you've noticed but there are quite a few bars in this town.'

'But this will be different don' you see. Sure there are a lot of bars, but dey are no' much, how you say '

She was searching for words.

'Chic. Up market?'

I suggested.

'Sure tha's the word Harry, up market! There's a few places but no' many, an' nobody has the money to spend on '

Again she shook her head in frustration as she sought the right expression.

'Doing them up!'

'Yeah, tha's whad I mean. Doin' them up!'

'No I suppose not!'

I thought for a moment.

'And where are we going to find a premises for this posh new watering hole?'
'What is 'posh'?'
'Smart, stylish.'
'Ok, so right here carino, in Paseo del Marti!'
'Right, fair enough. __Good area, can't argue with that, but__'
'I tell you why Harry! __Tha's you' next question yeah?'
'Well you don't know what the question is, but it's certainly one of them. On of a few in fact!'
'Because the Yankees are comin' back to Cuba, to Havana chico! Tha's why! __Castro don' like it but he needs the American dollars to survive, now that the communistas have gone.'
'Have they? I hadn't noticed!'
I grinned mischievously.
'You know wha'd I mean Harry, the *Russians* I'm talkin' about!'
I nodded slowly.
'Yes I suppose you're right. Old Fidel is backed up to the wall right now! __So yes you just could be right at that.'
'I'm sure about it Harry! We make it a 'posh' bar like you said. Instead of Cuban cerverza we give them Budweiser an' Millers an' Kentucky Bourbon instead of Barcardi!'
'A lot of people like Barcardi!'
'Sure, bu' we give them a choice.'
'Ok, but how may I ask, are you going to import all this American booze?'
'I talk to Mamen abou' this. She tell me it's possible, with the trade barriers gettin' easier now'
'They're not down yet sweetheart, not by a long way!'
'But they will be Harry. An' soon, believe me!'
I pursed my lips and nodded again, skeptically.
Lucia had a good point I suppose.
It was true that the tourists were coming back in increasing numbers. Slowly perhaps, but certainly our charter business was increasing with every month that went by. And maybe her friend was right, maybe imports of American beer and liquor might be easing slightly, but any really meaningful commodities most certainly were not. The yanks saw no problem in profiting on such innocuous items as booze, perhaps while the administration looked the other way. As they say, business is business! However the U.S. was a very long way from exporting sophisticated machinery and electronics, which might strengthen the Cuban economy.

'Yes, you just might have a good plan there Lucia. There's quite a lot of things to sort out, like I said, a premises of some kind__'

'I foun' a place, no more than a hundred metres from here.'
'Well that's a start.'
'I already talk to the guy abou' the rent, he can give us a good deal.'
'You *have* been busy sweetheart!'
'We can't sit on our asses Harry! If we don' come up with new ideas an' do somethin' about it then someone else will, __tha's for sure!'
Once again I couldn't help but smile at her unquenchable zest.
And who knows, once again maybe she was right. Things were changing in Cuba whether Castro liked it or not, so maybe her plan wasn't so crazy. A bar, or perhaps a restaurant that catered to the American taste didn't seem such a bad idea.

'Can I have some more coffee love?'
'Sure Baby!'
She stood up and bringing the coffee pot back to the table, she poured some more of the dark liquid into my cup.
'So wha'd you think Harry?'
She looked at me eagerly as she took her chair again.
For a few moments I stared out at the bright sunlight beyond the kitchen window.
'Yes it's a good idea. Needs a bit more research and attention to detail, but yes. Only problem is who's going to run it? We can't carry on with the boat charter business and run a bar at the same time, now can we Lucia.'
'Why not carino? __Vale, maybe we need some extra people to help out, but tha's ok! Plenty of people in Havana need work now, so we can give them that. We gotta' start thinkin' more like the capitalistas!'
'I am a capitalist honey, born and bred, I thought you knew that.'
She smiled softly.
'No you ain't a capitalist Harry, you're a good man. Tha's one of the reasons I wanted to marry you.'
'So all capitalist are bad are they sweetheart?'
'Come on, you know wha'd I'm sayin' chico!'
I gazed at her with a smile and with great affection.
'I'm kidding.'
'I know you are!'
I continued to stare at her.
'Do you know what I can't understand Lucia!'
'Wha's that?'
'How any god could have made a woman quite as perfectly beautiful as you are!'

She looked at me seriously and then getting up from where she was seated she moved around the table and dropped onto my lap, then she pressed my head between her breasts.
'Tha' was such a lovely thin' to say Harry.'
She whispered.
I put my arms around her and kissed her, and then I held her very close.

'So this deal of yours, like I said, maybe it is a good idea.
I'm no businessman as we both know, but I just have the feeling that it could work.
So to the next question! __How much?'
She was making breakfast for us now, and turned her head slightly.
'Ok! __I talked to some guys an' it's gonna cost abou' thirty maybe forty U.S.!'
I drew air in sharply through pursed lips.
'That's a lot of cash honey!'
'Yeah I know, more than I thought.'
She glanced at me hesitantly.
'I got about nine thousand now in my bank account, an' I thought that maybe twenty would do it, so we could be equal partners, __mas o menos!'
'We are equal partners sweetheart.'
'Oh I know that carino, but I wanted to be, oh I don' know, indepen'ent I guess!'
'Independent!'
I corrected her absently.
'Yes I suppose I know what you mean.'
I continued.
'But don't worry about it. I can finance this little plan of yours and if it takes off we can get our money back in a couple of years.'
'Your money you mean!'
'Ok if you're going to split hairs, __my money.'
'Split what?'
'Oh it's not important. Look Lucia.'
I leaned forward on my chair.
'I don't mind financing this, as I said, I think it is a good idea, so lets just get on with it, ok!'
'You sure Harry!'
I smiled at her reassuringly.
'No. I'm unsure, but we'll do it anyway.'
She laughed out with obvious joy.
'It's gonna' work Harry I promise you.'
'I'm sure it will love. __What are you going to call the bar?'

'I thought of that. El lugar en Marti!'
'The place in Marti.'
'Yeah, you' Spanish is getting better carino.'
'Not as much as it should be.'
It was easy to see and to sense her excitement, and I suppose I felt the same. Thirty or forty thousand was a lot of money in those days, but I could afford it and if Lucia was right about the coming changes on the previously isolated island, economically at least, then quite possibly it could be a winner.

There was a lot to do of course, not for me, not at first anyway apart from getting money transferred from my account in England to the account in Havana. Then there was the usual bureaucratic process, or nightmare might be a better word, that is almost always associated with a socialist regime when it comes to planning procedures.
First of all transferring the lease for the property and then the torturous game of gaining permission from the local council to open a new business. Fortunately Mamen, Lucia's friend in the government, was able to circumvent much of the red tape involved.

Lucia took on the job of managing the conversion of what was once an old tailoring shop into what finally became quite a luxurious café, which, after some discussion between us about the extra cost, eventually included a small restaurant facility.
Her forceful personality more than compensated for her lack of practical knowledge in organizing the work and supervising the builders, who were at first skeptical about a young woman being involved in what was essentially a male dominated role.
However her pragmatic approach and her willingness to learn, soon earned her the respect of all those concerned in the project.

It was necessary to employ an architect to present plans to the council, although once again Lucia imposed her strong will when it came to designing the layout of the café.
She knew a lot of people of course who were eager to have some useful and much needed work, in first of all emptying the old place of its antique fittings, taking up the old floor tiles and stripping back the cracked plaster on the walls and ceilings and then finally to completely replace the whole shop front.
It was then ready to begin the complete renovation and to refit and indeed revitalize the fine old colonial premises.

There was sufficient space for extra tables outside beneath the cloistered arcade with its series of stonework arches.
To my amazement the work was completed within three months and almost on budget.

There was an opening night with free drinks for invited guests, which included minor figures in the government and of course Mamen and her Father the police chief, together with a number of her many friends which included the man Diego, who managed the bar where we had first met.
It was a successful event with loud music and with the tables pushed aside to allow for dancing within the limited space.
Above the noise of talk and laughter and of course the incessant salsa music, I spoke briefly to the proprietor of the bar that was close to where Lucia had once lived in her dilapidated apartment.
'Diego, I hope you don't think we are stealing your business!'
I had almost to shout to make myself heard above the cheerful and good-natured celebration.
'No Amigo!'
He responded, putting his arm around my shoulder and uttering a deep chuckle.
'I see you' new menu Harry! My clients cannot afford your fancy prices here!'
He was probably right and it occurred to me at that point that we would be heavily dependent on the tourist trade to make the place viable. However Lucia with her unshakeable optimism dismissed my concerns at once.
'Don' worry carino! I got some kids handin' out leaflets to the passengers as soon as they walk off their luxury cruise ships!'

It seemed that she had thought of everything, and in fact she had!
Paseo del Marti was a magnet for visitors and the prime position of the bar very soon attracted an almost constant wave of thirsty, not to say hungry customers.
Within a week Americans and tourists from around the world began to drift into the immaculate new premises and in what seemed like no time at all the bar was busy from opening time in the morning until well after midnight.
I felt that I should take an active role at this point and suitably dressed for the part I took position behind the bar, occasionally dispensing drinks, but mostly to act as a one man welcoming committee, urging potential customers to partake of the new wide range of drinks.

'This isn't the bar that Hemingway used is it, by any chance at all?'
An elderly grey haired Englishman asked me in a studious manner, with his wife, at least I presumed that she was his wife, looking on expectantly.
'No sir I'm afraid not. That's in a different part of the town, although it's not too far from here.'
'Oh I see.'
He still looked slightly confused.
'We can make you a cocktail which was his favourite.'
I lied.
'That would be very nice! I'm afraid that my husband was obsessed with the man's stories.'
His wife intervened, glancing around as she spoke. She wore a bright flower patterned dress, white canvas shoes and a broad brimmed sun hat with ribbons tied beneath her chin.
'I must say this really is a very nice place you have here.'
She continued.
'And I must also compliment you on your excellent English young man.'
'Well in fact I am English madam!'
She gave me a nice friendly smile and a wink, which indicated very clearly that she wasn't as daft as her appearance might have suggested.
'Well that explains it then! __Could we have two of the cocktails which you just mentioned?'

To my surprise if not astonishment, the bar was virtually an immediate success. However we still had a fishing charter business to run and with me almost constantly now running the Café, a job which I found easier to adapt to than I had ever imagined, an obvious problem seemed to have arisen.
But a solution to this problem appeared almost out of the blue.

Chap. 8

'Harry, Mari-Carmen has a pro'lem with her job!'
Lucia remarked.
On one of my rare evenings off from managing the bar,
We were taking an evening stroll next to the sea wall, heading towards the old fort at the entrance to the bay.
'What kind of problem sweetheart?'
'A big one carino. She can only work for three days a week now!'
'But why?'

She shrugged her bare shoulders.
'The gov'men' cut her workin' hours.'
'Government!'
I corrected her.
'Ok the governmen' then!'
She replied irritably.
'Sorry love, you did tell me to help you with pronunciation.'
'Sure, but not all the bloody time hombre! __Dis is importan'!'
I grinned at her.
'Well at least you pronounced 'bloody' correctly.'
She relented at once.
'No I's me tha's sorry honey.'
I reached for her hand and squeezed it gently.
'So what's this about Mamens job?'
'The *government!'*
She said carefully.
'__don' have money to pay her, so they cut back her workin' time. Dis means she' short of cash.'
'Oh right, __well that is bad news. I thought she had a job for life?'
'So did Mamen carino.'
Lucia was thoughtful for a moment or so.
'I think we can help her Harry.'
'Sure, of course love. How much does she need?'
'No I don' mean that. I's not easy running the boat now with you mostly workin' in the bar.'
'Well we're sort of managing I suppose.'
'Sure, but I got a better idea! Mamen can help me with the charters and we can pay her!'
'Yes I suppose so, but what does she know about fishing, __or boats come to that?'
She turned to me with a broad smile.
'Wha' did you know before I teach you Harry!'
'Taught you!'
I corrected again, which this time earned me a sharp slap on my arm.
'Ok, it's great idea love. __I'll agree to anything you say if you stop beating me up.'
'Oh yeah baby, well maybe tha's jus' what you need!'
She pushed me back against the sea wall and flicking back her magnificent mane of dark hair she kissed me, and dug the outstretched fingers of her hands into my ribs making me gasp momentarily for breath.
'Yeah so perhaps tha's wha' you need Harry. I strip you naked an' beat your ass! Wha'd you think abou' that?'

She pressed her lips against my ear, whispering softly.
'How does tha' sound carino?'
I put my arms around her and pulled her close.
'Well if you put it that way Lucia, it doesn't really sound quite so bad at all.'

We got back to the apartment just over an hour later and were quickly in bed making love with a soaring passion.
Sex with Lucia always seemed like it was for the first time ever and then again so much better than the last!
It was after midnight and the sounds drifting up from the Paseo del Marti, just beyond the window, had diminished to the occasional subdued murmur of voices or from the odd taxi passing by slowly in the narrow traffic lane as it sought its last passenger of the evening.
A cool breeze lifted the curtains briefly and then there was total stillness.
I lay with my arm around Lucia's smooth naked body and felt utterly at peace with the world and everything in it.

'So tomorrow morning we 'ave some customers carino. I already tol' Mamen tha' she can come with me on the boat.'
Lucia commented casually as she made breakfast for both of us.
I poured more coffee into each cup and leaned back in my chair, opening the morning paper
'Good Lucia, it helps her, it helps us! But please be careful love!
Are they all men these people?'
'Two couples honey. From Kentucky.'
'Mmm ok, __anyway, like I say. be careful.'

The new arrangement, with Mamen assisting with the charters on the days when she had no work at the government office, seemed to be ideal for all concerned. For a month it all appeared to go well, although a couple of charters were perhaps longer than usual, with occasional overnight stops at small fishing ports along the coast.
It wasn't a problem as there was adequate bunking accommodation on the boat for at least six people, and Lucia would contact me by phone to say if they were unable to get back to Havana.

I woke up at nine on another fine, cool morning, but Lucia had already left an hour or so before.

She had written me a note in muddled English to say she would be back at about six in the evening and would come directly to the bar afterwards for something to eat.

When I arrived at the café at just after ten o'clock it was already busy, and it looked very much as though it was going to be another hectic day.

My prediction turned out to be correct!

At two o'clock I took a break and walked the short distance back to the apartment where I had a nap for an hour.

The novel idea of the siesta was something I had caught on to very quickly after arriving in Cuba.

When I returned the café was as busy as ever and I took a turn behind the bar, dishing out drinks to the now primarily American customers.

At six the place was packed, with the staff, which included me run off their feet!

By then I had half expected Lucia and perhaps her friend to arrive after a long day of fishing. At seven I was only slightly worried when she still hadn't appeared.

At just before eight o'clock, one of the waiters, who now seemed, unofficially at least to run the place, came to me to say that I had a phone call and that it was from the police!

I was instantly terrified if I was to be honest, although I made every attempt to conceal my feelings from the man, but when I took the receiver from him I had a lump in my throat and a grinding pain in my stomach.

'Harry how are you!'

Came the immediate and cheerful response.

'Er, yes, erm, __ is this the police?'

'Of course Harry! It's Raul, __Mamen's father.'

Then I recognized his voice and his excellent English.

'Look don' worry about anything. We had a call from Lucia's ship-to-shore radio, she knew you would be worried if she was late.'

'Are they ok?'

My voice was shaking.

'Sure, don' worry. She couldn't get to a phone to let you know. They ran out of gas and had to stop over to refuel in a place called Matanza, you wouldn't know it. It's a small place about eighty kilometers east along the coast. Too late for them to get back tonight, so they're all sleepin' on the boat.'

'But how? I mean__'

'Who knows Harry? Maybe the yanks got too keen lookin' for Marlin, went too far off shore maybe. Who cares, it's gonna cos' them more dollars for the inconvenience.
So anyway, like I say, you don' need to worry, ok Harry?'
'Er yeah sure and thanks er, __Raul. Thanks for letting me know.'
'No problem! __We mus' get together, have a beer or somethin'!'
'Yes, yes that's a great idea.'

With enormous relief I hung up the phone, although the churning sensation in my stomach persisted.
The bar was still packed, but now after my profound, if short-lived anxiety, I didn't have the energy or the will to continue being nice to half drunk Americans and explaining the best places to visit in Havana. I wasn't going to be much use for the rest of the night and I knew it.
I had a quick word with the waiter, who it seemed had quite naturally fallen into the role of manager, through natural selection I suppose. It had enabled me to take a back seat, partially at least, and to spend most of the time serving behind the bar.
'Pasqual I 'm going back to the apartment.'
'Sure Harry. You ok?'
He looked at me with what I was sure was genuine concern.
'You don' look er, __'
'No I'm ok, just er, I don't know, bit tired I guess. Can you erm, __'
'Of course! No pro'lem. Get some rest, some sleep. You feel better tomorrow I bet!'
He smiled as he spoke, laying a hand briefly on my arm.
He was a decent guy, who Lucia, with her instinctive way of evaluating people with considerable accuracy, had given a job after he had been fired from one of the hotels, for no other reason than it went broke. Like so many other enterprises in Castro's brave new society, once the money tap had been turned off.
Initially by the U.S., and then finally by Russia.
Cuba's only remaining patron appeared to be Venezuela, which once a wealthy oil-rich nation would also eventually succumb to lower world oil prices and economic pressure from the U.S.
They were difficult times indeed for Cuba, but thankfully not for us as we had cornered a small niche market, __or rather two!

I went back to the apartment, showered and then started drinking cold beer with the sole intention of getting drunk.

This would be only perhaps the third night after meeting Lucia almost a year before, that I would be sleeping alone. I knew that if I didn't get drunk then I wouldn't sleep at all!

I woke up at just after ten the next morning with a monumental headache and a vile taste in my mouth.
Forcing myself out of bed I wobbled my way to the bathroom and drank cold water from the tap, not a wise thing to do but this was an emergency. Then I threw water over my face several times. Leaning heavily on the edge of the basin, as my legs were in no condition to support me, I stared down into the water, my head thumping. At last I straightened up groggily and stared into the mirror, trying to recognize the image staring back at me. With a deep groan I turned away and crept unsteadily into the kitchen where I fumbled with the coffee pot and lit the gas stove with a hand that was shaking.
Sitting at the kitchen table I sipped at the strong dark coffee, praying for some magical relief to the throbbing pain behind my temples. After fifteen minutes or so, some Aspirin, and two more cups of coffee the agony began to recede slightly.
__Thankfully, even though the sun was rising in a clear blue sky beyond the window, it was another cool clear morning with a light breeze drifting in through the opening. I glanced casually at my watch. The big hand I noticed was on the eight and the small hand was somewhere between eleven and ten. It didn't register at once, but when it did it was very much like being hit in the face by a swing door.
Lucia! She should have got back by now surely!
The pain returned in full force at the sudden realization.
I leaned my elbows on the table, pressing my fingers hard on each side of my head and closing my eyes in an attempt to stop the self- imposed misery of my hangover.
Suddenly furious with myself I stumbled back into the bathroom, ripped off my shorts and got into the shower, turning the cold faucet on full.
I gasped as the water hit me, forcing myself to stand under the deluge for a full minute that seemed like thirty. Then I turned off the tap and still gasping for breath I leaned against the tiled wall with my eyes closed.
It had the desired effect, not entirely of course because I knew that complete recovery was going to take several hours. Nevertheless I was able to dry myself and throw on a pair of pants and a shirt.
Another quick glance in the bathroom mirror reassured me that I was still alive and after running a comb through my hair I almost resembled a human being again.

I thrust my feet into a pair of shoes and grabbing my keys, left the apartment and descended the stairs carefully, gripping hard onto the handrail as my feet slowly learned to walk again.
There was another welcome fresh breeze as I left the apartment building and crossed the tree-shaded avenue towards the café just a short distance away.

When I entered there were only half a dozen customers.
Pasqual was behind the bar as bright as a button. It was almost as though he hadn't left.
I took one of the stools as he walked across to me.
'Better this mornin' Harry?'
'Not really!'
I pointed towards my head.
'What have you got for a hangover?'
I asked him dismally.
'Coffee!'
'I've had two already.'
'Then one more won' hurt you! __And maybe Codeine, I'll fin' you some.'
The coffee did help oddly enough and I took two of the white tablets that Pasqual gave me.
'I'm worried about Lucia. She got stranded last night. Ran out of fuel. Do you know where Matanza is Pasqual?'
'Sure, it's down the coast some way.'
'How can I get there?'
'Taxi, but it's a lousy road could take you two hours, an' you have to get to the other side of the bay first.'
'Yeah that's true.'
'Can't you contact her?'
'Don't have a radio.'
'The police have!'
'Yes of course they do! __I'm not thinking straight Pasqual.'
'I'll telephone them for you.'
'No I'll walk! It's only a few blocks. A bit of fresh air might make me feel better.'
I eased myself off of the bar stool and headed towards the door, which at that precise moment opened, and there she was.

I can barely describe the sheer, overwhelming relief.
Entirely irrational of course, why would she not just suddenly turn up like this, I had no reason to expect anything else, nevertheless I hurried towards her and flung my arms around her.

'Lucia, I'm __ I mean, I was really getting worried.'
Her face broke into that now so familiar smile.
'*Why* Harry? Didn' Mamen's dad contact you?'
'Well yes he did, yesterday evening.'
'So wha' you panickin' about?'
'Not panicking exactly, __well__'
'I'm glad you' worried carino! It means you care about me!'
'Well of course I do!'
I looked over her shoulder. Mamen was smiling knowingly.
'Hi Mamen. Everything ok?'
'Sure Harry, we're fine, bu' you don' look so good.'
It was Lucia who stared at me now, holding me at arms length.
'No tha's right, you don' look too good at all honey, wha's wrong with you' eyes? An' you look sort of __palido! __You ok harry?'
She looked concerned now.
'Not really.'
I sighed deeply.
'Had a few beers last night.'
She nodded her head slowly, turning to her friend.
'You see chica, I'm away for one day workin' hard an' this man wanders around the bars geddin' borracho, __geddin' drunk!'
'No seriously Lucia it wasn't quite like that__'
'Tha's wha' *you* say muchacho!'
She winked at Mamen as she led me back into the café.
'Hola Pasqual, que tal, todo bien?'
'He smiled at her.'
'Si Lucia, todo regular.'
'Can you get some breakfas' for my 'usban' and for me an' Mari-Carmen!'
She looked at me.
'Did you have breakfas' Harry?'
'No er, not yet.' I mumbled.

We had taken a seat at a table outside the café on the cloistered walkway. I drank deeply from a second large glass of cold water while the two women sipped at coffee.
'So what happened love?'
'You know wha' happen! We ran out of gas an' had to spen' the night in Matanza!'
'Bit uncomfortable wasn't it?'
'Not too bad. The customers slep' in the cabins up front and Mamen an' me sleep on the bench seats in the main cabin.
We had some drinks, I made some food__'

She shrugged.
'It was ok Harry, jus' for one night.'
'Did they catch anything?'
'One Marlin only. __Two hundred pound!'
'Bloody hell. Hardly worth the trip!'
'No no' really. We sold it in Matanza to get rid of it. Then we set off at sunrise, abou' six.'
'You did well then! __Eighty kilometers!'
'No I's a bit less, abou' seventy maybe. The sea was calm, so no pro'lem.'
'Good, at least you're safe.'
I turned to her friend.
'So how was your trip Mamen? Enjoying the new job?'
'It's ok Harry. New experience for me.'
'What about the clients? You were supposed to be taking them out again today, wasn't that the plan?'
'They ain't going nowhere today Harry! They all got drunk on Barcardi las' night. Now they at the hotel, in bed prob'ly sleepin' it off!'
'Oh right! So you lost a days money then.'
'We los' nuthin' carino. They paid for today an' for the extra gasoline. __I make sure of that.'
She took a roll off notes from the pocket of her shorts, waving it at me. I had to smile. __Lucia, the quintessential business woman!'

'Ok so now what?'
I exclaimed after we had finished eating.
'Now I go back to the apartment an sleep!'
Lucia remarked with a wide yawn.
'You too Harry. You look like you need it!'
Mari-Carmen grabbed at her overnight bag.
'I'm going to get a taxi and do the same as you!'
'No, espera Mamen! I gotta pay you firs'!'
She took out the wad of cash again and peeled off some notes.
'Here you go chica. Two days money.'
Her friend kissed her as she stood up.
'Gracias Lucia, An' thanks for this I see you soon yeah! __Bye Harry.'
'So long Mamen. Say hello to your dad for me.'

She caught a cab almost at once. Then it was just the two of us at the small table outside the Café.
'So, __bit of an adventure then!'
I remarked, just to fill what felt at least like a gap of some sort.

'No' really.'
'No problem with the boat?'
'No. __Apart from runnin' out of gas.'
'Good! __Well.'
I attempted a smile as Lucia continued to stare at me.
'Why did you get drunk las' night Harry?'
'Oh I don't know. One beer led to another I suppose.'
'Where did you go?'
'Nowhere! As soon as I got the call from Mamen's father I went home.'
'You went home.'
'Well where do you *think* I went Lucia?'
'I don' know.'
She started playing distractedly with a small spoon on the table, turning it over and over as though it was some precious, newly discovered artifact.
'Look, after I got the call from Mamen's dad, I was, __I don't know, shook up I suppose. __Worried!'
'You didn' need to be.'
'Maybe, but I was! So I went home and got drunk!'
She smiled at me then, and reaching out she ran her fingers across my hair.
'We were all ok Harry.'
'I know that, but__ the thing is, that was one of the few nights that we hadn't been together. I missed you and I was concerned about you, and I knew that I wouldn't be able to sleep. So__'
My voice trailed off because there was nothing much else that I could say.
'I miss' you too Harry.'
Lucia remarked after a few moments of silence.
'An' you' right. It was only a coupla' times we been apart since we got married.'
She looked up at me again and smiled.
'How's you' head?'
I shrugged.
'Not too bad now, now I've had something to eat and drunk about a gallon of water.'
Those lovely eyes gazed at me, and once again I found her completely irresistible.

I swear that every time I looked at her I fell in love all over again.
Was that normal? Who knows, who cares, but that's how it was.
Yes that's exactly how it was. I had never really understood the meaning of the word until I met Lucia, but now she was my life and nothing else seemed to matter.
No I'll correct that, nothing else mattered at all!

'Let's go home carino. I'm tired, you' tired, let's jus' get some sleep.'

So that's what we did.

The thing is, unless you have lived in a country where it's hot most of the time and where rain is a welcome respite.
Where it's never freezing or even that cold. Where miserable damp weather never even existed. Where it's not overcrowded and congested, like the major cities in England.
I mean with houses built on top of each other, people crammed together in close proximity.
Sure it was crowded in Havana, but it was different.
In England there was no real cohesion, or social contact.
Who has time for social contact when your life is regulated, formalized, dependent on the strict regime of getting on a bus or a train each morning to go somewhere you don't really want to be, but you have to because that's the conditioned game as written by __well who knows the answer to that, apart from the faceless wealthy bastards who ultimately devised the plan in the first place, whoever they are!
In Cuba I felt as though I had the freedom to do virtually whatever I wanted. Was I one of the lucky one's, maybe so.
The best choice I ever made, no, the second best, was to leave England and embark on my limited adventure, and to end up on a truly beautiful island like Cuba.
Poverty? Oh yes, you had better believe it, there was poverty alright, but in spite of all this my, ok, subjective opinion was that generally people were happier!
Under Castro, people's lives had improved, albeit for a relatively short period. Would it continue, only God knew the answer to that!
Karl Marx's grandiose social ideals didn't actually work, that was the bottom line, nothing new there!
Good sentiments perhaps, impossible to implement!
He was a philosopher and that's all that he was!
A successful architect of social change? I don't think so.
But there, I suppose I'm rambling a bit now.

Lucia and I went back to the apartment, but instead of going to bed, which would probably have been the sensible thing, we sat together talking, Talking and talking about everything, during which we had a few

Barcardi's. mixed with real orange juice and with plenty of ice, best way to drink it as a matter of fact!
Not wise perhaps, but it was worth it because we talked and debated and discussed just about everything.
What better way to spend time, except for the more obvious way of course. Then we did go to bed, by which time it was getting late, and we were both exhausted, and I at least slept as never before!

I discovered a short time later that the latest fishing trip Lucia had made with her friend Mamen, wasn't actually that at all.
It was only just over a week later in fact, and it was purely by chance.
I didn't know too many people of course in Havana and my command of Spanish was at best rudimentary, although it was slowly improving.
A guy at one of the hotels in Havana called the apartment to say that he had some more clients for us the following week.
'Ok.' I responded and grabbed at the book that we kept for reservations.
'How many?'
'Jus' two senor, for two days.'
'Ok, give me the details!'
He did just that and I wrote it down carefully in the notebook.
'Thanks Antonio, this is repeat business I can see. That's what really matters. If they're happy they'll come back.'
'Oh they' happy senor. Most of them anyway!'
'Good! We didn't get feedback from the two couples from Kentucky. I mean they only caught one fish, but Lucia went to a lot a lot of trouble__'
'From Kentucky?'
'Yes! About two weeks ago, bit less maybe. It was supposed to be two days but ended up as one.'
'No senor Burgess I don' have a record of that. The trip for them was cancelled.'
'Cancelled?'
'Si senor.'
'Do you know why?'
'No senor.'
'Oh right ok, but the trip did go ahead.'
'Maybe it was through a different hotel mister Burgess.'
'Yes that must be the answer, double booked probably.'
I glanced through the record book again.

'Well no, in fact it's here clearly enough Antonio, they booked the trip alright, through you it says, no sign it was cancelled. Maybe my wife made a mistake here.'
'I guess that she did senor. __So can I say that these new people have a reservation?'
'Er, well yes of course, just a slight mix up here. I've probably got it wrong somehow.'
'Perhaps. Bien senor Burgess, y gracias!'

Right, well the man was clear enough I suppose. There was a mistake, simple to make with all the business we were doing.
There was no point in discussing what seemed a trivial matter with Lucia so I didn't bother.

The charter business was better than perhaps either of us could have predicted. Lucia and I both agreed on that.
And the new café? __Well that had taken off like the proverbial rocket.
In an essentially impoverished country we were making good money. I did speak to Lucia about the question of taxation but she was as always unconcerned.
'Honey don' worry abou' this! Mari-Carmen has foun' us a good accountant. In these difficul' times I's not a problem to be makin' money. Fidel is wakin' up to the real world!'
I dare say she was right. The halcyon days of support from the defunct USSR were history now. Did this mean that the hideous corrupt regime of the Batista days would return?
My guess was no!
Poverty and happiness was better than poverty and misery and I was quite sure that the people of Cuba understood that.

I never really thought anymore about the conversation that I had had with the desk clerk at the 'Vista del Mar' hotel. It didn't seem important.
In fact the matter would never have re-emerged had it not been for a chance meeting with someone who I had never seen before.
It was late evening a few days after my conversation with the hotel clerk, and a woman came into the Café and asked for Lucia.
I didn't know her of course, and there was no reason why I should have.
'I'm sorry, but Lucia is not here at the moment. Can I help at all?'
I remarked with a suitably courteous smile.
'Would you like a drink, coffee perhaps?'
The woman was I suppose, what one might expect of the average tourist, well dressed, American accent clearly defined.

The best thing I could have done, and what I should have done perhaps was simply to have told her that Lucia was not around and just left it at that.

'No thanks, a "Millers" please, just a small one.'

I obliged, filling a glass with cold pale beer from the elaborate chrome tap, one of three that dominated the marble counter top.

'I was wondering when we could charter your boat?'

She continued.

'My husband and I that is. We've spent almost a month in this wonderful place, with our two friends and we were really hoping to do some fishing for a couple of days. I know how busy you are, but your reputation__'

She shrugged expressively.

'Well that's good to hear and absolutely no problem at all. We can certainly arrange a couple of days for you__'

'I mean we did have a trip organized__'

She continued.

'__but it was cancelled a week or so ago. You had some slight problem with the boat I was told, these things happen of course, but if it's resolved now__'

'Er, no no, it's business as usual! If you can give me your name and where you're staying__'

'Sure! At the,__well what used to be the 'Marriott'.'

'The 'Vista del Mar you mean.   Yes, still quite comfortable so I'm told.'

'Sure it's ok.__Are you English?'

The woman replied with a curious look.

'I'm surprised you noticed!'

I smiled at her at once as I spoke.

'Bit of a giveaway really, the accent, but yes I am English. Currently resident in Cuba.'

'Ok, I don't mean to be rude,__inquisitive I mean.'

'No of course not. It must seem,__well a bit odd I suppose.__A bit like Hemingway.__How did *he* end up here for god's sake!'

'Are you a writer?'

'Good heavens no!'

'Ok!'

She nodded her head uncertainly.

'So__'

'Yes, I run this place and my wife runs the charter business. So anyway what I will do is to tell her to contact you in the morning and make some firm arrangement for a trip. I assure you that you won't be disappointed. Lucia is an expert fisherman,__or woman I should say!'

'Well that's great! That's all I really wanted to know!'

'Ok so your name__'
I had a pen ready and a note pad.
'It's Louise, __Louise Clermont.'
'Sounds a bit French, the name I mean!'
'It is! __So that will be me and my husband together with our two friends.'
'Fine! Where are you from Mrs. Clermont? __Purely out of interest.'
'Well, the states obviously. __Kentucky!'
I gave no indication at all of my total surprise.
'Right, ok! __Never actually been to America. __Big country of course! Perhaps one day, who knows.'
She glanced at me with an expression that suggested the discussion was over.
'Ok then, so that's settled.'
She glanced at her watch.
'My husband is meeting me outside shortly.'
'Ok, I won't keep you then. __Lucia will call you at your hotel in the morning Mrs. Clermont. At which time she will be able to give you a firm date for your trip.
My sincere apologies for any previous inconvenience.'
The woman smiled.
'How much for the beer?'
'On the house.'
'Thanks, I'll expect a call tomorrow.'
With that she left, and I could see her and I presumed her husband get into a taxi outside in the street.

Well, was that a coincidence, a real coincidence! Four people, with at least two of them from Kentucky!
I had certainly never been completely stupid, and this new information had stopped me in my tracks. The point was what the hell was I going to do about it! And the business of the boat breaking down? Well that was the first I'd heard about it!
There didn't seem to be any obvious explanation, none that I could see anyway.

'You ok senor Burgess?'
Pasqual interrupted my thoughts with a look that implied limited concern.
'Er, yes of course Pasqual.'
'Senor I was hopin', jus' for tonight to get back a little early__'
'Of course! It's eight now anyway, and it's a bit quiet for a change.'
'It's my wife Harry, she's er__'

110

'Yes I know. Wonderful news Pasqual! Congratulations to both of you. Your first yes?'
'Yes it will be our first.'
'Then get going! I'm closing up in an hour anyway.'

The thought still persisted and it still made no sense.
I would have to talk to Lucia when I got back to the apartment and there seemed to be no way around it.
What the hell was I going to say and more importantly what was *she* going to say.

It was dark when the last customers left at just after nine.
With distinct nervousness I closed up the café and began the short walk across the terraced central pedestrian area of the street, where a number of people were strolling beneath the floodlit trees or relaxing on the numerous carved stone benches.
With my stomach churning now, I let myself into the apartment building.

'Hi Lucia.' I called out, closing the door to the apartment.
'In here Harry!'
Her cheerful voice came from the open door of the kitchen from where a delicious smell of cooking permeated the air.
'Hi baby!'
She kissed me lightly when I entered and went back at once to stirring pieces of marinated chicken in a large pan.
'That smells bloody good!'
I commented, forcing a smile.
'Cajun chicken! __Hot and spicy, jus' like me!'
'Can't argue with that.'
I responded, my heart sinking as I spoke, because the small kitchen table had been covered by a pristine white cloth, and there were two plates with cutlery set out. A small vase of flowers had been placed in the centre with a single brass candle stick next to it with the candle waiting to be lit.
'You wan'na beer honey?'
'Er, yeah, that would be great. __You look beautiful by the way.'
She smiled at once.
'Thanks baby!'
'What's the occasion?'
'No occasion, I jus' wan'ed to make myself look nice for you an' cook you some good food.'
She went back to stirring the pan.
'Get a beer for me as well carino!'

She called out as I rummaged in the refrigerator for bottles.
'How did it go today Harry?'
'Oh ok, bit quiet for a change.'
'Tha's good. but I thought you' be back sooner than this!'
'Pasqual asked me if he could go a bit earlier. Wanted to get back to his wife so I said I would close up.'
'Oh sure, yeah! She's pregnan'. She only got abou' two month to go now.'
'That's right.'
I pulled the caps off of the bottles and handed one to Lucia.
'First baby, so he's pretty excited.'
'For sure I bet! __When you gonna knock me up Harry?'
She gave me a coy smile before lifting the bottle to her lips.
'Well it's not my fault love. You're using that er,__'
'Diaphragm you mean. __Not anymore carino, not for more than a month, so now I's up to you!'
She presented me with another meaningful smile and suddenly I felt embarrassed without knowing why.
'Bloody hell! __I mean, that's really pulled the rug from under me!'
'Pull the *what?*''
'Oh it's just another daft English saying. It means like surprised, __shocked I suppose!'
She stopped what she was doing and walked across to me.
Still holding the bottle of beer, she put her other arm around my waist and kissed me on the mouth.
'Well who knows chico, maybe I already got a bun in the oven!
But for sure, after you' hot and spicy chicken, you got hot an' spicy me to deal with tonight.'

If it was possible my heart sank even lower, when in fact I should have been ecstatic.
I decided that I had to broach the subject that was tormenting me without putting it off any further.
With my courage failing rapidly I knew that it was now or never.
'Sweetheart someone came into the bar earlier on. She wanted to book the boat for a couple of days.'
'Ok babe! Did you write it all down?'
'Yes I did.'
'Why didn' she call me?'
'I don't know, maybe she tried. The guy at the Vista hotel usually tells potential customers to call in at the Café if they want to arrange a trip.'
'Ok, so?'
'I said you would ring her in the morning and sort it out.'

'Fine!'
'There's four of them apparently, __two couples.'
'Ok.'
She had gone back to stirring the chicken pieces in the thick, dark sauce, the aroma of which was wonderful, although now I had absolutely no appetite.
'Said her name was Clermont, __Louise I think. __From Kentucky she said!'
Lucia briefly stopped what she was doing then continued stirring slowly again.
After a few moments she removed the large wooden spoon and laid it carefully on a plate. Then she turned to me.
'What else did she say Harry?'
I tried to avoid her eyes, but I couldn't.
'That the original trip was cancelled just over a week ago. Something about a problem with the boat.'
It was still a struggle to meet her eyes directly.
'Look at me Harry!'
I did, but it wasn't easy.
'So what d'you make of all this carino?'
'Erm, well I don't know *what* to make of it. I was hoping you could tell me.'
She turned to the stove again and switched off the gas.
Then she took one of the chairs at the kitchen table.
'Get some more beers Harry, we have to talk!'
I did as she said retrieving two more cold bottles from the fridge. Then, feeling acutely nervous, I sat opposite her.

'I'm no' gonna' lie to you Harry, not anymore. Believe me, I feel real bad about that. You done so much for me carino and I should have been straight with you, but the pro'lem' is I couldn't.
This is such a big thing an' I jus' had to do it.'
'Do *what* for Gods sake?'
She took a sip from the bottle, perhaps to help her say whatever it was that seemed so difficult. Certainly she was struggling with something and I could feel the tightness returning in the pit of my stomach.
'Lucia whatever it is, it can't be that bad surely!'
Her face changed somehow, an expression I had never seen before. She tried to smile but it didn't work.
'Lucia come on! I love you, what else matters!'
'Well maybe you won't, not after I tell you.'
'Well, *tell* me then for Christ's sake!'

I wasn't getting annoyed exactly, but I was certainly getting scared.
She hung her head for a moment, her mass of dark hair almost covering her face.
Then she looked up.
'Mamen and me took the boat out a coupla' weeks ago, but we didn' go fishing. We went around the west side of the island.'
'Which island?'
'Cuba Harry, *this* island!'
'Went where?'
'Somewhere you wouldn't know. I's on the west coast, a place called Cayos de Buenavista, jus' some little islands with lots of, how do you say, bahias?'
'Bays, inlets. __Islands? Why would you go there for God's sake? __And it's got to be, I don't know, a bloody long way, I mean__'
'Abou' two hundred kilometers!'
She interrupted.
'We had to sail at night to get there and back.'
'Good God! __But the point is *why* Lucia?'
'Yeah well this ain't easy to say. __We were takin' guns Harry!'
'*Guns!* __what the hell do mean, guns!'
'Lots of guns. The boat was loaded up!'
I couldn't believe what I was hearing.
'Guns for *what* Lucia! The revolution is over isn't it!'
I was still trying to understand, or struggling would be a better word.
'No! __Here maybe, but in Central America, people want freedom. Nicaragua, el Salvador, Panama. You know this Harry you jus' gotta read the papers!'
'No, I still can't believe this! You say that you're smuggling guns to bloody Central America!'
'No not quite Harry, We hide them on one of the small islands an' then some guys pick them up.'
'What guys?'
'Revolutionaries.'
'Communists you mean!'
'She shrugged.
'Call them what you like Harry. They're freedom fighters!
Fighting agains' the U.S. agains' the CIA, against the criminal bastards, the dictators paid and backed up by America. It never stops. Although one day maybe!'

I was stunned to say the very least, and virtually speechless!
Smuggling *guns!* No, this wasn't possible. It couldn't be possible!

At last I found my voice again.

'This is madness Lucia. What if you were caught by the authorities, __ by the police?'

'Well that ain't gonna happen__'

'Not this time maybe, but you must stop this crazy business, and stop right now Lucia! __ I can't allow you do this again.'

'Carino you don't get it. It's the authorities as you wanna' call them who are paying for all this, supplying the guns, everything!'

'*What!* __That's impossible!'

'Honey it's Castro. He wants the revolution to continue in these places, you mus' know this. What do you think Guevara was doin' in Bolivia!'

'Look, I don't know anything about him, or about revolutions or about politics, or about any related subjects Lucia. I never have. __ And to be honest I don't fucking *want* to know!'

She stared at me for a long time before saying anything. It was the same kind of reproving look that I once used to get from my father, only for entirely different reasons of course.

'Harry you' lucky, you have money. You can do pretty much what you want! Bu' mos' people in this world don't have nuthin'!'

'Anything.'

I corrected her sheepishly.

'Harry I'm bein' serious!'

There was an element of anger now in her voice, maybe not anger exactly, but certainly something like it and I didn't want to provoke her, I just wanted to know what the devil was going on.

'You told me once Lucia that you weren't political, that you weren't a communist.'

I said quietly.

'Harry I'm not a communist. It doesn' work! I's failed in Russia and I's failin' everywhere 'specially in South America, an now I's failin' here in Cuba, although Fidel will never accept that.

No carino, I'm not a communist, but I believe people should be free an' be able to lead a decent life.'

Perhaps she was right. In our hearts I suppose that's what most of us want, to have the freedom to live a more or less happy existence. So she vehemently denied that she was a communist or even a socialist, come to that, and I believed her.

'But these people you're dealing with *are* communists Lucia!'

'No! They are anti-capitalist, anti corruption, anti-U.S. The Yankees have interfered for too long in South, an' especially Central America because I's

what they want! It suits the big companies, the fruit growers, the people who wanna' cut down the rain forest, exploit the oil reserves in Venezuela an' the gulf.
I's abou' money Harry, abou' makin' the rich richer. Tha's what I's all abou', tha's what I's always about carino! __I's the same ol' story!'

Yes, maybe she was right. I was slowly beginning to realize that I had been leading a sheltered life in England, quite happy to remain ignorant, or more likely indifferent to what goes on in the world.
It had been a conscious choice I suppose, to shove such matters to the back of my mind.
For most of us who have a comfortable life and don't have to worry about where our next meal is coming from, the plight of others hardly seems relevant.
The difference was of course that I *should* have been aware!
The remarks made by my headmaster some years before were returning to haunt me.

'So tha's the story carino. __Now you know!'
She tipped back the bottle and took a long gulp of beer.
Neither of said a word for some time until Lucia finally broke the silence.
'It was Mari-Carmen who come to me with this!
If the yanks know that Cuba is supplyin' arms to the revolutionaries they would come down hard on this country. Jus' when things are gettin' a bit better, with the tourists comin' back here an' some trade, ok no' much, an' no' much with the U.S., but I's gettin' better. If they discover this it would be back to the blockade.
Cuba is in a bad way Harry. The embargo by the Yanks is killin' this country!'
She shook her head, her thick dark hair sweeping across her shoulders.
'You jus' don' see carino! What the Americans really wan' is Cuba the way it was, with the big companies runnin' the show again, controlin' everythin', makin' big profits an' payin' lousy wages to the people. They wan' the return of the casino's, an' the whores back on the streets again. You gotta' think abou' what America is doin', not only to this country, but in the world Harry! Always tryin' to__ I don' know, __fuck up small countries, like__how do you say!'
In frustration, as she groped around for the right expression, she thumped the table with the palm of her hand.
'Ok I know what you mean love!'
I intervened, coming to her rescue at once.
'De-stabilize the smaller nations, that's what you mean!'

'Is tha' what I mean? __Ok then tha's what they're doin'!
They say they're tryin' to save the world, but tha's not true Harry!'
She gazed at me, once again with apparent frustration.
'Why don' you know all this stuff?'
She lifted her shoulders slightly.
'You' a smart man, so why don' you see wha's goin on in the world?'
She was right of course and I had to agree.
I felt a slight sense of guilt at what was in fact an accurate comment.
'Well you've got me there sweetheart, and I don't have any defense.'
She relented, but only slightly.
'Harry I love you, you know that, but you gotta wake up carino. The world is a shit-hole. Prob'ly it always has been, but we gotta stand up an' try to change things.'
'So is that your contribution to changing things Lucia, is that what it is, shipping a few arms for the freedom fighters? More wars!'
'Yeah, if you like! __I's no' much, but I's somethin' a' least!'
'How do you know that the guns are getting into the right hands?'
'We think so. We can't be sure although the Cuban security service is in contact with the rebels over there so I guess they know what they're doin'.'
'But it seems like an amateur venture almost. A small fishing boat like ours delivering weapons to __well wherever!'
'But tha's the point carino! There are others doin' the same thing, like you say, small boats, but keepin' close to the shore. Not easy for the American coastguard to do somethin' about it, even if they see us. They can't stop every little boat in Cuban waters.'
'No I suppose they can't.'
I thought for a few moments.
'But how do the guns get delivered to these Central American countries?'
'I shouldn' be tellin' you this Harry. __None of it, but I guess I's too late now.'
She hesitated.
'They pick them up by sea-plane from the cayos.'
'I see.'
I couldn't resist a smile.
'Yes I see! Very crafty Lucia! It's a short flight to Belize or Nicaragua.'
'Yeah. __So now you know!'

Yes I certainly did, but the shock at this news had hardly registered, in fact it hadn't sunk in at all.
For several long moments nothing was said as I tried to get things straight in my head.

'You said that Mamen was involved!'
'Yeah. Mamen is communist. She always has been. She believes in Castro an' Marx an' all that bullshit, but at leas' they tried to make some changes in the world. There's a lot of sufferin' Harry, not jus' here or in South America, but in Africa an' a lot of other places.'
'So she's been brainwashing you!'
'Wha's brain washin'? wha's that Harry! __I can *think* for myself, I always have done!'
I could see now that she was starting to get angry. With her back straight, her hands flat on the table she leaned towards me.
'I don' need some chica like Mamen to tell me abou' injustice an' poverty Harry, I can see that here everyday an' in the countryside too, 'specially now the Russians have gone. Fidel is desperate but he don' give up the struggle!'
'No perhaps not.'
I said quietly.
'The point remains you're taking enormous risks by what you're doing Lucia. You're right about my lack of knowledge in these matters, or perhaps indifference would be more accurate.
What I do know is that the Americans are pretty ruthless when it comes to the communists or to anyone who they see as a threat to their system.'
I drew a deep breath.
'How many of these gun-running trips have you made so far?'
'Three times now!'
She commented without any hesitation.
'I see! __Lucia I want you to promise me that you won't ever take these risks again! Not ever!'
She looked at me in a way which told me immediately that that was never going to happen.
'I can't do that Harry!'
I looked at her steadily.
'You must, if I'm of any importance to you at least. I care about you very much Lucia, you cannot surely have any doubt about that!'
'Sure of course not Harry, I know tha's true, but don' you see, this is real life here! Sure we are happy together an' we love each other, I know that, but we are lucky.'
'Yes we are. I could never say otherwise, but this venture is crazy not to say dangerous! What would I do if something happened to you? I can't even bear to think about it.'
I paused as I tried to think of some way of explaining to her what was in my head, some eloquent inarguable statement to convince her somehow of

the enormity of what she was involved in and at the same time to convince her to stop.

It had to be a strong argument, but at that moment I just couldn't find the right words.

'So it was Mari-Carmen who put you up to this!'

'She didn' put me up to it like you say!'

I shook my head.

'But you told me__'

'It wasn' just Mamen, it was others as well. Her father knows all about it. He don' like his daughter takin' these risk', but he can't stop her. So he organizes the weapons and gets them loaded on board. He's a good man an' he want's what we all want. Some kind'a freedom for the people, a chance to live decently. Harry you have no idea what its like to live under a dictator!'

I smiled feebly.

'Well we came close in nineteen forty!'

She smiled as well, relieving the tension to some degree.

'Yeah, you sure did!'

Again we were silent, that is until I could make the only sensible comment that I could think of.

'I want you to stop this Lucia, for me if for no other reason. __Promise me!'

By the look in her eyes I could tell almost at once that I was wasting my time.

'I can't carino! This is somethin' I have to do. I love you Harry, but we're fighting for a principle, for the right to live with self-respect an' without fear.'

I shook my head in increasing despair.

'You told me once that you didn't care about politics. That communism was failing!'

'Yeah communism is failing, sure, that doesn' mean that there is no differen' kind'a life to capitalism and greed. We have to try Harry, an' keep tryin' until we find another way.'

I had no chance and I was beginning to realize that.

So what could I do now? Give her an ultimatum? But what kind?

"If you don't stop this now I'm leaving and I'm going back to England!" The problem was I didn't want to go back to England, and more importantly, so much more in fact, was that I couldn't leave Lucia. I had never been quite sure exactly what 'Catch 22' actually meant, but now it was becoming clear.

'This is madness Lucia! The risks are__'
Again I shook my head impotently.
'If the Americans discover this they will come down so hard on this country, just when things are beginning to improve.'
'But don' you see Harry! If we get caught it's just' me an' Mamen in a small boat. The Cuban gov'men' will, __how d'you say, deny about us!'
'Disown you!'
'Ok whad'ever! __So then__'
'So then you'll be in an American gaol, or worse, and I shall never see you again! Is that what you want Lucia?'
I suppose my sheer frustration was showing very clearly now.
She smiled her brilliant smile with no hint of concern.
'Tranquilo Harry! We have a special plan for that.'
'A plan!'
'Sure if the coastguard find us we sink the boat!'
'You *what!* __Lucia you can't be serious, that is complete nonsense! You sink the boat, then you swim to the shore, is that right! __About twenty kilometres! Brilliant idea!
If you don't drown, the sharks will get you!'
'Come on carino, i's not so crazy. Firs' of all we keep close to land, never more than abou' fifteen kilometres, an' we always carry a life raft, you know that Harry.'
'It's still bloody daft! __And if the coastguard catch you, which they could quite easily__'
'An' prove what Harry?'
'They won't need to prove anything. They will take you both on board and what then? Sail you back to Havana and wave you goodbye? I don't think so! They'll arrest you on suspicion of__ I don't know, terrorism or something. Anything! Then, well God only knows. You'll certainly be banged up somewhere or other. The Americans get very nervous when it comes to supplying arms to the opposition.
You simply don't *know* what might happen.
Never seen again is a distinct possibility!'
It seemed I had silenced her, for a moment at least. Then she spoke again but now her expression was serious.
'Harry we know this. We' not daft like you call it!'
'Well that's a relief, so stop this crazy bloody game before something unthinkable happens!'
Her expression was unchanged.
'Are you mad at me Harry?'
'Yes I bloody well am! First, because you never told me what you were up to, second, because you still seem intent on doing it again!

What do you expect Lucia? I'm your husband and I love you. That should mean something surely!'

Her manner changed at once and she reached across and took my hand.

'It *does* carino, you mus' know this. I never loved a man before you. __You change' my life, you make me happy, you are good to me. __A good man!'

'So stop then! __Promise me Lucia before something terrible happens.'

I got the impression from the look in those delicious brown eyes that I was just a small innocent boy and that I didn't understand the profound lesson that she was trying to teach me.

'Harry I can't! __I am, __how do you say, commit to this now, is tha' the right word?'

'Near enough.'

'You' angry with me now an' I'm angry with myself for makin' you unhappy. You don' deserve this!'

'No, I'm inclined to agree with you.'

I didn't feel sorry for myself, but for her. Good causes are one thing, putting her life at risk for them was another.

Senseless, that's how I saw it. Martyrs are revered, and there have been plenty of them, but of course they are all dead!

My view of life was to get through it relatively unscathed and to look after yourself and those close to you. Life is short enough surely.

It takes a certain type to be a 'Jesus Christ' or a 'Che Guevara' and that type certainly didn't include me!

'So you're continuing with this__ this, mad idea of yours?'

I withdrew my hand slowly as I spoke.

She looked at me sadly.

'I guess so Harry.'

She responded almost timidly.

'You guess so! __Is that a yes or a no?'

'Harry I have to do this thing!'

'No you don't. You have a choice which you've obviously made.'

'Don' be angry, please Harry. Without you I don' know what I would do.'

'Again, you have a choice!'

Her head dropped forward and she stared at her hands, twisting the single gold ring on her finger back and forth.

I considered for a few moments.

'Was this the idea right from the start Lucia, about buying the boat I mean and shipping guns?'

She looked up at once.

'No Harry, never! It was jus' to do with the fishin'. Believe me, this last year almost has been the best in my life. You mus' believe that.'
'Lucia I don't know what to believe anymore.'
I pondered the matter in silence for almost a minute, or maybe it was longer. Then I stood up.
'I'm going out!'
I left in that moment with Lucia calling out to me as I strode along the passageway to the door of the apartment.
'Harry, carino please__'
They were the last words I heard before I slammed the door and headed down the staircase.

Chap. 9

In the street outside the apartment I caught a taxi.
I knew the government office where Mari-Carmen worked having been there a couple of times with Lucia to meet up with her for one reason or another. I also knew that sometimes she worked until quite late.
My Spanish wasn't up to much, but I knew enough to be able to ask the girl on the reception desk if I could speak with her briefly.
When I arrived however there were a few lights still on, but the office was closed.
Then I remembered that she only worked three days a week because of the recent budget cuts, although I didn't know which days.
However I did know where she lived and told the driver to take me to the other end of Havana away from the port, a quiet part of town where she kept a small house.
It was dark now, apart from the light of a few streetlamps, when I paid off the taxi.
Approaching the neat little terraced house I rang the bell.
After no more than a second or so Mamen appeared at the door dressed in an old pair of jeans and a tee shirt. It was the first time I had seen her in casual dress as she was normally on her way from work or dressed up for a night out with Lucia and I.
'Harry! I er, __I'm surprised to see you.'
She held the door partially open, not perhaps with the purpose of closing it again, but neither with the intention to admit anyone.
'Mamen can we talk?'
I asked at once.
'Well yes Harry. Is Lucia__'

'Lucia's at home. I just left there.'
'Yes. __I mean of course.'
With a mixed expression she drew open the door and stepped to one side, allowing me to enter.
'Would you like a drink Harry?__Russian 'Coke', it's not very good but that's all I have in until I get to the market.'
'No it's ok, some water maybe.'
Mamen led me to a small room lit by a single table lamp, at the rear of the house where there was room for some bits of furniture, a dining table with four chairs and not much else.
She brought me a glass of water and sat opposite at the small table giving me a smile that said neither one thing nor the other.
I didn't waste any time.
'Mamen! Lucia told me today about what you've both been doing!'
'Doing?'
She glanced at me nervously.
'Running guns for Central America!'
'Oh!'
'Yes. __Bit of a shock!'
'I'm sure it was.'
'I want her to stop!'
'I see. You said this to her obviously!'
'Very clearly.'
'I know what her response would have been Harry.'
There was a distinct edge of resolve in her voice.
'This is insane Mari-Carmen! You could both be killed don't you realize that?'
'Yes we do realize that. __Sometimes Harry we have to make a stand about things in life. There is more suffering than you can possibly imagine in__'
'I heard all this from her an hour ago and I'm not interested. She is my wife and I care about her. What she is doing, what you are both doing is madness. You don't have a husband so I wouldn't expect you to understand.'
'You're wrong Harry, I do understand. No I'm not married, but if I was I would still be loyal to the cause. For me it's a way of life.'
'For you maybe it is Mamen, and what you do is entirely your business, I am not being critical here, but I don't want Lucia dragged into this. If you care about her as a friend then you must discourage her.'
'I can't do that!'
'You mean you won't!'

'I mean__what I mean is that Lucia is her own woman! Yes I spoke to her some months ago about this plan. About helping the people of Central America to fight for a better life__'
'Influenced her you mean!'
'You can't influence Lucia. You should know that by now.'
'I've never needed to. We agree about almost everything.'
'A perfect relationship then. You are lucky Harry!'
'Yes maybe I am. I certainly consider myself as being fortunate, not least of all by meeting Lucia! __I love her very much, but I'm sure you know that.'
'Then you are both lucky because she loves you, and now that she is pregnant your marriage is truly blessed, because now__'
'*What?* __*What* did you say Mamen?'
She raised a hand slowly to cover her mouth and an almost fearful look appeared in her eyes.
'You didn't know.'
She whispered the words.
For several seconds I was unable to respond. It was simply shock I suppose and the complete inability to accept what I had just heard.
Lucia was pregnant! No, it still didn't register.
'I have some wine in the fridge.'
The girl said quietly
'I'll bring you a glass.'
It seemed that she just wanted to get out of the room for a few moments, perhaps to allow me to take in what she had revealed, purely by accident. When she left I stared out into the darkness beyond the window into a small garden that was overgrown with several palms and a lemon tree, heavy with fruit. It was beautiful and unspoilt, not that it really registered very much because I was still overwhelmed by what I had just heard.
Mamen returned with a bottle and two glasses. Setting them on the table she half filled each glass.
'I am most sorry Harry, I should have been the last person to tell you this.'
'When did you know?'
'Two days ago. __She was overjoyed.'
'Too overjoyed to tell me quite obviously.'
'No Harry you mustn't say that. She was I'm sure just waiting for the right moment.'
'Maybe.'
I stared out into the garden again, lost in my thoughts.
'Anyway. Salud!'
She had raised her glass and was attempting a smile.

I picked up my glass like an automaton and she touched her's against it briefly with a dull clink.

'My very best wishes and can I say good luck and very good health to the three of you.'

I sipped listlessly at the wine without even tasting it.

'She's on her own.'

'What do mean!'

There was an element of alarm in her voice.

'I mean at the apartment. __She was cooking something for us.

'I left in, __well, in a hurry.'

'I see.'

'I was angry. Angry with her, and with you!'

'Yes. She was afraid to tell you, not about the baby, but about the er__'

'The gun running you mean, yes I'll bet she was!'

'She knew that you would find out eventually.'

'Well in view of this latest news perhaps she will come to her senses at last. __I bloody well hope so anyway.'

Mamen said nothing. She was staring at her glass, slowly twisting the stem.

'Like I say, what you do with your life Mamen is your affair, but you're going to have to find a new partner, *and* a new boat! This simply can't continue. __From now on__'

The phone rang, startling me, and her, because she spilt some wine on the table trying to reach for the receiver.

'Ola Lucia, si. __Si, el esta aqui.'

She glanced at me.

'Lo siento Lucia, le dije, me refiero a__Si__si Lucia.'

Again she looked at me uncertainly, listened for a moment longer and then passed the phone.

'Harry!'

'Yes.'

It was easy to tell that she was crying.

'Harry come back, __please!'

'Ok. __I wanted to talk with your friend. She told me something that was __well, a bit of a shock.'

'Come home Harry, come home now carino!'

'Ok, I'll see you shortly.'

I handed the phone back to Mamen.

'I'd better get going.'

I sighed deeply and taking another sip of the wine I stood up.

'Believe me, I will do everything in my power to stop this Mamen!'

She nodded hesitantly, and perhaps her silence indicated that she was taking me seriously. Maybe, __I couldn't be sure.
'I'll let myself out. __Thanks for the wine.'
Normally I would have bestowed the traditional kiss to each cheek, but not tonight.

Lucia must have been watching the street for my return because as soon as I let myself into the building she was leaning over the banister rail staring down at me as I began to ascend the stairs.
When I reached the first floor she almost threw herself at me, her arms wrapped around my body so tightly I could hardly move.
She was crying again and I could feel the dampness from her tears through my shirt.
I held her gently.
'Well, if this is the welcome I get whenever I go out, I must do it more often!'
I added a soft laugh as I spoke.
'Carino, don' do that ever again! I was so worried! I checked all the bars in Paseo de Marti, I even walked to Miguel's café thinkin' you might be there. He paid for a taxi to bring me back.'
'Sorry love, I was angry! Still am, __a bit anyway.'
She looked up at me, her lovely face wet from the flow of tears.
'Why did you go to Mamen's place?'
'Why do you think? I'm just as angry with her!'
She released her grip, and with an arm around my waist led me through the open door to the apartment.
'Your lovely food is spoiled now!'
'Sorry.'
'Tonight was suppose' to be special for you Harry! I got some Cava too, real Spanish stuff!'
'I see. Hence the nice dress and you looking like an angel.'
'Exactly! Then you run out!'
'Walked out.'
'Ok walked out, I's the same! I was gonna give you a lovely dinner, get you a bit borracho, __como?'
'Drunk.'
'Yeah drunk. Then I was gonna' take you to bed an' make love to you. Then carino, I was gonna tell you the won'erful news that now you already know about!'
The table in the kitchen was still set out for two, the single candle still unlit. The large pan of chicken was now cold on the stove with a bowl of salad waiting nearby.

I sighed as I regarded the scene that had been so carefully planned and now I understood what it was all about.
'The chicken is ruined!'
Lucia commented sadly.
'No it's not. __Light the gas I'll stir it for you. A bit of extra water, it'll be fine.'
I gave her an encouraging smile.
'No lemme do that! You open the Cava, I can never know how to get the thing out.'
'No problem, but first of all what about a kiss!'
'I'm no' sure you deserve one chico!'
Her back was turned to me as she lit the stove and began to stir the contents of the saucepan.
I put my arms around her waist and kissed her neck.
'Promise me you won' walk out again like that Harry.'
'If you promise me that you won't even *think* about this crazy arms smuggling business ever again!'
'Harry__'
'No Lucia! There's two of you to think about now remember.'
She reduced the heat under the pan and twisted round in my arms.
'Are you pleased Harry? __abou' the baby.'
She was staring up at me her deep brown eyes searching mine, although of course there was nothing to search for.
'What do you think sweetheart! I wish I had heard the news from you, but it doesn't matter now. I'm so happy__so __elated, I can't even describe to you properly how I feel.'
'What does elated mean?'
'Figure it out!'
Whether she wanted me to or not I kissed her and the response was what I expected, or at least what I'd hoped for.
'I love you Harry!'
'I know that. This is the most wonderful thing, apart from meeting you of course. __What, almost a year ago.
And just by chance in a bar, and in a place that I barely knew existed. It's a strange world indeed.'
'So you' pleased yeah?'
'It hasn't sunk in yet properly, but at this point I just want to run down the street shouting for joy!'
She smiled at last.
'The cops will arrest you for acting loco!'
'Who cares!'

I kissed her again only this time she sighed and pressed her body firmly against mine.
After a few delicious moments I released her.
'I'll sort out the wine, you get the food ready, ok.'

The dinner that Lucia had made was excellent, but over quickly.
We sat opposite each other at the small table.
I lit the candle and in the subdued glow we exchanged occasional comments as we ate, her eyes engaging briefly with mine in the odd provocative glance that said more than words ever could.
I moved the small vase of flowers to one side and by accident or otherwise her fingers brushed against mine, the momentary contact inducing something close to an electric surge.
With a hand that shook slightly I poured the Cava into tall slim flutes and as we drank I felt just the slightest touch of her toes against my foot and then moving slowly upwards beneath my trouser leg, scratching invitingly at my skin. She peered at me over her glass with a seductive look and a devilish smile that reduced me to a quivering wreck.

We almost raced to the bedroom and with my heart pounding I undressed her slowly and with a sublime desire that was impossible to describe.
I sat on the edge of the bed stroking her glorious bottom, pressing my face against her smooth flat belly.
Then we were making love, franticly, almost aggressively and with an agonizing passion.
Having sex with Lucia just seemed to become more and more exquisite with each occasion, which hardly seemed possible somehow.
Finally sated we lay close to each other.
My fingers were between her thighs, slowly caressing the moist silky soft opening to her vagina.
'So eventually our new child will have to squeeze out through this beautiful little place here?'
'Tha's how it works carino!'
She whispered.
'I can't imagine it somehow.'
'Well I's not gonna be easy muchacho, an' it will take a lil' while for me to get back in shape for you' nice cock again.'
'Not too long I hope!'
She laughed softly.
'No, no' to long. An' I got other ways of takin' care of that, which you know abou' very well carino!'

We were silent now. With my arms around her she lay with her head on my shoulder and I listened to her slow regular breathing until I knew that she was sleeping.

Staring up at the ceiling I kept turning over in my mind the situation that remained, or seemed to remain, unresolved.

I recalled what Mari-Carmen had said, of her obvious dedication to freeing the dispossessed of the world, as hopeless and impossible a dream as that certainly was.

More importantly, of her belief that Lucia was equally dedicated to what seemed to me would always be a lost cause.

But now, expecting our child, would she realize not only the futility but also the dangers, not just to herself, but to the tiny living being inside her. I was optimistic. I had to be! The alternative was unthinkable, but at that moment, if only to get some sleep, I forced myself to look on the bright side.

'Can I see Raul Vasquez, it's important!'

My lousy Spanish was good enough it seemed, because the copper on the desk at Havana police headquarters responded at once.

'Your name senor?'

'Harry Burgess.'

'Perhaps you can say in what connection senor Burgess, its possible that I may be able to assist in__'

'No. It's a private matter.'

He scrutinized me carefully with that typical policeman's look that I presumed was universal.

After a few moments he picked up a phone and spoke into it with garbled words that I barely understood.

He listened and then returned the phone to its cradle.

Then he looked up with what seemed very much like a smile.

'Take the lift senor, __third floor. The commandant will meet with you.'

Mamens father greeted me with a broad smile and a handshake.

'Hello Harry, it's good to see you again. __Quite a long time!'

He added in his excellent English.

He looked immaculate as always in his dark green uniform, poished black boots and the obligatory pistol tucked firmly in its holster at his waist.

'We'll talk in my office. Do you want some coffee?'

I thought quickly.

'Ok that would be nice. Thanks senor Vasquez.'

'Raul! __No formality Harry, we know each other well enough now.'
A few doors along a brightly lit passage way and he ushered me into a surprisingly large office.
'Well, this is quite er, grand!'
I remarked.
He took a seat behind an equally large desk.
'What did you expect? I'm the boss!'
He grinned warmly.
It wasn't difficult to like the man.
From the first time I had met him on our boat on the day that the two Americans were shot dead, he had displayed an equitable and friendly manner that I was quite sure was genuine.
If I had been guilty of the murder of the two alleged fishermen then no doubt I would have seen a completely different side to him.
He picked up a phone and asked for coffee to be brought, then he lit a cigarette.
'Have a seat Harry. Incidentally I have visited your new café a few times. It's very impressive. __Good tapas as well.'
'Yeah we've er, tried to make an effort, Lucia and I.'
I returned his smile.
'There are a lot of cafes in Havana so we had to create something a bit different. __The yank's like it anyway!'
'I'm sure they do. We gotta keep them happy, especially the way things are right now! We badly need some good business in this town. The economy is__'
He finished his sentence by doing a short nose-dive with his hand.
'Yes so I hear, since the Russians pulled out of Cuba!'
I replied. He grimaced.
'I never liked the bastards Harry. Arrogant! No manners!'
Again I smiled.
'I wouldn't know. They left before I got here.'
'Sure, you didn't miss much, but we miss the money of course.'
'But things are slowly getting better, are they not Raul? With the tourists and a bit of foreign trade now.''
'Too slowly my friend. __Too slowly.'
At that moment an elderly woman brought in coffee on a tray.'
'Gracias Maria!'
He cleared papers away and she set in down on the desk.
When she had left, the police chief leaned back in his chair taking a long draw on his cigarette.
'So how can I help you Harry?'
I bent forward to take one of the small cups.

'Is it ok if__'
'He gestured with the cigarette.
'Sure, help yourself.'
I sipped at the strong dark liquid, not knowing quite how to broach the subject.
'I saw Mamen last night, briefly.'
'You did?'
'Yeah, erm, __look she told me some things that I'm still struggling to come to terms with.'
'Ok. Like what?'
I cleared my throat nervously.
'I'm not sure quite how to put this, but she, that is to say she and Lucia have been well, erm__'
'Carrying guns for us!'
'Yes exactly.'
'You knew that I knew about this Harry!'
'Yes. Lucia told me.'
He heaved a deep sigh.
'Vale! I was sure you would discover this sooner or later. It was just a question of time.'
He seemed to consider for a moment.
'This is secret stuff my friend. If the Americans discover this it will set Cuba back for years, an' we can't afford that.'
'Yes I'm sure you're right.'
Again he was thoughtful.
'What do you think about this country Harry?'
'Think, well__'
'I mean do you like it here, do you like living here?'
'Yes, very much.'
'Don' you wanna go back to England?'
'No.'
'Not for a visit?'
'I haven't thought about it.'
'Lucia said that you love this country!'
'Lucia was right.'
'But you might wanna go back at some time, to see your family maybe?'
'As I said, I haven't thought about it.'
He stubbed out the cigarette and reached at once for the packet.
'The thing is Harry we can't let you go back. __Not for a while at least.'
He continued, reluctantly it seemed.
'If this gets out, this business with the arms, we are in deep shit!'
'You think I'll spill the beans, is that what it is?'

'No Harry! But what I think don' matter. I'm sure you understand that there are others__'

He pointed towards the ceiling.

'_who are behind all this. I just do what I'm told to do.'

He released a deep sigh.

'If you wan' my opinion, for what little value it has, this whole scheme of arming rebels in central America is a wasted, an' futile enterprise.'

He lit another cigarette, drawing in a lungful of smoke and regarding the glowing tip for a moment.

'But there it is. Like I say I'm just following orders.'

He glanced at me carefully before continuing.

'Harry I was a senior officer in the police during Batista's time, not in his nasty intelligence service I gotta say, I kept far away from those bastards those__'culos'! I'm not a communist Harry, but I am a socialist. I believe this country is a lot better under Fidel, he just needs to compromise a little more, an' supporting revolutions in Nicaragua an' others is not gonna work out.'

'Well I'm sure you know more than I do about that, I'm not political, but Mari-carmen confesses to being communist and Lucia, __well, Lucia is Lucia!'

He smiled with obvious affection, perhaps for both women.

'Mamen is her own person too. I don't try to discourage her now.'

He gave a short wry laugh.

'That's assuming that I could! I gave that up a long time ago. __You know women Harry!'

'I'm slowly finding out.'

'Listen! I've been married for almost forty years. You can't win and you never will, trust me on that!'

I smiled and was beginning to feel a distinct affinity with the man.

'It seems I have a lot to learn Raul.'

'Sure, but you're young, you got plen'y of time.'

I was silent as I tried to think what to say next and how to say it.

'I only found out about all this yesterday, and only by chance. The point is I don't want Lucia involved in all this. It's dangerous, very dangerous. I don't think she realizes.'

The police chief nodded slowly.

'If the US coastguard catch them Raul, I dare not even think about what could happen.'

Again he nodded.

'It's a possibility, but only slight. As long as they keep within Cuban territorial waters they should be ok!'

'Do you think that would deter the Americans! I doubt it, even with my limited knowledge of these things.'
He sighed and drew again on his cigarette.
'Harry, do you think that I haven't tried to explain this to them! This was never my idea remember.'
'But you said__'
'What I said was Harry, that I get instructions to do certain things. I'm not ask' for my moral opinion on these matters.'
He glanced at me carefully.
'Look amigo, I'm lucky. I have a good, well-paid job, which some of the time I get satisfaction from. But if I start questioning my orders I'll wind up shining shoes on the Paseo de Marti.'
'Yes I see your point.'
'I never offered this job to them!
Mamen, who as you know works for the government, came to me and said that she had already volunteered. She'd spoken to some guy in her office and it was all settled. I tried to talk her out of it, and your wife as well.'
He shook his head.
'Like I said, I might as well have saved my breath. What little I have after smoking these!'
He gestured again with the cigarette.
'Yes, I get it Raul.'
I hesitated.
'There's something else as well. __Lucia is pregnant!'
The police chief's expression altered at once.
Beneath his large mustache his lips parted in a broad smile displaying fine white teeth.
'Harry that is wonderful news! I congratulate you my friend!
'Thanks. Bit of a shock really.'
'When did you discover this?'
'Yesterday.'
I told him when, but I didn't tell him how.
'So now things have changed for you.'
'They have, for both of us in fact. So now she has got to abandon this__ *crazy* idea.'
'What has she said to you?'
'Nothing Raul. Not yet anyway. Can you try to persuade her?'
He spread his arms.
'I can try, but really it's up to you now!'
'Yes I know it is, I was just hoping for a bit of support.'
The man nodded.
'I will talk with her again. And with Mamen as well.'

'Do you know when the next trip is planned?'
'Next week!'
'Jesus! As soon as that! I've got to stop her somehow.'
Raul nodded.
'Well good luck with that amigo. I will do what I can, but__'
Again he raised his hands submissively.

I thought for a moment.
'Incidentally Raul, what happened about the two guys on our boat, the one's who got shot. Were they American agents?'
'Harry I don' know anythin' about them, __an' neither do you amigo!'
His stern look indicated that that particular matter was permanently closed.

It was ten o'clock when I left the police headquarters. Outside it was a cool cloudy day with rain threatening and a strong wing gusting from the sea.
I stood outside the building, planning in my head what I was going to say to Lucia, __or trying to anyway.
It wasn't easy, Raul was right of course, Lucia was a strong woman. I would just have to be stronger!

Lucia embraced me as soon as I returned to the apartment, throwing her arms around me, holding me close.
'Carino, where did you go? I was worried. I called the café but they said you weren't there!'
'I went for a walk.'
'You didn' go for a walk Harry, I know you.'
'I did as a matter of fact, to think about things.'
'Vale. Ok.'
She remarked with a doubtful expression.
'And then I dropped in to see Mamen's father.'
I added casually, as casually as I could anyway.
'Raul!'
'Yes.'
'To talk about what?'
'You know what Lucia! This crazy business you're involved in!'
'You shouldn' have done that Harry'
'Why not? I'm desperate! Who else can I talk to?'
'You can talk to me carino!'

She had released her grip and was glancing up at me with that 'no nonsense' look that I now knew so well.

'I tried that. It wasn't very successful if you remember!'

'But this is between us. I's nuthin to do with Raul!'

'What! Of course it is. He plays a direct role in all this. Look! __I don't want you making these bloody trips again Lucia!'

'Ok.'

She responded simply.

'Ok what?'

'Ok I won't!'

I stared at her for several moments.

'Do you mean this. __I mean are you serious?'

I dropped into a sofa while she stared down at me, her arms folded.

'Yes I'm serious. After next week, __tha's the last one.'

I sighed and closed my eyes in mute desperation.

'Lucia *no more trips*, __that's it!

'Ok Harry. __After nex' week!'

'No you're not listening! No *more* Lucia. Please! No more__suicide missions, which is what they are! Don't you get it? You could be killed, don't you see that! Dead __floating in the sea, you and our unborn child!'

She sat next to me at once reaching out for my hand, or trying to because I drew it away from her.

'You can't go through with this Lucia, it's madness!'

'What did Raul say to you?'

'He was very sympathetic, but he said he can't really stop you, or though he said he would try. He's just following orders, government orders I suppose.

Anyway it's not him I'm worried about it's you, don't you see this?'

She paused, and once again I felt like the kid in school who couldn't understand the current lesson being taught.

'Harry I's not as dangerous as you think. There are radar stations on the coast that can tell if the US coast guard is in the area. We keep close as we can to the shoreline, we drop the guns on one of the islands an' then we start back. I's easy Harry!'

'You make it sound easy, but I don't believe it! The Yanks are not stupid! They must know this is going on and if you're caught! __Well we've been over that already haven't we.'

I was getting angry again, which for me was a rare condition.

Before embarking on my epic voyage to the Caribbean I had always breezed through life cheerfully, uncontentious, always taking the middle path. So I suppose it was my in my nature.

Never having been faced with controversy or any serious problems it had never been necessary for me to make difficult decisions.
This was a new and unfamiliar dilemma, but for the first time in my life I was determined to impose my will, whatever the consequence.

'Harry this all planned, everything is organized! Mamen has arranged everything the weapons are stored an' waitin' to be loaded on the boat.'
'I don't give a fuck! You're not going and that's it!'
She got up from the sofa again and I could see that she was getting angry as well. As she spoke she started waving her arms in that typical Cuban way that was now so familiar to me.
'You jus' don't get it, do you Harry! __You' rich so you don' un'erstan' what I's like to live in poverty!'
I stared at her, getting angrier now by the second.
'Oh I see, so I'm rich, is that it! Well I must apologise for that mustn't I! For buying the boat you wanted, for this nice apartment as well, for setting up the café, which is now doing ok as a matter of fact, in addition to providing employment for people! Yes I'm deeply sorry for being rich as you call it, not that I am rich actually, certainly not in the way that you mean!'
'I didn' mean it like that__'
'Then you shouldn't *fucking* say it should you! Why the hell do you think I'm concerned about you and this idiotic gun running lark? Why Lucia? The question is rhetorical because you know why, it's because I love you. So in other words you're not__fucking__going! Now is *that* clear enough for you!'
Without realizing it I was also on my feet now, confronting her face to face.
She looked at me with an expression that was very close to contempt.
'You can't talk to me like that Harry! Wha' we are doin', Mamen an' me is importan' for thousan's of people that don' have no food an' don' have no freedom!'
'It's you that doesn't get it Lucia! Like I said, I don't give a fuck! It's you I care about, so you're not doing this anymore. If I have to I will march down to the port right now and sink the bloody boat on its moorings, so don't try me!'
Her eyes narrowed in a look that I had never seen before.
'You would do that would you! __Is tha' what you are sayin'?'
'Try me Lucia, __just try me!'
She continued to stare at me, partially I think in disbelief.
'You never talk to me like this before Harry.'
'I never had reason to!'

She seemed to relent if only slightly.
'I'm sorry I said that to you, abou' havin' money I mean!'
'That's ok, I forgive you, but you're still not going!'
She sank down onto the sofa again drawing her bare feet up beneath her, propping a hand against her lovely face.
At that moment she looked so beautiful that it took my breath away.
'Ok Harry, you win.'
'Meaning?'
'It means I'm not gonna make the trip.'
She replied quietly.
'Uh! At last you're being sensible!'
I heaved a sigh.
'Do you want some coffee?'
'Ok Harry. __Then I'm going out!'
'Out where?'
I asked with an air of suspicion.
'Jus' to the café. I said I would help out, one of the girls is sick.'
'Fair enough, I'll make the coffee.'
There was a difficult silence between us. I made coffee for us both and carried it into the living room where she was still sitting, hunched up on the sofa.
'Do you want something to eat?'
'No. I get somethin' from the café.'
'Ok. __What time are you coming back?'
'Abou' four I guess.'
'Fair enough.'

We drank the coffee in virtual silence.
The row had taken its toll on both of us and it was probably better if she was out of the apartment for a few hours, time for both of us to cool down. It was the first real argument we had had since we were married and I suppose it had to happen at some point.
It wasn't a nice feeling however, even though I felt no compunction to make amends. Not yet anyway because I still felt angry about the whole thing and slighted regarding her comment about my so-called wealth. It was true that we didn't need to worry about money, but I could hardly compare myself with the Rothschilds, not by a very long chalk!

'Thanks for the coffee. I gotta tidy myself up now.'
'Ok.'
'I won't be back later than four, ok Harry.'

'Sure. Bring something back with you then we won't have to do any cooking tonight.'
'Ok.'
She disappeared into the bedroom returning five minutes later.
She had brushed her hair, tightened it into a bunch at the back of her head and had put on some fresh lipstick.
She was standing in the doorway and looked wonderful, although I didn't mention the fact.
I had taken a seat on the sofa again and was pretending to read a book.
'I'm ready now so I see you later yeah!'
There was a brighter note in her voice now, which I also didn't acknowledge.
I looked up briefly.
'Ok Lucia. I'll see you later.'
She paused for a moment and then turned away. I heard her heels clicking on the tiled floor of the hallway then the door opening and after a short delay closing again, leaving me with an uneasy silence.

Had I been too hard with her, too unreasonable?
I tried to remember everything that I had said, which wasn't easy.
Whatever it was it had to be said, no feelings spared.
The whole idea was ridiculous! Two young women running guns, in a *boat,* and during the night!
No it was crazy. If I had known sooner I would have stopped it, or tried to at least.
Why would they put themselves in such danger, there was the mystery. Or was it. The truth was I suppose that I had no real idea of what they were trying to do. Fighting for freedom was a completely alien concept to me with my comfortable English upbringing. Such matters were confined to the television screen or written about in books that I had never read.
So maybe Lucia was right. As the devils advocate for a moment I caught a glimpse of what they were perhaps trying to do.
For a second or so I was plagued with uncertainty.
I got a beer from the fridge and pulled the cap.
Our bedroom had a balcony with an ornate cast iron balustrade where there was just enough room for a small table and two chairs.
The tall glazed double doors stood open, the fine net curtains billowing inwards on a steady breeze.
Carrying the bottle I sat outside taking one of the small spindly chairs and staring down through the railings at the Paseo de Marti directly below.
Across the tree-lined boulevard with its small sounds of activity, I could see the café a hundred metres further along. It seemed to be busy, with

people coming in and out almost constantly. I imagined Lucia greeting customers with her wonderful smile, handing them menus with her usual cheerful comment.

I had an immediate impulse to run across the street, burst into the café and throw my arms around her.

Not a good idea under the circumstances.

I gazed along the paseo at the aging but still elegant buildings on each side of the street, wondering for a moment what this town would be like in another twenty years or so. Probably much the same I guessed. There seemed little likelihood of a sudden influx of cash investment and so the lovely old buildings would probably continue to slowly deteriorate. Castro would pass on eventually as we all do. Who would replace him? Someone who would buckle under to the U.S.? I doubted it somehow. People now had a taste of relative if not complete freedom. Fidel had provided the populace with health care and schooling, something they could never have dreamed about under the previous corrupt regime. My feeling was that only a very few wanted a return to the days of the casinos, the live sex shows, the rampant prostitution. The days when this lovely old colonial town was seen as the Sodom and Gomorra of the Caribbean and a safe refuge for organized criminal elements.

I truly hoped that those days were over forever, realizing instantly that I was making a political statement, if only to myself.

I finished my beer slowly, still deep in thought, which was broken suddenly by a few isolated drops of rain that fell randomly, plopping in large globules that burst on the surface of the small metal table, and on to me, dropping vertically in cold sharp stabs that melted into my shirt.

I stood up slowly, moving into the bedroom and closing the doors against the breeze that had now turned into a gusting wind.

Once again I was isolated in silence, overcome by an instant and unfamiliar sense of loneliness and something close to depression.

Never prone to such emotions, I shook myself and returned to the kitchen, retrieving anther bottle from the refrigerator.

Walking back into the large living room I switched on the television for no other reason than to drown out the silence.

I dropped into the sofa and stared unseeing at the antics of 'Tom and Gerry'.

Before I knew it I had fallen into a deep dreamless sleep.

I was jerked out of it by the sound of the door-bell, with its noisy urgent sound that could surely wake the dead.

With a groan I pulled myself upright on the sofa, glancing at my watch.

One-thirty, I had slept for almost an hour.
I got to my feet kicking over the empty beer bottle and sending it clattering across the floor. Muttering a curse I retrieved it and headed towards the entrance door.
'Yeah, who is it?'
I grunted irritably, still only half awake.
'Mamen!'
The single word response from the intercom, banished the last remnants of sleep.
'Mamen! Er, __hold on.'
I pressed the button releasing the latch to the building entrance.
Gazing stupidly at the small bottle in my hand I hurried into the kitchen and dumped it into the waste bin.
Then, hurrying to the sink I sloshed cold water onto my face, wiping it dry with a towel just as I heard a muted tapping on the door.
When I opened it Mari-Carmen was standing almost demurely clutching her bag. Her hair and her light jacket were saturated.
'What happened to you?'
'It's raining.'
'Oh er, yes, __ok come in.'
I found a clean towel in the bathroom and carried it into the kitchen where Mamen had taken off her wet jacket. She was seated at the kitchen table where the previous night Lucia and I had eaten the excellent meal she had cooked, partially at least, both of us more hungry for sex than for food!
'Here, dry your hair. Do you want some coffee?'
'Thank you, yes. Where is Lucia?'
I put a kettle of water on the stove and began cleaning out the glass coffee maker.
'At work in the café.'
I opened a packet of fresh coffee and began spooning it into the cafetierre.
'I see. __I spoke to my father earlier on. About an hour ago in fact.'
'Oh, is that unusual?'
I commented. I was in no mood for conciliation, but she ignored the heavy sarcasm and continued.
'He said that you had visited him at the 'policia' earlier today.'
'Yes I did.'
'And that you asked him to try and persuade Lucia not to make our planned journey next week.'
'That's absolutely right.'
She fell silent and for nothing better to do I stared at the kettle of water, waiting for it to boil.

'He said that he agreed with you and because of Lucia's condition, that I should also persuade her not to go.'

'To which you replied?'

'I can't speak for Lucia. If Lucia wants to make this trip then it's her decision!'

'So presumably I should have no say in this either, is that correct?'

The water had boiled and I filled the coffee maker, pressing the filter into the top.

'You don't understand the importance of all this Harry.'

'Obviously not! What I do know is that I don't want the woman I care very deeply about risking her life for an uncertain cause, not to mention the life of our child!'

She sighed deeply and stared down at her hands.

'Some things are more important than the lives of individuals.'

'To you maybe, not to me! If you were in a similar situation Mamen you might well think differently.'

Again she seemed to relent slightly.

'What did you say to Lucia about this?'

'What did I say to Lucia? Well that shouldn't be too difficult to figure out. We had an argument this morning, a very noisy argument.'

'I'm sorry.'

'You should be. Involving her in this bloody nonsense, which is what it is!'

'Harry you don't understand '

'Look Mamen I'm getting a bit weary of being told that I don't understand! By you and by Lucia! My priorites are clear and simple. For my wife to embark on this fools errand, which is what it is, is madness and nothing less. She's *pregnant* for Christ'sake!'

I had raised my voice now, my earlier anger beginning to return.

Instead of counting to ten I carried the cafetierre across to the table and found a single cup and saucer.

'Do you want any milk with that?'

'No thanks.'

'Sugar!'

'Just a little.'

I obliged, taking a shaker from a cupboard and a spoon from a drawer, easing myself into a better temper.

Mamen was silent as she poured some coffee and added a small level of sugar.

'I'm sorry Harry, I can understand how you feel. My father seems to be on your side in this and perhaps you're both right.'

She stirred the coffee slowly.

'What has Lucia said?'
'She said she's not going now, __thank God!'
'I see.'
She sipped at the hot dark liquid.
'Well then, that's that! __But there is something else.'
'Which is?'
'The boat, __your boat. I still need it. The arrangements have all been made with the people in Nicaragua. We, __I can't let them down on this, they need these weapons urgently.'
'To kill people!'
'To defend themselves, you have no idea of the conditions__'
'I don't want to know.'
'No, ok Harry, but I still need the boat just the same.'
She wasn't exactly pleading, not exactly.
I pondered for a few moments, drew a deep breath and released it again.
'Take the bloody thing! __But we want it back, and in one piece! If the people behind this, __behind you, want to take advantage of my generosity then they can pay for a new boat if the yanks decide to sink it! You'd better tell them that.'
'Yes ok, but that's not going to happen.'
'Let's hope not.'
I attempted a smile. In addition to being a friend of Lucia, Mamen was a nice enough person. I had always liked her, whatever her crazy political beliefs.
In any event, if I had not agreed to let her take the boat it would probably have ended up in another massive row with Lucia.

'What time is she coming home?'
'About four.'
'Is it ok if I dry out for a bit before I leave?'
'Sure. How did you manage to get so wet? Didn't you get a taxi?'
'I did, but the man wouldn't drive down the paseo.'
'Why not?'
She shrugged.
'Who knows. I had to get out at the corner and make a run for it.'
'Miserable bastard!'
'That's what I thought. If it had been Lucia he would have driven her anywhere she asked and then walked her to the door with an umbrella.'
She smiled ruefully, and I couldn't help but smile with her.
'Have some more coffee. Do you want something to eat?'
'No it's ok. I'll dry out for a while then I'll be on my way.'
I thought for a moment, watching as she filled her cup again.

Then I found a cup for myself and sat opposite, filling it from the cafetierre.
For ten minutes or so we talked about general unrelated matters. Steering well clear of Cuban politics.

'You're pleased about the baby of course!'
She said.
'Yes I am. It's wonderful news, not to say unexpected. I haven't quite taken it all in yet.'
'I'm sorry you had to hear about it from me.'
I smiled again, shaking my head.
'Doesn't matter, it was just__accidental I suppose.'
We were both silent again.
'You're surely not going on your own Mamen! I mean on this mad voyage you're planning next week?'
'No, I erm, someone from my office is coming with me.'
'Does he or she know how to drive the thing? In addition to the cargo that you'll be carrying?'
'He said that he can.'
'And the cargo?'
I gave her a skeptical look.
'I haven't said anything about that yet.'
I shook my head.
'Is he able to navigate?'
'He says so.'
'Ok.'
I shrugged in acceptance and walking across to the window I looked out at the heavy grey clouds.
'Still raining! Quite heavy as well.'
I heard the sound behind me as she got to her feet.
'I'll get moving now Harry.'
I turned to her.
'In this!'
'It won't last. I'll walk across and see Lucia for a moment.'
'Ok, well let me find you an umbrella at least.'
I walked out into the hallway and rummaging in a cupboard I retrieved a brolly.
She had followed me, pulling on her jacket.
'Ok then. Good luck next week.__When are you leaving?'
She took the brolly from me.
'Thanks.__We're not sure yet.'

'Well, I wish I could talk you out of it Mamen, but I think I'd be wasting my time.'
'That's just what my father said.'
'I'll bet he did!'
She swept a dark limp strand of her hair to one side with small slim fingers.
'Ok then Harry, I expect I'll see you again soon.
'Sure.'
This time I kissed both of her cheeks before opening the door to the apartment.
'Can you ask Lucia to bring some beer back with her?'
'Yes I will.'
In the large airy open stairwell the sound of her heels echoed from the stone steps as she descended. I waited next to the banisters, giving a brief wave before the heavy carved door to the front entrance closed with a dull thud behind her.

Chap. 10

'Harry!'
'Yes.'
I had been woken by the phone at the side of the bed, fumbling to reach it in the darkness, forcing away the remnants of a profoundly deep sleep.
'It's Raul.'
Sitting on the edge of the bed now I groped around like a blind man for the switch to the bedside lamp.
'Raul!'
Pressing the switch I squinted at the sudden rush of light, still barely awake.
'Yes. __ Get dressed Harry.'
'What!'
'As quickly as you can.'
'Raul, what is this?'
I glanced at my watch on the small bedside table, trying with difficulty to focus on the numerals. It was three o'clock.
'What the hell's going on?'
'Get down to the port Harry as quickly as you can! I will try to delay them.'
'The phone went dead.
'Raul!__Hello__'

I passed my hand over my face, still squinting in the artificial light.
'Bloody hell! __ Shit!'
I mumbled impotently.
'Lucia!' I twisted round on the bed to wake her.
That's when I had the most profound shock, because her side of the bed was empty.
'In the bathroom maybe.' I thought. 'Or the kitchen, getting some water.'
I reached for my trousers and pulled them on, still half drugged with sleep.
'Lucia!' I called out.
I got to my feet slowly. The bedroom door was closed. I opened it and walked out into the darkened hallway.
The door to the bathroom was also closed and I tapped on it gently, no response.
I pushed it open, but again there was darkness.
With growing anxiety I turned towards the kitchen.

It was like being hit with an iron bar, because once again the room was empty and devoid of light except for the glow of a street lamp through the window.
So where was Lucia!
In the bedroom I threw on a shirt, picked up my watch and forced my feet quickly into a pair of shoes.
Slamming the door to the apartment I ran down the stairs and out into the deserted street.
The air was cool as a result of the rain that had continued into late evening, the pavements were still damp.
It wasn't far to the port, fifteen, perhaps twenty minutes and I started to run.
An old bicycle was propped up against a tree in the paseo, which wasn't unusual in this town. I grabbed it and raced off again cycling like a mad man towards the port.

Normally it would have been in virtual darkness at this time of the night. But as I arrived I could see an area of bright light hollowed out in the blackness at the edge of the quayside.
It came from the headlights of a large van and those of a police car. I dumped the bike and approached the scene slowly on foot.
Several figures in uniform were loading packing cases onto our fishing boat, and a number of police were watching a short distance away.
I entered the circle of light and one of the policemen turned, seeing me at once because I had made no attempt at concealment.
He approached me slowly, his hand on the gun at his side.

'Espera! Que usted quiere senor!'
I barely heard him as I drew nearer to the boat.
'Hombre!'
Louder this time, only now he had drawn the pistol and was pointing it downwards towards the uneven paving.
'Sanchez!'
A quieter voice now, but with a strong authority.
'Tranquilo!'
It was Raul, emerging slowly from the shadows.
I turned to him, to the sound of his voice.
'That was quick amigo. Muy Pronto! At first I thought you would never wake up, the phone must have rung for a minute at least.'
'Yeah I was er,__had a few drinks last night.'
I lied.
'I um__I nicked a bike Raul!'
'Nicked?'
'I stole a bicycle!'
He laughed softly.
'You could get jail time for that!'
I was in no mood for humour.
'What the hell's happening Raul?'
The boat will be ready to leave in half an hour Harry. I said I would do what I could to help, now it's up to you!'
'Where's Lucia?'
'On board with Mamen.'
'Jesus Christ!'
'Go and talk to her Harry!'
I hurried towards the boat, jumping down onto the rear deck, where boxes were being manhandled and shoved in position against the stern. A further crate was being stowed below into the main cabin.
When the two uniformed men carrying it disappeared from view, the opening was filled again almost at once.
It was a woman's shape emerging slowly from the open hatchway, clearly illuminated in the stark artificial light. A head of dense black hair at first and then Lucia's shapely body in jeans and a tee shirt.
She shielded her eyes against the headlights from the van, then, clearly shocked she saw me.
'Harry__'
'What the bloody *hell* do you think your doing!'
She was rooted to the spot and the two men appeared again, pushing past her to take yet another wooden box that was being lowered from the quayside.

'How, I mean__'
'Because I have at least one friend in this town! That's how!'
She lowered her face and looked up again, turning for a moment to see Raul staring down at us his hands in his pockets, his cap pushed back on his head.
'I see.' She breathed the words quietly.
'We have to talk about this Harry.'
'You're bloody right we do!'
'Come below.'
She turned and I followed her.
The main cabin was stacked up with cases and marked with various numbers and the stenciled letters CCCP.
We had to clamber around them to get to the bow of the vessel where there was a small toilet and shower room and a cramped forward cabin with bunk beds, that until recently had only rarely been used.
We squeezed into the cabin and I pushed the door closed.

'What do you think you're doing Lucia!'
My voice was level and controlled, unlike the thoughts that were racing through my head.
'I have to do this Harry!'
'Why! I spoke to Mamen a few days ago, she told me she had found someone to go with her. Some guy so she said.'
'There was no guy Harry.'
'So it was just another lie, is that right. To keep me in the dark until you'd both left! The stupid Englishman who understands nothing!'
'Harry__'
'No Lucia!'
I shook my head in something approaching disgust.
'How am I supposed to feel about this? __This deception. Don't I mean anything to you?'
I stared at her in utter despair.
'I was out of it when Raul called me this morning, __dead to the world. Why was that Lucia?'
'Listen Harry__'
'Did you put something in my tea last night before I went to bed, because we both know I wasn't drunk!'
She lowered her head.
'I'm sorry carino, you don' un'erstan'__'
'Look if anyone else tells me that I don't understand I'm going to be guilty of murder!'
'Harry listen!'

She had raised her voice now and there was fire in her eyes.
'I have to do this thing. The revolution never stops, don' you get it! People are sufferin', like my mum an' dad suffered. They joined Fidel to fight for a better life, an' died for it! __My brother too.'
'Your brother? I didn't know you had a brother!'
He was a coupla' years older than me, shot by Batista's secret police, his fuckin' murderin' gangsters! __He was twelve years old only.'
I leaned back against the bulkhead in the small, claustrophobic cabin.
'I didn't know about that.'
'Tha's because I don' talk about it.'
I couldn't see what was in her eyes because her head had dropped forward again, but grief was clearly evident in her voice.
For some moments we were both silent.
'Lucia don't you understand that I love you, that I care about you. Doesn't that *mean* anything? I don't want you risking your life! __It seems that you've lost quite enough already.'
'It's not as risky as you think Harry.'
'No! Well maybe you've been lucky so far, but luck has a curious habit of running out!'
I paused as I tried to think what to say next.
'Do you love me Lucia?'
She looked up at once.
'Of course I love you! You mus' know that! __You are everything to me!'
Her clear brown eyes even in the dim light from the bulkhead lamp told me all I wanted to know.
I attempted a smile.
'Well, almost everything it would seem.'
'Harry__'
'Look I have the solution to this__'
At that moment there was the sound of another crate being noisily lowered into the main cabin and then a light tap on the door.
I opened it to see a man in military uniform.
He looked beyond me towards Lucia
'Senora, todo esta cargado!'
'Bien! Gracias.'
Lucia murmured.
The man turned away and I closed the narrow door again.
'Harry look__'
'I know what he said! __Listen, this is the plan. I will go instead of you. __Me and Mari-Carmen!'
'No Harry__'

'What do you mean no? __Look I can sail the boat and I can navigate. I can also look after the engine, which you can't. If it broke down, what would you do?
I've picked up quite a lot over the past eight months or so.
Show me where we're going and that's all I need to know.'
'Carino no, I can't let you do this!'
'Why Lucia? Too risky? You said there *was* no risk!'
'No, I mean that__'
'You have two choices here Lucia! It's either me and Mamen or Mamen and me! __No other choices available!'
'No Harry__'
I interrupted before she could say anymore.
'So there's really no point in you going now Lucia, especially as you're carrying our child. What reason could you possibly have? It's only two days in total, __that's what you told me anyway!'
'Harry!'
'What's it going to be Lucia, because I'm not getting off this boat!'
She ran her hands through her long, lustrous dark hair in obvious frustration.
'You can't do this carino!'
'Oh I certainly can, so decide now!'
'You don' have ID!'
'Don't need it!'
'You don' have any clothes!'
'I'll manage!'
'You won' fine the place.'
Her resolve was slipping.
'Point it out on the map. I'll find it all right. The Englishman is not as daft as you think!'
'I don' think you' daft carino!'
'Settled then. Lets go up to the wheel-house and you can explain to me. __Where's Mamen by the way?'
'She'll be here soon.'

Lucia spread out the chart and showed me the exact point at the south-western end of Cuba, a group of tiny off-shore islands where the crates of weapons were to be dropped.
'You jus' hide them in the trees close to the shore, ok.'
'How are they going to locate them?'
'There is a small radio beacon, it gives out a signal every thirty seconds on a pre-set frequency. Jus' leave it on top of the boxes, they will find them ok.'

Mamen arrived after another five minutes or so. I watched as she spoke briefly to her father and then embraced him.
Carrying a large bag over her shoulder she dropped down onto the after deck and began to make her way up the steps to the wheel-house.
'Lucia I've brought some more food, just in case. __We should__'
She stopped short.
'Harry!'
'Hello Mamen!'
She looked from me to Lucia and then back again.
'Change of plan! I'm the skipper on this trip.'
She turned to Lucia again uncertainly.
'You and Harry are going to Maria la gorda. You can explain to him what to do when you get there.'
Mamen seemed lost for words.
'Don' worry chica, This man knows what he's doing, I taught him everything.'
'Except about engines!'
I commented.
She nodded with a half smile on her face.
'Sure! Except about engines.'
'Have we got plenty of fuel?'
I asked her.
'Plenty! __Enough to get there and back.'
'Good. So lets get moving.'
I skipped down the steps to the lower deck and called up to Raul who was still standing on the edge of the quayside.
'Raul, thanks!'
'No problem amigo!'
'Look could you__'
'Take Lucia back to your apartment? __Sure thing.'
Then she was standing next to me.
'Harry I'm sorry.'
'You should be! __We're partners remember, __in everything!'
She put her arms around me and kissed me briefly.
'I'm really sorry Carino!'
'Ok. Just don't do it again!'
'I love you Harry. Please be careful!'
'I certainly will be. I guess I've got everything to look forward to now!'
I gave her a hand to climb up onto the quay where she turned and stared down at me.
'Cast us off will you love!'

I said with a smile.

Raul untied the bow-line, while at the same time Lucia released the stern.

I jumped back up the flight of steps and started the engine, pulling back the throttle as soon as it caught.

I leaned over the side and saw Lucia standing next to the police chief in the bright pool of light from the two vehicles.

'She raised her hand and called out something that was drowned by the noise of the engine.

I gave her a quick wave and then turned to the helm, moving the control slowly into gear.

With the wheel hard over the boat moved slowly out into the darkness of the bay.

I glanced back briefly. Still in a halo of light, Lucia stood alone now her hand raised once more. Then I turned away, steering the boat towards the sweeping beam of the lighthouse at the entrance to the harbour.

Still feeling tired, I turned the helm to port, as we passed the lighthouse.

It was just after four o'clock, two or perhaps three hours more or less before sunrise.

In the dim, ghostly green glow of the compass, I set the course westwards, yawning widely. A half moon lay close to the horizon draped in a few wispy clouds and casting a faint light across a virtually flat sea.

In silence Mamen sat on the upholstered stool next to me.

She hadn't uttered a word since we cast off, but that was ok because I was in no mood to talk to her.

After half an hour of silence as we ploughed at full speed through the water, I turned to her.

'Can you get me some water from the fridge!'

Without a word she slipped off the stool and went below deck.

When she returned she handed me a cold plastic bottle.

'Harry__'

'You had better get some rest. In three hours you can take the wheel. I didn't get much sleep last night!'

Again she went below and above the noise of the engine I heard the door to the forward accommodation slam shut.

I took a good swig from the waterbottle, staring ahead through the windscreen into the darkness.

It was quite exhilarating to turn and watch the sun rising almost directly behind me.

First a faint orange glow against a deep cobalt sky and then, emerging from a fringe of low dark cloud, a perfect red arc that widened slowly as it began its relentless upward journey.
In half an hour I could feel the warmth on my back.
Earlier I had found a waterproof jacket and had pulled it on against the cool night air. Now I discarded it, throwing it over the back of one of the two elevated chairs, bolted to the deck in front of the control panel.
I glanced at the compass and took a quick look at the undulating hills of Cuba, less than ten kilometes away. Easing back on the throttle I made my way quickly to the deck below and then down into the main cabin, squeezing between the crates of cargo.
I rapped on the door to the for'rd cabin, waited for any sound then knocked again and opened it.
Still dressed, Mamen was struggling out from beneath a blanket on one of the bunks.
'Ten minutes ok, then you can come up and give me a break!'
I said curtly, closing the door again.

Shortly afterwards she appeared and slipped onto the chair next to me. I barely glanced at her before turning to concentrate on the vast open sea in front of me.
'Harry__'
She began, but I was in no disposition to embark on any conciliatory discussions. Apart from anything else, I was dog-tired, exhausted after hours of navigating in near darkness.
'Watch the compass! I've written the bearing on the edge of the chart here.'
I pointed to the scribbled figures.
'Keep the same distance from land, we don't want to stray beyond territorial boundary. __Also watch the sonar, there's plenty of depth beneath us, but__well, just keep your eye on it!
I'm going below to get some sleep. Wake me if there's a problem!'
I eased myself off of the comfortable seat in front of the wheel, where I had been fighting against the creeping fingers of sleep for the past several hours.
Without another word I went below deck.

Firstly, in the hot cramped engine space where I had to bend slightly to avoid the ceiling, I checked on the cooling and pressure gauges and then the oil level.
The old diesel engine was rumbling away happily and I left it to its task.

In the for'rd cabin I almost fell onto a bunk, and almost at once into a deep slumber.

I woke with a start and glanced at my watch. It was almost noon and I had slept for more than four hours.
I listened carefully. Apart from the noise of waves against the bow and the constant sound of the engine I could hear nothing that might have disturbed me.
I lay on my back for a while staring upwards as random thoughts drifted through my mind.
Then I shook myself and swung my legs over the side of the bunk, ducking my head to miss the one above.

Mamen was seated at the helm where I had left her.
The sun was at its peak, but a fresh breeze was blowing across the starboard side bringing a welcome coolness to the air.
To the south, large banks of dark cloud were building up over the island and it looked very much like more rain was on the way.
I mounted the steps to the wheelhouse slowly, refreshed by a sound undisturbed sleep.
'Anything happened?'
I asked taking the elevated seat next to her.
'No. A radio message from my father that was all.'
'Ok, well you can take a break now.'
'No it's ok I don't need__'
'Take a break! When you have a few moments you can make some food for both of us.
She glanced at me nervously and then dropped down from the seat and went below.
I was in no mood to converse with her, still angry, both with her and with Lucia for the deceit of which they were equally guilty.
A few minutes later she called up to me from the lower deck.
'What would you like Harry, there are some__'
'Anything!' I responded, before she could say anymore.
She hesitated and then disappeared into the main cabin again.

I stared out across the broad blue expanse of sea in front of me.
It felt good somehow to be out on the boat again after more than a month. Away from land, buildings, people and all the complications and diversions of living in a town, even one as small as Havana.
I reflected once again on how I had ended up in a place that was as different from North London as it was possible to imagine.

I had no regrets at my impulsive decision to sail away on a cruise liner with no real idea of what to expect.
It could have turned out differently of course, if I had never left the ship in Havana and decided to stay for a week or so. If I had never, purely by chance met Lucia, if I had never__.
Well the options, the permutations were of course endless.
If I didn't have the financial resources, I could never have embarked on my travels, although even that wasn't true of course. Throughout history people have always ventured into the unknown for one reason or another, many with barely a penny in their pockets.
No, I had no regrets even though I had no real idea what the future held for me.
Why was I so different from my father for whom a safe predictable life style had seemed essential to him, though perhaps not so different to my mother who had never been further than the coast of northern France on the occasional weekend trip organized as always by her husband.
I remembered that she'd always had her head in a book of one kind or another, which certainly included those of far off places.
A woman of few words however, she rarely revealed her thoughts, not to me anyway. Perhaps I should have asked her.
In spite of all that she was a kind and thoughtful person and I missed her. I had sent the odd letter to them both over the past year assuring them that I was well, but saying very little about my new life in Cuba, certainly never revealing my marriage to a beautiful woman of mixed race, which I knew would be something of a shock to say the very least!
In addition to which, it suddenly occurred to me, they were soon to be grandparents.
I resolved in that moment to write to them and tell them the whole story as soon as I returned to Havana, although the promise was soon forgotten.

Mamen brought some food up to the bridge, sandwiches and a large mug of coffee, which in silence she set down on the broad shelf behind the controls.
I was certainly hungry and began to devour the bread and cheese and something else with the flavour of cured ham. Whatever it was it was tasty enough and I soon cleared the plate.

To my relief, as I had no desire to speak to her, Mamen had gone below again.
I made a quick calculation in my head. If it was two hundred kilometers to our destination as I had been told, then we had covered more than half the distance, which meant that we would arrive in another five hours or so.

I finished the coffee and felt better, more awake and more alive, as a result no doubt of the caffeine injection.

My mind began to wander again as I considered the exciting if somewhat daunting news of Lucia's pregnancy.

I had no idea how to deal with it. It was a new and alien concept, which I struggled to accept as reality. How would I come to terms with that? What does one do with a newborn child, I certainly had no idea.

There seemed to be no easy answer and the more I thought about it the more disconcerting it all became.

The feeling, the mixture of fear and elation, became more overwhelming the more I thought about it, and at that moment I wished with all my heart that Lucia was here with me.

I was startled out of my reverie by Mamen's voice.

Without me being aware, she had come up from the lower deck again and was standing behind me.

It was something of a shock, which I managed somehow to conceal.

'Harry.'

I turned slightly in acknowledgement of her sudden appearance and then gazed ahead again gripping the wheel of the boat.

'Harry I'm sorry for deceiving you__'

'You should be.'

'It was wrong.'

'It certainly was.'

'My dad made that very clear to me. You have a strong ally there.'

I didn't respond as there seemed no reason to and I was in no mood for polite conversation.

'Harry you must understand__'

'Listen Mamen, if anyone else uses that *bloody* word again I will not be responsible for my reaction!'

'Ok I'm sorry, it's just that__'

I interrupted at once.

'And don't try to re-word the statement. That's like an insult! I'm, not interested in your socialist causes Mamen.'

'Humanitarian causes!'

'Call it what you want. To me, currently, it's supplying arms that are going to be used for killing people.'

'No it's so much more than that Harry, You don't__'

She stopped short just in time.

'It's the evil of capitalism and what it does to the under-privileged and the exploited in this terrible world that we live in.'

'That's your view! Without capitalism as you call it, without the profit motive, nothing would ever bloody well get done.'

'That's simply not true Harry! In the ideal Marxist world the commune cannot fail to be successful.'
'Oh really! Well where's the evidence? Russia has fallen apart as a result and that's a fact! The place is in economic ruin, even I know that. __Me, the man that doesn't understand!'
'Yes mistakes were made, but__'
'But nothing Mamen! You need to change those rose-tinted socialist spectacles of your for something a little more__practical!'
She must have sensed that I was getting angry again.
I was in no mood for her crap and she must have felt it.
At that moment I just wanted her to leave, to go back down to the main cabin again and leave me to my current muddled thoughts about bringing up a small child.
She didn't however and remained where she was, gripping the back of the other seat.
I continued to gaze ahead at the advancing seas without speaking.
A quick glance to port showed me that we were still only ten or perhaps fifteen kilometers from the shore.
Looking ahead again I noticed for the first time, what appeared to be a faint shape on the distant horizon. I focused on it for several moments as it seemed to grow larger.
Beneath the control panel there was a large shelf space that contained some charts, a small compass, some fishing reels and other nautical junk.
I rummaged around and found a pair of binoculars, dragging them out.
I leaned over the side of the vessel and focused them on the still indefinable shape in the distance.
For several moments I continued to gaze at it.
Then uttering a curse, I tossed the binoculars back where I had found them. Reaching for the throttle lever I pulled it back so that the sound of the engine was reduced to little more than a low rumble.
'What's happening?'
Mamen whispered the words, thinking perhaps, however absurdly, that we were being overheard.
'No one can hear you, not yet anyway. Get some rods from below and shove them in the starboard sockets. I reckon I've got about five minutes to get these four crates in the stern below deck.
I almost jumped down onto the afterdeck and began to untie the boxes. We almost fell over each other in the panic, however it was easier than I thought to drag the crates across the deck and slide them down into the main cabin. Mamen located two fishing rods and set them up in position, while I dragged the crates into what little space was left in the for'rd bunk cabin. Then I raced up on deck again.

The shape of an approaching vessel of some kind was now clearer or though still some distance away.

I grabbed the binoculars and stared at what now appeared to be a ship of some kind, a long sleek vessel, grey in colour.

For a full minute I continued to scrutinize the image as it drew nearer. At last I lowered the binoculars, wrapped the strap around them and stowed them away again. Then I turned to Mamen.

'US coast guard!'

'It can't be! We're in territorial water surely!'

'Yes we are, but that doesn't make much difference to the Yanks! They do whatever they want. __I said this to Lucia.'

'So what do we do now?'

There was a distinct element of alarm in her voice.

'Well we could make a run for it to the shore, but that will just arouse suspicion, and we don't want that. We'll brazen it out. They're heading directly for us so fingers crossed.'

'What does that mean? Fingers crossed.'

'It means pray!'

The small ship was perhaps only a couple of kilometers away now and the numbered markings on the bow were clear, as was the small gun turret on the fore deck.

'They will probably try to reach us on the radio, if they do let me do the talking. We're fishing and that's all, ok!'

She nodded silently.

In no time at all the U.S. ship was surging past us, the smooth line of the bow slicing effortlessly through the water almost as though it didn't exist. I could see various men in uniform looking down at us over the handrail. Behind us it made a sharp u-turn and in no time at all was sailing alongside, the bridge of the vessel towering above us.

A loud speaker suddenly burst out deafeningly.

It gave a marine radio call sign demanding that we made contact at once.

I turned on the radio, holding the receiver against my ear as I tuned into the frequency.

A man's voice came through clearly, the American accent equally apparent.

'This is the U.S. coastguard. I am Lieutenant Foster can you tell me what you are doing here?'

'Yes good afternoon, we're fishing.'

'Fishing!'

'That's correct, we are within Cuban territory I believe!'

'We know where you are!'
Came the curt response.
There was a pause.
'You have an English accent.'
'Yes, that's because I'm English!'
I tried to make my voice sound as lighthearted as possible.
'Not much luck so far today I'm afraid.'
I continued.
' __The fishing I mean.'
'What's an Englishman doing in Cuba?'
'I live here, __well for the past six months anyway. This is my wife!'
I gestured for Mamen to move to the open side of the wheelhouse where she could be seen, while I stood next to her.
'She is Cuban! We are enjoying what I suppose could be described as an extended honeymoon!'
Again I attempted to inject an element of humour in my voice.
It was an effort that appeared to work, because the officer responded in a lighter fashion.
'Where you from?'
'London. __North London.'
'Yeah! __I visited once. Nice place, but the beer was warm and weather was the opposite!'
'You get used to it!'
'And they don't know how to cook steaks!'
'Well having been to the states, I'm inclined to agree with you.'
'Who owns the boat?'
'No idea. It's hired by the day.'
'Which port?'
I was fumbling for an answer, when Mamen whispered in my ear.
'Puerta Esperanza, my wife tells me. Not easy to pronounce!'
'Sure!'
There was a short silence. Then the man spoke again.
'Ok you have a nice day now. __Good luck with the fishing.
Like a greyhound the sleek vessel seemed to leap forward in the water, accelerating away and heading north.
With my heart thumping painfully, I switched off the radio and replaced the receiver leaning back against the control panel.
'Shit, that was close!'
'Do you think they'll be back?'
Mamen asked, looking as scared as I felt.
'Who knows? Maybe. __The Yanks are not stupid. My guess is that they might know something is going on!'

'Do you think they might track us?'
'Again who knows!'
'They shouldn't have been here.'
'They know that and they obviously don't care. If the Cuban military know they're here I don't suppose there's much they can do about it apart from make a complaint to the U.N.!'
After a few minutes the naval vessel was virtually out of sight and I pushed the throttle to maximum again.
A short burst of dark smoke from the exhausts in the stern and we were on our way again, the little boat ploughing its way through the light waves.
'Right the sooner we get this nonsense over with the better!'
It's about another four hours to the keys, so lets hope the Americans have lost interest. I guess we'll know soon enough.'

Keeping a sharp, not to say nervous lookout to the north we pushed on solidly towards Cayos de Buenavista.
There was no sign of the coastguard ship again and as the sun began to drop towards the horizon we finally made it to the string of tiny uninhabited islands densely covered with sparse vegetation and innumerable low lying trees.
I glanced at the detailed chart. The island we were headed for was the largest and the last in the chain.
'So what now?'
I asked her.
'We motor round to the south side of Buenavista. There's a tiny inlet.'
She pointed on the chart with a pen.
'Look, just here. There's enough room for us to pass through and just enough for a sea-plane. It's cut off almost completely. We generally unload right here, and stow the boxes a few meters from the shore.'
'Ok, You're the navigator now.'
In less than an hour we were approaching the western end of an island getting close to the low shoreline that was capped with densely packed trees. If there was an inlet then I couldn't see it!
'Are you sure we're in the right place Mamen?'
'Yes. Just keep going.'
With the engine almost idling we continued in flat seas close to the featureless strip of land in which I continued searching for the slightest breach in the unbroken shoreline.
'Look there! There it is!'
Mamen whispered.
'Get in closer now.'

I did as I was told and sure enough a narrow inlet almost completely disguised by the low forest of greenery gradually appeared no more than two hundred metres away.

I glanced at the sonar.
'Not much water beneath us!'
'There's enough, just keep going!'
I eased the vessel even closer as the narrow inlet became clearer. I guessed that it was no more than twenty metres across, certainly enough room for us to pass through and also I estimated, to accommodate the wings of a small seaplane.
'How the bloody hell did you find this place?'
I murmured.
'By searching on maps.'
She replied simply.
We passed easily through the narrow entrance and into a smooth featureless river that stretched away in front of us.
'Ok now pull over to the left against the shore. It's easy to tie up on the trees.'
I eased the boat against the low bank where a virtual jungle grew right up to the waterline.
'Right. Keep it against the bank I'll tie up!'
Mamen had already descended to the lower deck and carrying a line she clambered over the side onto dry land. I eased the engine into neutral and waited as she tugged on the line drawing the stern end of the boat hard against the shore and then coiling the rope around the trunk of a tree.
I made my way quickly to the bow and threw another line across to her. In no time at all she had repeated the exercise, pulling the front end of the boat against the bank and tying it off again on a tree trunk. Finally I killed the engine.
She stood on the shoreline her hands on her hips.
'There, I told you it was easy!'
I couldn't resist a slight smile.
'Yes you did.__Now what.'
'We unload the boxes and carry them into the trees.'
'How far?'
'Five or six metres is enough. Nobody ever comes here.'
'I'm not surprised, pretty bleak place.'
'Which is why we chose it.'
I nodded.
'Ok then lets get this done. Sooner the better, then we can start back before it gets dark.'

It took a little over an hour for us to manhandle the fifteen or so crates from the boat and carry them into the dense mantle of trees, stacking them up and then covering them with a tarpaulin in the more than possible event of some rain. Mamen had tucked the radio transmitter between two of the boxes and switched it on.
'How long will the batteries last?'
I asked her.
'A week at least, but these will all be picked up almost certainly tomorrow, early morning I should think.'
'Ok, so lets get moving then!'
The mooring lines were released and I started the engine.
The river was slightly wider than the inlet and it was relatively easy to turn the boat around. Then I eased the throttle forward and we headed towards the narrow opening.
Mamen had switched on the radio and tuned it in to a frequency.
Then, picking up the receiver she spoke into it briefly in rapid Spanish of which I understood not one word.
Then she replaced the hand-set and switched it off.
'Who was that?'
'My dad!'
'What did you say? You might have been overheard.'
'That we caught some fish at last and that we're on our way back.'
She was smiling as she spoke.
I glanced at her skeptically.
'Well we're not back yet!'

We had a quick snack of bread and cheese and some salad and it was just getting dark as we passed the last of the 'cayo's', the elongated group of islands that lay just west, off of the farthest tip of Cuba.
Then it was full speed ahead, back to Havana.
With the sun disappearing slowly beyond the horizon behind us the weather looked good, with an almost flat sea and barely a breeze as we headed eastwards into the oncoming darkness.
I glanced at my watch. It would be ten or maybe eleven hours I estimated before we reached the harbour, which would mean that we should arrive at roughly seven the next morning.
I felt a distinct sense of relief that the job was done and that we were on our way back.
I missed Lucia immensely. With our disagreement forgotten, temporarily at least, I couldn't wait to see her again.

It occurred to me at that moment that she had made this same journey with Mamen on three previous occasions, journey's which unlike ours had been uneventful, or so I had been told.
I shuddered to think what might have happened if the coastguard had boarded us earlier, but they hadn't, so no point in speculating about what might have been.
With our course clearly set I checked on the engine again to see that all was well. Then it was homeward bound.
Mamen took the first watch while I had a much-needed rest in the cabin below.
At one o'clock the following morning I woke refreshed after a sound sleep of almost four hours.

Taking the steps up to the wheelhouse, I took over the wheel from Mamen who was clearly eager for a break and wasted no time in going below, plainly exhausted after what had been a demanding day previously, and a long night at the helm.
For the next four hours or so I navigated the little boat through virtually calm water in a night that was as black as ink with only a few isolated stars for company and the mesmerizing, but somehow comforting sound of the engine.

We were heading almost directly east, and dawn would not begin to break ahead of us for at least another two, maybe three hours.
Maman appeared suddenly on the bridge carrying two mugs of strong dark coffee.
At that point in the early morning it tasted better than I could have imagined, together with a packet of biscuits, which we shared hungrily between us.
'Quiet night Harry?'
'Yep! Just me and the ocean!'
In the subdued light of a half moon and the dim glow of a million stars, the sea ahead of us was now as flat as a millpond and with the total absence of a breeze.
'It's quite beautiful really isn't it, the night, the stars, the isolation?'
Mamen commented quietly.
'It's always here, but of course we rarely see it. It makes you realize what a beautiful planet we live on. Something we don't think about nearly as often as perhaps we should!'
I took a sidelong glance at her.
'Your very philosophical this morning!'
I said with a smile.

'Yes, perhaps.'
She replied thoughtfully, her blue eyes gazing straight ahead.
With the glow from the instrument panel reflecting on her fair hair and her pale smooth skin, she looked quite different somehow.
Her expression seemed to be relaxed, maybe even contented, a contrast to her usual look of veiled concern about the world, and about politics with which she seemed to be permanently preoccupied.
'How come you're not married Mamen?'
'I don't believe in marriage.'
She said reflectively.
'Oh I know that you and Lucia are very happy, I suppose I just have other priorities.'
'Solving the problems of humanity!'
I offered, together with another smile.
'Doesn't mean you can't have a partner, does it?'
'I do have a partner.'
'Really! Now I am surprised. I've never met the man and Lucia's never mentioned him.'
'That's because he is a 'her'!'
She turned her nice face for a moment and grinned.
'Ah, that explains it. __ That it's a 'her' I mean.'
She was still smiling at me.
'Explains what?'
'Well I mean um, __er, I'm not really sure what I mean.'
'You're not embarrassed are you Harry?'
She was teasing slightly.
'No of course not! But I thought that __I mean I heard__'
'That I was with a man?'
'Yes, that's what I was told.'
'He was a bastard!'
She said quietly.
'A lot of men are!'
Mamen glanced at me.
'You're one of the exceptions.'
'Well thanks.'
'Lucia told me that.'
'Well I should bloody well think so! __ I do a lot for that woman.'
I turned to her with a grin.
'Anyway Mamen, there's no reason why you can't bring your partner with you the next time we all go out to a bar and get drunk, is there?'
'No I suppose not.'
'Good! Settled then.'

We pushed onwards with the partial shape of a flat yellow moon suspended on an invisible string in front of us, almost inviting someone to reach out and touch it.

It was utterly peaceful, with the boat cleaving through the calm water and creating two perfectly symmetrical bow waves that drifted away in a regular series into a possible infinity.

The ragged, mountainous shoreline in pin-sharp clarity, was touched as though with random brush strokes by soft golden moonlight.

I groped around for the binoculars again, focusing them on a distant point of land which I knew was Havana.

'I can just about make out the beam from the lighthouse. We should be there in just over an hour.'

I remarked quietly, both of us I think feeling a comforting sense of relief as we neared the end of our journey.

Then suddenly, unexpectedly, it all went terribly wrong.

Chap. 11

The thundering sound of the old diesel engine was augmented gradually by another similar sound, which was instantly recognizable.

I spun round to see two large powerboats bearing down on us from behind, one on each side.

They were big, built for speed, with curved windscreens over low streamlined accommodation. Fast motor launches that drew next to us in seconds.

'Cut your engine mister Burgess!'

A man's voice with an American accent bellowed loudly from a megaphone, and we were suddenly blinded by spot-lamps from both vessels.

On the decks of the two boats several men, similarly dressed in dark clothing, were carrying weapons, which we all knew that they would never need to use, the implicit threat being more than sufficient.

I cut the engine at once as the two boats drew nearer.

"Mister Burgess!" The man had said!

I felt a sharp chill engulfing me at the sound of my own name. How could they know that?

For the second time in my life I felt a deep sense of fear.

One of the launches drew alongside and grappling hooks were used to hold the two vessels close together.

'Climb on board Burgess!'

The megaphone again.

I hesitated and stood close to Mamen, who was staring at them defiantly.

'*Now* Burgess! Unless you want to go down with your boat!'

I turned to Mamen.

'Come on!'

I whispered to her.

'We don't have a lot of choice. There's nothing they can prove Mamen. No evidence.'

I took her arm and we dismounted the steps to the lower deck.

'What the hell do you want?'

I called out with feigned bravura.

'You first Burgess!'

One of the armed men said quietly, ignoring my feeble response and at the same time lifting his gun.

There seemed little choice and I clambered over the side onto the other boat.

At once I was grabbed by two men and handcuffed.

I struggled with them, turning to face to Mamen again.

She was standing next to the bulwark of our boat, which to my horror was now slowly drifting away, the two men having released the grappling irons.

When there was some distance between the two, a man on the other powerboat lifted a rocket launcher and fired a missile at the waterline of the 'Lucy'. A huge explosion blasted a jagged hole in hull and almost at once the little boat began to list to one side.

A second missile took care of the emergency dinghy that was lashed to the foredeck.

'*MAMEN!*' I cried out to her as our boat slowly settled bow first into the sea.

A sharp jab to my stomach dropped me to my knees, and I gasped for breath.

She still stood on the after-deck defiantly. If she was at all fearful it certainly didn't show.

'*Viva Cubanos!*'

She called out in a last rebellious shout.

Then the engines of the craft beneath us burst into life with a roar.

I managed to call out to her one last time as we raced away, still struggling against the two men who held me.

Then a gloved fist struck me with a punch in my face that knocked me almost unconscious and I was dragged below deck.
I never saw the 'Lucy' as it finally slipped beneath the surface.

My handcuffs were released, I'd been given a towel to wipe the blood off my face and now I was seated in a comfortable chair in a wide modern cabin. It took a few moments to focus on the man sitting opposite. He was dressed incongruously in what looked like an expensive tropical suit and an open necked shirt.
I tried to speak but no words emerged, as I was still dazed by the sharp blow to my face.
The man leaned towards me. He was holding a glass in an outstretched hand.
'Here, whisky! You look as though you need it.'
Still dazed I took the glass and sipped at the contents, feeling a sharp stinging pain from the cut in my lip.

'How the fuck did you ever get involved in all this Harry?'
The man was leaning back in a leisurely manner, his hands on the armrests of his chair.
I sipped at the whisky again ignoring the pain, then I spoke out with uncontained fury.
'You *fucking* heartless bastard! You've just killed that young woman, my wife, __without a second thought.'
'Not unless she's a good swimmer!'
His smile seemed almost friendly.
'We were fifteen kilometers offshore and in the dark. I wouldn't give much for her chances!'
'Neither would I.'
He replied in the same level tone.
'Who the hell are you.'
I murmured.
'That's hardly relevant. What is relevant is my first question. How the hell did you get mixed up in all this? You're not political, that we know.'
'Mixed up in what?'
I remarked without much confidence.
He released a long sigh.
'You took a whole load of Russian made weapons to Cayo Buenavista tonight.'
He waited, but there didn't seem much point in responding.
'We traced you all the way from Havana Harry.'

'Perhaps you did. There were no guns, we were fishing. We were also intercepted by the U.S. coastguard, they didn't seem particularly interested.'
'They just wanted to make sure you were on your way. We didn't know exactly where you were meant to drop them off, not until last night that is. It was a good location by the way, easy to get to in a seaplane by Sandanistas, or some other activists, __once they picked up the signal.
__Anyhow, they won't be making any more gun running trips. We're taking very good care of that situation!'

It seemed utterly pointless to lie anymore. In my acute naivety it had never occured to me, not even once, that the Americans would know our every move. I was suddenly overawed by my own shortsighted stupidity.
And now Mamen was dead!

'Why did you have to kill her, leave her in the sea __in the dark?
That was fucking __inhuman!'
'The woman on the boat? __Your wife you said. __But she's not your wife, is she Harry!'
I hesitated.
'No.'
I murmured quietly.
'No she's not. __Lucia Jose Martinez! That's your wife. Ex-hooker, who is now we presume, tucked up in bed where you should be if you had any fuckin' sense!'
He sighed again.
'I don't get it Harry, I really don't! Do you want to explain?'
'There doesn't seem much point really!'
I felt somehow resigned to what I was quite sure was soon going to happen, specifically that I would shortly be dumped over the side, hopefully with a bullet in the head as the thought of drowning slowly in the darkness was terrifying. My mind turned to Mamen again and I shivered involuntarily.
'Oh there is a point! Assuming you want to stay alive that is.
Then it's back to the UK for you Harry, which you should never have left to begin with!'
He stared at me with a questioning look.
'Why Cuba? That's what I don't get!'
'Pure chance.'
I responded.
'Yeah, well maybe it was.'

He leaned forward, resting his arms on his well-tailored legs.
'I can think of much better places to visit, not that it's important.
Like I say we know you have no political agenda, so we assume that you just wanted to see something of the world. You just chose the wrong place to visit that's all.'
He paused.
'We know quite a bit about you Harry, more than you might imagine. And this Cuban girl of yours, the one you married, she's quite a woman, I have to admit!'
'If you assure me now that she won't be harmed I will do literally anything that you ask.'
I was pleading with the man unashamedly, and I meant every word I had said.
'We'll get to that!
__Look Harry my job, __our job is to try and keep a lid on these little skirmishes in Central America. It destabilizes the status quo, __meaning American interests.'
He smiled as he spread his hands apart.
'Harry these people don't *know* what they want. If they had power they'd like as not fuck it up! Just look at the record. These guys couldn't run a delicatessen never mind a country.
Chile, for instance! With inflation on it's way to the moon, something had to done there, and we did it! __Cuba, another prime example!
Castro is fucked now that the Russians have pulled out.
You've seen the place Harry. No economy now to talk of. __Free schooling, free health cover?'
He shook his head.
'How long is that gonna last? __Where's the money coming from?'
I lowered my head, perhaps because I could hardly argue with the man.
'Castro's a dreamer!'
He continued
'Ok he was a brave guy, no one can say otherwise, but he's out-moded by history now.'
Still I said nothing, as there seemed nothing worth saying.
No doubt he would get to the point eventually.
'What I'm trying to tell you Harry, is that the socialist idea doesn't work. I don't want to give you a lesson in politics here, just to explain that these countries in central and South America have vital resources that can benefit the world.'
'Including the U.S.!'
I intervened.

'Sure why not! We've invested in these countries to help them exploit their resources.'
He shrugged.
'Why shouldn't we expect some return? That's what capitalism is all about!'
I had no response for him. In fact I was hardly listening now. Instead I was thinking about Mamen. Still young, still in her twenties, abandoned to a fate that I shuddered even to think about.
I imagined her in total darkness, floundering helplessly in the water, her strength slowly diminishing.
For a few moments I buried my head in my hands.

Perhaps he knew what was going on in my mind because he spoke again.
'She was meant as an example Harry. __To you!
Sure we could have arrested her, probably given her jail time, or sent her over to some legitimate military authority in Central America, in which case she's probably better off were we left her, better than being in some filthy shithole prison and gettin' raped solid every day.'
'Or you could have let her go. She was just a young idealist, 'fighting for freedom' so she told me. You threw her life away just now like an empty cigarette packet, __as though it was nothing. That's contemptible!'
He regarded me with a level gaze.
'How many lives in Central America have been lost over the past decades Harry? Young lives on both sides. Her's was just one more.
We can't allow communism to flourish so close to our borders, it's a threat to the U.S. and to the free world. You need to take a look at the bigger picture. We have a duty to ensure that these regimes don't gain a foothold, so we intervene when necessary.
People like Pinochet, Somoza, Norieaga, and yeah Batista. Not nice people, in fact I'll go further, they were fuckin' assholes all of them! __I met Noriega once, he was repulsive, a fuckin' animal!
Jesus, I wouldn't let these people anywhere near my family, or in my neighbourhood come to that!
The point was, they were effective in policing their countries and keeping order!'
'You mean stifling dissent!'
'If that means keeping out the commie's, __sure!'
He gazed at me with all the smug confidence of a poker player with a full hand.
'I'm still waiting for you to tell me how you got involved in this fucking mess in the first place Harry. We're pretty certain that you're not the revolutionary type, so there's some mystery here!'

I sank back in my chair feeling desperately tired suddenly.
'There's no mystery, __ and you're right, I'm not involved or even remotely interested in politics. It was just__. I was helping someone out that's all! __Nothing more than that!'
He shrugged.
'Well whatever reason you had, it's ended you up in some very deep shit!

There was a long pause while I was, no doubt, given time to contemplate my situation.
'So now what?'
'So now you go back to Havana.'
'To *Havana?*'
I replied, completely mystified.
'Sure.'
'And how am I supposed to get there?'
'In a small rescue dinghy, similar to the one we just destroyed on your boat.'
'I see. And what am I supposed to do in return for this__favour?'
Again he fixed me with the same unwavering look.
'There are two ways here. First alternative, we put a bullet in your head and throw you overboard.'
'Well thanks for the bullet, there's a lot of sharks around here!'
'I urge you to take me very seriously Harry!'
'I am! Believe me.'
'Good. Second alternative. You go back to Havana and keep your ear very close to the ground.'
'Spy you mean?'
'Yeah that's exactly what I mean. There are a lot of subversive elements in Cuba who still believe, mistakenly, that socialism can succeed in Central America as well as their own country.
They're like mosquitoes, they never give up and as we know they're not easy to find, and they're not easy to swat!
So your job will be to watch out for them and tell us who they are. Simple as that!'
'I get it.'
'Not all of it you don't Harry. If you fuck up, if you don't get results in a reasonable time frame we kill your wife, then we kill you!
Now the second thing is, we want to know when and where these arms caches are being stashed. We know that different locations are being used every time and it's not easy to know exactly where.

We got lucky with your boat and managed to trace you. We had a good result there, but we need more good results!'
'I see. So you're not asking for much then!'

It was like a nightmare that I knew couldn't possibly be real and that at any instant I would wake up, except of course that it wasn't!
At that precise moment I had to admit to myself that the prospect of a bullet in my head seemed quite tempting.
The events of the last hour had left a disgusting taste in my mouth and quite suddenly I didn't want to live on the same planet as the man who had just laid out my future for me, nor indeed the faceless leaders and politicians behind him, those ultimately responsible for Mamen's dreadful end.

'Ok, so you can throw me over the side now if you want to.'
'No problem, if that *is* what you really want. But we still kill your wife, so maybe you should think about that.'
He stared at me again as he waited for the only response that I could give.
'How do you people live with yourselves? How do you sleep at night?' I commented impotently.
'Was that a yes or a no?'
'I don't have much of a choice do I.'
'Good that's settled! __As to the answer to your question, I sleep very well at night. I have a lovely family, two kids at a good school. We have a nice house and we live very well. America is a great place. __Best country in the world!'

I felt utterly defeated and was left with a distinct feeling of nausea.
There was nothing that I could do but go along with his plan, although how I was meant to accomplish what he wanted was, at that moment, far beyond me.
I shook my head in sheer exasperation.
'How the hell am I supposed to carry out this __espionage, for want of a better word? I don't know anything about anything to do with the people you say you're looking for. I can't even speak the bloody language properly.'
'Oh you'll think of a way Harry. Somebody must have put you up to this gunrunning trip, so I would say that was a good place to start. And anyhow, there's nothing like a challenge to stimulate and inspire. __And you've got one hell of a challenge my friend! One hell of an incentive!'
I knew I was wasting my time, but I said it anyway.

'How can you even think about killing my wife, she's entirely innocent, and as a matter of fact she's also pregnant!'
He shrugged, and there was no change in his expression apart from a nasty grin.
'Even more incentive for you to get this right then Harry!'

In that instant, as he uttered that last phrase I felt for the first time in my life an entirely new emotion, if emotion was the right word.
It was a feeling of complete anger like no other before.
No not anger, rage, blind red rage that overwhelmed me to the exclusion of anything else.
I wanted to tear his body apart while he still lived, rip him to pieces in sheer elation, and bathe in his blood.
The sheer frightening force of my anger propelled me from where I was sitting directly towards him.
Amongst other things on a large desk behind him there was a paper knife, which I grabbed at and with more strength that I ever knew I possessed, I flung myself at him throwing my free arm around him and pressing the blade hard against his neck, so hard that it drew blood.
'*No!*__ 'Listen you fucking arsehole, I don't care if I die but you should *never* have threatened my wife!!'
I blurted out my response without thinking, whispering the words through tightly clenched teeth, my mouth close to his ear.

He was certainly taken off guard, no question of that, but when he spoke it was, surprisingly, with a total absence of fear.
'No! What does that mean Burgess? You don't have a fucking choice here!' He murmured.
'But I do, you're so wrong. __Look I said I would do what you ask as long as you leave my wife out of it and I meant that, that's the truth! Otherwise there's no deal. Believe me, I am a desperate man! You can kill me, sure, but if I'm dead you get nothing! That should be clear enough, even to a shitbag like you. I said I would cooperate and meant it, as long as my wife is left out of this!'
At that moment the door burst open and the two men who had dragged me below deck were instantly leveling pistols at me.
Without hesitation the man I was grasping raised his hand to them.
'It's contained!
He shouted the words at the two men, still without any apparent fear.
'Get out and shut the door!'
Still they hesitated, their guns pointed directly at my head.
'Now I said! Do it now. __Put your guns down and leave!'

They relaxed at once without a word and then left the cabin closing the door firmly behind them.
Still in the same controlled tone he now spoke quietly to me.
'Ok Harry you made your point, so now let me go before I break your fucking arm.'
I had run out of strength. It just drained away as I realized that there was really nothing that I could do.
My impulsive, but impotent display had achieved nothing.
I did as he said dropping the paper knife to the floor and staggered away from him, sinking back into my seat, my whole body trembling with rage or fear, or perhaps both.

He sat straight in his chair and taking out a handkerchief, wiped away the small amount of blood from his neck, regarding it disinterestedly for a moment.
'Right Harry, nice try, and you made your point. You got more guts than I thought!'
'Extreme circumstances call for extreme measures.'
I remarked, my voice almost certainly betraying the terror that I now felt inside.
He regarded me silently for several moments.
Then he nodded slowly.
'Ok now listen very carefully, because what I said just now still stands.
Your wife dies if you don't go along with this.
Let me explain further.
We will take her and we will transport her to a jail in Mexico, which she will never leave. Now at this moment we have a good relationship with the Mexican government, and I can tell you that it isn't very receptive to Cuban revolutionaries, trust me on that.
Also, Mexican jails have a pretty *bad* reputation. Your wife is an exceptionally beautiful woman Harry, no one could argue with that. I leave it to your imagination as to what will happen to her in one of their filthy lock-up's, with guards who will be more than anxious to, shall we say, __entertain her!
After a week she will *pray* to be dead!'
He paused, no doubt to allow his words to take effect.
'This is one sure way to get you to do what we want Harry, and if you fuck with me even this much!'
He held up a thumb and forefinger with the tiniest gap between them.
'Then I will personally shoot you and take time about it. __After we prove to you of course, that your wife is no longer in the land of the living! __So are we clear now?'

'I had never felt so frustrated and helpless in the whole of my life.
I knew that there was nothing that I could do or say that would make any difference to his resolve.
With a feeling of utter revulsion for the man and a sense of being completely beaten, I nodded slowly.
'Ok then, I'll do whatever I can. Or though at this point I have no idea how.'
'Good we understand each other. You'll think of a way Harry, trust me.
'Necessity is the mother of invention!' You heard of that phrase?'
I didn't respond as there seemed to be no point.
'So, you know what you have to do, and I don't need to waste anymore of my time.'

I searched for something else to say, something that was at the back of my mind, at the same time struggling to regain some kind of composure.
'Alright then, as you say, we have a deal!'
 But how long am I supposed to keep up this ridiculous fucking "James Bond" act. Eventually I'm going to get caught, so I'm going to be dead anyway!'
'We thought about that so we'll make it a little easier. __Find us one high level activist who's trying to put a spanner in the works, into American interests. Just one! Maybe he or she is behind these shipments, who knows! And there is something else. Two guys got shot some months back, __our guys. We don't know who did the shooting, not yet anyway, but maybe you can help us with this.
We need to know who was responsible. We're pretty sure they were out on a boat somewhere when it happened.'
He allowed this to sink in before continuing.
'In addition to this, let's say, two, no let's say three locations where these guns are being hidden and when its gonna' happen, then that's your job done.
If you're careful and you do as we ask, you should be able to stay alive.
Then, like I say, you and your wife can go and live in England where you belong.'
'Thanks, but I'd rather stay in Cuba!'
'Maybe not, __not after they find out who's been leaking information to us!
If all goes well, and for your sake it had better, call us from the UK and we'll make sure our little secret never gets out.'
He paused with the same half-smile on his face.

Was there even the slightest element of compassion in his manner, I doubted it, certainly none that was apparent.

A last question occurred to me suddenly.

'Supposing it had been my wife who had made this trip tonight instead of me?'

'Then it would have been the same deal Harry, exactly the same deal! Except that it would have been you in a Mexican slammer gettin' the shit kicked out of you!'

The same self-satisfied smile accompanied his reply.

'We'll give you and maybe your wife some time to work things out, __ but not too long. I'll give you a number to call when you have something to tell us. So now it's up to you!'

'And how do I explain rowing ashore in a life raft and the loss of our boat, in addition to the death of a close friend?'

'We are going to drop you off at about I would say, eight kilometers from land. That should give you plenty of time to think of something.'

That was it. The interview was over.

I was thrown into an inflatable just over an hour after we had been intercepted. Then the boat that had picked me up sped away, vanishing into the night.

In the distance I could see faint individual pinpricks of light from the shore and much further to the east the clear, but faint beam from the lighthouse, sweeping through the darkness, beyond which on the far horizon, the suggestion, just the merest evidence of the beginning of a new day.

With a feeling of almost suicidal bleakness I took hold of the short oars and began to row.

Chap. 12

By the time the tiny craft drifted up onto the pristine white sand of a deserted beach, two or closer to three hours later, the sun was already beginning to rise into a clear blue sky.

Not exhausted, but certainly weary, I dragged the dinghy up onto the sand before slumping down on my backside onto the beach, drawing my knees up to my chest with my arms clutched around them.

My head fell forward as I considered once again what might have happened if I had not taken Lucia's place on this trip. It was pretty

obvious, as the man, whoever he was, had said, that it would in fact have made little difference. But if, unlike me, she had refused to cooperate __?
I shuddered to think what might have happened. Perhaps she would have suffered the same fate as Mamen, or perhaps shipped off to some hellish prison somewhere. If that had happened then I really wouldn't have cared very much what my own fate might eventually have been.
But now of course it was up to me to ensure that in spite perhaps of what the agent, the spook, or whatever he was, had said, that she would remain safe, and as much as I was determined to achieve that, I still had no idea at all exactly how!
Once again I was overwhelmed by the darkest feelings imaginable.

I looked up suddenly. A small boy had wandered down onto the beach. He carried a primitive fishing rod and a canvas bag.
With barely a glance at me crouched on the sand, he dropped the bag next to him, rummaged inside for bait and then cast the line with some expertise, over the light incoming waves, dropping the hook some distance away into the deep blue water.
With some effort I struggled to my feet and in tortured Spanish I asked him where the nearest town was.
He pointed back up the beach to where a few palm trees leaned over towards the sea, the fronds drooping listlessly.
'Dos kilometros en esa direccion.'
He remarked, turning his attention at once back to the fishing.

From the top of the beach a narrow sandy pathway led straight through a tangle of trees and bushes and I started walking.
Eventually the tree cover diminished and a group of buildings appeared some distance away. The pathway merged eventually with a roughly tarred road that led into what was no more than a small village.
In a square, an ancient church with a large bell suspended in a crude stone arch above it, took up one side of the plaza, surrounding it, primitive buildings, houses and a couple of shops, and opposite the church a bar with a faded sign and a striped canopy that tilted precariously to one side.
Several lines of lottery tickets were taped to the window inside, waiting to be sold, perhaps to a lucky winner.
I walked across the square and into the bar, which had maybe half a dozen customers.
Their conversations halted at once as they stared in silence at what I realized quite suddenly was my grossly disheveled appearance. There was blood on the front of my shirt that was torn in places, and my jeans were stained with patches of engine oil.

The barman held a brandy bottle poised in one hand and a glass in the other, which he was about to fill.
For a few moments he looked frozen in time.
I spoke up, breaking the heavy silence.

Puedo, er, puede llema er, para policia!
'Policia!'
The man replied giving me an uncertain glance.
'Yes, Si, it's um, muy important, __importante!'
Still looking at me suspiciously he put down the bottle and reached for a phone behind the bar.
'Ingles?'
He grunted the question.
'Yes, Ingles!'
He shrugged his shoulders and pressed in a number.

Within minutes, or so it seemed, two uniformed officers wandered into the bar. The proprietor nodded in my direction where I was sitting at a small table nursing a glass of water.
They strolled across to me with bored, unconcerned expressions.
'Que pasa?'
One of them said, the thumbs of both hands tucked behind his belt.
'It's difficult, erm, Explica. Er, ahi esta, er, chica, erm, dead, __ muerto!'
I pointed in the direction of the sea.
'Muerto?'
He repeated. Now I had his attention.
'Si, yes. Er, I take you, __in coche!'
'Cual coche?'
He spread his hands.
'No, oh shit! I mean in your car! En er, tu coche!'
'Hay una chica muerta en mi coche?!'
He responded.
The few customers now listening intently to the exchange, burst into laughter, which was shortly echoed by the two policemen.
I buried my head in my hands.
'Oh bloody hell!'
I looked up at them both.
'Listen!'
I shouted the word.
The smiles on their faces dried up at once. Replaced by that universal look that all police officers seem to adopt when they are challenged.

'I mean can you Puerde contacto Er, el capitan, er jefe of policia in Havana! Raul Vasquez!'
'Raul Vasquez!' The man repeated stupidly.
'Yes, yes! Raul Vasquez! Capitan de policia, in Havana! It's muy, __very importante!'
The man had a mobile phone and taking it out he pressed in numbers and after a pause, he spoke rapidly into the device. Turning his back on me he strolled the length of the bar and then back again, pausing to listen and then speaking again in rapid Spanish. Again he appeared to be listening, stopping dead in his tracks. Then he walked across to where I was still sitting and passed the device.
I pressed it against my ear.
'Raul is that you?'
'*Harry?*'
'Yes. Can you come here, like now!'
Where the hell are you? I've been trying to contact you on the boat! __What's happened.'
'Something awful.'
'What do you mean Harry?'
'How soon can you get here?'
'Get to where? Where the hell are you?'
'I don't know, er, hold on!'
I passed the phone back to the copper.
'Hablar por favour!'
I urged him.
He listened and spoke into the phone again briefly. Then he switched it off, regarding me now with distinct curiosity.
Then he pointed towards me with the phone.
'You __er, wait here! Si.'
'Sure, si!'

The next half an hour felt like a year.
The barman, without me asking, brought a glass of dark rum across to where I was sitting.'
'Drink!'
He remarked, with a clear element of sympathy in his voice.
I did as he said, coughing on the strong fiery liquid.
The two policemen had walked outside. Through the glass I could see them sitting at a table in deep conversation.

Then there was the sound of an approaching car that burst suddenly into the plaza, drawing to an abrupt halt outside the bar.

I saw Raul as he climbed out and walked across to the two officers. I got up at once from where I was sitting and hurried outside.

The two coppers were on their feet now in animated conversation with Raul, then he turned and saw me.

'Harry! What the hell happened to you? And Mamen,__where is Mamen?'

'Raul I'm so sorry!'

I approached him slowly, almost cautiously.

'I don't know quite how to tell you this. __Mamen is dead!'

He stared at me in silence and with obvious disbelief.

'I'm so sorry Raul. I couldn't, __it was impossible to save her.'

He removed his cap slowly.

'Tell me what happened.'

His voice was steady, although not much above a whisper.

'It was about four o'clock this morning. I don't know who, but__. A ship ploughed into us in the dark. We had navigation lights so how they couldn't have seen us I have no idea. Mamen was on the lower deck on the port side. What she was doing there I'm not sure. Perhaps she had just come out of the lower cabin, I don't know. I was on the bridge of course. The boat, the ship whatever it was just cut us in two. It was so quick you can't imagine. I don't know *why* they didn't stop, __they must have known__surely they must!'

I paused, gazing at him directly.

I hated lying to the man. I wasn't responsible for Mamen's death but oddly at that moment I felt as though I was. It was the lie I suppose and I despised myself for not telling him the truth of what had happened, but then if I had__.

He was still staring at me perhaps only half believing.

How I managed to continue looking him in the face I shall never know. Maybe it was sheer will power, because I knew that at any cost I *had* to convince him!

'Lets go inside Harry. __We'll talk inside.'

He led the way back into the small room. A brief word between him and the proprietor was all it took.

In seconds the other customers left the bar, leaving just me and the same two officers who had followed us inside.

'Sit down Harry.'

Raul and I took one of the tables. He turned to the proprietor who was still hovering uncertainly behind the bar.

'Dos Cervezas.'

He said, still in the same level tone. Then, turning to me.

'What happened to Mamen?'

I responded without hesitating.

'I can only presume that she drowned or was killed by the impact. It collided with us in the afterdeck, portside, just below the steps to the wheelhouse.'

Did you see anything of the other boat Harry?

'It was grey.'

'Any markings?'

'None that I could see.'

'How could you tell the colour if it was dark?

'From the lights in our cabin below. Mamen had been making us both some coffee.'

'And you didn't see a name on the other boat, or markings of any kind, words, numbers.'

'There wasn't time Raul! As soon as it hit the lights went out almost at once. It was total darkness. I called out to Mamen but there was nothing! Not a sound! In seconds the boat was going under.

I managed somehow to get to the foredeck and release the liferaft capsule. The next thing I knew I was in the water.'

I stopped as the barman set two small bottles on the table and retreated to his sanctuary again.

The room was completely silent now. I picked up a bottle and drank half the contents.

'What then Harry?'

'I climbed into the life raft. I knew there would be a torch somewhere in the kit and found it almost at once, then I started to search for Mamen. I called out to her but there wasn't a sound I looked around on the surface but there was no sign, not of anything just a few bits of debris from the 'Lucy'.'

'What about the other ship?'

'By the time I found the dinghy and then the torch it was some distance away, no onboard lights, only navigation. It seemed to be heading towards the shore then it turned in a wide circle and headed off to the north.'

'How quickly?'

'Fast, like *very* fast. When it hit us it was over in an instant. There was no time__no time to do anything.'

'Grey you said Harry.'

'Metallic grey, that's the only thing I can be sure about.'

'Metal? A metal hull?

'Almost certainly!'

He thought for a moment.

'And Mamen?'

'No Raul!'

I shook my head.
'Believe me I searched around until dawn, there was no sign of her, nothing! There was no point in looking any further.
I found some oars in the inflatable and started rowing.'
Again he seemed deep in thought.
'I spoke to my daughter. It must have been when you were both on the way back. She said a US coast guard boat had intercepted you.'
'That's right! It was on the outward journey. I gave them the story that we were fishing and they swallowed it. __We were very lucky!'
'Maybe.'
'Yeah maybe! __I know exactly what you're thinking.'
'They were violating Cuban territory.'
'I mentioned that to them in a roundabout sort of way, just to make the point. __Raul, they do what the fuck they want!'
'Yes you are right my friend.'

The story was simple enough, the lie easy to cover.
I was overwhelmed with shame for my dishonesty, not to say grief at the loss of the young woman.
Raul must have seen that, not the guilt but the grief. It would have been difficult for anyone to tell the two emotions apart.
There followed a long silence while Raul seemed to be staring into nothing.
'Are you ok Harry?'
He said at last
'Yes I suppose so. I got whacked in the face by something, apart from that__'
'You look terrible.'
'Yes I suppose I do.'
'Where is the life raft?'
'Not far from here on the beach where I left it, assuming it hasn't been stolen by now.'
He released a deep sigh, the only evidence so far of his own grief.
Or perhaps he hadn't taken it all in yet, which seemed more likely.
'Finish your beer, then we'll go and pick it up.'
'No. I've had enough. __Let's just go.'

The car was in fact and old Jeep with a covered rear end and painted in regulation green with the police insignia on the side.
In no time at all we had driven through the trees along the dirt track and pulled up on the top edge of the beach.

The boy was still fishing and turned to look at us for a moment without much interest.
Raul and I trudged down through the sand to the water's edge, where the bright orange dinghy still lay like a beached whale.
'I suppose we had better take it back with us.'
He remarked absently.
'I'll give you a hand. Although I don't know how you're going to get it in the back of your car.'
Raul turned to the boy and called out.
'Oye muchacho, tienes un cuchillo?'
The boy searched in his bag with his free hand and took out an old cooking knife. Raul took it from him, walked back to where the dinghy rested on the sand and was about to plunge it into one of the sides.
At once the boy called out to us, dropping his rod on the sand.
'Caballeros! Puede quedarme con el barco?'
Raul straightened up, glancing at the boy.
From his appearance, the threadbare tee shirt, the worn, faded denim shorts, his lack of footware, it was obvious that he was from a family of limited means, assuming he had a family.
'He was here when I landed Raul. He could have stolen it, but he didn't!'
The police chief turned to the boy again.
He was perhaps seven or maybe eight and was gazing from one to the other of us with a pleading look.
Raul smiled at the boy.
'Por supuesto! __Tomalo!'
The young lads face broke into a wide smile. His fishing forgotten for a moment he raced across at once and began to drag the orange inflatable further up the beach.
It was his lottery win for the day, perhaps for many days or even years to come.
'Gracias senors!'
He called out.
'He should be in school!'
Raul observed with obvious compassion.
'Schooling is free in Cuba.'
'If he was at school then he wouldn't be able to catch fish.'
I commented.
Raul sighed deeply and then turned to stare out at the sea.
'Did Mamen speak to you before__'
'No. She had been making coffee, it was her turn to take over the helm.'
'Before then?'
'Not much really. Small talk. __I asked her why she wasn't married.'

He nodded slowly.
Then he turned and began to trudge through the white sand, up towards where he had left the car.
'We must get back to Havana!'
He said quietly.

What was I going to say to Lucia?
The question tormented me on the drive back to the Capital, which was closer than I had imagined.
Raul and I hardly said a word, but I suppose that there wasn't much to be said. God only knows what was going on in the man's mind.
He dropped me outside the apartment and to my total surprise he stretched across the wheel and offered his hand.
'I'm sure you did what you could Harry.'
I took it at once, still with an acute sense of guilt.
'I'm so sorry Raul.'
I got out and slammed the door and he drove away at once.

I couldn't remember if I had taken a key with me when I had rushed out early the previous morning. Was that all it was, a mere day and a half ago? It seemed like a year.
If I had taken a key I certainly didn't have it now.
I rang the bell to our apartment and waited, then I rang again.
Shit, I would have to walk across to the Café, looking like a survivor of a ship-wreck, which of course was exactly the case.
I was about to press the bell a third time when I heard the rattle of doors opening almost directly above.
I looked up to see Lucia gazing down at me over the metal balustrade.
My emotions were so confused I was unable to speak.
'Harry!'
She shouted my name.
'Wait carino!'
She disappeared and a few moments later I could hear her wrestling with the lock.
Then the door opened and there she was.

She stared at me in undisguised horror.
'Harry! What happened? __Madre mia!'

Neither of us moved for a few seconds. Then she walked forward slowly and took my arm, drawing me gently into the cavernous hallway and closing the door.
'Raul called me.'
She murmured nervously.
'When?'
'Earlier. About an hour and a half I guess.'
'What did he say?'
'That he was on his way to meet you, __along the coast somewhere.'
'Anything else?'
'No.'
She was still gazing at me with clear concern.
Suddenly I felt more weary than I could ever recall.
'Let's get upstairs love.'
Lucia must have seen or sensed at least, because she held my arm, supporting me with both hands as we slowly ascended the steps to our apartment.

I dropped into an armchair in the living room feeling now totally exhausted.'
'Harry do you want something, a drink maybe?'
'No, er, __a beer would be nice.'
She hurried out and came back with an opened bottle and a glass, which she handed to me, half filling it with beer. Then she sank to her knees in front of me.
'What happened carino?'
'Did Raul say anything?'
'No! __Tell me Harry.'
I hesitated, fearfully.
'Lucia I don't know quite how to say this. Mamen has been killed!'
With a sharp intake of breath she covered her face with her hands so that all I could see were her eyes, which said everything.
I told the same lie I had told to Mamen's father, almost word for word, and she listened without interrupting.
When I had finished explaining I slumped back into the chair.
'I'm desperately tired Lucia! I've got to sleep, for an hour or two at least.'
'Yes Harry.'
She said quietly.
'Get those dirty clothes off and take a shower. I'll come with you.'
I stood in front of the bathroom mirror and saw at once why both Lucia and Raul had been shocked by my appearance.

The cut on my mouth was now surrounded by a huge bruise, my shirt, torn in places was covered with streaks of blood and my pants could never be worn again.
I undressed wearily and stumbled into the shower.
When I had finished cleaning myself I dried slowly and walked naked into the bedroom, collapsing at once into the bed.
I felt Lucia climbing under the sheet behind me. Then, in an instant I was asleep.

After a deep dreamless slumber I woke up suddenly, believing for a moment that I was in another world.
Lucia lay behind, me her arm around my waist.
'Harry?'
'Yeah.'
'Are you ok?'
'I'm not sure yet.'
'Can you tell me anything else Harry. __About Mamen I mean?'
'Sure, give me a minute or two while I try and figure out where I am.'
'Don' talk crazy Harry! You're here. __With me!'
'I know love, it's just__'
I groaned and swung my legs over the side of the bed, sitting for a moment, my head bowed forward as I recalled the last twelve hours or was it twelve days or twelve weeks. At that moment I had no clear idea.
I reached for a dressing gown that was draped over a chair. Then I stood up and pulled in on.
'Get me a drink honey.'
'Sure. Go and sit down I'll bring it to you.'
In the living room I almost fell onto the sofa and stared out of the window. Dark clouds were grouping close together and it looked as though it was going to rain.
Lucia came into the room after a few minutes. She also wore a dressing gown now and was carrying two small glasses.
'Some whisky Harry.'
'Just what I need love!'
I attempted a smile.
'How is your face, does it hurt much?'
'Not really.'
'So we have no boat now carino!'
'No. __We can replace the boat, but not your friend!'
'What did you talk about before__'

'Nothing really. We took turns at the wheel on the way to the island so there wasn't much opportunity to talk I suppose. And anyway I was still furious, both with you and with her!'

'I'm so sorry Harry!'

'Yes, well there it is. What's done is done.'

I sipped at the whiskey, which at that point was just exactly what I needed.

'So you dropped the guns at the island and hid them.'

'Yeah.'

'No problems?'

'No.'

'Then you started back. __But still not speaking with Mamen.'

'We took turns at sleeping for a few hours, then she came up on deck at about three thirty I suppose. We talked for a while__'

'What about?'

'I asked her why she hadn't married and she told me about her girlfriend.'

'Laura.'

'She didn't tell me her name. Said she didn't believe in marriage.'

'No. I'm surprised that she told you. __About Laura I mean it is still not, __how do you say?'

'Acceptable, is that what you mean?'

'In Cuba yes. __She cared about her very much!'

'Mmm. Well there it is. You will have to tell her, __the girl I mean.'

'Yes I will, yes I will have to tell her an' tha's not gonna be easy.'

I was silent and stared out of the window again.

'More rain coming!'

'Yeah. It's that time of the year Harry. __Hurricane weather.'

She paused.

'What happened after you both talked?'

I breathed out heavily.

'It was about four by then I suppose. I could just about see the beam from the lighthouse so I guess we were about thirty kilometers away, maybe more. Then Mamen went down to make us some coffee. I heard her coming out onto the rear deck about ten minutes later. That's when we were hit.'

'With no warning, nuthin'!'

'No. With no warning! Didn't even hear it coming. __Cut the boat in half and took Mamen with it.'

I took another sip at the whisky.

It was getting easier now to tell the lie. I was almost starting to believe it myself.

'Do you think it was an accident Harry?'

'No. __The more I think about it the more certain I am.

There were no lights on the ship, only port and starb'd navigation. It had to be deliberate!'

'It could have been an accident.'

'No, no chance!'

I paused again.

'Let me tell you the whole story Lucia. On our way to the island we were intercepted by the U.S. coastguard. They came alongside about halfway through the journey. Didn't say much__'

'You mean they *stopped* you! They came aboard!'

I smiled at her grimly.

'Lucia if they had come aboard I wouldn't be talking to you now. __Would I!'

'No I s'pose not.'

'There's no 'suppose' about it! __No, in fact I spoke to them on the radio-phone. Told them that we were fishing and they seemed to believe it, at least I thought so at the time. __Now I'm not so sure!

So maybe it was they who rammed us, I really don't know Lucia.'

She was deep in thought for some time.

Then she took both of our glasses and walked back to the kitchen.

'I need another of these Harry. I guess you do as well.'

When she came back she handed the glass to me and sat half turned towards me on the sofa.

'We didn' hear from the guys who were meant to pick up the weapons.'

I shrugged.

'Maybe they haven't arrived yet.'

'No, maybe.'

She looked down at the glass that she was cradling in her hands.

'I can't believe that Mamen is dead.'

'No, it's not easy love.'

'Raul must be__broken!'

'Yes I'm sure he is. He didn't show any emotion, not to me anyway, but he must be, well, like you say. __It's a terrible thing, maybe it hasn't hit him yet Lucia. __Does he have other family?'

'A daughter, three years younger.'

'And his wife of course.'

'Yes.'

'Christ, I don't envy him. Having to break the news to them both. You should go and see him Lucia, him and his family.'

'I shall.'

She was silent again.

'Do you see now Lucia! What might have happened if you'd gone with her!'

'Don't Harry, please!'
'It has to be said, like it or not! __Raul tried to convince Mari-Carmen not to go and this is the result!'
'Harry__'
'*No* Lucia! This is what happens when you get mixed up in politics! __I want you to promise me right now that you will never get involved in anything like this ever again!'
'Harry you don' understand__'
'What did I say to you about using that *bloody* word!'
I could feel genuine anger rising again.
'I don't want to know about *any* of this! __Mamen is dead and it could quite easily have been you as well! So don't tell me I don't understand Lucia!'
She said nothing and was staring down at her glass again.
In fact neither of us said anything for what seemed like an age.

'Get your coat!'
'What?'
'We're going for a walk. I've got to get out of here!'
'It's raining Harry!'
'I don't care, we'll take an umbrella. I need something to eat.'
'But I'm not dressed!'
'So get dressed! How long does *that* take?'
She looked at me uncertainly. I had never spoken to her like that before and judging by her expression I might well have been a completely different person.
'Come on let's go!'
It was a command now.
I got up and walked back into the bedroom.
Tossing the dressing gown onto the chair I took fresh clothes from a drawer.
Lucia had followed me silently. Disgarding the dressing gown she began to pull on a pair of jeans, giving me another doubtful look.
The sight of her lovely naked breasts made my heart jump painfully and in that instant I wanted to wrap my arms around her, but now was not a good time.
Still without a word, she took a tee shirt from the wardrobe and pulled it over her head.
'We're going to need a waterproof coat, so you can find them as well while you're there!'
I remarked in the same sharp, off-hand manner.
Without replying she began to rummage again in the wardrobe.

On a dresser there was some note paper and a pen.
I walked across and scribbled a brief message.
When she turned, her face had the same peeved expression and she avoided my eyes as she handed me a weather-proof jacket.
At the same time I handed her the note.
She looked at it and then raised her head at once to stare at me in acute surprise. She seemed about to speak, but I already had my forefinger pressed against my lips.
I had written just a few words.
"Don't say anything! Just come with me!"

'Right come on lets go! I want to get something to eat.'
I spoke to her again using the same blunt tone.
Walking quickly into the hallway I grabbed an umbrella and opened the door to the apartment, ushering her through before following her and slamming it shut.

'Harry what's going on?'
She whispered to me when we were on the street.
'I'll tell you later!'
'Are we not going to the Café?'
She was holding tightly onto my arm as we passed our bar on the opposite side of the road.
'We'll stop somewhere else. Just keep walking.'

Chap. 13

The rain was sweeping in on a blustery wind when we reached the old sea wall and the waves were growing in strength, bursting against the breakwater and sending dense spray cascading across the road that ran the length of the broad promenade towards the fortress at the harbour entrance. Hunched together with the umbrella angled towards the sea, we walked at a brisk pace until we reached the ancient fortification where we took refuge from the constant downpour.
We sat close together on a bench seat, sheltered from the wind and rain. Lucia still clinging to my arm, looked up at me expectantly.
'Harry tell me what's happening, your note jus' now___'
'We may well be overheard in the apartment!'
'Overheard?'
Her brow was creased and she stared at me with a confused expression.'

'Maybe! __Listening devices are very easy to install.'
'*What* Harry! Wha' d'you mean, listenin' devices?'

I hesitated as I rehearsed in my head what I was going to say to her, recalling every word that the man on the motor launch had said to me, whoever or whatever he was. CIA, NSA? __How would I know, never having come into contact with any such murky organizations.
At that moment I felt just as fearful as Lucia appeared to be.
I reasoned that I could trust no one except her.
It seemed logical enough to me, and so I began.'

'Sweetheart listen to me carefully. Everything, well almost everything I told you in the last hour or two is a lie!
Also what I said to Raul!'
Her expression was now one of total shock.
'Yes, Mamen is dead! That's the only thing that is true.'
She seemed about to speak.
'No, don't say anything honey, just listen!'

For the next ten minutes I related everything that had happened on the journey back from the remote island near the western tip of Cuba.
She barely spoke and when I had finished she drew even closer, holding on to me with both hands.
'Harry, I can't believe this!'
'Neither can I! __Do you know what 'Catch 22' is honey?'
I remarked quietly.
'No.'
I barely heard her whispered response.
'It doesn't matter.'
I heaved a deep sigh and put my arm around her shoulder, holding her close.
'What are we going to do Harry?'
She whispered again.
'The short answer to that love, is that I have absolutely no idea!'

LUCIA P.201___

We sat in silence listening to the wind and behind us the waves crashing against the sea wall.

An occasional taxi drifted by searching for a fare, which in the current weather conditions seemed a fruitless quest as the area around the old fortress, normally busy with tourists, was deserted.

'What he has tol' you to do is like er, __treason! Is that the right word Harry?'

'Something like that! If I was Cuban it would be.'

'But if they catch you! __Madre mia!'

'Yeah! Madre mia is right.'

'They will shoot you carino!'

'I'm sure they will.'

'But I's no' your fault!'

'I doubt if the authorities will see it like that.'

'No I guess not.'

She rested her head against my shoulder and gripped tightly on to my hand.

'I's all my fault!'

She whispered suddenly.

'No it wasn't really love. __What I should have done is drag you off the bloody boat instead of taking your place. That would have been the sensible thing. Then Mamen would still be alive!'

I turned and smiled down at her, at her lovely face framed by the hood of her weatherproof jacket.

'We'll sort it out somehow Lucia.'

Her liquid brown eyes looked directly into mine.

'I love you Harry!'

'And I love you sweetheart. Don't worry I'll think of something.'

We sat there for perhaps half an hour, huddled together and barely speaking.

It was oddly peaceful, just the two of us sitting in silence and for a while I tried at least to push the current dilemma to the back of my mind, but it was of course impossible.

'Harry, maybe you should go to Raul an' tell him about this whole thing!'

'Mm, the problem with that is I don't know who to trust. Even Raul!'

'He is a good man Harry.'

'Maybe he is, but I remember something he said to me quite recently. Which was that he didn't support the current thinking of the Cuban administration with regard to supplying arms to rebels in Central America.'

'Did he say this to you!'

'Yes he did. I don't believe that he would ever betray his country, but that was his personal view.'

'Harry he would never say anything, to betray you I mean. I am sure of this!'
'And I'm sure you're right. But this is literally a life or death situation here! I can't trust anyone, __except you of course.'
We both fell silent again.
'So now you gotta be a spy for them!'
'Looks that way.'
'But how you gonna do that Harry?'
'That's what I told the guy on the boat. He said I would think of something. That my life__ and more importantly your life depended on it.'
'I'm not afraid of those bastards Harry. They ruined my country and now they're tryin' to do it again!'
'Yes I guess they are.'

The rain had eased slightly although the wind was gaining in strength and the sound of the waves on the other side of the fortress was increasing. It was comforting somehow, the temporary isolation, clinging together under the sheltered niche in the castle wall. It would be short lived of course because soon we would have to return to the apartment and to reality, to grim reality.
I still had no idea how I was going to achieve what was demanded and for a moment I felt acute fear creeping through the whole of my body.
Perhaps Lucia sensed yet again what was going through my mind because she nudged me and when I turned to her she presented me with her wonderful smile.
'Don' worry about this carino, we'll figure somethin' out between us, so don' worry!'
Looking at her my heart lifted, if only for a moment.

We hurried across the broad wind-swept area around the fortress during a brief respite before the rain started up again and were about to cross the perimeter road and make a run for it back into town. Luckily a taxi appeared and we both waved at it frantically.
The driver dropped us off outside the café in the Paseo de Marti and we climbed out of the cab into a renewed downpour.
There were only a few customers inside, mostly locals.
Discouraged by the weather, the tourists had no doubt retreated to their hotel rooms to write their postcards and make their overseas phone calls back home.
We greeted the man who was serving behind the bar and took a table at the far end, the dining area, currently deserted, as it was the wrong time of day for eating.

It was almost six o'clock now and I was seriously hungry, not having eaten anything since the previous evening.
When the waitress came up to us I smiled up at her.
'Hello Consuelo.'
'Hola Harry.'
She replied, returning the smile.
'Whatever is best on the menu today I'll have it!'
She turned to Lucia who responded at once
'Tendre la misma Consuelo.'
We had taken off our wet coats and tossed them on the bench seat on the opposite side of the table.
For a while we were both silent, both preoccupied, probably with the same thoughts.
'Poor Mamen!'
Lucia remarked in an isolated moment.
'It would have been more human at leas' if they jus' shot her. Not leave her like that in the sea, an' in the dark. It mus' have been so terrible for her.'
'Yeah! They were trying to make a point. That's what the arsehole who spoke to me said anyway.
They certainly made the point all right! _ The horrible bastards!'
'So now Harry you don' wanna talk to Raul, is that right.'
'Not until I've at least thought about this properly.'
The waitress brought us a drink at that point. A few words of gossip were exchanged between her and Lucia and then she left us again.
'What the hell am I supposed to spy on Lucia? I don't know a damn thing about what's going on in this country.'
'It will be the arms shipments carino. Tha's what they want to know abou'!'
'Oh that makes it easy then. I'll give Fidel a call tomorrow and meet up with him. I'm sure he'll want to tell me the whole story!'
Lucia was thoughtful for a few seconds.
'You know tha's not a bad idea Harry when you think about it.'
'Of course it isn't! I'm full of good ideas.'
'No you don' understan' me Harry!'
'There's that word again!'
I remarked in a serious tone, softened at once with a broad grin.
'No no carino, I mean I's really not a bad idea!'
'I don't follow?'
She sipped at her Barcardi drink, white rum and pineapple, a favourite now of both of us.

'Wha'd I mean is this! __Go to Raul, tell him the whole story. The truth I mean abou' wha' happen' to Mamen!'
'Are you serious! If I go down to police headquarters and tell him that, you'll probably never see me again!'
'Harry don' be loco, *listen* to me! You know Raul, 'e's a good man. Tell him everythin'! About this CIA guy or whatever, Level with him, isn' that what the gringos say! Whad 'ave to got to lose hombre?'
'Everything,__meaning you!'
'Tha' was nice carino, but tha's not gonna happen.'
'You can't be sure of that Lucia.'
'We can' be sure about anythin' in this life, but sometimes you jus' have to take a chance. Mamen used to talk about her dad a lot.
I never met him too often, but I jus' got this feelin' about him, tha's all I can tell you!'
I pondered for a while on what she had said.
Maybe she was right, there was no way of knowing.
One thing seemed probable I suppose. I could not be banged up in a Cuban jail for telling the truth about something that wasn't my fault to begin with. That was my hope at least!
I sighed deeply.
'Listen Lucia! If Raul tells me quite openly that he doesn't support Cuban involvement in Central America, what does that tell you?
Perhaps it means that he might try to prevent any arms supply.'
She stared at me incredulously.
'Harry do you *really* believe that?'
I was forced to look away.
'No. No I don't.'
'Now you' talkin' sense!__Harry, a lot of people who support the gov'ment don' think we should get involved in the fuckin' mess in those countries.
I's gonna bring nuthin but trouble, an' we got plen'y of that ya!__Already I mean!'
'I know what you mean sweetheart.'
Again I lapsed into my own thoughts.
Even if I confided in Raul what could he do?
I couldn't see how he could possibly help in the desperate situation in which I was now apparently trapped. Even though, as he had confided, he was against suppling arms to these fractured nations, even if he knew when and where weapons and God knows what else were to be smuggled, there was no way that he would tell me!
It was absurd to expect that he would, the man was a Cuban national for Chist's sake, a patriot!

No, I could think of no reason on earth to suppose that he would pass on such information.

'Anyway Lucia, I can't see the point in going to Raul. He can't do anything__'

'Harry you don' know 'till you ask him! Go to him carino, tell him everything that happened las' night, maybe he will come up with somethin'. __What else can we do?'

I shook my head, in desperation more than anything else.

'Can't we talk to Mamen's__er, friend first. Maybe__'

'Maybe what Harry!'

Again I had no answer.

I picked up my glass and took a long sip.

'Ok Lucia, you win. I can't see what good it will do, but I'll go and see Raul in the morning.'

Her face brightened at once.

'Thanks Harry, we have to start somewhere.'

'Yeah, I suppose you're right. __We'll see what happens tomorrow.'

I barely slept that night. The occasional rumble of thunder over the distant mountains felt like a portent of some kind.

I stirred constantly in bed as I tried to think of some way to extricate us from what seemed an untenable situation and from which there was no apparent escape.

My sole concern was for Lucia, and only for her.

The promise that the man had made to me seemed somehow demonic. To be willing to take the life of someone who was quite innocent and for no other reason than to gain some obscure political end was to me incomprehensible.

Once again I felt as though I didn't want to exist on the same planet with such people. 'Human being' seemed the wrong expression to use in the context!

But of course that's exactly what he was, a human being.

The very thought only increased my already acute depression and once again I turned over beneath the sheets.

'Harry can you not be still carino!'

Lucia complained sleepily.

'I can' get no res' with you tonight!'

'Sorry love, I'll go and sleep on the sofa.' I whispered.

I started to get out of bed, but she put her arm around me at once, holding me back.

'No Harry, lay with me.'
She kissed my shoulder.
'I's not the same now, sleepin' on my own. Try to get some res' honey, don' worry abou' things.'
I lay still now, for no other reason than not to disturb her.
Eventually, in the early hours, I finally fell asleep.

Once again I found myself in the central office of the 'Policia de Habana', ascending quietly in the 'Otis' elevator, one of the very few previous worthwhile imports from America, apart from the cars I suppose.
Raul was waiting as before, as soon as the doors slid open.
I stepped out and took his hand.
'Raul I'm so sorry for, __well for Mamen.'
'Let's go into the office Harry.'
I followed him and entered the now familiar room, which had a panoramic view across downtown Havana and beyond that the Caribbean.
'Siddown Harry.'
He said quietly as he closed the door and took his own seat behind his cluttered desk.
'Raul, er, Lucia has asked me of course to convey her condolences and her __enormous sadness.'
'Thank you amigo.'
'When will the er, __'
'Funeral. __No' much of a funeral Harry. Mamen will be the only one not present. But we must celebrate her memory at least.'
'Yes of course.'
I muttered awkwardly.
'So there will be some words in the church. I'm no' religious, but my wife is, so __if you can come, both of you.'
'Of course we'll be there.'
He stared out through the window at the expanse of sea beyond the breakwater.
'Lucia said you have a younger daughter.'
I made the comment for no other reason than to keep up a dialogue of some kind.
'Juanita! Yes. __It's not good in my house at the moment. You know Harry, if you hadn't come down to the port a couple of nights ago__'
'If you hadn't warned me you mean! __Yes, I hardly dare to think about it.'

He took a packet of cigarettes from a drawer.
'Of course we sent a boat out to search the area yesterday, but__'
He shrugged his broad shoulders.
'Raul I couldn't even tell you where it was exactly.'
'I know that! But we had to make an effort of some kind.'
He paused while he lit a cigarette.
'Raul__'
'The thing is Harry it could only be the U.S. coastguard from what you told me, but to prove it is near impossible!
A guy from the government said that if we knew for sure, then we could complain to the U.N. I don' know, but maybe__'
I interrupted quickly.
'Raul I have something to tell you, and this not going to be easy.'
I could feel already the creeping fingers of fear at the back of my neck, but I had no other choice than to continue.

I told him everything that had happened two nights before, leaving out nothing.
When I finished there was complete silence in the large office.
I felt acutely nervous not to say fearful, and I was quite sure that he was aware of that.
'Do you want some coffee Harry, or maybe something stronger?'
'Erm, yeah. Coffee would be good right now. __Thanks Raul.'
"For not taking out your gun and shooting me in head", was my immediate thought.
He picked up the phone and spoke into it briefly.
'Why didn't you tell me this right from the start amigo?'
'Because I needed time to think, because I didn't know who to trust! If I say anything about this to anyone they are going to kill Lucia! That's what he said, the bastard on the boat! __He made it very clear, and I have every reason to believe him.'
He nodded slowly.
'I think I would have done the same as you Harry.'
'Lucia means everything to me Raul!'
'I'm sure of that.'
Again he was thoughtful.
'You are in a clef' stick my friend. A rock an' a hard place, isn' that what they say, these Yankees?'
I gave him a rueful look.
'That's precisely what they say!'
He sighed.
'Madre mia! __What do we do about these fuckin' people!'

I could think of no useful response so I kept quiet.
The same woman as before arrived with a tray of coffee.
She set the tray down on his desk in silence and left.

'Is there anythin' else you can tell me about these men Harry. Somethin' you forgot maybe.'
'No. __It's not something you forget about easily.'
'I guess not, but think anyway.'
'Other than the number he gave me to contact him!'
'Yeah so you said, an' which number was that?'
'I should have explained that further. He said it would be easy to remember as it was the date when I was born!'
'Your *birthdate!*''
'That's right. Fourteenth of December, nineteen sixty three! Impossible to forget, which is obviously why they chose it!
How the hell he knew that is a mystery!'
'Vale! The CIA know everythin'! __But what about a regional code? Some states in America have half a dozen or more!'
'Vermont, only one code! __Again all of it easy to remember and I suppose easy enough for them to manufacture a contact number.'
'Yeah I guess so Harry. __Very clever.'
He scribbled the number in a notebook.
'I do hope you're not going to give him a call!'
'No, of course not'
He smiled at last, albeit grimly.
'So what now Raul? I have a limited time span to, as he put it, come up with something. Then, __well he made it quite plain!'
'You haven't contacted him yet?'
'No.'
'Maybe you should.'
I lifted a hand in response.
'Why? I don't have anything to tell him.'
'You can say that you are doing what you can to find some information, looking for possible contacts. And you can ask him for some time. Weeks maybe, or a couple of months.'
'Yes I suppose so. __Yes, that's probably not a bad idea.'
'Better you contact him I think. Meanwhile Harry I will give this some though. I will also talk to some people who know about these things.'
'For God sake don't let the cat out of the bag Raul, I mean__'
'I know what you mean Harry, don't worry! __Have you spoken to anyone about this, apart from Lucia?'
'No.'

'Good. If you do speak to anyone, then stick to the original story that you tol' me, it makes sense! But only if you think you have to. It would be best of course if you say nothing.'
I nodded in agreement.
'Raul, I can't be sure of course, but maybe our apartment is bugged.'
He nodded thoughtfully.
'We'll check it out Harry.'
And after a brief silence.
'There is somethin' else that you should know amigo!'
I glanced up at him again.
'The plane, the sea-plane tha' was meant to pick up the weapons from the cayo this morning! It was shot to pieces before it could take off again.'
I was speechless for a moment.
'Jesus Christ Raul! __How?'
'An F15 would be my guess.'
'Bloody hell, the poor buggers.'
'Yes my friend, I doubt if they knew what hit them, but there it is. These are nasty people we are talkin' about!'

I finished my coffee quickly and stood up.
'I'll get going now. Once again Raul, both Lucia and I are deeply sorry for what's happened, it's the worst possible tragedy!'
'I know that. __In a way I feel responsible for her death. I should have done what you did, forbade her to go. What I mean is physically stopped her! But I didn't and now I must live with that.'

There was no answer I could give, no words of comfort, because he was right. It was a terrible load that he would have to carry.
Any platitudes I might have offered would have been empty and meaningless and so I said nothing.
Raul had also got to his feet.
'Let me know about the er, funeral. __I mean the__at the church.'
'Sure Harry.'
I offered my hand again which he took with a firm grip.
'I'll come down with you.'
He said.
'There's no need Raul.'
'There is a need my friend. We don't know who is working for the Americans. You might have been followed here, which will make them suspicious. So I will come down with you.
Put on a show for them.'

He grinned cheerfully, perhaps relieving for a moment the profound grief, which he must have felt, no matter how well he concealed it.

On the street outside the 'Policia' we engaged in some insignificant small talk for a few moments. Then we shook hands again and to my surprise he embraced me briefly and I responded at once.
'We'll make it look good for them amigo!'
He whispered.
We separated and I smiled at him.
'Absolutely Raul! Let us know when__'
'I'll call you.'
Then he turned and walked back inside the building.

Maybe it was just an act that he had put on, but somehow I felt that it was rather more than that.
As Lucia had said, he was a good man.
At some point in life you have to trust someone, and I felt inside somehow that I could trust Raul.

'You saw him Harry?'
'I did! And I told him the whole story.'
'An' he was ok about it?'
'Yes. I wasn't sure what his reaction would be, but yes he was ok. There is to be a service of some kind in church in Mamen's memory, we will have to go to that.'
'Sure. Do you know when?'
'No, he's going to call us.'
'Ok.'
She released a long sigh, relief of some kind, or so it seemed.

Lucia had made some lunch for us both and after we had finished eating we left the apartment and took a stroll.
We sat for a while on one of the ornate carved stone benches, located on each side of the paseo.
On the paved area between the two rows of trees, a group of young people were dancing with considerable expertise to the recorded sound of salsa music, the infectious, rhythms drifting across to where we were sitting.
'I wish I could dance like that!'
I muttered, watching their precise gyrations with envy.
'I'll teach you carino!'

Lucia said putting her arm around my shoulder.
'Impossible. I've got two left feet. Anyway with this current business hanging over us I can't think about anything else.'
'Harry don't worry. We'll figure it all out somehow.'
'I hope you're right sweetheart.'
'Sure I am, so cheer yourself up muchacho!'

Nothing seemed to bother Lucia for very long. She was intelligent and knew the considerable risks we were both facing, but somehow she seemed to rise above it.

'Are you sure the apartment is bugged Harry?'
'Well we have to assume that it is. We certainly can't search the place because then they will know of course.'
'Tha' means we can't make love then Harry, not with these nasty people listenin' in!'
'Well we can, we just have to be quiet about it.'
She leaned over and kissed my ear.
'Tha's impossible carino!'
She whispered.
I smiled ruefully.
'Well it certainly won't be easy, that's for sure!'

I sighed deeply as depression closed in on me again.
'It's turned into a nightmare love, this whole bloody thing!'
'Come on Harry, we will get through this somehow.'
The expression on her face lifted me for a moment. Her undying optimism about everything was as always, inspiring.
I smiled at her.
'What would I do without you?'
'I don' know honey. Fine' you'self a nice English girl maybe! Live a nice quiet life!'
She gave me a wicked grin.
'There's no woman to compare you with Lucia! Not in England, not anywhere. __And I'll put up with the nightmares! Who needs a quiet life anyway!'
She squeezed my arm and her lovely brown eyes stared into mine.
'You always say nice things to me Harry.'
'That's because I love you.'
She rested her head on my shoulder.
'How are you feeling sweetheart? I mean with the new baby.'

'No differen'. A bit sick in the morning tha's all, nothing much, it's early yet Harry. __Jus' wait a coupla' months when my belly is fat an' I'm moanin' at you all the time. You won' fancy me too much then I bet!'
'That could never happen, I mean never!'
'Ok we'll see. In six months time I'll remine' you abou' this!'

We were silent for a while, watching the fluid, complex movements of the pairs of dancers, which they practiced with such apparent ease.

'Are you going to see Mamen's friend?'
'Tonight. __She knows all about it now, Mamen's mother tol' her everythin' that happen'.'
'Are you going on your own?'
'Come with me Harry, I's gonna be difficult! Anyway you were the las' person to see her, so she will wanna talk to you.'
'Yes I suppose so.'
I must have looked downcast again because she grasped my hand.
'I's better if you are with me Harry. __Anyway, come on, let's walk for a while.'
We stood and continued strolling slowly along the broad marble paved walk-way at the centre of the paseo, that was almost completely shaded by the trees. There had been some rain earlier in the morning, but now the sun was out in force again with just a few white clouds wandering slowly across a brilliantly blue sky.
'What else did he say to you, __Raul?'
'Not much really. Although he did say that I should call the man, __the CIA guy or whatever the bloody hell he's supposed to be. __Fucking monster, that's what he really is! __With his nice house and his nice family!'
Sensing my anger she squeezed my arm.
'Don' let it get to you Harry, tha's jus' what they want. To weaken you!'
'I get so furious when I think about what he has said and what he has already done. I swear I could murder the bastard!'
'But you mus' not Harry! Get angry I mean. It stops you thinkin' clearly.'
I breathed out heavily.
'I suppose you're right, but it's not easy. You weren't there love!'
'Harry never mind that! You need to think straight, to__foco? I don' know the right word.'
I nodded.
'Focus! It's the same, more or less. Yeah you're right, focus on ways of killing the bastard!'
'Harry!'

She glanced at me reproachfully.
'Ok then, enough of him!'
'But you didn' say why carino.'
'Why what?'
'Why you should call him!'
'Oh just to, I don't know, bargain for time Raul suggested. At least until Raul, or one of us can come up with something.'
'But I already come up with somethin'!'
'You did!'
'Sure!'
She gave me a radiating smile.
'Jus' 'cos I gotta nice ass doesn't mean I'm dumb Harry!'
'I can't see the distinction to be honest. Anyway you're far from being dumb sweetheart.__So what's the plan?'
'Jus' to tell them where to find the guns an' stuff like that.'
I looked at her skeptically.
'Oh I *see!*__Well I certainly missed that one didn't I! But I must agree that you do have a beautiful bottom!'
'Harry I'm bein' serious!'
'So am I!'
I grinned at her.
'You don' see it carino!'
'Well not at the moment that's true, but perhaps when we get back to the apartment__'
She gave me a playful slap.
'Behave you'self Harry, an' listen!
I'm sayin' that we tell them where they can locate some weapons. Like maybe in the same place around Buenavista, or some other similar place.'
'Yes that's what I thought you meant.__So is that your brilliant idea?'
'No you still don' get it Harry!'
She took my hand and drew me towards another of the stone benches shaded beneath a Jacaranda tree where she sat staring up at me.
'Siddown Harry an' lemme tell you!'
She commanded.
'Go on then love, tell me everything about this plan of your's.'
'Ok look, the gringos want to find guns, yes! Well we got plen'y of guns Carino.'
'We? I presume you mean the government. Anyway how would you know that?'
'Because Mamen tol' me once, an' the person who tol' her was her friend Laura Torres. She works for the governmen' as well.

The problem is not the gun's, I's getting them to the rebels in Nicaragua or some place else.
That's the reason you got caught Harry.'
'No, I, __I mean we, got caught because some bastard told the CIA about us. A Cuban probably.'
'Tha's true. They will fine' who it is at some time tha's for sure.'
'No doubt they will. But that doesn't help us much now, does it.'
'No it doesn', but listen to the plan first. If we can stash some arms somewhere, an' then let the yanks know where they can fine' them, then that lets you off the hook! __Isn' that right!'

Lucia had a point, but there was a rather obvious drawback.
'Lucia, why would the Cuban authorities allow the Americans to just wander onto Cuban territory and snatch a pile of weapons just to save my neck? __And yours as well, which is of far more concern to me! Also, guns are expensive.'
'Well in the firs' place carino, they owe us somethin' for riskin' our necks with all the previous trips we made for them! __An' there was quite a few! Also I believe that Raul will support us in this! He lost his daughter for the cause. A cause which he don' support anyway! __An' there is another thing Harry I jus' thought about.
If the Yankees are chasin' after boxes of guns in one place, they might not be lookin' in another!'

Now Lucia really did have a point.
'Yes I see what you mean. That's a not a bad idea love I have to admit.'
She gave me huge cheerful smile.
'I tol' you I wasn' dumb Carino!'
'Well we've been over that! __So now we have to think about this very carefully in case there's a pitfall of some kind.'
'What's a 'pitfall'?'
'A pit is a hole, and one that we don't want to fall into.
But I have to admit it seems like a bloody good plan on the face of it, __yes, the more I think about it.'

I stared across the paseo, barely noticing the single line of slow moving traffic as I considered what she had said.
'Ok. I'm going to meet up with Raul again tomorrow and see what he thinks. But we musn't forget that I've got to uncover some undercover agents that this arsehole seems to think are threatening American interests! That just might be a little more tricky.'
'One thing at a time carino!'

'Yes maybe. Meanwhile perhaps you can apply your considerable intellect to that particular problem.'
'Think about it you mean?'
'That's exactly what I mean love!'

The more I thought about Lucia's plan the better it got!
Whether we could convince the bureaucrats in the Cuban administration was another matter however. But that would be Raul's job, providing I could convince him of course.

We continued our stroll along the paseo and then turned and walked back again, during which time I turned Lucia's inspired idea over and over in my mind as I attempted to find some fault with the plan. In spite of my efforts I could find none!
Lucia hardly spoke as we walked, perhaps she understood my preoccupation and decided to leave me to it.
Eventually we arrived at our nice little café.
It was still busy with the usual midday diners and we took a seat outside at one of the half dozen tables beneath the arched walkway.

I was still deep in thought when the manager, Pasqual appeared from inside, greeting as both with a subdued smile.
'Hi Harry, __Lucia. How goes it?'
He was slowly acquiring the verbal mannerisms of the predominantly American customers, which was slightly irritating, but I suppose understandable in the circumstances.
'No bien Pasqual!'
Lucia responded at once, with a sad expression.
She turned to me.
'What do you want carino?'
'Oh, just a drink love! __Whatever you're having.'
She spoke to him in rapid Spanish.
'What happened to the boat Harry?'
Pasqual remarked, turning to me.
'I heard you had an accident of some kind!'
I shook my head.
'Don't ask Pasqual, it was a total disaster! I was lucky to get back in one piece.'
'So the boat was lost, __I heard this anyway.'
'At the bottom of the sea, about twenty, maybe thirty kilometers along the coast.'
He looked shocked.

'Madre mia! How did you get back?'
'Life raft!'
'But Mamen didn't make it! Tha's what I also heard.'
'No she didn't, which is a bloody tragedy.'
He nodded sadly.
'She was a good person. I spoke with her quite often when she came into the café. It's a terrible thing Harry, I'm really so sorry.'
He shook his head as he murmured his condolence.
'How did it happen?'
'A boat ploughed into us in the night.'
I gave a minimal shrug, maintaining an expression of deep concern, which wasn't entirely contrived.
'How it could possibly have happened I have no idea. Our navigation lights were clear enough, so__'
Again I lifted my shoulders briefly, picking up a menu in an effort to end the conversation, but he continued.
'But at night Harry, I mean__'
He was persistent and I could have told him that I didn't want to discuss it, but not wanting to arouse any kind of doubt, rumours or speculation I decided that it was better to give the man an explanation of some kind.
'Yeah. The thing is Lucia wasn't feeling too well, so Mamen agreed to come with me on the boat. One of the main pumps wasn't working properly. The repairers in Regla couldn't do it for a couple of weeks, so I took it further down the coast to get it changed.'
I attempted a grin.
'You know what it's like in this town Pasqual! Trying to get anything done.'
'I sure do Harry.'
'The thing is, it took longer than we thought to do the work, so we decided to make a nighttime run of it, just to get back.
I didn't want to leave Lucia on her own.'
He turned to her with some concern.
'You ok now guapa?'
'Sure Pasqual!'
She presented a brilliant smile.
'I wasn' feelin' to good cos', well, __point is we jus' discover' that I'm pregnant!'
The man's face lit up at once.
'Tha's fantastic Lucia! Congratulations, __to both of you. Felicidades, tha's wonderful news!'
'Yes we are both very happy, except if it wasn't for Mamen.'
'Sure, of course. __Er, I'll get your drinks.'

He disappeared into the café and I gave Lucia a quick glance.
'Did that sound, __well, plausible?'
I said quietly.
'Sure, good thinkin' Harry! We need to be careful what we say. People roun' here are a bit, __como se dice?'
'Nosey!'
'Yeah, nosey.'

Pasqual returned a few minutes later with two glasses.
'There you go!'
He set a glass in front of each of us.
'How is your wife Pasqual?'
I asked at once, in an effort to deter any further questions.
'She's ok amigo. Not long now!'
'No I guess not! What are you hoping for?'
'I girl I guess! But it doesn' matter. If the child is healthy that's the only importan' thing!'
'Of course it is. Please give our best wishes to your wife.'
'I will Harry, an' thanks.'
He left us then, to my relief.
Other customers had taken a table outside further away from us and he went to attend to them.
'He's ok.'
I observed.
'Bit of a gossip, but he's good hearted.'
'Yeah sure, I guess so.'
Lucia responded thoughtfully.
I glanced at her at once, more or less reading her thoughts.
'What is *that* supposed to mean?'
'Nuthin' Harry.'
She presented a wide-eyed smile, almost daring a response of some kind. I knew her well enough now to know that there was something on her mind.
'Come on!'
Now it was my turn to provoke a response.
'No nuthin' Harry, really!'
'Mmm, there's something going on in that head of your's!'
'No really carino. __Drink your drink!'
There was no point in pursuing it. I knew that if she wanted to, she would say something eventually.

'Lets get back Harry.'
'You ok love?'

'Sure, jus' a bit tired tha's all. I didn't sleep to well again las' night.'
'That was my fault. __Sorry sweetheart.'
'No not jus' that Harry. An' also I hardly slept at all when you were on the boat the night before. __I shouldn' have put you through that.'
'History now love! __Anyway it was my idea, and in spite of everything that happened I'm deeply relieved that I went instead of you! The alternative is unthinkable now!'

It was mid afternoon when we walked across to the apartment.
As soon as we had closed the door behind us, we both went directly to the bedroom. Removing just our shoes we virtually fell onto the bed.

This time I slept deeply and without dreaming for almost three hours.
When I woke up quite suddenly, Lucia was still out to the world.
I slid carefully out of bed so as not to wake her and crept out of the room into the kitchen where I made some coffee.
Then I sat at the kitchen table and thought again about what Lucia had said earlier.
It still seemed like a bloody good idea and as much as I tried I could find no fault with it!
The problem of course was firstly convincing Raul and then Raul convincing whoever it was in the government who would need to approve what was in fact, an unusual plan. Unusual to say the least!
My initial confidence lapsed slightly as I continued to think about it.

I made the decision and reached for the phone to call Raul.
On the very point of dialing the number I suddenly realized and carefully replaced the receiver. Maybe the place *was* bugged.
I stood up and walked across the living room to the single large window that looked out onto the Paseo.
The sun was low in the sky now with long dark clouds hovering above it. More rain was certainly on its way.
Switching on the TV, I turned the volume down so as not to wake Lucia. Then I slumped onto the sofa to watch the local news for no other reason than to try and improve my Spanish.
There was the usual government line about the increasing U.S. sanctions on Cuba with some shots of Castro surrounded by cheering admirers, accompanied by the usual revolutionary propaganda and with renewed threats to refer yet again to the United Nations.
For a moment I felt a brief surge of sympathy for the man, still unbowed by the vast strength of the Americans and their obvious determination to isolate the beleaguered island.

Then there was a local piece of news that brought me bolt upright from where I had been relaxing.
The body of a girl had been found on the long curved breakwater north of Havana. She was named as Laura Torres!

I stared at the screen in disbelief, even after the televised images had turned to the result of a local baseball game.
Then my head fell forward and I felt the most profound grief for a young woman who I had never even met. A grief that strangely was even greater than I had felt for Mamen. The pointless waste of another young life.
Overcome with a sudden rage I grabbed at the phone again, pressing the code and then the numerals of my date of birth.
Almost at one it was answered. It was a womans voice, a recording.
"Your call will be returned shortly."
That was it. The line went dead, replaced by the dialing tone.
I slammed the receiver back on the cradle, but within less than a minute it started to ring and I grabbed for it again.

I recognized the voice instantly, the man on the motor launch.
'Glad you called Harry__'
That was as far as he got before I released my pent-up anger in a single burst.
'Why the *fuck* did you have to kill *her!* You ruthless bastard!'
'Now hold on! We went over this! We could have killed both of you, __and your wife. This was clearly explained to you Harry!'
'I don't mean Mamen, you *know* who I mean!'
'You better calm down Harry before I forget about this deal we have! __Now, will you tell me what the fuck you are talking about!'
'Her friend, Mamen's friend! She was found washed up near the sea wall in Havana! Who else could have done it!'
In my blind anger I realized that I had partially pissed in my trousers and saliva was leaking from my mouth.
I felt instantly disgraced and humiliated at what was no more than a display of weakness and perhaps fear on my part.
'Don't tell me it wasn't you! You fucking__'
I had to force myself to be silent, to stem the pointless flow of words.
'Like I say Harry, you had better calm down. __I mean for your own good.'
His tone was calm and level, but then he was in his natural element where the arbitrary death of innocents was of little or no significance to him.
'So first of all lets get this straight! Who are we talking about here?'
I struggled to control my voice.

'Her girlfriend, her, partner. Mamen's partner. The girl you killed, remember.'
'I've no idea what you're talking about!'
'Don't '
I began, then I took a deep breath.
'Torres. That's her name, Laura Torres!'
'The name means nothing. If she's dead, whoever she is, we don't know anything about it.'
His tone had softened slightly, but only slightly.
I didn't quite know how to respond and remained silent.
'Burgess, this is nothing to do with us, this girl, Torres or whoever. We know nothing about this ok, so now can we talk about the real business here! For instance how long do we have to wait for you to get your act together. How long before you get some information for us?'
'Erm, it's not easy '
'We never said it was.'
'I'm going to I er, need some time. A month, maybe two.'
'Ok two months! You know what we want Harry. I suggest you get on with it. And next time you call use a pay-phone!'
The line went dead.

For several moments I stared at the device in my hand.

'Harry?'
At the soft sound of her voice I turned my head sharply to see Lucia standing in the doorway.
She looked half asleep and was slowly sweeping her dense black hair away from her face with her long fingers.
'Who was that on the phone carino. You were shouting!'
She started to move towards me as she stared at my face.
'Look at you Harry! What happened?'
She sank on to the sofa next to me, putting an arm around my shoulder and resting her other hand on the top of my leg.
She glanced down at once as her fingers touched the warm dampness on the front of my pants.
'Wha's wrong with you chico! You wet yourself!'
Slowly I replaced the receiver. Then I buried my head in my hands.
'Harry please talk to me, you' scarin' me baby!'
I lifted my face and turned to her.
'I think we should leave Cuba! Get the first plane out of here!'
'Carino you ain't makin' any sense. Talk to me Harry!'
I shook my head in sheer desperation.

'Look at me, now I've pissed myself! __We have to get away from here Lucia. Back to England!'

I realized suddenly that if the apartment was bugged then it was all over. I cursed myself for my own stupidity.

She held on to me tightly.

'Ok honey, we will do whatever you want, but you mus' tell me what's happened!'

'Oh shit! Look at me Lucia.'

Breaking away from her arms I stood up.

I've got to change my trousers, __I just can't believe I did this!'

I took a quick shower and put on some clean trousers and a shirt before returning to the living room where Lucia was still seated, a look of deep concern on her face.

'Tell me harry, please!'

'Mamen's friend, __her partner! She's dead Lucia!'

'*What!* __Harry you' not makin' any sense!'

'It was on the TV. Her body was found on the breakwater at Malecon.'

'Laura? No this can't be true surely!'

I sank on to the arm of the sofa with a sudden feeling of total exhaustion.

'We must go the police now. __Find out exactly what happened.'

'Sure. __Sure we'll go now. I'll get my coat Harry.'

I heard her rummaging in a cupboard in the hallway and she returned dressed in her weatherproof jacket and holding a coat out for me.

'I think it's gonna rain again. __Lets go.'

I put on some shoes and dragged on the coat, then we left the apartment without another word.

It was spotting intermittently with rain as we left the building, but with luck we managed to catch a cab almost at once.

We sat in the silence in the back of the taxi, then I felt Lucia's hands gripping mine.

'That was stupid of me, blurting out about leaving! __I just forgot for a moment, I__'

'Oh *fuck* them Harry! Who cares! __Anyway we ain't leavin'!'

She was staring ahead with that expression of defiance that I now knew so well.

I managed to force a smile.

'No, you're right love.'

'Who was that you were talkin' to on the phone Harry?'

I glanced at the driver.

'Our American friend, the one I met recently.'

'Oh him! Ok, well we'll talk about him later!'

It was nearly dark when we got to the large imposing building that served as the 'Policia' headquarters. The rain was more persistant now as I paid the cab and we both hurried inside.
I hardly expected Raul to still be in his office and when we asked at the desk we were told that he'd already left.
Lucia explained to the sergeant why we were there and that the girl that had been found, Laura, was a close friend.
He regarded us blankly and then picked up a phone.
Speaking for several seconds he then handed it to Lucia and made himself busy elsewhere, perhaps to provide some privacy.
"Raul" was the only word I clearly understood before she launched into a rapid dialogue exchange.
After a full minute she handed the phone back to the policeman.
'Gracias!' She said to the man, adding a brief smile.
'Lets go Harry!'

Outside we sheltered in the entrance from the rain, which was even heavier now. Glistening vertical streaks against the darkness reflected in the bright lights that illuminated the station building.
'What did he say Lucia?'
'We are to meet with him at his house in the morning. Nine o'clock!'
'Was it Mamen's friend?'
'Yes.'
She seemed subdued.
'Let's get a drink Harry. A beer or somethin'.'
We made a run for it, across the wide forecourt and then crossing the main street between light traffic, quickly entering the first drinking place that we came to.

We sat at the bar and I ordered two beers.
'Are you ok with this now?'
I gave her a skeptical sidelong glance.
'Sure! __No more Barcardi though.'
'Absolutely.'
I took a long welcome gulp from my glass.
'Christ, I needed that! __Sorry about all the drama earlier sweetheart. __But I just wanted to kill the bastard!'
'It wasn' him Harry!'
'No, that's what he told me. __But how do you know?'
'It was suicide, tha's what Raul tol' me jus' now.'

'Suicide! __ God that makes it even worse somehow! How does he know for sure?'

'There were witnesses, __ abou' half a dozen Raul said.

She climbed over the sea wall, walked across the rocks an' jus' threw herself into the water. The sea was really heavy they said. A big wave jus' picked her right up an' threw her back againt the rocks again. __ It was terrible! She had so many differen' injuries__'

I lowered my head and sighed, feeling genuine remorse for a young woman who I had never met.

'You know what it's like there when the sea gets up Harry!'

'Yes. __ Pretty horrible way to go! Poor bloody girl.'

I finished my beer and asked the barman for another.

'Her and Mamen must have been very close.'

'They were really in love Harry. I didn' say much to you because__'

She shrugged.

'I didn' know how you thought about that, __ I mean women together in that way.'

'It makes no difference to me at all love!'

'No I guess not. __ Cuban men are__ well, Cuban men I s'pose. __ Muy machisimo! They don' like that kinda thing.'

'Maybe not! We take a different view where I come from. Most of us do anyway.'

We both fell silent, both I suspected for the same reason.

'What else did Raul say?'

'Not much. __ We'll talk with him tomorrow carino.

I feel really tired now Harry. I was in such a deep sleep before, then I wake up an' hear you shoutin' down the phone!'

'Was I, __ yes I suppose I was. Sorry love.'

She gave a weary smile and lifting my hand she kissed it with great tenderness.

'It doesn' matter. __ Drink you' beer an we get a cab, yeah!'

'Yes. I'm feeling a bit tired myself now. It's an early night I think.'

Early on Sunday morning, after a long uninterrupted sleep, I was woken by Lucia.

Her lips were pressing against my neck and her smooth limbs were wrapped around my body.

'Harry!' She whispered.

'I need you chico! Muy pronto!'

Her hand moved downwards to grasp my cock, which needed very little encouragement in responding.
In seconds we were making love ferociously.
Lucia held a corner of the bed sheet against her mouth to stifle her cries when she came, thrusting her groin hard against me.
Moments later she pressed her hand over my mouth as I experienced the same overwhelmingly exquisite feeling that defies all description.
Gradually our mutual tension subsided and we relaxed against each other in utter contentment.
'Do you think they heard that Harry?'
Lucia whispered again, breathlessly.
'Depends where they hid the microphones I suppose!'
I held her close, suppressing a laugh.
'I don' care anyway carino, it was worth it!'
'If that means utterly bloody wonderful then I have to agree with you.'
She smiled and then kissed me.
'You' right Harry, __ it was bloody wonderful!'
She turned her head for a moment.
'Did you *hear* that!'
She called out.
Now we both burst into laughter.

Raul looked very different without a uniform.
He was wearing a neat pair of light coloured trousers and a blue shirt open at the neck.
'Come in please. Welcome, both of you.'
He smiled broadly as he opened the door of his house to us.
There was the usual handshake and a kiss on each cheek for Lucia.
'Welcome to my home__Please come through.'
We followed him to the rear of the house and into a large comfortable room.
'Please sit. __I must say that you look very beautiful Lucia.'
He remarked as each of us took a comfortable chair.
He turned to me.
'You don' mind me sayin' that Harry?'
'Yes I do. She gets far too many compliments!'
We both laughed and Lucia looked confused.
'What you sayin' about me Harry?'
'Nothing love.'
'Your husband was agreeing with me Lucia.'
'Mmm!'

She gave me a skeptical look.
'My 'usband talk to fast sometimes. I don' always understan' him.'
If there was any initial awkwardness it was quickly dispelled by the brief, cheerful exchange.

'Let me get you something. Coffee maybe.'
'Not for me Raul. We were up quite early this morning and had some breakfast.'
I turned to Lucia.
'Honey?'
'No, gracias Raul.'
He took an armchair by a window that looked out onto a well-kept garden, his expression was now serious.
'First of all my friends.'
He began.
'The death of Mamen's er, __friend was so terrible!
I won't give you the detail, but it seems certain, thank God, that she died almost at once. She was thrown so far back against the breakwater that the sea could not reach her again.'
He paused.
'Did you ever meet her Lucia?'
'Only once, __Harry, no! We were supposed to meet with her las' night to, I don' know, to talk I suppose about Mamen.'
She raised her hands almost submissively.
'I'm so sorry Raul! __About Mamen, about everythin'.'
'No need Lucia.'
He smiled warmly at her.
'She had her ideas, her beliefs, I tried to persuade her otherwise, but perhaps it wasn't my business to do so!'
'I was never much of a revolutionary I suppose. Just a simple policeman.'
At that moment a woman entered the room. Tall, attractive, well dressed. In her early fifties I guessed.
I got to my feet at once as did Raul.
'This is my wife, Maria.'
I offered my to her hand at once.
'I'm pleased to meet you, __er, encantado senora!'
She smiled as she took my hand.
The smile was clearly an effort and Raul filled what might have been an uncomfortable gap.
'My wife speaks only a little English Harry.'
'That ok, I only speak a little Spanish!'
I responded, returning her smile.

'Will I get some drink for you?'
The woman asked.
'No no, gracias senora.'
I replied at once.
'Then I will leave you.
She turned briefly to Lucia.
'Hola Lucia.'
'Hola Maria.'
Lucia's reply was subdued and wisely perhaps she added nothing.
The woman left us then, closing the door behind her.

Now the atmosphere in the room was quite obviously tense.
'You can understand that Maria is __broken by what has happened. The loss of our daughter is something that is impossible to bear, but somehow we must. We have our younger daughter to think about now and we must bury our own feelings, as difficult as that may be.'
He hesitated.
Raul was a tough character, no question; in his job it was a necessity. I couldn't even begin to imagine what was in his mind or indeed that of his wife and there was nothing that I, or Lucia could say that was of any use, so we said nothing.
Raul spared us by continuing at once.

'It was suicide of course, there is no question of that!
There were a number of pedestrians who saw the whole incident.'
He reflected briefly.
'I think perhaps it was a wish, or a desire of some kind, for her to be closer to__ well I expect you can figure that out easy enough.'
'Yes we can Raul, of course.'
I intervened quickly.
'When I first heard about it I thought at first that it was the Americans who were responsible.
I phoned the number I was told to use and, __well I suppose I lost my temper.'
'You sure did Carino.'
Lucia murmured.
'You spoke to the man! The same guy__'
'Yes Raul! __And made a bloody fool of myself.'
'No carino you didn' make a fool! __Mos' likely it could have been him that killed Laura, the same as__'
She stopped short.
'What else did he say Harry?'

Raul intervened.
'He denied it of course!'
'Yes he did. __Anyway it wasn't him, I know that now. I have two months to get him some answers Raul. That's what he said.'
'Two months!'
Raul nodded.
'Yes. __Now, my extremely clever wife here, has come up with what appears to me to be an ingenious plan.'
'Get on with it Harry!'
Lucia remarked.
'I am love! I'm just explaining to Raul__'
'She's right, get on with it Harry!'
Raul said with a grin.
'Jesus I'm outnumbered here. __You explain Lucia!'
Which she did, while Raul listened attentively.

When she had finished talking Raul was silent. Then he lifted his eyebrows, tipping his head to one side and then to the other.
'Yes, it's not such a bad idea.'
He said at last.
'The problem will be in convincing those in power.
I can't predict their reaction of course, but I will do what I can to persuade them. That is after I have had a day or so to think about all this properly in case we, or rather you, have overlooked something.'
'That's fair Raul.'
I said at once, glancing at Lucia.
'The key thing could be as you suggest. To offer a gift of arms with one hand and deter the yanks from looking elsewhere.
We will see. I will think about this carefully and then discuss it with those concerned.'
He smiled.
'I'll let you know as soon as I can.'
'Great. That's all we can ask.'
I turned to Lucia again.
'What do you think love?'
She nodded.
'Gracias Raul.'
She said quietly.

'There is this other question of course.'
He continued.

Delivering a person, or maybe two who are involved in espionage on behalf of the Cuban government. That is going to be very difficult for very obvious reasons.'
'Any ideas Raul?'
I asked him.
'None my friend! We cannot hand over our own agents, whoever they are and even if I knew the identities of such individuals I would certainly never reveal them. Not to the CIA or too anyone else for that matter!'
'No of course not.'
His manner changed at that point.
'And I have to say to you Harry that if you do manage to discover such details for yourself, which I very much doubt, we will then, quite obviously, be on opposing sides. I'm sure that you understand that.'
'Yes I do Raul. __We both do.'
He nodded.
'Is there anything else?'
'No. __Thanks for your time Raul.'
Lucia and I both got to our feet at almost the same moment.
'The service for Mamen will be next Tuesday morning at ten o'clock at the Iglesia Purisimo. You will know where that is Lucia.'
'Yes I do. We shall be there.'

There was hardly a word between us in the cab on the way back from Raul's house.
Both of us I suspected, were preoccupied with the same thing.
Namely, that I was expected to give information about Cuban undercover operatives to the C.I.A., or whoever. Information, which I knew, would be virtually impossible to discover.
Even if by remote chance I managed to do so, then I was in deep trouble, __and if I didn't__?
Raul was correct when he had said to me the previous day in his office that I had no room to maneuver.
It was a situation that, the more I thought about it, the more difficult if not impossible it now seemed.
Perhaps I should never have told Raul the truth, but at least now with his support we might have found an answer to half of the problem.
The other half however, seemed infinitely more intractable!

'Think about somethin' else Harry!'
Lucia remarked.
'Not easy love! __This character, this __spook, call him what you want__'

'Bastard?'
Lucia offered.
'Ok, bastard then! He seems to think that I know who is behind all this__'
I glanced at the back of the drivers head.
'__ridiculous game.'
'Even Raul doesn' know carino. His job was jus' to make sure the goods got delivered!'
"Yes I'm sure that's true. Maybe you're right love, I'll be better off thinking about something else!'

We fell silent again for a while.

'Shall we get another boat Harry?'
"Another *boat!*'
Sure why not. The insurance will pay us out.'
'You mean you *hope* they'll pay us out. I have serious doubts!'
'Why you got serious doubts? The police will give a statement to the insurers, an' like you say, job done! __Ain't that right?'
I breathed out slowly, barely listening to what she was saying.
'Oh I suppose so. I haven't really thought about it.'
'Well think about it then!'
'It's not the money Lucia. I can afford to buy another boat. It's just that, __well, are you sure that's what you want?'
'Why not? We were makin' good money before, right?'
'Yes sure, but we have the café now don't we?'
'I don' wanna work in a café Harry an' neither do you!
The café run' itself now. With Pasqual an' Consuela, an' the others in the kitchen, the café is doin' ok.'
'I suppose so.'
'Don' keep sayin' "I s'pose so!" like that!'
She made a face, mimicking my expression.
'I's negative hombre!'
'Yes, I___'
I stopped myself in time from repeating the same phrase."
'__guess you're right. I just haven't really thought about it.
I've got other things on my mind at the moment.'
'If you keep thinkin' about that you will drive you'self loco! I think we should start to look for another boat. Like soon!'
I smiled at her, at her unquenchable enthusiasm for all things that she considered worthwhile.

And maybe it wasn't such a bad idea. Find a new vessel and get out to sea again. I would have to bury my current fears of drowning it was true, but yes, the more I thought about it.
'Yeah maybe you're right love. Maybe we should get another boat. It was good fun, the fishing, I have to admit. I was really starting to enjoy it. __And yes, we were making a decent profit!'
I nodded slowly.
'Ok then love, start looking whenever you like.'
'Tha's good. Tha's what we need Harry. A new__er, como se dice?'
She wrinkled her brow.
'A new enterprise!'
I suggested.
'Well not new exactly, but an improvement on the old one. __Yes, I think it's a very good idea of mine!'
'Of your's!'
She remarked indignantly.
'Sure, I think I deserve most of the credit here.'
That comment earned me a painful dig in the ribs.
'Have you got something in mind?'
I asked after I got my breath back.
'Not yet! First I go to the insurance company. After that we can start lookin' for somethin'!'

The next morning Lucia left the apartment early to consult with the marine insurers. With her obvious command of the language and her assertive manner I was quite sure that she was best suited for the task.
Meanwhile I walked across to the café to get something to eat.
It was quiet, not unusual at that time on a Monday.
I took a seat near the front of the café and smiled at the waitress as she walked across.
'Buenas dias Harry. What would you like?'
'Hello Consuela. Some coffee and some breakfast as well. __Is Pasqual around?'
'In the kitchen, I'll go get him for you.'
A moment or so later he appeared and walked across to where I was sitting, giving his usual broad, friendly grin.
'Hi Harry, how are you?'
'Hello Pasqual, I'm still recovering, it was a very nasty experience.'
'I'm sure it was.'
'How's the wife?'

'She's good. Gettin' close now.'
'Tense time for both of you.'
'Yeah, you can say that again Harry.'
More American colloquialisms, not that it mattered and I chided myself for the unnecessary thought.
'Pasqual, have you got the book for the boat reservations?'
'Sure I'll get it for you.'
He went behind the bar and rummaged beneath it, returning shortly afterwards with the large bound notebook that we used for recording the fishing trips.
'You won't be needing this anymore I guess!'
He commented, dropping the book on the table in front of me.
'We certainly will Pasqual. We're buying another boat!'
'You're buying a boat!'
'Yep, why not? It was a nice little business venture.'
'Sure, but that's a big investment Harry.'
'The one we lost was insured of course, so what we recover from that will go a long way to paying for a new one.'
'You're getting a new fishing boat Harry?'
Consuela had returned with a cup of strong black coffee, which she placed on the table.
'Sure, why not! Not new maybe, but we'll see what comes up.'
I looked up at her and grinned.
'Can't stand still when it comes to making money'
'No you're right. I think it's great. __Do you want to eat yet Harry?'
'Give it ten minutes Consuela.'
She left us and returned to the kitchen.
'So that's why I wanted to see the upcoming fishing trips Pasqual, __have a seat.'
He took the chair next to me and I opened the book to the current page of reservations.
'Now look we might have to cancel a few people, but I wanted to see what's coming up over the next month or so and try to reorganize, shift things around a bit. For instance this party of four from Georgia for next week, we can't possibly accommodate them now, but perhaps we can offer them a later date, give them a discount of some kind, a sweetener. We don't want to lose the business. So see what you can do there, ok.'
'Sure Harry! How long do you think before you get moving again?'
'Sailing again you mean! __I'll take a guess and say a month.'
'As soon as that!'
'Could be. Lucia said there's a lot of boats for sale at the moment because of the poor Cuban economy, let's hope she's right!'

I glanced down at the column of reservations.
'Now, it appears that there's a few bookings coming up next month and we don't want to lose them. If it comes to it we'll hire a boat for a week or two. __ So now Pasqual, can you call these clients up as soon as you can and juggle things around somehow?'
'Of course Harry.'
'Good. We don't want to lose the custom so do what you can.'
'What if they ask about the delay?'
'Well don't tell them the truth for God's sake! That will *really* put them off. Just say that we're purchasing a newer craft, more sophisticated, more comfortable. Whatever comes into your head.'
'Sure Harry.'
'Who usually answers the calls from clients?'
'Me. Or if I'm not here Consuela, she's quite capable of making reservations and her English is pretty good.'
'Yes it is, she's quite fluent. How did she manage to pick it up?'
'The same as me, she has relatives in Florida. Goes back every few months to see them.'
'That explains it. __ Ok Pasqual I leave it to you now. Assume one month ok, before we're ready to ship out again. __ What's this?'
I took out a large envelope that had slipped from between the pages.
'Receipts for diesel fuel. __ Lucia keeps them in here so she can check on what's being spent and how many miles your covering on the fishing trips.'
I broke into a smile.
'That's my wife all right, thorough to a fault!
Right then. Any problems, let me know.'

The following Tuesday was the service of remembrance for Mamen. A sombre occasion, which was not easy for either of us and far less so, I was quite certain, for her immediate family.
A surprising number of people attended, none of whom we recognized.
'Do you know any of these people?'
I whispered to Lucia, as we crowded into the small ancient church.
'No. Mostly I think they are from her office,'
An old Padre gave the blessing and then spoke quietly to a hushed audience.
His words even to me, the ultimate non-believer, were oddly reassuring and even comforting, and left me with a new and unfamiliar feeling about life in general.

Even more so to Lucia it seemed, because when I turned to look at her she was crying silently with tears coursing slowly down her cheeks.
I reached down and grasped her hand, feeling a strange prickling sensation at the back of my own eyes.
It was a very odd sensation indeed.

There was no wake afterwards or whatever expression Cuban's use to describe a wake. No reception, no groups drinking to Mamens memory. Instead, outside the church, the congregation, singly or in small groups spoke briefly to Raul and his wife, who I had seen briefly at his house just days before. She was holding tightly to their younger daughter as though she might, by some act of spiritual intervention, be taken from her.
We waited until last before approaching and offering our own condolences. Lucia, still tearful embraced the woman and then the small daughter, holding her close for several moments.
I could think of nothing to say to the man. Instead we simply shook hands in silence.
As we left them to take a slow and perhaps reflective walk back to the Paseo de Marti, Raul called out and I turned to see him as he caught up with us.
'Now is not a good time Harry, but I need to speak with you. Perhaps later on this afternoon.'
'Sure. Er, __ just give me a call Raul.'
He left us and we continued walking back towards where we lived with hardly a word passing between us, engrossed perhaps with our own thoughts on the tragedy.

Raul called me later that evening.
'Thank you both for coming to the church today.'
He said at once.
'How could we not come Raul. It was, __ I thought the padre's words were, I don't know __ inspiring somehow.'
'Yes. I'm not religious but I have to agree with you. __ He is a good man!'
He paused briefly.
'I have some news on the other matter we discussed. Your idea was favourably received Harry and is now under consideration. I will let you know more as soon as I can.'
'Well that sounds like good news. So you'll __ '
'Yes, I will contact you my friend.'
'Thanks Raul. Look forward to hearing from you.'

We found a new boat within a week, just by trawling through the small ad's in local newspapers.
It was a fine looking craft, slightly larger than the "Lucy" and with more accommodation and decent toilet and shower facilities, another added bonus.
It cost just a little more than we had paid for the vessel that was lost, so Lucia was right about the sharp downturn in the Cuban economy and the sheer number of boats that were for sale.

'What do we call her Harry?'
Lucia has asked.
'What about "Lucy Two"!'
I suggested.
'Is that bad luck maybe carino?'
'Maybe! Although it wasn't the boat's fault that it sank.'
'I think Maria, after Mari-Carmen. What about that?'
I nodded agreement.
'Sure, why not love.'

After the payout from the insurers I was out of pocket by just a few thousand. We had the boat overhauled and repainted and there was some more cash to pay out, but the boat was newer than the previous vessel by about five years and better appointed, so there wasn't really much to complain about.
After another three weeks the vessel was ready for sea and the first American clients.
It was little more than the month that I had promised Pasqual.

The first trip out on the new vessel was very successful, better than we'd hoped for.
Now there was enough room for six people to sleep comfortably on board and we were able to avoid the usual tedious task of trying to find a convenient hotel. We simply moored up for the night in one of the numerous small ports along the coast and were able to set off again promptly the following morning.
Thanks to Lucia there was a good catch of Marlin to please the clients and everybody seemed well satisfied with the two days of fishing.
The American couples assured us of a return within the next three months or so, even leaving us a good cash deposit for the next trip.

'These yankee's seem to have a lot of spare time on their hands!'
Lucia commented as the four middle-aged people caught a cab back to their luxury hotel in Havana.
'Not all of them love, just the rich ones!'
I responded with a reflective grin.

A week later I met up briefly with Raul.
We met in a bar some distance from Havana, in an out of the way pueblo. It was Raul's idea.
"In case someone is curious!"
He commented, dressed in casual clothes for the same reason.
We sat at a table in a secluded corner and had a few beers between us.
'Harry!' He began.
'The people I've spoken to have accepted the idea of planting some weapons for the yanks to find.'
I was elated and it must have shown.
'That's a big relief Raul, I don't mind admitting. A very big relief!'
'I'm sure of that. It wasn't so difficult to convince them because of your additional plan to leave an even larger cache elsewhere, perhaps at the same time, that can be collected the following day or perhaps a little later. So it will take the heat off, as the gringo's like to say!'
'That's great news Raul. Will they accept the idea of more than one load?'
'Weapons are expensive, but they have agreed to three separate operations, assuming all goes well.'
It was a huge weight off of my mind.
Half the battle at least had perhaps been won.
'I think they realise that it's as much in their interest as yours. Getting weapons to Central America is no easy task and this plan, this diversion, if it works, will make life a little easier for them.
So there it is! As you know I don't agree with supplying arms to these people, but my opinion is of no consequence.'
'I know that Raul.'
'You still need to solve this other problem however, which I have already spoken to you about. You know my views on this so there's no point in going over it again. However I'm still considering the matter.'
'No. No point at all. __Anyway thanks Raul.
Incidentally who is going to put the cheese in the mouse trap, for want of a better expression?'
'You are! The Americans will not be surprised by your participation, in fact they might even expect it.'

'That's true I suppose. And if they decide to sink my boat again?'
'That isn't likely Harry. You will be the goose laying the golden egg. The previous atrocity was meant, we believe, purely as an example.'
'Yes that makes sense. __The problem is who is coming with me on these trips. I can't do it on my own and it cannot be with Lucia, __in fact it will certainly *not* be with Lucia, not after__'
I stopped short at once.
'No of course not! It will be someone else, somebody probably unknown to you. It's not important.'
'Fair enough. When is the first trip?'
'In one month more or less. __We don't want to make it look too easy.'
'No I guess not.'
I pondered for a moment on everything that had been said, then I lifted my bottle from the table with a brief gesture to the man sitting opposite.
'Salud Raul!'
He lifted his at the same time,
'Good health Harry. __And good luck.'

Lucia was as pleased I had been when I told her of my conversation with Raul, but not so pleased when I told her that it would be me who was making the delivery of guns.
We sat together in the Paseo, so that we could talk with some degree of privacy.
It was fine and warm after several days of heavy rain. Lucia looked incredibly beautiful in her favourite light green dress and I told her so, although she was undeterred by the compliment.
'Harry this isn' fair carino! No' after what happen' before.'
'Look love don't worry about this. Raul has said that he has someone else who will be coming with me.'
'Someone else! __Who someone else?'
'He didn't say love and it doesn't matter.'
'No Harry It does matter. __I will come with you!'
'Don't even think about it Lucia! It's all been arranged and organized.'
'Harry I will be ill with worry for you!'
I put my arms around her and kissed her.
'You don't need to be sweetheart. Better brains than mine have thought about this. Believe me, it's all been very well planned.'

In spite of Lucia's obvious concern I was resigned to my assignment if not exactly eager. It had to be done and that was that!

The next thing was to call the number in Vermont again, something for which I felt the most extreme distaste.

The sound of the American's voice induced instant revulsion, which was probably irrational. However the call had to be made, and complying with his previous instruction I used a public phone box in the paseo.

In seconds the call was connected and the man's now familiar voice came on the line.

'What have you got Harry? Something good I hope, for your sake!'
'A consignment in about two weeks time.'
'When exactly?'
'They weren't specific.'
'We need an exact date!'
'Well I could hardly ask for an exact date, now could I! No more than ask for a delivery address. __Let's face it, I'm not being employed by Fed-Ex!'
'Don't be smart Harry!'
There was a definite underlying threat in his response.
'Then don't ask stupid questions!'
Had I exceeded myself, gone too far? In that precise moment I didn't actually care, such was my abhorrence of the man.
'I'm going to swallow that Burgess, but don't try me!'
'Look, they're hardly going to tell me when and where, now are they! I'll probably get a day's notice, maybe two. When I do I'll call you again.'
There was silence for a few moments.
'Ok Harry, but if you fuck with me you'll regret it.'
'I'm already regretting the whole bloody business.'
'Well you should have thought of that before you started all this! __Incidentally, why are they trusting you with another cargo?'
'Why not? I delivered the last one successfully!'
'So they didn't ask if you were a little nervous at all, knowing what happened last time?'
'What happened last time could have been an accident couldn't it? That's what I told them anyway. We were cut in two by a large ship in the dead of night. Could have happened to anyone.'
'You have a point there! __So this is the story you gave them.'
'Yes.'
'And they swallowed it?'
'Yes they did. I initially explained everything to her father, who just happens to be the chief of police in Havana.'
'We know who he is. __So you convinced him as well.'
'That's what I just said.'
There was a long silence on the other end of the line.

'Ok Harry, seems like you gauged this just about right.'
'They've also paid for a new boat. An added inducement I suppose.'
'So you had no problem in convincing them to let you continue with this crazy plan?'
'It was they who convinced me! Hence the new boat. Also Mamen, the young woman who died, was a close friend of my wife, so for that reason I said I would do a few more trips for them, well for her really, she was a dedicated young woman, although I doubt if that will mean anything to you! I said I would do a few more deliveries until they had organized another team. So that's the story.'
Another pause, shorter this time.
'Ok Harry, that seems reasonable enough.
Now what about this other business. Any progress on that?'
'You don't ask for very much do you! The answer is no. That's going to take some time as I said to you before. At the moment I don't know anything.'
Another silence.
'Ok then. __Contact me when you know the date and where you're making the delivery.'
The line went dead.

I met up with Raul again in secret two weeks later at the same venue.
'It's all set amigo. Two days from now your boat will be loaded and you leave at about the same time. Early morning.'
'What about the man who's coming with me?'
'He'll be there. He knows what he's doing and he also knows everything there is to know about navigation.'
'Ok and what about destination?'
'Buenavista again, different location! I presume you've spoken to the C.I.A. asshole.'
'Yes, a couple of weeks ago.'
'What did you tell him?'
'Only that we were making a delivery very soon.'
'Good. Don't contact him until the day before you leave.'
'What about the location?'
'You don't know the location! Tell him you won't know that until you're under way. You will have to contact him by the on board radio.'
'Ok. __Raul, supposing they decide to destroy the boat en-route as it were, with me in it! That could be a possibility!'

'No Harry. They don't want the guns, they want the people who are collecting them, the Sandanistas or whoever the hell they are.'
'Sure, of course, I'm just being paranoid.'
I added a nervous laugh.
'Harry, without inside knowledge, which you are providing, they don't know where these pick-up points are going to be.
It's almost impossible for them to discover where and when these shipments are going to be made, and how and *when* they are going to be collected!'
'They knew about us before Raul, __about Mamen and me! I'm sorry, I don't mean to__'
'Don't be Harry. It was no fault of your's, if it was anyone's it was mine! __I should have stopped her.'
He fell silent and I left him to his thoughts for a moment. Then he spoke again.
'Do you think they're suspicious?'
'By *nature* I would say Raul! The point is they've put me up to all this and if I don't do what they want, both you and I, __and Lucia, know what the consequences will be.'
He nodded sadly.
'Yes Harry I know that.'
He attempted a smile.
'Good luck my friend.'
'Oh I'll be ok Raul. They want to keep me alive, __for the time being anyway.'
I thought for a second.
'It would be very nice to know how they knew about our fateful trip last time Raul? __Very nice indeed.'
'Yes it would be Harry, as you say.
This CIA agent must have a contact In Havana, it's the only conclusion I can make!'
'The "CIAsshole" you mean! __Hereafter to be known as!'
We both laughed, a little grimly perhaps. Then we finished our beer.
'Well, like I say, good luck amigo! __Thinkin' about it Harry, don't let him know when you're leaving until a couple of hours before. The less time he has to think, the better!'

The delivery went smoothly. Ten days later at just after four in the morning we left the port of Havana and headed west again.

My companion, who was probably only slightly older than me, gave his name as Alfredo, apart from that he said very little.
He might have been working for Cuban intelligence although I had no idea, and he certainly wasn't saying, not I suppose that it mattered. Taking turns at the tiller, there was little time to exchange any more than the briefest of small talk.

We reached another inlet further west on Buenavista, which, as before, was equally as difficult to locate amongst the low lying, densely packed trees on the small island.
From a tiny inlet we unloaded the boxes, carefully fixed the radio sensor, covered everything with plastic sheeting and left at once, starting back to Havana on full throttle.

Lucia was waiting for me on the dockside when we arrived in early morning, the sun just a shallow semi circle glowing red on a clear horizon. As soon as I climbed up onto the quayside she threw her arms around me. She kissed me, pressing her lips hard against mine.
'Harry! __You ok carino?'
'Sure I'm fine. My companion didn't have much to say though, so it was a bit boring! __How did you get here?'
'Raul brought me.'
I looked up then and saw him leaning against the bonnet of a police car. He eased himself upright and strolled across to us with a wide grin on his face, white teeth gleaming below his bushy mustache.
'Everythin' ok Harry?'
'No problems. Had to outrun a frigate and dodge a couple of torpedoes otherwise it was pretty quiet.'
'Harry don' joke abou' that, I's no' funny!'
Lucia looked genuinely concerned, and behind her Raul pulled a good humoured face, and lifted his eyebrows.
'How did you get on with your companion, __your companero?'
'Well he didn't say much Raul.'
'He was *told* not to say much!'
'Right, well he certainly did what he was told.'
I glanced across to where the same man was tying up the boat and lowering fenders over the side.
'Right, so now I'll give you a lift back to your apartment.'
'What about the boat?'
A sergeant will take care of that. He will drop the keys back at your place after he's secured everything. You mus' be tired my friend.'

'Just a bit!'
'Then let's go!'

When we got back to the Paseo de Marti I asked if Raul would like to come up for some coffee, but as Lucia began to open the door to the building he declined.
'I think your wife has got some other ideas amigo, an' nuthin to do with coffee!'
He whispered, giving me a wink and another broad smile.
'We'll talk soon Harry.'

He was right about that. Lucia's homecoming greeting did indeed make it all very worthwhile.

Several weeks later I was still waiting apprehensively for news from Raul about the next gun running exploit.
He had given no hint at all of when it was meant to be, probably because he didn't know, which I suppose made the waiting even more stomach churning.
But there was nothing I could do except wait, and try to keep the nervousness to a minimum.
Lucia had gone to the hospital for a maternity check-up, to which I was not invited.
'I's boring chico! I sit around for hours, they tell me everythin's ok, then I come home. __In a few months it will be differen'. Then you can come!'
So instead I walked across the street to the bar to get some early breakfast.
Pasqual was on duty, but not looking his usual cheerful self.
His wife had given birth to a boy just over a week before and I put it down to another sleepless night.
Another girl was serving customers, someone I didn't recognize.
'Hi Pasqual, how's the missus and the new addition?'
'They're fine Harry. He sleeps like __well, like a baby.'
'Not keeping you awake then, not yet anyway.'
'No, he's a little sweetheart!'
'Who's the new girl?'
'My cousin, she's helping out while Consuelo is in Florida.'
'Oh yeah that's right, I forgot.'
'An' when she gets back she's got a problem amigo! I haven't tol' her yet. Didn' want to mess up her holiday.'
I was instantly curious if unconcerned.
'What happened?'

'Her place was robbed yesterday, __las' night in fact.'
'Good God!'
'Yeah. Her neighbour called me early this morning. I only live a block away so I got there before the "Policia".'
'Shit! __Is there much missing.'
'Well they turn' the place over tha's for sure!'
He was reverting back to his Spanish accent, dropping his 'd's and 't's at random.
'Did they take much?'
'Her vecino say's no' to much. Television set, a radio, some ornaments, she thinks only cheap stuff, an' stuff from her kitchen as well. An electric kettle saucepans, a coffee machine__'
'*What!* __Why bother? Was junk like that worth getting caught for?'
'Times are hard in Cuba Harry! They took food as well, accordin' to the vecino, __sorry, the neighbour.'
'Bloody hell! Did they make a mess of the place?'
'Yeah pullin' out drawers an' cupboards, but no real damage. When the policia have finish' we will clean the place up for her before she returns.'
'When is that?'
'Nex' week sometime! It won' look so bad when we finish.'
'No I guess not. Look Pasqual we'll pay to replace what's been taken ok.'
'Tha's very generous senor, she didn' have much to start with.'
'No. So let us know what it all comes to as soon as you can alright. Including the television. __She lived alone didn't she?'
'Yeah I think so Harry. __Anyway what can I get you?'
'Some coffee and some breakfast. Whatever's on the menu.'
He left me to ponder on Consuelo's bad luck. She was a nice woman always cheerful, good with the customers. We would make sure that we replaced everything that she lost in the burglary.
As long as "Cartier" jewelry wasn't involved in the theft of course, which seemed highly unlikely.

When Lucia returned from the local hospital I related the story to her about the burglary.
'Bastardos!'
Was her immediate, predictable and fierce reaction.
'Don't worry love. Pasqual and a neighbour are going to tidy the place up and I said we would get some new things to replace what she lost.'
'Sure Harry. That would be the right thing to do. She don' have much money.'
'She isn't with anyone is she? Pasqual say's no.'
'I don' think so.'

'How old is she do you reckon?'
She shrugged.
'I'm no' sure. Forty, maybe forty two.'
I pondered again on Consuelo's dilemma for a moment or so, then I looked up at Lucia with a smile.
'So anyway, everything was ok at the hospital love, yes?'
'Yeah like I tol' you! Sittin' for two hours, then ten minutes with the doctor. __Madre mia!'
'But everything's ok is it?'
'Sure Harry, everything is ok!'
She smiled her brilliant smile.
'Nothin' to worry about carino! __So I'm gonna take a shower now.'
'Ok love.'

She disappeared into the bathroom and just moments later the phone rang. It was just approaching midday.
I had an acute, almost instinctive feeling as I lifted the receiver.
'Burgess?'
My ominous intuition was correct.
'Yes.'
I replied at once.
'Call me back on a payphone, like now!'
I half suspected what he was going to say as I pocketed some change and picked up my keys.

Five minutes later I was at an outside call box in Paseo de Marti.
I dialed the usual number and was put through to the man in seconds.
'What's going on Burgess?'
'With what?'
'The items you planted, and we know that you planted them, they're still there.'
'How can you know that?'
'We know, that's all that matters!'
'Ok, so what does that have to do with me?'
'I'm not sure. They need these guns that I do know. So why are they still laying there.'
'Look! You asked me to make the delivery. I told you where it was going to be and at considerable risk to myself! If they haven't been picked up yet that's hardly my fault. Why don't you pick them up yourself, I thought that's what you wanted.'
'Don't be smart Harry, you know what we're after.'

'I can guess. __And my other guess is that after you destroyed a seaplane and whoever was on it. Maybe the people who want these weapons are now being just a little bit cautious! You could hardly blame them for that now could you.'
There was a distinctly heavy silence, which lasted to the point at which I thought I had been cut off.
'Hello!'
'Still here Harry.'
'I don't know exactly what you want me to say, because__'
'When is the next shipment due?'
'I don't know and that's the truth. I don't find out what's going on until the last minute you should know that. There is no reason why they should tell me in advance, now is there. __Maybe they don't trust me entirely. I mean why should they?'
'Yeah.'
I could almost hear him thinking.
'We have you on a tight leash Burgess, you should remember that.'
'I could hardly forget! __Look, as soon as I know when the next shipment is I'll tell you. That's the deal isn't it?'
'Sure that's the deal. I wait for your call Harry.'
'Like I said as soon as I know, then you will be the first__'
The line was dead suddenly.

I thought for a second or so, then I rummaged for some more change and called Raul at his office.
'Hello Raul it's me. Do you fancy a drink I'm at a loose end.'
'I'm busy Harry!'
'Ok, um, well in fact it's a bit more than that.'
There was a moment's silence from the policeman.
'Sure, ok then Harry, where are you?'
'The Paseo, near the café.'
'Fine, I'll pick you up in fifteen minutes.'

He drove us to some run-down bar on the outskirts of town and parked in a side street.
Dressed, perhaps for obvious reasons, in civilian clothes he walked ahead of me into the scruffy ill-kept premises. The only reason for the bar's existence seemed to be that it served the porters who worked all hours in a nearby fruit market.
It wasn't particularly busy and we found a vacant table in an isolated spot by a window that hadn't been cleaned for some considerable time.

The bare cracked tiles of the floor were strewn with cigarette ends. On two of the walls, large, once colourful posters announced upcoming bullfights in Madrid and Valencia, aging announcements of Corridas, with men in elaborate costumes and exaggerated poses. The posters were now curling at the corners and covered with a deep patina of nicotine.
A young disinterested woman with untidy dyed blond hair strolled across to us.
'Dos cerbeza, y, __'
Raul murmured, glancing for a moment at the rows of lottery tickets sello-taped to the window.
'__este!'
He peeled one off.
'I never figured you for a Lottery man Raul?'
'Oh, just now and again amigo. __You never know.'
He added with a smile.
'Buena suerte!'
The woman remarked with little enthusiasm, strolling off to bring the beer.
'Well you certainly take me to some nice places Raul!'
I commented skeptically.
'The only people who come here are workers from the market, that's the reason Harry, one of them anyway.
So what's so urgent?'
Raul asked as he lit up a cigarette.
'The bastard from American intelligence! I spoke to him a few minutes before I called you.'
'He want's to know when you're taking the next shipment, is that correct?'
'Exactly.'
'Let him boil in his own fluids for a while Harry.'
'Sure, as long as he doesn't try to boil me in mine!'
'That isn't going to happen. He doesn't want to start an international incident, that's not how these guys work.'
'Also he was asking about the weapons I dropped off. He reckons they are still there.'
Raul grinned.
'Well he'd better check again because they've gone'
'Gone!'
'With the wind! __Don't ask me how.'
Now it was me who couldn't resist a smile.
'That won't please him.'
'We can be certain of that!'
The girl returned with two bottles of beer, dumping them unceremoniously on the stained wooden table between us.

'So I just wait now until the next delivery, is that right?'
'It won't be long Harry, I'll let you know in good time.'
'Sure.'
'By the way Raul, I expect you know anyway, but the girt who works in the café for us got robbed a couple of days ago.'
'Consuelo, yes.'
'Made a real mess of her place according to Pasqual.'
'Yes they did. He said that you and Lucia are replacing a lot of the things she lost.'
'The very least we could do I suppose. She doesn't have a great deal of money.'
He nodded slightly and stubbed out his cigarette.
'The thing is Harry, I needed to talk to you about this.'
He looked serious.
'About the burglary you mean! Don't tell me that you think I did it!'
Once again I was unable to suppress a smile.
'You're on our list of suspects Harry.'
He gave me that policeman's look.
No of course not, but listen it's a bit more complicated than that.'
'How do you mean?'
He glanced up at me as he reached for a second cigarette.
'This is between us Harry, I believe I can trust you.'
'Yes of course you can, but what's all the bloody mystery?'
'When does she get back?'
'Day after tomorrow I'm pleased to say! She's been very useful to us. Very good with the customers.'
'I'm sure she is. Look Harry this is not easy to explain, so you must bear with me, as you English like to say.'
'Of course! You sound very secretive.'
'How long has she been working for you?'
'About six months maybe.'
'Who employed her?'
'I did. She came in one day just after the Café opened and asked for a job, very polite very personable. We needed someone so I took her on.'
'Look Harry this will sound crazy, but it was us who broke into her apartment!'
'*What!* You're not serious surely Raul!'
'Not me personally, a team from the station.'
'You broke into her apartment!'
'Yeah, like I said, it sounds crazy.'
'Yes it does.'
He drew hard on the cigarette.

'Harry we know there are agents working undercover in Cuba. It's been going on for years. It's what the CIA or the NSA, call them what you like, that's what they do. If *anything,* a country, a group of people, anything at all that smells of communism gets near their back yard they're on high alert. Instead of cooperating or helping or trying to adapt they crush it out of existence, or try to!'

'Well I suppose that's true enough.'

'Believe me, it is true enough!'

'So are you saying that Consuelo is *part* of this! __ conspiracy, whatever it is?'

He gave a slight shrug of his broad shoulders.

'Well we can't be sure, not absolutely.'

'No evidence you mean!'

'No. No real evidence.'

'Raul I don't get it! How can you break into the girl's place, turn it upside down, nick all her stuff__'

'Nick?'

'You know what I mean, pinch, steal, and with no evidence. That doesn't sound like you Raul.'

'Harry this was a separate operation organized by Cuban intelligence, I knew nothing about it until afterwards. But if you're asking for my opinion I think they were right!'

'But you just said__'

'I know what I said Harry! We pinched her stuff, as you call it, to make it look like a normal theft. They are not uncommon in Havana!'

He continued quietly.

'Amigo these people are very clever, but if it is true and she is caught she is dead. __Muerto! She will know this.'

'Are you going to tell me what you're getting at Raul?'

'Be patient my friend.'

He drew on his cigarette again.

'Did you know that she has family in Miami.'

Yes, she mentioned it to me a couple of times.

'But she never visits them.'

'She's there now!'

'In the States, yes Harry. In Miami no!'

'I don't get it.'

'Ok. We, or rather Cuban agents have kept a watch on her for more than a year now. She returns regularly about every two or three months to Florida.'

'Yes I know she does.'

'Just for a few days.'

'It was a week this time!'
'Ok, but she doesn't stay there.'
'What do you mean?'
'She has been followed! As soon as she arrives in Miami she catches an interstate bus.'
To where?'
'Who knows could be anywhere. Not that far distant though. She always returns within a couple of days. __So Georgia maybe, Alabama. We don't know.'
'You could have followed her.'
'We didn't need to! If she's travelling north on an interstate and she claims to have family near Miami, then why the hell would she do that?'
'Yes I see your point I suppose. __What I don't get is why you suspected her in the first place. Why you went to all the trouble of following her to Florida.'
'Not us, the Cuban security service.'
'Ok whatever!'
'They only confide to us what they think we need to know, so I can't answer that Harry. I shouldn't be talking to you about any of this, but because of the circumstances I suppose__'
I considered what he had said for some moments.
'I suppose they know all about me and this current business as well, is that right Raul?'
'Yes they do Harry.'
Again I pondered on what he had said.
'I presume that you, or whoever it was, turned her place over to try and find evidence of some kind?'
'That was the idea!'
'And did they?'
'No, it seems not.'
'Huh, so you're no further forward then!'
'No.'
That seemed to put an end to the discussion, momentarily at least. I grasped one of the bottles and took a long pull of cold beer.

'How is your wife Raul? Dare I ask.''
'She is broken Harry.'
'Yes. __Daft question really!'
'No' not daft as you say amigo, I appreciate your concern.'
There was an awkward silence, which I didn't quite know how to fill. Raul had turned his attention; reflectively it seemed, through the smeared

unwashed window at the continual activity in the market place on the opposite side of the street.

It wasn't difficult to imagine what he was thinking and I wished that I had kept my mouth shut.

Perhaps out of some sort of reverence, I glanced down for a moment at the unwashed floor of the bar where a cockroach was rummaging amongst several fag ends, God knows why, but that's cockroaches for you, the sole survivors of the next world war, so perhaps they know more than we do! Raul's voice jerked me out of my aimless contemplation. When I looked up he was his familiar self again, regarding me with one of his of his warm broad smiles.

'So tell me. When are you going back Harry?'

'Going back? Er, when you say "going back" I presume you mean to England.'

'Yes that's exactly what I mean. How long have you been in Cuba?'

'Almost a year I suppose.'

'You don't miss your country?'

'No.'

'That's a pretty strange thing to say my friend.'

'Yes I suppose it is.'

'Your parents are there?'

'Yes.'

'Brothers and sisters maybe?'

'Just me Raul.'

He shook his head, regarding me now with a quizzical look.

'But why Cuba Harry? What made you decide to come here?'

I took another long pull at the beer.

'Pure chance really! I got on a cruise liner bound for the Caribbean and this was the first stop.'

'How did you meet Lucia?'

'In a bar, just over a week after I arrived.'

'That was quick! Muy pronto. __Love at first sight Harry?'

The policeman's smile indicated nothing other than the cheerful observation of a good friend.

'Literally! You know the rest of the story Raul.'

'Yes I do amigo.'

'__Anyway the thing is I can't go anywhere now. Not until this latest bloody business is resolved. The American arsehole has made that very clear!'

'It will be resolved some way or another Harry, perhaps with our help.'

'I wish I could share your optimism. God knows what his reaction will be when he discovers that the weapons we delivered have been snatched from beneath his nose! He will not be a happy man I suspect.'
'That is no fault of yours my friend. You told him where they were to be hidden and I've no doubt that he checked the location within an hour of you dropping off the crates.'
'I'm sure he did.'
'So don't worry about it!'
He presented another reassuring grin, which did actually have the desired effect, at least short term.
'Would you like some food Harry?'
'What *here*! Are you serious?'
'Can't you smell the cooking?'
'Er, yes I can I suppose now you mention it, but__'
'Harry this miserable little place would close in a week if it wasn't for the market. If the food was lousy the porters would go elsewhere to eat.'
He beckoned to the bored looking woman behind the bar.
'Make your mind up amigo; it will start filling up for 'comida' very soon. The paella is fantastic by the way!'

Raul was correct. The food was extraordinarily good and for twenty minutes or so we barely spoke as we demolished plates of the traditional rice dish, strongly spiced and mixed with a generous assortment of freshly caught sea-food.
By the time we had finished, the small café was packed with men waiting for their lunch, and a strong hint from the young waitress suggested that it was time for us to move on.

We climbed back into Raul's car, utterly sated with the excellent food we had just eaten.
'I'm just about ready for a siesta now Raul after that.'
'Me too my friend, but I must return to the policia central. I shall sleep for an hour in my office.'
I glanced at him.
'Can you do that?'
'I'm the chief of police. Who's going to stop me?'
He gave me another of his broad smiles as we started back to the centre of town.

Raul dropped me off at the bottom end of the Paseo de Marti.
I needed to walk and to stop somewhere and get some cold water to drink after our huge feast.

Also I needed a chance to think carefully about something that was at the back of my mind, a recent and at the time insignificant event that was now picking away at me relentlessly.
It was an innocuous discussion with Pasqual some weeks before, a discussion that I had virtually forgotten about.

I stopped at a bar in the paseo and got a bottle of water and a glass, sitting at a table outside in the now quiet boulevard. Most of the residents of Havana having returned home for the traditional midday break.
The more I thought about the detail of the conversation between the café manager and myself, the more cogent the theory seemed to become, but at the same time the more unbelievable.
However at this point that was all it was, just an unsubstantiated theory! There was only one way to be sure.

I paid for the drink and continued walking slowly along the tree-shaded Paseo where now just a handful of tourists, dressed up for the part, ambled along taking photographs of themselves and of the lovely, but decrepid old buildings.
Would they ever be restored and repaired I wondered, would there ever be the financial resourses available? It was up to Castro and the virtually bankrupt communist regime, it didn't look hopeful, but who could say what would happen in the next ten years or so?

I arrived at our little café, which was as busy as always and took a seat at the bar.
Pasqual was taking orders for food at the spacious rear end of the room. Eventually he hurried back to the bar, preoccupied with his order pad on which he was scribbling away hastily.
He tore off a couple of pages and thrust them through the narrow hatch to the kitchen, calling out curtly in Spanish to whoever was working in the enclosed space beyond.

'Harry how are you?'
He greeted me at once.
'Would you like something to eat?'
'I've had something Pasqual. Look I know you're busy, but Lucia and I have to present some figures to the accountant in the next day or so.'
'For the Café?'
'No, the fishing business. Can you give me the reservation book, just for a day or so, we need to do a bit of cooking of our own!'
I gave him a sly wink.

'Sure Harry, of course!'
He took a key from his pocket and unlocked the small safe under the counter.
'How's the family Pasqual?'
'Great Harry!'
'The new arrival keeping you awake yet?'
'So far so good amigo.'
'Well, lets hope it lasts.'
He handed me the book.
'Would you like a drink Harry?'
'No, we're in the middle of sorting out these accounts so we had better get on with it. I'll see you later.'

When I got back to the apartment Lucia was sleeping.
There was no need to disturb her and I walked quietly into the kitchen and closed the door.
Tossing the book on the kitchen table I made myself some coffee, found a pen and sat down at the table.
First I removed the large brown envelope from the book and emptied it out onto the space in front of me. Then I began to sort through the pile of fuel invoices.
I tore out a clean page from the back of the book and slowly began to note each invoice in date sequence.
There were quite a few receipts to go through, but in just over an hour I had listed all of them writing down the exact dates and the amount of fuel that had been taken on board.
Then on a separate page I began to list the trips that had been made since we first started almost a year before, once again in order of the times when we had shipped out.
I checked through the receipts for a second time and then stuffed them back into the envelope.
With the separate pages in front of me I began to compare the two, now with very a clear idea of what I was looking for.
And indeed I found it!

I shoved the receipts and my written lists into the ledger and closed it, leaving it in the centre of the table. Then I crept into our bedroom, slipped off my shoes and climbed carefully into bed, so as not to wake Lucia, moving close to her invitingly warm body.
In seconds I was asleep.

'Harry, wake up careno!'
Lucia's lips were close to my ear as she whispered the words quietly.
'Come on mister, it's almost six!'
I groaned and stirred beneath the sheet, still more into a deep dreamless sleep than out of it.
'Where did you go Harry?'
'Oh yeah er, the CIA guy called as soon as you went in the bathroom. I left you a note.'
'I saw it, but you were out for a long time carino, and I fell asleep.'
'Sorry love.'
I turned over in the bed and kissed her as she continued to stare down at me.
'I'm getting up now honey, I'll make you some coffee.'
She left me to recover from my semi comatose state.
After a few moments I swung my legs over the side of the bed and sat up, yawning massively. Then I got slowly to my feet and followed the sounds emanating from the kitchen.

'What is the book doing here Harry?'
Lucia remarked, setting two mugs on the kitchen table.
'Oh that! Yes well I need to explain that. __And a couple of other things as well, but what about some coffee first, I'm gasping here!'
At once she plonked the cafetiere in the centre of the table, the palm of her hand hovering over the plunger.
'You wan' your coffee fuerte, or you wan' it weak chico?'
She was gazing at me, leaning forward with one fist bunched on her hip and an expression that I now knew very well indeed.
'No that's fine love, no hurry at all.'
I declared quickly with a wide disarming smile.
She took a chair opposite.
'Ok, so what's with the reservation book?'
'Oh that. Just going through the fuel invoices, that's all.'
I pointed a finger to my ear and then placed it across my lips.
The accountant wants the details of our expenses. We don't want Castro stinging us for tax do we love.'
I gave her a knowing wink.
'So that's where you were!'
'As well yes, er, picking the book up from Pasqual. __Finished with it now so we can walk over to the café afterwards and return it.'
'Nuthin' else?'
'Just the call from our American "friend".'

'Him! __What did he want?'
'I expect you can guess the answer to that one love.'
'Yeah I guess so. __Bastard!'
The last word was offered clearly to the room, just in the event that it was overheard.
'Yes, well that was the other reason why I went out.'
Lucia's anger was clear and palpable and I reached across and squeezed her hand in an attempt to both reassure and to try to calm her, which wasn't easy.
'Look honey we'll return the book back to Pasqual and then go to the supermarket, we need to get a few things, ok?'
I squeezed her hand again giving her another deliberate wink.
She caught on at once and smiled her lovely smile, which in itself was well worth my efforts.

'*Consuela!* __No Harry I don' believe it!'

After dropping the reservation book at the café, we had taken our usual route to the sea wall at Malecon and were strolling along the wide pavement towards the fortress.
The evening was warm and almost without a breeze, with a calm almost flat sea lapping gently onto the rocks. The sun was still just above the horizon, but a few early stars were already clearly visible on the eastern side of a deepening blue sky.
At my announcement of the latest revelation Lucia had stopped in her tracks turning sharply to face me.

'Well that's what I was told honey!'
I responded defensively.
'Well its bull-shit!'
'Maybe it is love!'
'No *maybe* Harry!'
'Sweetheart I find it just as difficult to believe as you do. I'm just relating what Raul said to me.'
'Well Raul is talkin' out of his *ass!*''
'Raul is an intelligent guy Lucia. He's also impartial when it comes to politics or anything else come to that. He's just making the point that's all. And that's the reason I picked up the book from Pasqual, just to check out the possibility.'
'What possibility?'
'I explained this already.'

'Explain it again!'
Lucia was staring at me, not in annoyance exactly, but not far short.
'Ok I will! __Look if you compare the dates on the fuel invoices and the bookings for the fishing trips it's pretty clear.'
Lucia had backed against the low parapet of the sea wall and in an easy movement hoisted herself up in a sitting position on the edge, still regarding me skeptically.
I continued.
'On the three occasions when you and Mamen took the boat out late at night to carry guns further along the coast to the cayos, you had taken on full tanks of diesel the previous evening, right!'
She nodded.
'But during the day that followed there were no trips registered in the book. The following evening when you both returned you filled up again as you normally would, ready for a fishing trip the next day.
So on three occasions__four in fact, including the last trip that I made with Mamen, the last tragic trip I should say, it indicates as clearly as daylight that we took on full tanks but didn't apparently go anywhere, according to the book at least!
Do you see what I'm getting at? __We were almost permanently busy during that six or seven month period, but with any sense at all you can see just by looking at the record that on four occasions we used up a truck load of fuel but didn't take anyone fishing!'
I looked at her in silence waiting for a response of some kind, but there was none, not for some moments.
'Ok, so anyone could have figured this out Harry!'
She said at last.
'Yes certainly! Anyone who was interested and had access to the information, in other words the record ledger!'
She was silent again, which I felt obliged to break.
'Look sweetheart, it isn't conclusive. We can't prove that she went through the book and put two and two together. Also they found nothing in her apartment so there's no real evidence so far about anything.'
Leaning back on outstretched hands she turned her head to one side, glancing along the coastline towards the old fort and the lighthouse on the opposite promontory of the narrow inlet, then she looked back to me suddenly.
'What do you think Harry?'
'What do I think? Well, I don't know it all seems a bit, I don't know, airy-fairy!'
'Airy what?'

'Sorry love. stupid expression meaning a bit vague, no proof of anything. Just thought I should tell you about it that's all.'
'Sure.'
She jumped down to the pavement again taking my arm.
'Let's walk to the castillo, I need to think carino.'

We took our usual stroll in virtual silence. Lucia turned her head out towards the sea occasionally, returning to stare again at the pavement in front of her.
We reached the old fort and still with barely a word spoken took a bench seat facing the sea.
'How can we prove that Consuela is spying on us?'
Lucia said at last.
'Well, like I say, we don't know that she is__'
'But *if* she is?'
'Then I've no idea!'
'Pasqual could have figured out the same thing, couldn't he. He has the key to the lock-up where the book is usually kept.'
'I suppose anyone who works in the café could have love! During the day the book is often left lying around under the counter.'
'I'm no' sure about that Harry.'
'What do you mean?'
'You say you took the book back to the apartment.'
'Yeah, so what?'
'How long did it take you to look through the fuel bills compare the dates and then look through all the reservations over seven months?'
'I don't know honey. An hour, maybe longer, I wasn't counting.'
'The other people working in the café wouldn't have the time would they, not without being noticed.'
'Um, no I suppose not.'
'So only Consuela or Pasqual would be able to do that, wouldn't they carino.'
'Well, yes I suppose your right. __But Pasqual?'
'Why not Harry!'
'Er, no. Once again I suppose you're right.'
She was gazing at me intently now and it wasn't difficult to tell that her active mind was churning away rapidly.
'Maybe that some person or other is watchin' us Harry, apart from the bastard gringo I mean. It doesn' take a genius to figure out how far the 'Lucy' could get on full tanks of diesel. So whoever it was figured out what was going on an' the night you set out with Mamen was 'mal suerte', __the night we ran out of luck!'

'You mean Mamen ran out of luck!'
'No you as well, both of us, an' yes, Mamen of course, __poor Mamen.'
She stopped for a moment.
'Look at the fuckin' mess we're in now Harry!'
The expression in her deep brown eyes had an unfamiliar element of uncertainty, perhaps even fear. It was a look that I had never seen, or perhaps noticed before.
At once I took both of her hands in mine.
'Lucia, I don't want you to worry about this. If anything is going to happen then it will happen to me not to you. I made a deal with this piece of shit the night I was captured. I said I would do anything he wanted as long as you were left out of it and he agreed to that!'
I felt no shame in lying to her.
'But carino it was my fault, all of it! An' Marie Carmen I s'pose. Now you are __ sufrimiento, como se dice?'
She struggled with the word.
'Suffering? Do I look as though I'm suffering?'
I laughed at once and it was genuine. I put my arm around her and pulled her close. I had lied to her of course about what the spook had said to me that night, but there was no way I was going to tell her the truth.
'Look stop worrying! The only thing you have to worry about is this little nipper in here!'
I stroked her belly gently.
'Nipper! Is that wha' you call it?'
It was her turn to laugh, much to my relief.
'Yeah, another silly English expression. The other thing is we have Raul to support us. Because of his daughter he is as much involved as we are and he's an intelligent man.'
'Yeah I guess so Harry.'
We both relaxed, and for a while we watched yet another spectacular Cuban sunset. At that moment there seemed no better way to pass the time and for a few minutes our problems were forgotten.

'You don't really think Pasqual is involved in all this, do you sweetheart?' I asked her at last.
'I dunno Harry, who knows wha' to believe?'
'No I suppose not.'
I fell silent again, turning the whole business over and over in my mind.
'Raul said that the last load of guns has been taken by someone.'
'Taken by who?'
'He didn't say or didn't know. The rebels from Nicaragua or wherever I suppose.'

'So the Yanks didn't intercept them?'
She remarked in surprise.
'It seems not. And that's going to put the spook in a very bad mood indeed.'
'It sure will honey!'
She was grinning widely.
'How the hell did they do that I wonder?'
I asked her.
'The cayos can be pretty dangerous carino. Like a __swamp.'
'A marsh you mean.'
'If tha's wha'd it is! There are lots of lagoons an' like I say places where you can sink quite easy.'
'But why would anyone wander around there? Surely they would have just taken the weapons and left.'
'While the U.S. coast guard waits around for them and then destroys the seaplane or the boat, jus' like last time!'
'Yeah I see what you mean. So__'
'I dunno Harry. Maybe they took the guns deeper into the cayo and hid them again. Just leavin' the beacon for the yanks to find.'
'Never thought of that. Yes, quite possible I suppose.'
'They will only get away with that one time. The Yankees are no' stupid.'
'No I guess not. So it will be interesting to see what happens next time.'
'Has Raul said anything to you about that Harry.'
'Nothing. That's the reason our CIA friend phoned me today.'
'He's getting impatient yeah?'
'Exactly.'
Now it was Lucia who looked thoughtful.
'I worry about you doin' these trips carino.'
'Well at the moment love I don't have much choice, do I?'
'Because of me!'
'No, don't say that. I'm doing this to get us both out of trouble and there's no reason why it shouldn't go according to plan. I've just got two more trips to make__'
'You' forgettin' one thing Harry.'
'No I'm not! He wants me to give him the name of a Cuban agent. I haven't forgotten about that, but one thing at a time honey.'
'But Harry if it wasn't for me__'
I put my arm around her at once and held her close.
 'Look, just forget about that ok! I love you Lucia, we're together and we help each other no matter what, and we'll find a way around this. "All for one and one for all"!'
She attempted a smile.

'Wha' does tha' mean?'
'I can't be bothered to explain. __Now give me a kiss!'

It was almost dark when we made our way slowly back to the paseo and little more was said until we were inside the apartment.
As usual we put on the radio when we wanted to talk about something that we didn't want to perhaps be overheard.
Lucia got a couple of beers from the fridge and two glasses and we sat opposite each other at the kitchen table, talking in hushed tones.
'Can Raul be sure that Consuelo is travelling further north when she gets to Miami?'
'He says so love.'
'Maybe her family live there someplace, not in Florida'
'Nope! That doesn't fit either. She's told me herself a couple of times. They're in Fort Lauderdale it seems, so she said anyway, but who knows!'
Lucia shook her head.
'It's jus' that all this is so difficul' to believe Harry.'
'Yes I agree.'
So what do we do if it is true?'
'Nothing. What can we do, __fire her?'
'No. No I guess not. __What will you say to her when she gets back tomorrow?'
'Ask if she had a nice time, what *else* can I do?'
Lucia nodded her agreement.
'She has a nasty surprise waitin' when she gets home in the morning carino.'
'Pasqual is going to be there when she arrives, just to soften the blow. Anyway most of her stuff has been replaced now.'
'She will be suspicious Harry, __that is if she's really working for the Americans.'
'No doubt she will love.'

We both fell silent, both preoccupied with similar thoughts, and me at least with how the hell I was going to extricate myself from what at the moment seemed an insoluble situation. Specifically, how I was supposed to discover the identity of a Cuban agent responsible for organizing arm shipments to Central America, a daunting if not impossible task. The prospect caused me to shudder involuntarily.

'You ok honey?'
Lucia was smiling at me.
'Sure!'

'You seem like you__well like you' thinkin' abou' somethin'.'
'No not really, just about how to be a dad that's all! Haven't had much experience up to yet.'
She laughed at once.
'That's gonna be easy, easier than you think hombre.'
'Well I bloody well hope so love.'
She continued to stare at me with a slightly amused expression.
'Lets go to bed Harry!'
'It's early love.'
I glanced at my watch.
'__Barely after eight thirty.'
'So bloody well what!'
She exclaimed.
'I wanna make love to you!'
I didn't need a great deal of coaxing.

The procreative act, that wonderful physical experience, which in humans culminates in a frantic crescendo of emotion, physical feeling and the most sublime satisfaction, is familiar enough, nothing new there at all, except that with Lucia it transcended all of that. It wasn't just simply coital, mere blind insatiable lust, no it really was a passion beyond any possible description.
Two individuals becoming one, perhaps in spirit, whatever that meant?
I knew that I loved her more than anything, and I was certain beyond any doubt that her feeling for me was the same.
Just to look at her in an unguarded moment or feel her hand touch mine in the most casual manner seemed to ignite some incomprehensible joy within me that I could never quite explain.
I often wondered about the extraordinary circumstances which brought us together. Was our meeting accidental? The longer we were with each other the more I became convinced that it wasn't, which makes very little sense in the familiar world we all live in.
"We were destined to meet." Is an overused cliché, but I believed it absolutely however absurd it sounded.
Our chance encounter, if that's what it was, seemed entirely logical to me, and now I just couldn't imagine my life without her.

Afterwards lay close to her listening to the familiar sounds from the paseo drifting up through the partially open window of our bedroom.

Her arm rested contentedly across my body and her head was buried against my neck, her abundant hair flowing across my shoulder like a dark river.

'You ok carino?'

She said after a minute or so.

'What do think?'

I whispered. She squeezed my arm gently.

'Who is going to meet Consuelo when she gets back Harry?'

'Who knows, Pasqual maybe or one of her friends. It can't be one of us. That would be a bit too obvious!'

'I didn't mean from the ferry, I meant in the café.'

'Oh right! __Me I suppose. You've got some people, some clients arriving from the U.S. on Thursday if I remember correctly.'

'Yes I have, so I won't be here, unless you want to take them out fishing.'

'No you're better at it than I am, but who's going to lend you a hand?'

'Alberto said he would come with me.'

'The guy we bought the "Lucy" from.'

'Yeah, he's got nuthin' much to do these days and I think he's short of cash.'

'What about the money that was left to him by his brother?'

'All gone I s'pose. I don' think there was much left over after he buy that fancy yacht.'

'Ok, well keep him off the booze. Make it clear to him before you leave. If the customers want to get drunk that's their business but Alberto needs to stay sober!'

'You leave Alberto to me carino, I know exactly how to deal with that hombre!'

She shifted slightly in the bed drawing me closer.

I gave a short laugh and turned to plant a kiss on her forehead.

'I'm sure you do love.'

'We lay in contented silence again.

After a while the sound of laughter and music almost directly below the window started up.

'What's going on now I wonder?'

I asked Lucia as the sounds grew louder, or though by no means unpleasantly so.

'Bailando practica! __Dance training for the fiesta next week.'

'Not *another* fiesta!'

'Don't you like fiestas Harry?'

As she spoke she gripped my chin and squeezed it as she might a small boy.

'It's not that love, just not used to it that's all. We only have two fiestas a year in England, Christmas and Guy Fawkes!'
'Who, which Guy?'
'Er, __ oh forget it. It will take too long to explain.'
'Ok, __ so give me a kiss then chico an' lets see if you are in the mood again!'
With the familiar delicious feeling of arousal returning instantly I turned to her.
'For you sweetheart I'm always in the mood.'

'Consuelo! How are you? Como esta?'
I greeted her as soon as she entered the café.
It was three in afternoon and we were busy, with a room full of customers and more at the tables outside.
'Thank you Harry, I am well.'
She managed a smile. And walking behind the bar she rummaged beneath it for a clean apron, which she began at once to fasten around her waist.
'Look Consuelo, you don't have to work today, you've had a long trip. Go home and rest, we can manage ok. I'll see you in the morning.'
'No boss you have customers. Anyway I need to earn some money.'
She tied her long dark hair in a tight knot at the back of her head and the rapid transformation to waitress was complete.
She was slim and although not overly attractive she had a nice manner and did her job well.
I spoke up again before she had a chance to say anymore.
'Consuelo we heard about the break in at your apartment. It was really bad luck. I know that Pasqual cleared the place up for you__'
'Yes. __ You and Lucia have been really kind Harry. Pasqual said that you had replaced a lot of the stuff.'
'Forget it, that's what friends are for! Look are you sure you want to do this__'
She had already picked up an order pad and a pen, shoving them into the deep pocket of her apron.
'Yes I'm sure Harry. So who's waiting for food?'
I shrugged.
'Ok you're right I suppose, it is a bit hectic and Pasqual won't be in until this evening. There's two tables outside, I haven't had a chance to get to them yet.'
With a quick smile she turned and hurried towards the open door at the front of the Café.

An hour later the pressure had eased and I had a chance to speak with her again. She had a taken stool at the bar and I had a cup of coffee ready to put in front of her.
'So how was Miami?'
I remarked cheerfully, not to say as casually as I could manage.
She sipped at the coffee.
'It was ok. __Muy differerente!'
'I'll bet it was. How's your family?'
'They are good Harry.'
'Missing Cuba?'
'I don' think so. They have a good life in the U.S.'
'Good. If they're happy that's everything I suppose. __Er, I take it you went back to your apartment.'
'Yes. Pasqual met me at the port and took me straight home. To soften the blow I guess. He and his wife have been so kind. They even put some flowers on the table and in the bedroom.'
I thought I detected a catch in her voice. If I did, she recovered at once.
'And thank *you* again Harry for all you've done.'
I gave her a broad smile.
'No problem! You will have to go to the police at some point.'
'Por que?'
Again I shrugged.
'Well they will know more about the burglary than anyone I suppose and who knows, maybe they have some leads as to who was responsible.'
'I doubt it Harry and anyway the things you replaced are better than the things that were taken!'
She gave a cheerful laugh that was almost convincing.
'Right, so there you go then, but I still think you should go to the policia, they'll think it a bit odd if you don't.'
'Tomorrow morning then, early if that's ok.'
'Of course it is. I don't suppose they have much information, but you never know. Anyway Pasqual will be here to cover for you.'
I gave her what I hoped was a comforting smile.

It seemed impossible to believe what Raul had told me just a couple of days before, Consuelo an agent for American intelligence, no it couldn't be true! She was the most unlikely spy I had ever met, not that I had actually met any of course, and anyway how would I know!
I suppose that spies are chosen *because* they are unlikely!
A small group of potential customers entered chattering together and taking an empty table. Consuelo started to rise from where she was sitting.

'Finish your coffee, I'll take care of them.'
I remarked at once, hurry around from behind the bar.
For now, any thoughts about conspiracies, spies and undercover agents were forgotten, but only briefly.

It was funny how it happened. An unexpected revelation from an unexpected source, but I'm racing ahead now.

Early the following morning I met Pasqual in the café and engaged him in innocent conversation; "How's the wife?" "How's the newborn son?" etc, gradually steering the conversation around to Consuelo.
"Did you meet her from the Miami ferry ok?"
"What was her reaction when you broke the news about the burglary?"
He was forthcoming about everything, voluble in fact because that was Pasqual. No reason why he shouldn't be I suppose. My curiosity was perfectly understandable after all.
'She seems like a nice girl.'
I added.
'Has she got a partner, a boyfriend maybe?'
'Maybe, I'm not sure Harry. I've never seen her with anyone.'
'Leads a quiet life then!'
'It seems that way. We invite her to our place for something to eat once in a while and she always comes alone so who knows?'
'No absolutely! Look I'm not being nosey at all.'
'Nosey? What is this?'
'Yeah you know, over curious.'
He broke into his familiar congenial grin.
'No more than Carmen and me, which is why we always ask her to bring someone when she visits us.'
'But she never does.'
'No.'
'Mmm. __Anyway it's not important.'
I pondered for a moment.
'Where is she today?'
'At home, I told her to rest and come in early this afternoon. That's ok isn't it boss?'
'Sure. You know what you're doing Pasqual.
Look I think I'll take a walk around to her place. You know, see if she needs anything else.'
'Sure, I think she'll appreciate that Harry.'

So that's what I did, or though not for the reason I had given to Pasqual. I was hoping that I might just by chance find out more about Consuelo, some clue maybe as to what she was up to, if indeed she was up to anything!

Her apartment was no more than a few streets away and I was there in no time at all.

It was in a three storey tenement block close to Pasqual's place and given its shabby appearance didn't seem a very likely target for a burglar, although given the economic climate in Cuba I suppose anywhere could be described as a likely target.

There was no door at street level, an open invitation perhaps to anyone passing by. A stone archway led through to a small flagstone clad courtyard with an ancient communal well at the centre. Surrounding the area on four sides, the open stairway and narrow balconies with ornate wrought iron balustrades lead upwards to the apartments. The circular well with a pulley suspended from a rusted iron framework above it, still seemed to be in use, as an old woman was lowering a bucket into it attached to a rope.

'Buenos dias senora!'

I greeted her.

She barely turned to look at me, preoccupied perhaps with her task.

'Buenos dias senor!'

She responded in a voice that was as cracked and broken as the stone steps that I now began to mount to the second floor.

At Consuelo's apartment I knocked softly on the paneled wooden door that was long in need of a coat of varnish.

I heard the sound of voices from inside, brief and muffled, then some movement, then a long silence. I tapped again and almost at once the door opened and there she was. Her hair was unbrushed and she wore a dressing gown, the lapels of which she clutched tightly together just below her throat

'Ola Consuelo. This isn't a bad time is it? It's not really important so__'

Her serious, perhaps nervous expression transformed at once into a smile.

'No Harry of course not, I'm just surprised to see you.'

'I had some free time so I thought I would just call in quickly and see if there was anything else we could do for you.'

'That's er, really very kind.'

She glanced briefly over her shoulder.

'Pasa por favour!'

She exclaimed at once, reverting perhaps unconsciously to her native language.

'Well if you're sure__'
I walked past her into the narrow, dingy passageway.
'Just go straight through Harry.'
She urged, closing the door behind her.
In the small cramped living room that I had already visited a couple of times during her recent absence, a man, smartly dressed, stood by a table in the centre of the room. As I entered he picked up a small battered brief case.
Consuelo was close behind me. Was she slightly flustered or was it my imagination.
'Or er, Harry this is senor Mahoya, from the insurers.'
'Ok!
I smiled at the man.
Consuelo spoke rapidly to him in Spanish, at the same time retracing her steps to the front door and ushering the man ahead of her. She opened the door again and with a brusqe "Adios" closed it behind him, returning at once to the living room.
'Can I make you some coffee Harry?'
'That would be nice. I've had two already this morning but what the hell!'
I followed her into the kitchen, which barely had room for one person let alone two.
'Are they going to pay out?'
I asked her.
'The insurers I mean?'
'No, in fact I wasn't covered.'
'So__'
'He was trying to *sell* me insurance. I told him no because I can't afford it. The premiums are crazy, I mean really high. I don't have anything that's really worth stealing anyway, apart from what you very kindy replaced while I was away.'
'How did he know your place had been broken into?'
She shrugged.
'Who can say? Word gets around I suppose.'
'Yes I suppose you're right.'
She turned to me with a smile.
'Everyone's looking for business in Cuba these days. __Here take your coffee and go and sit down.'
Although the living room was small if was filled with light from the single large window that overlooked the street.
I took one of only two upholstered armchairs that had seen much better days, and dropped into it. Consuelo joined me after a few minutes, taking

the other chair and drawing the dressing gown loosely around her slim body.

'I had only just got out of bed when he arrived and started banging on the door, so this is the reason for my casual appearance.'

I nodded and sipped at the coffee.

'Incidentally, did you call in at the police station yesterday?'

'Er, no. I didn't really have time. I had planned to visit them before I go to the café this afternoon.'

'Good. Don't forget, it might seem odd to them if you don't.'

'I promise.'

She smiled again.

'Thank you for calling in like this Harry.'

'It's a pleasure, as I said, if there's anything else we can do__'

'Not really, you rescued me from the insurance guy at least, so thanks again for that.'

'What about if I send someone round to put a new lock on your door, the one you've got looks pretty feeble.'

'They got in through the bedroom window.'

'I know. You probably noticed that's been properly secured now.'

'I did notice, and thanks.'

I spoke slowly and with a satirized glance of severity.

'Consuelo if you thank me again I shall fire you!'

'Ok, but anyway Harry__'

'No anyways! __ So that's the door sorted out, is there anything else?'

'No I don't think so, what has really made the difference has been the moral support from you and Lucia and from Pasqual and his wife. To arrive back here after Florida and find everything very much as I left it was__, well I can't tell you__'

I sensed an onset of tears and intervened at once.

'Yes Florida. So did you enjoy it?'

'Of course, it was good to see my family again.'

'I'm sure it was. Much chance to travel around?'

I was fishing, with little hope of success.

'Not really. No time.'

'No I suppose not.'

We chatted for half an hour about nothing in particular, at which point it seemed the right moment to make an exit.

' Right, so anyway what I also meant to say was would you like to come over to us at the weekend and have some dinner and maybe a glass or two of wine. Don't say no or Lucia will be disappointed and indeed so shall I. So if you wish to retain your position with us, then the answer must be yes!'

Again her rather plain features were transformed by a smile.
'Thank you Harry, of course I accept.'
'Bring your boyfriend along.'
'Which boyfriend?'
'So you have a choice then!'
'No, I mean I don't have a boyfriend!'
'I find that hard to believe Consuelo.'
'It's true anyway.'
'Ok so just bring yourself.'
'I will, and, __well er,_'
'Don't say 'thanks' again!'
I warned her with a touch of humour and pointing a finger.
'Or else! __Saturday, around seven, ok?'
'Sure. __Would you like a drink Harry, a beer or somethin'?'
'No er, I have things to do so I'd better get going.'
She stood up slowly and I followed her to the door of the apartment. Opening it she turned to me.
'I really appreciate you coming over like this Harry.'
In the same instant she had put a hand on my arm and reaching up she kissed me lightly on the cheek.
'Well, no problem! If there's anything you need just ask us.'

As I left the old woman I had seen earlier was feeding a cat on the opposite balcony.

I didn't believe for one moment the story about the insurance salesman, who would!
As I began a slow walk back to the Paseo de Marti the man in the suit with the black briefcase played a major role in the confused scenario that had formed in my head.
So if he wasn't selling insurance then why was he there? And why was Consuelo in a dressing gown? Was he her lover maybe? I had an instinctive impression that he wasn't. So no, it made no sense, none of it.
I stopped at a panaderia and bought some bread to take back to the apartment. The girl behind the counter had to ask me twice for the money, preoccupied as I was with my visit to Consuelo's claustrophobic little flat. I paid her and left the shop. Or at least I was about to leave the shop, but stopped dead in my tracks.
Across the street the man with the brief case was poised on the kerbside staring along the busy road. After a few seconds a car pulled up next to

him. Without hesitating he pulled open the door, got in and the car drove off again.
What the bloody hell was that all about? I wondered.
Maybe the driver was also selling insurance and they were both off to look for more potential customers.
Yeah right!
Even more confused I left the panaderia and walked at a faster pace now, back to our apartment.

I turned into the now familiar paseo, still deep in thought.
However odd the circumstances related to me by Raul in the dingy bar in downtown Havana, however strange the circumstances I had just encountered in Consuelos apartment, I still found it difficult to believe that she had a part in a conspiracy that even now was entirely unclear.
I don't know, but you get a feeling about people that makes it difficult if not impossible to believe that they are involved in some pernicious plot or another. I had very serious doubts that Consuelo was participating in some undercover role, as indeed did Lucia, whose judgment I trusted implicitly and not just because I loved her. But then who was the guy with the briefcase?
Overwhelmed by the tangle of facts, or perhaps fiction whirling around in my mind I hardly noticed when a car drew up to the kerb where I had reduced my walking speed to a mere amble.
Nor did I notice when the door opened and the driver, a man in a tee shirt and jeans got out and stood in front of me on the wide pavement, which I had been staring down at almost without seeing, but when he spoke I was brought sharply back to earth.
'Get in the car mister Burgess. Someone needs to talk to you!'
I glanced up at once, hardly realizing what was going on.
'What?'
I remarked.
'You heard! Just a moment of your time, get in the car!'
He had opened the rear door.
'Who the hell are you?'
I almost stammered the words.
'I won't ask you again mister Burgess.'
The expression on his face convinced me at once that he meant what he said.
I ducked my head and climbed into the back seat. The door was slammed shut, the driver got behind the wheel and we drove off in the opposite direction in which I had just been walking, with my head stuck firmly in the clouds.

'How's it going Harry?'
In the interior that was obscured by dark tinted glass to the side and rear windows I turned at once to see that I had company, someone I recognized instantly and with considerable shock not to say distaste.
'*You!*''
'Yeah me! I though we should touch base just to make sure that you're still in the same game.'
It was several months now since that dreadful night, but he was exactly as I remembered him. Still arrogant, still totally composed. It was the American on the motor launch, the man who had been responsible for the death of Lucia's friend Marie Carmen!
I was at a loss for words and he probably knew that.
'What were you doing at the woman's place just now? Are you fucking her Burgess?'
'She's an employee.'
'We know that. That doesn't mean you're not fucking her.'
I was determined to remain calm in spite of the fear I now felt in the very centre of my stomach.
'I'll ignore your nasty tasteless comments, whatever your name is. She was burgled recently, I called to see if there was anything I could do for her.'
'We know that as well, __that her place was broken into I mean. Why was that do you think Harry?'
'How the hell should I know! To steal things seems a safe bet!'
'No that's fair enough I guess.'
He glanced briefly out of the side window.
'How's business Harry, The little café doing ok? Still in the fishing game so it seems.'
'Are you really that interested?'
'No, not really. What does interest me is your cosy relationship with the cop, Raul Sanchez. Do you want to put me in the picture there Harry?'
'If your spies did their job properly you would know that he is the father of the woman you killed.'
'Oh we do know that. What we're not sure about is whether or not he knows what you know! I mean about how she died. Do you want to talk to me about that Harry.'
'As far as Raul is concerned the "Lucy" was cut in two by what I thought was a cargo vessel and his daughter was killed by the impact. I told you all this.'
He nodded slowly, his closed lips in an exaggerated downturn.
'Yes you did, and yeah that's plausible I guess. __Sure that fits ok, now to more important matters__'

'If it is what I think is then I don't know! That's the short answer. Look I can't control this! When they want us to move some stuff for them then they call me. What else can I say to you?'
'What happened to the last shipment Harry?'
'How the fuck should I know! I tell you when and where I make the delivery, what else can I do?'
'The last shipment got lost.'
'What do you mean got lost? I delivered it exactly where I said and I'm quite sure you checked on that as soon as we left the cayo.'
I felt pleased with myself at what I hoped was the convincing way in which I protested my ignorance.
'Oh we did, but then it just__'
He raised his hands like a performing magician.
'__disappeared!'
'That's your problem not mine!'
'Maybe,'
He stared at me levelly.
'Burgess, If I find out you're double dealing us, __well I don't have to be more specific than that, now do I!'
'Look I know what I've got to do and I said that I would do it. You just have to be patient. In addition, you can't expect me to know what happens to the weapons once I drop them off!'
He nodded again thoughtfully.
'Ok, so let's see how it goes next time.'
He spoke quietly to the driver.
'Pull over here.'
The car drew up to the edge of the road. By now we were next to the breakwater on the edge of town and just a short distance from the old castillo.
'So that's our little chat over with.'
He paused.
'Don't fuck with me Harry, I'm sure I don't need to remind you of the consequences.'
He leaned across and opened the car door, as he did so I caught, as before, the same strong offensive whiff of stale cigars.
'Right, now get out!'
As soon as I left the car it pulled away at speed in the direction of the port.

But I had noticed something, not absolutely certain mind you, but pretty much. Like ninety five percent certain!

You see the thing is in Havana there are very few new cars. When the U.S. cut off all relations with Cuba it also cut off supplies of numerous items, virtually everything in fact, cars included!

As a consequence the vehicles that they were left with after the revolution suddenly became much valued and therefore carefully preserved.

There were a few imports of Russian vehicles, but they were lousy. Badly designed, badly built, completely unreliable and as such no match for the lovely old Buicks the Chevrolets and the Fords. These were now lovingly cared for, restored and maintained.

If spares were not available they were ingeniously manufactured in backstreet workshops.

Generally thirty or forty year old cars now looked as though they had just left the showroom, such was the care lavished on them.

Deep in thought again I wandered over to the sea wall and hoisted myself up on the edge, sitting half turned to gaze out at the tranquil turquoise waters behind me.

It was the car that gave it away, the car that I had just been unceremoniously ejected from.

It was German, there were a few German cars still around of course, but they were vintage. This one looked fairly new.

Nothing strange about that really as a few new cars could often be seen on the streets of Havana, driven by tourists who had brought them over with them on the ferry from Miami.

The colour also was unremarkable, a sort of metallic dark grey.

But this was the point. I was certain that I had seen the car twice in the same day, almost within the same hour in fact. It was the same car that had picked up the insurance salesman just a few streets away from where Consuelo lived.

Was I sure? Not completely because it's not the sort of thing that you would normally notice, why would you want to?

I think it was the colour, the drab grey and unobtrusive, but not, if you know what I mean, given the bright pastel shades of most of the cars in Havana.

I struggled to picture the scene I had witnessed from inside the panaderia, tall guy, black hair, dark suit, standing on the edge of busy pavement with pedestrians passing in both directions.

Then the car drawing up at the kerbside, the passenger door opening then closing again then pulling away slowly into the traffic.

Was it grey? I felt certain that it was. Tinted windows? Hadn't noticed, no reason to.

I wracked my memory trying to recreate the image, which was as recent as no more than a single hour before.
Yes it was the same car, I was sure of it.

I continued staring out at the sea as I considered the significance of this new situation. If I had got it right, and it was still an "if" then the theory about Consuelo's role in all this would appear to be proven, or at least heavily reinforced.
I wanted to talk to Lucia. To tell her what I had observed, but she had taken a group of people out fishing and wouldn't be back until at least seven o'clock that evening. Should I talk to Raul about it?
Perhaps not, not yet anyway.
Once again I concentrated on reconstructing the images of the past hour and the more I did so the more certain I became that my supposition was correct.
I knew that it was important to try and remain impartial.
Right from the beginning when Raul had first told me about Consuelo's possible involvement I had been skeptical. Even now I found it difficult to imagine that she could be involved in something like this, it was counter intuitive knowing her as well as I did, but then did I really know her at all?
I desperately wanted Lucia to be here so that I could share what I knew, or thought that I knew. Her common sense approach to most things was exactly what was needed, but I would have to wait until that evening when she would return from the fishing trip.

I slipped down from the breakwater on to the pavement, crossed the road and lost myself in the labyrinth of tatty streets, heading back by instinct towards the centre of the town.
Stopping at a bar I sat at a table and ordered a glass of Spanish brandy. Normally I never touched the stuff, but I needed to calm myself down even if it meant getting a bit drunk.
The brandy didn't help much and I continued turning over and over again in my head the events of the past hour or so.
Consuelo a spy for the Americans, for whichever secret service was involved! It was the first time that I had really thought about it seriously and no, it still seemed ridiculous.
Maybe I had got it all wrong.
The business with the guy in the dark suit and the briefcase, the possible similarity of the car, Raul's revelation about Consuelo's visits to Florida! All of it was circumstantial, but put it all together?
Well right now I wasn't sure about anything anymore and the brandy was not having the desired effect. As a result of this I ordered another.

The measures dished up in Cuban bars were nothing like the "teaspoon" doses dispensed in English pubs and very soon I began to feel the effects of the alcohol. After a third glass my mind had turned to mush, but at least it had turned my thoughts away from the current dilemma. Instead I started to think about Lucia, picturing her wonderful naked body lying next to me. Then slowly I began to make love to her. Now this was a far more desirable diversion and all thoughts of Consuelo drifted away.

I finished the brandy and left some money on the small table where I had been sitting. Then I stood up, or at least tried to stand up. I felt the guy behind the bar staring at me and because of this I made a concerted effort to control my legs and managed a fairly straight line as I walked out of the bar.

I stood unsteadily on the kerb and fortunately didn't have to wait too long before a taxi pulled up.

I slumped into the back seat and gave my address to the driver in a voice that I barely recognized.

I made a firm mental note not to drink Spanish brandy ever again.

In the apartment building I had to grip firmly onto the handrail as I made my way carefully up the tall staircase to the first floor.

In the apartment I almost fell onto the bed and was asleep, or more probably passed out, within seconds.

I woke up about four hours later felling groggy, but sober at least.

I glanced at my watch, six thirty. Rousing myself I rolled out of bed. In the bathroom I threw cold water over my face, which helped slightly. Then I made myself some strong coffee.

Lucia wouldn't be back until at least eight o'clock, maybe later than that. Seated in the kitchen I stared into space trying to get my head back on track as the events of the day crowded in on me again.

It was the car, the bloody German car!

Was it the same one? Now I wasn't sure anymore, the memory seemed to have faded.

Once again I re-ran the whole episode through my mind, trying desperately to recall the incident in detail.

Was it the same? Yes I felt certain somehow that it was and if I was right then Consuelo was working for the C.I.A. or whatever agency the man, the arsehole I had spoken to earlier belonged to.

So now what?

I remembered that I had invited her to dinner on Saturday. Could I cancel it? No, not a good idea, we would have to go through with it now and put on an act, and that wasn't going to be easy.
I would have to explain all of this to Lucia when she got back and I wasn't looking forward to it.

I decided to meet Lucia at the port as soon as she returned; anything was better than sitting around in the apartment and driving myself nuts, with one speculation crowding in on another and, assuming that Consulo *had* been spying on us all these months, no clear idea for a solution.
Why would she do this anyway, she was a Cuban national?
Ok there were dissenters to Castro's regime, there were bound to be, with the majority of them now living in Florida, but we had given her a job, I remembered her pleading look when she first came to the café. Jobs were scarce and I was pleased to be able to help her out.
If she was a spy then it seemed a very nasty way to repay us.
But then there may have been a reason.
Let's face it, I had effectively been blackmailed into service by the low-life piece of excrement who I had spoken with just a few hours ago. So maybe Consuelo was in a similar situation. The clear comparison I suppose was that I was playing a similar double role
I heaved a deep sigh, partially I suppose of despair with the human race and the things we are capable of.
Not all of us perhaps, although in particular circumstances who can say, perhaps any one of us is corruptible.
I reflected yet again on how much my life had changed since leaving England and the safe sanctuary of "normal" existence without all the complexities in which I was now totally entangled.
Perhaps I should have taken my fathers advice and accepted a safe job in the civil service, it would certainly have been less complicated, but then I thought about Cuba and about Lucia and any reservations I may have had evaporated at once.
No. Whatever might happen in the future I had no regrets.

I met Lucia in the port and helped to tie up the boat alongside as soon as it arrived, which was later than I had expected.
There was a great deal of "goodbyes" and "thank you's" for her from the cheerful group of four Americans, before they climbed ashore carrying their travel bags, which I helped them lift over the gun-nel.
Lucia jumped nimbly onto the dockside with a broad smile on her lips and embraced me at once.

'Nice surprise Harry!'
'Well I was twiddling my thumbs so I thought I would come and meet you. How did it go?'
'It went really well carino. More clientes muy contento!'
She gave a final wave to them as they hailed a taxi.
I glanced over the side of the boat to see the glistening bodies of three large Marlin lying motionless on the rear deck.
'Good. Not a bad catch!'
I commented.
'No it was ok.'
She turned and called out to Alfredo who was stowing fishing gear into a locker.
'Alberto take the fish over to the cold storage and get what you can for them. I'll see you tomorrow.'
'Sure thing Lucia. __Hola Harry.'
He called back and I raised my hand to him briefly.

In the taxi on the drive back to the town centre, Lucia looked really happy, even elated.
'You had a good day then?'
I grinned as I glanced at her.
'Yeah, it was great Harry. The yanks were really nice and gave us an extra hundred bucks.'
'Good result then. Do you think they'll be back?'
'It's a sure thing Harry. They want to go out again in two months time.'
'Great. Will you be able to take them fishing in two months time, given your current condition?'
'Sure, why not!'
'No fine, if you're happy with that.'
I was reluctant to spoil her cheerful mood and decided to keep my latest news to myself, at least for now.
'What about Alberto, was he ok?'
'Sure! He was a big help. He had a couple of beers with the clients, but yeah, he was ok.
Harry shall we go out somewhere to eat?'
'Where, the café?'
'No, to a restaurant. I've got fifty dollars burnin' a hole in my pocket.'
'I thought you said it was a hundred!'
'I gave half to Alberto, he worked very hard today.'
'That seems fair. Ok love we'll get changed and go out somewhere.'
Which is what we did. There was a decent restaurant in the street facing the Capital building that we had used a few times before and we caught a cab

just after nine pm arriving ten minutes later. The restaurant was popular, but luckily we managed to get a table.

We had a pleasant meal and chatted together about various things, mostly about Lucia's fishing trip, but I excluded still my meeting with Consuelo and later with the American. I didn't want to spoil her obvious pleasure and decided to postpone my own news until the following day.

The following day however was not quite what I had expected.

We walked home in what was a wonderful warm evening our arms linked tightly together like two young lovers, which I suppose is what we were. Although we were married and had been together for almost a year it felt, to me at least, as though we were on a first date.

Feeling the smooth skin of her arm and the warmth of her body close to me, all thoughts of the events and revelations of my day faded away and were replaced by a feeling of total contentment.

It wouldn't last of course, but I made the most of it while I could.

We went to bed almost immediately as soon as we got back to the apartment, both weary from what had been, albeit for different reasons, an exhausting day. We made love with delicious urgency, which although brief was eminently satisfying.

Afterwards both of us fell at once into a deep sleep.

The next day started with a row, well not a row exactly a heated argument would be the best description. It was all over who should have tidied up the apartment in her absence, me being the accused.

Lucia had left home at seven the previous morning and quite reasonably I suppose expected me to do the clearing up.

I didn't say anything of course about why I hadn't done what I really should have done, and so I was subjected to Lucia's hot-blooded invective, unwisely taking a defensive stance, which on reflection was a bad idea.

She was right of course! Although she was unaware of it, my getting drunk and falling asleep for four hours while she was sailing around on the high sea's looking for Marlin, was inexcusable.

If I had told her the full story then of course the argument and my subsequent 'crucifixion' would have been avoided, but for some reason I shied away from telling her the story even though I wasn't sure exactly why.

She had barely cooled down when I kissed her cheek and mumbled that I had to get going, having agreed to help out at the café that morning.

'Bye Lucia! Love you sweetheart!'

I called out as I left her in the kitchen, clearing away things from the previous day.

'Love you as well!' She murmured without turning her head away from a sink full of dishes.
As I descended the long staircase to the ground floor I cursed myself for not revealing what had happened and paused for a moment considering whether or not to go back up to the apartment and spill the beans.
Some obscure motive told me otherwise however and I continued down, letting myself out onto the street and closing the door quietly behind me.

I crossed over the paseo and walked into the café which was unusually busy. It was Pasqual's morning off and Consuelo was dashing about trying to serve a couple of dozen customers.
'Sorry Consuelo. Got up a bit late this morning!'
I apologized breezily.
'If it happens again I'm gonna fire you!'
She remarked, giving me a nice smile as she spoke.
'Can you take some orders at the back there Harry. They been waitin' for ten minutes.'
I picked up an order pad from behind the bar and hurried to the brightly lit dining area at the rear of the café.
'Buenos dias. What can I get you?'
Folding back the pad, I began unclipping a pen from the breast pocket of my shirt.

After an hour or so we managed a short break and Consuelo made us both a drink.
'Any more insurance salesmen been around looking for business Consuelo?'
I asked her, sipping at the strong dark liquid that now after living in Cuba for more than a year, I was firmly addicted to.
'No, _er, if they do they'll be wastin' their time.'
'Sure, I guess so. _So how was your holiday in Florida? I forgot to ask you.'
'No you did ask me, _it was good.'
'Did I?' Yes you're right, of course I did, but you must miss your family a lot!'
'I get to see them every three months or so, so it's not so bad.'
'Er, no I suppose not.'
I felt like an idiot. What was I trying to get out of the woman, a confession of some kind! If so I was certainly going the wrong way about it. I hurried on with a different tack.

'Incidentally, I'll get the carpenter over to your place first thing tomorrow. We need to get a new lock on your door. I meant to call them yesterday, but it slipped my mind.'
'That's ok, no hurry boss.'
'Well there is, the sooner the better really. Like I say I meant to do it yesterday but with Lucia out on one of her expeditions it just erm__'
'How is your wife Harry? __With the pregnancy I mean?'
'She's fine, yes really well, but I worry about her going out on these fishing trips in her condition.'
I shrugged.
'But you know Lucia! She's a determined woman.'
Consuelo smiled, with clear affection it seemed.
'Yes she is.'
I glanced up to see new customers taking seats at a table outside.
'Oop's! Here we go again.'
I remarked at once, relieved at the respite and also at being rescued from my clumsy comments.
At that same moment as I was hurrying outside to attend to the newly arrived group, Lucia suddenly strolled in from the street.
Pleased to see her after our previous disagreement, I presented a conciliatory smile.
'Hello love! __Look I'm sorry about earlier on, it was entirely my fault and__'
'No Harry, it was me. I shouldn' have yelled at you.'
She kissed my cheek lightly.
'Look I've got to see to these people then I need to tell you something. Something which I should have told you yesterday.'
'That's ok carino.'
She remarked brightly.
'We'll talk later. I'm jus' gonna speak with Consuelo, I haven't seen her since she got back from Miami.'
Outside beneath the wide covered walkway I greeted the new customers.
'Buenos dias!' I remarked in my poor Spanish, even though the four people seated at one of the tables were quite obviously American.
'What can I get you?'
'Are you British?'
One of them, a woman, dressed up typically for the part of a tourist asked coyly.
'I am as a matter of fact. The proverbial fish out of water! Would you like some coffee, or we have English tea if you prefer__'

At that exact moment there was the sound of a voice raised sharply in protest and then a crash followed by the noise of chairs or maybe a table toppling over, then a woman's scream.
The four heads in front of me turned in unision to gaze in some surprise through the plate glass window of the café.
Suddenly Lucia emerged, marching out through the open doorway.
'Lucia, what__'
'She's fired!'
She commented with a satisfied grin on her face.
'I'll see you later Harry!'
Without looking back she crossed over the paseo with a purposeful stride, heading directly towards our apartment.
Unable to speak I turned to look inside the café where customers were assisting a prostrate figure. Chairs had been knocked over and several plates were smashed on the tiled floor.
With some shock I realized that the person being helped to her feet was Consuelo.

In total confusion I rushed back inside the café.
'Consuelo! Good God what's happened!'
She was on her feet now still being supported by two women, the front of her white shirt was torn and there was a steady trickle of blood from her nose. Her hair was disheveled and hung rather pathetically across her face.
I pulled a chair upright and taking her arm sat her down gently.
Grabbing at the napkin dispenser from a table I pressed some tissues carefully against her nose.
'What in Gods name has happened Consuelo?'
She was trying hard to hold back the tears and I put my arm around her shoulder.
'It was your wife, she just__punched me! I__I mean__'
The tears no longer found any resistance and welled from her eyes in a steady flow.
'*Why* for Gods sake? Why would she do that!'
'I don't know Harry. She just said "My husband belongs to me!" then she__'
That was as far as she got. Her shoulders hunched forward and she was now at the mercy of her emotions.
I continued to hold her tightly. One of the cooks had wandered out from the kitchen wiping his hands on a tea towel, an expression of amazement on his face.
'Pepe, can you just take over for a while, sort the customers out!'
'Er yeah, sure Harry!'

Still bemused he whipped off his chefs cap and hurried outside to the four Americans, who were still gazing through the window at what was, it had to be said, a completely bizarre scene.

'Thank you for your assistance.'

I said to the women who had come to her aid, adding the best smile I could manage.

'Please have anything you like from the menu with our compliments.'

I repeated the phrase in tortured Spanish, which they seemed to understand. With concerned expressions they returned to their table. Gradually, still with the low buzz of concerned chatter, the café slowly got back to normal. I continued to comfort Consuelo until she also managed, at least partially, to regain her composure.

I helped her to her feet and walked her to the door.

'Look, get back to your apartment Consuelo, I'm really sorry about this. I don't know what this is all about, but I certainly intend to find out!'

'Lucia said that I don't have a job here anymore!'

She turned to me, still tearful, pressing tissues against her face.

'Ok well look, let me sort that out, but for now go home and rest.'

I took out a couple of twenty dollar bills and pressed them into her hand.

'Let me get you a cab.'

'Is my nose broken Harry?'

She asked, her voice quivering.

I gave it a cursory glance.

'Well I'm no doctor, but it seems very unlikely.'

I waited at the kerb until a taxi appeared then I helped her inside with a smile and another comforting remark.

'Don't worry about this Consuelo, just leave it all to me.'

When she had gone I turned to the Americans who still looked slightly bewildered.

'Sorry about all that, slight domestic issue it seems. Please have coffee or whatever else you would like on the house.'

With a conciliatory glance at the four people I walked back into the café. Still totally confused by the whole incident I spoke quickly to the cook.

'Pepe can you manage for half an hour?'

'Sure, of course Harry.'

'Give Pasqual a ring and ask if he can help us out for a while. I know it's his day off, but__'

I lifted my shoulders.

'Give him my apologies.'

As soon as I got back to the apartment I hurried inside and closed the door.

'Lucia!'
I called out to her at once.
'In the kitchen Harry!'
Her response was immediate and casual, betraying no evidence of the little drama that had just been enacted.
When I walked through the open doorway Lucia was standing over the oven engrossed in some cooking recipe or other, with numerous ingredients and pots of spices strewn around on each side of the counter top.
'Does that smell good Harry, or am I a Chinese woman!'
She commented without turning her head from the task.
'Yes to the first, and most certainly no to the second! __Lucia what the hell was that all about just now? I can't believe you did that!'
'She's out Harry! I don' want her back in the café!'
'Well you made that bloody plain and no mistake! What the devil were you thinking of?'
'Anyone who thinks that they can share my husband has me to deal with carino!'
'Share? Share what for Christs sake? __You're not making any sense!'
'Ok, share your *cock!* Is that clear enough for you! Does that explain why I punch her in the face?'
My mouth fell open and for a second or two I could think of no response.
'*What!* __Lucia what the bloody *hell* are you talking about?'
Now she did turn to me. Was that a slight smile I detected on those beautiful lips? No, that couldn't be right.
'I'm bloody hell talking about you and her! Wha'd you think hombre.'
'Me and Consuelo! Having an *affair!* __Come on Lucia, be serious please!'
'So why then were you at her shitty apartment yesterday mornin'? An' why was she in a dressing gown when she answered the door? Tell me that Harry!'
She was holding a large wooden spatula, weighing it up and down in her hand. I expected her at any moment to throw it at my head.
'Oh *that!* __Christ almighty, is *that* what this is all about!'
'Yeah tha's exac'ly wha' 'dis is all about! __You were there weren't you Harry! Don't tell me you weren't.'
I was completely off guard, which was hardly surprising.
'Well no, I mean yes, __yes I was there! This is what I wanted to explain__'
'So while your pregnan' wife is out fishing and trying to earn some money, you're fuckin' the waitress is that right carino?'

'No, no of course not Lucia! That's crazy! I mean, well anyway how did you know that I was at Consuelos apartment?'
'Oh tha's easy, my aunt tol' me. She lives in the building. She saw you walk up the stairs and saw you go into her flat. Isn' tha' whad you Ingles call it. a flat!'
'Oh *that!* Ok now I get it! The old woman who was getting a bucket of water from the well, I said hello to her.'
'Sure she's old, but she' no' stupid. She tol' me abou' the whole thing! She call me up this mornin' an' tol me everything.'
For some odd reason I still had the impression that she was smiling about something, maybe it was the lull before the impending storm.
'Look Lucia, you've got this all wrong I can explain '
'Not interested! I'm making this special for you Harry, I don' know why, but there it is. Anyhow I need some pimientos so I'm going out to the grocery shop, an' you can do what the fuck you want!'
Before I could respond she smiled, openly this time. Then she winked and put a finger to her lips, after which she stabbed it several times towards the door.
Initially bemused, It took a second or so for me to catch on.
'Er. I'm coming with you!'
I blurted out the words.
'Like I say Harry, you do wha' the fuck you want!'
She wiped her hands, picked up her bag from the kitchen table and headed straight for the door with me following her like an automaton.

Outside on the paseo she headed directly for the small greengrocers shop a few doors along from the apartment.
'I really did wanna get a couple of things Harry. After, we can get a drink or somethin' an' talk!'
'Ok, but not in our café love! At the moment I think that might cause a bit of a stir!'
I waited as Lucia bought a few things, paid the man and then I followed her out of the shop, turning left on the Paseo.
Another hundred metres or so and I followed Lucia as she entered a small bar that I had never even noticed before.
'Ola Enrique!'
Lucia called out to a man who was polishing glasses behind the counter.
'Dos cervezas!'

There was no problem finding a table, as the place was empty.
'I think you must know just about everyone in Havana Lucia.'
I commented.

She laughed at once.
'Not everyone Harry.'
She remarked as we took our seats.
Two bottles were brought to us and dumped unceremoniously on the table between us.

'So carino!'
Lucia began.
'Now you un'erstand! I mean abou' the little performance jus' now.'
'I do now sweetheart. Bit disconcerting at the time though.'
'Discon_what?'
'Troubling!'
She chuckled again.
'Sure, but we want to give the bastards listenin' in somethin' to think about, don' we!'
'Yes I get it now. So you don't really believe that I was having it off with Consuelo?'
'Chico, I don' know if you notice' but Consuelo is not the mos' beautiful woman in the worl', but quite possibly I got that title! You agree carino?'
Now it was my turn to laugh.
'Yes, __how could I not!'
'In which case chico__'
'Ok you made your point!'
I grinned at her.
'__But maybe she's good in bed! __OUCH!'
Lucia had given me a sharp kick in the shin.
'Bloody hell Lucia!'
'You not suppose' to even *think* abou' that hombre!'
'I'm not, I mean I wasn't! __Shit, are you going to get to the bloody point or what!'
'Ok Harry I get to the point! Consuelo is workin' for the yanks!'
'I know, I already told you this.'
'No. You said that you *thought* she might be! Tha's a differen' thing.'
'No, I'm sure of it now. This is what I wanted to tell you last night, but we were having such a nice time together and I didn't want to spoil it for you. __Or for me come to that.'
'I guessed there was somethin' on your mind carino.'
She paused with that all-knowing look that she had.
I took a sip from the ice-cold bottle.
'Ok, so who's going first?'
'Going where?'

She asked wide-eyed and for Lucia, an uncharacteristically vacuous expression.

'No, what I mean is, who is going to tell their story first.'

'Oh vale! So you start Harry. You go first.'

I told her everything about my visit to Consuelo, about the guy posing as an insurance agent and then my meeting with the American. Last of all I explained my theory about the car that he had turned up in, even more certain now that it was the same vehicle that had picked up the man with the briefcase.

'I'm certain of it Lucia. About Consuelo's involvement.'

'So am I.'

She responded.

'How can you be sure? You weren't there.'

'I didn't have to be there!'

'That makes no sense love!'

'No I guess not!'

She turned her head and called out to the barman.

'Enrique, pasa por aqui un momento!'

The man strolled across to where we were sitting, wiping his hands on a cloth.

For several moments they spoke together in rapid Spanish, of which I barely understood a word. Then Lucia turned to face me again.

'It was a Mercedes and it was a dark er, come se dice "gris"!'

'Grey. Dark grey, yes it was I didn't notice the make although I thought somehow that it was German. __ But how the hell did he know that?'

'Yesterday he was standing outside smoking a cigarette. He saw you get in the car.'

'Well how would he know it was me? He doesn't know me from Adam.'

'Who is Adam?'

'No, I mean__ oh it doesn't matter. What I'm saying is, he doesn't know me for Christ's sake, he's never seen me before.'

Again she smiled with the same knowing look.

'Harry, believe me, everyone knows everyone in this street!'

I raised my hands in submission.

'Right. I believe you. Everyone in this town knows everyone in Havana it seems!'

The barman looked from Lucia to me and then back again.

'Otra cosa chica?'

He enquired.

Lucia looked up at the man.

'No, gracias Enrique.'

With a brief nod he wandered back behind his bar again.

I pondered for a moment.
'But you said that you believe that Consuelo is spying on us, for want of a better word. How can you be sure of that?'
'Well that was suerte, __lucky.'
'Yes I know what suerte means. So how?'
'Like I say it was jus' luck Harry. Raul phoned me at sea yesterday on the radio, it was abou' seven o'clock las' night when we were on our way back.'
'Raul? Why would he phone you?'
'Because he tried to contact you firs', but obviously you were somewhere else! He knows something is going on of course and tha's the reason.'
She paused and called out to the barman again.
'Enrique!'
She pointed to her bottle.
'Dos mas por favour!'
I intervened impatiently.
'Go on, so what did he say?'
'That an official had called him las' night, a guard at the port where the ferry to Mexico docks. He was checking the cars driving onto the boat and he noticed a guy who was almost certainly the one you described. The same guy who was at Consuelo's apartment.'
'Well how the bloody hell could he know that!'
'Because Harry, the man is a suspect. He is Cuban but they think he works for the CIA so they have his picture. Tha's how the official noticed him.'
'Jesus Christ! __What about the car?'
'No! The car was registered in Havana. An old Studebaker.'
'But *Mexico!* Why Mexico?'
'Because he probably had papers to get him across the border into the States.'
'So why not go directly to Miami?'
She spread her hands apart.
'Well tha's obvious carino!'
'Yes I suppose it is, if he wants to cover his tracks I guess. __Bloody hell eh! That official was pretty sharp to have noticed him, wasn't he! '
'Sure I guess so, he's probably connected with Cuban intelligence. I reckon he was tol' to pass on the information to the policia.'
'Yes, no doubt he was. __But hold on a minute. How did they connect him with Consuelo?'
'I don' know Harry, you better ask Raul. Maybe they follow him to her apartment, who can say?'

'No, maybe you're right.'
I heaved a huge sigh.
'So that, I suppose, is pretty conclusive. About Consuelo I mean.'
'Sure it is Harry. Tha's why I fired her today.'
'Might have been better to keep her on board, mightn't it love? I mean if she really is a spy, which now seems highly likely!'
'Maybe. I never like' her anyway. __Also she want' to get in your pants careno!'
'What complete nonsense Lucia! __Absolute rubbish!'
She nodded sagely.
'No, I's not absolute like you say. I know women Harry. I see the way she look at you!'
I couldn't argue with her and I didn't try.
'So that's that then. Why didn't you tell me all this last night?'
'For the same reason you didn' tell me.'
When I smiled at her it was with considerable affection.
'You're quite a woman Lucia!'
'You better believe it hombre!'

I met with Raul the next day.
It was in a room in a government office, the same building where Marie Carmen had once worked, a large grim looking place in the centre of town close to the capital building.
'If anyone was following you Harry__'
Raul said.
'__they won't get no further than the entrance.'
We shook hands warmly.
'How are you my friend?'
He asked with his familiar grin.
'I'm ok Raul. Why are we meeting here of all places?'
'For the reason I jus' gave to you amigo!'
'Oh right. __So what is this place?'
'The oficina de impuesto. __Tax office!'
'I thought Mamen worked for the trade delegation?'
'Differen' department!'
'Ok, now I get it. __How's things with you Raul?'
'No' too bad Harry. One day at a time my friend,'
I gave a brief nod.
'Yes I suppose so. __Can I ask how your wife is?'

'Pretty much the same, she's not going to get over this and neither am I. It's gonna take a long time to, I don' know, __accept it I suppose. Mamen was dear to us, as any daughter would be.'
'Of course.'
'An' now *you* have a child on the way.'
'Yeah. Lucia told you?'
'She told my wife. They keep in touch quite a lot now, since er__'
He left the sentence unfinished and taking out his cigarettes he lit one with his familiar relish.
'You don' mind this Harry?'
He held up the cigarette as though it was a precious relic of some kind.
'No it's ok. I shall probably get cancer by default, but what the hell!'
I smiled at him warmly. He was a good man and the longer I knew him the more my liking for him increased.
He leaned forward in his chair.
'So my friend, the web of intrigue is spreading it seems.'
'Looks like it mate!'
'I tried to contact you yesterday.'
'Lucia told me. I was involved with a couple of things which I shall now relate to you in case you don't know about them already.'
I told him the whole story, from meeting Consuelo at her apartment to the confrontation with the man who had been responsible for the death of Raul's daughter.
He nodded as he listened without interruption.
'At some point there will be a settlement between me and this American.'
He remarked quietly, almost as though he was confiding with himself.
'So. This woman Consuelo. Now we can be sure that she is on the CIA payroll.
'Looks pretty certain Raul.'
'So you must keep an eye on her Harry. Watch her every move, at the same time be careful my friend. When you see her in your café it must appear as though nothing is out of the ordinary.'
'Well that going to be a bit difficult!'
He raised his eyebrows.
'Why is that?'
'Because Lucia fired her this morning.'
'Fired her!'
His eyebrows rose a few more millimeters.
'Well, in a manner of speaking. She punched her in the nose and laid her out on the floor of the café!'
'*What!*''
He looked at me in amazement and then burst into laughter.

'I don' believe it Harry!'
'Well you'd better believe it because that's exactly what happened. I should know because I was there!'
Again he laughed, shaking his head in surprise, or was it amusement.
'Your wife is er, pretty fierce my friend!'
'She's that alright!'
He was still shaking his head.
'You' better tell me what happen'.'
'I just told you. __Lucia floored her with a single punch.'
'Yeah, but why, for what reason?'
I drew a deep breath.
'She told her that she believed she was having an affair with me__'
'With *you!*''
'Yes, I mean no, she wasn't. __I mean I wasn't! It was Lucia's clever idea to make sure she didn't come back again. In other words she fired her.'
'Madre mia! __Your wife Harry!'
'Yeah. That's Lucia all right! Although I'm not sure it was such a good idea, it could make the arseholes behind all this a bit suspicious.'
'Yes it could.'
I shrugged.
'There's not much we can do about it now.'
'No I s'pose not.'
He lapsed into silence for a while, drawing slowly on his cigarette.
'You could offer to conciliate. Say to her that you explained everything to your wife and that it was all a misunderstanding.'
'If I do that Raul, it might be me who ends up on the floor with a bloody nose!'
'Oh I don't think so Harry.'
He commented, still with obvious amusement.
'You don't know Lucia! The point is she doesn't like Consuelo and she really believes that__well, that she has her eye on me as it were.'
Again he grinned, giving me a sly wink.
'Is that true amigo?'
'I don't bloody know Raul. I'm not interested in the woman!
To me she's just a waitress in the café, a bloody good one at that. I'm sorry to lose her.'
He took a more serious stance.
'The fact is Harry, she is safer where you can watch her don't you agree? It is also easier to feed her false information.'
'What false information?'
'Anything that might come up! You know the old saying about keeping your enemies closer than your friends.'

'Yes I know I've already thought about all this.'
I bit at my bottom lip.
'Yeah, maybe you're right Raul. I'll talk to Lucia.'
He stubbed out the cigarette and reached for the packet again.
'Any chance of some coffee around here Raul?'
'I doubt it my friend. This is a government office, they're on a tight budget. Mamen was only working three days a week before __well, before.'
'Yes I knew that. That was the reason she started helping out with the fishing charters.'
He nodded reflectively.
'Now the thing is Raul, can you explain to me how you knew about this Cuban agent working for the yanks, the so-called insurance salesman?'
'That is easy my friend. The Americans bugged your apartment and we have bugged the woman's, this waitress, Consuelo Hernandez. That was part of the "burglary" operation.
So when this guy turned up at her place we heard everything that was said. She mentioned his name several times during their discussion, before you arrived of course, and that was how we made the connection.'
'I see. Now it makes sense.'
Raul nodded, drawing deeply on his newly lit cigarette.
'Incidentally we have now removed the listening device from your apartment.'
'Well thanks, that's good news I suppose. The problem is they will know that!'
'So who cares Harry. They forced you to do a job for them, an' you can't get out of that, but that doesn' mean they can just ruin your private life, listenin' to everythin' that you do.
To hell with them, __fuck them Harry. Don' worry about it!'
'I'll try not to.'
He drew slowly on his cigarette and eased himself back into his chair.
'So Yeah, It was fortunate that the official at the port authority recognized this guy as he left for Mexico. That was a piece of luck.'
'But why so Raul? It would have been easy to make the connection, the man would have had to show his passport surely.'
'His false passport you mean.'
'Oh right, now I get it.'
Raul continued.
'If the officer concerned hadn't noticed the man's face from records we probably wouldn't have known about his little trip to Mexico.'
'So was he arrested?'
'Of course not! What would be the point of that?'

'Er, no, I see what you mean.'
'And for more or less the same reason Harry, it would be better if you could get the waitress back into her job.'
'Like I said, I'll do what I can to convince Lucia.'
'Good! Let's hope that you can. It's important Harry.'
We were both silent for a while.
I was still gasping for some coffee as Raul lit yet another cigarette.
'So is that it Raul?'
I asked him, anxious now to get away from the stuffy, austere environment of the government building, not to say the fag smoke.
'Not quite. There is another shipment pending. It will be next week, Thursday probably. I will confirm the exact day for you.'
'Ok so I'll give the American a call and tell him.'
'Yes.'
'Who's going with me, the same guy as before?'
'Yes it will be the same man.'
'Fair enough. So one more trip after this and that's it!'
'Let us hope so. __ But you still have to comply with their other demand Harry.'
'Don't remind me! I think about little else and I'm still no further forward with a solution. Even if I knew of someone who was working for Cuban intelligence how could I betray them?
In addition to which I would almost certainly be bumped off for my efforts. So if the CIA doesn't kill me the Cuban authorities will!'
I grinned wryly.
'If that isn't "Catch 22" I don't know what is!'
Raul nodded, his face was serious now as he stubbed out his half finished cigarette.
'In addition to which I will have to return to England and I don't want to do that. __ In fact it's the very last thing I want to do!'
'It hasn't arrived at that point yet Harry. It is a problem as you say, but we will get our heads together on this.'
He smiled.
'Every problem has a solution!'
'Well I hope your right.'
Raul took a bundle of papers wrapped in a folder from a drawer.
'This is your alibi for being here today in case you are confronted. The approved accounts for your business activities, signed off by the tax authorities. This was the reason that I asked you to bring a briefcase.'
'Oh right. How much tax do I have to pay I wonder?'
'None I should think, not under the circumstances.'
He stood up and held out his hand.

'It's good to see you Harry. You and Lucia must visit us soon, don't forget, please! My wife would be happy to see you again.'
'Of course we will, and yes, soon. Goodbye Raul.'
'Adios my friend.'

On the way back to the apartment I could think of nothing else but the final millstone imposed on me by the CIA agent. The compliance with what seemed an insurmountable problem, the more I thought about it the more depressed I became.
I had decided to walk rather than catch a cab. It was a fine day with a pleasant breeze blowing across town from the sea, although I barely noticed it, wrapped up as I was in this intractable dilemma.
After a reflective and deeply troubled stroll of twenty minutes or so I was letting myself into the apartment building, my mood darkened by the enormity of what I was meant to accomplish in order to keep myself, and more importantly Lucia, alive.
I suppose that for many weeks now I had pushed the matter to the back of my mind, but my discussion with Raul had now brought it sharply into focus.

As soon as I entered I heard the sound of voices, female voices.
I closed the door and called out.
'In the salon Harry!'
Lucia's voice, familiar, cheerful, warming my heart instantly.
'Hello love.'
I greeted her as I entered our large living room.
She was seated on a sofa, a glass of what looked very much like white wine in her hand. When I saw who her companion was I was deeply surprised, or maybe shocked would be a better word because it was Consuelo!
'Hi carino. How did you get on with the gente de impuestos?'
Lucia asked brightly.
'The what?'
Confused, I struggled to respond.
'Oh the tax office you mean. __I er, I don't know, I haven't looked at the papers yet. __Hello Consuelo.'
'Hello Harry.'
She gave me a relaxed smile.
'So you don' know wha' you have to pay!'
Lucia again.

'Erm, no is the short answer! The woman's Spanish was too much for my limited vocabulary I'm afraid. I just grabbed the accounts records and made a run for it!'

As I spoke I laid the small briefcase I was carrying on top of a dresser.

'How are you Consuelo? I have to say I'm a bit surprised to see you after__'

Lucia interrupted at once.

'I asked Consuelo to come over Harry. First to apologize for my quick temper an' to say sorry for gettin' it all wrong.'

'Er, well good. I mean yes, as I explained to you Lucia__'

'It's all sorted out now Harry. The book is closed on the whole thing!'

'Ok, I'm glad to here it!'

I had turned to Consuelo again. Evidence of a large bruise around her nose had been partially concealed by makeup.

'Yes Harry, everythin's clear now.'

Lucia went on.

'An' she has agreed to continue with us at the café.'

'I see. Well that is good news!'

I smiled at the other woman.

'You would have been difficult to replace Consuelo.'

In some relief I spread my arms apart.

'So, that's that then! Are you the only two drinking or do I get a glass. I think I deserve some alcohol after being in the "ministry of fear" for an hour.'

Lucia got up at once.

'I'll get you a glass Harry.'

I took an armchair, sinking into it with a sigh.

'Consuelo I'm delighted this has all been resolved. Lucia is, __well, very __protective is the right word I suppose.'

'I can understand why Harry.'

She regarded me in a way that was not difficult to interpret.

I had never noticed before, so maybe Lucia was right after all.

'Yes, well__incidentally are you still ok for dinner with us here on Saturday?'

'I can't Harry. Something has come up. An old friend of mine, she is not too well I'm afraid.'

'I'm sorry to here that. We must arrange another time then in that case.'

'Sure, I look forward to that.'

Lucia returned with a full glass, which I took from her and sipped at with genuine relish.

'God I needed that!'

I remarked. I felt genuine relief that Lucia had obviously re-thought the whole question of retaining Consuelo. At that point I had no idea why she had changed her mind, but she apparently had and that was all that mattered.

Consuelo set her empty glass on a low table in front of her and stood up.
'Thank you for the wine Lucia. I'm so pleased that this has been settled and of course for getting my job back. Things are pretty tough in Havana at the moment and I wasn't quite sure what I was going to do.'
Lucia also got to her feet.
'It was my fault Consuelo, all of it!'
She shook her head.
'A stupid thing to do, I hope you can forgive me.'
She walked across and kissed the other woman lightly on the cheek.
'Yes, a very good result!'
I intervened, presenting a broad smile to both women.
'So can you be at the café in the morning Consuelo?'
'Of course Harry.'
And turning to Lucia.
'Thanks for your hospitality Lucia. I shall see you tomorrow perhaps.'
She picked up her bag and Lucia walked her to the door.
Mumbled comments were exchanged and then I heard the door close as the women left.
When Lucia returned, her expression and indeed her mood was one of clear frustrated anger.
I spoke up at once before she had a chance to say anything.
'Well I'm glad that's all sorted out then love! Got to keep the staff happy.'
'Harry__'
She began, but I interrupted before she could say anything.
'Tell you what, let's go for a walk honey. Take a stroll down to the castle, it's a lovely day and we can get some lunch somewhere.
She looked up at me, and her expression softened at once.
'Ok,__tha's a good idea carino.'

As soon as we were outside on the paseo Lucia went off like a firework.
'That puta! I could fuckin' *kill* her Harry, I swear to you I could!'
'Well, understandable love, but probably not a good idea!'
'You don' know what it was like, I had to crawl up her *ass!*'
'I'm sure you did. All in a good cause though sweetheart!'
'Harry! __'

'All right, calm down Lucia, you did the right thing. In fact when I met up with Raul earlier he said that we should try and get her back on board again, whatever our feelings or suspicions might be about the woman. He also said that we don't need to worry anymore about being overheard. His people have taken care of the listening device.'
'Tha's good news carino, really good news!'
Yes. Anyway, what made you change your mind about taking her back?'
'It was Pasqual. He call' me up and pleaded for her.
He had talk' with her an' she tol' him the whole story. He said it was impossible that she was havin' an affair with you, which ok, we know that, but he said that she needed the job.
Ok, well who bloody cares anyway if she needs the bloody job, but then I started to think abou' what you had said, an' you were right carino, so, tha' was the real reason.'
I grinned at her and took her arm.
'Right decision love! Actually, when I told Raul what had happened he was quite amused.'
'I'm not amused Harry!'
'I know that sweetheart. __Look, you did the best thing, I know it's frustrating, but we're in deep shit Lucia.'
I put my arm around her shoulder as we walked and her mood softened slightly, she tried to smile, but I knew that she was just as concerned about our predicament as I was.
'What are we gonna do Harry?'
I blew out a long breath of air.
'I don't know love, but I'm working on it. __Raul told me that there is going to be another arms shipment next week by the way.'
'Nex' *week!*''
'Yeah. I called the spook from a phone box on the way back and told him. Don't know the day yet, but it's all set up.'
'I don' wan' you to go Harry!'
'That makes *two* of us who don't want me to go.'
I squeezed her lightly.
'Don't worry about it Lucia, I know what to do and how to do it. I'll be back before you know it!'

We took our usual route through the backstreets and emerged opposite the breakwater.
Crossing the road we both sat on the edge of the low wall, turning to stare out at the sea.
'This fuckin' mess is all my fault Harry! __I know I keep sayin' this but__'

Lucia spoke quietly and with a serious tone to her voice. I turned to her at once.

'Look we've had this conversation already, forget it Lucia! You were acting for the best reasons, __for what you thought were the best reasons anyway. It's history now. So now we just have to come up with some brilliant idea. Simple as that!'

'If you discovered abou' someone, like who was workin' for Cuban intelligence, what would you do Harry? __Would you tell the Yank about it?'

'That's a tough one. I had the same conversation with Raul this morning, unfortunately he doesn't have a solution yet either.'

We were both silent, staring out over the beautiful blue waters of the Caribbean. The sea was stirred up now by a lively breeze, creating occasional waves that dashed themselves into an oblivion of white foam on the rocks below the parapet.

In the distance, with the backdrop of a perfectly blue sky, a cruise liner inched its way slowly from the east just below the horizon, taking its time because it had all the time in world.

I recalled my own voyage of discovery a year before, approaching the island with no idea what I would find and of course with no conceivable notion of the future that lie ahead.

In spite of the current and apparently insoluble problem that I was confronted with, I had not a single regret.

I had met Lucia who had given my life meaning and more joy than I could ever have imagined.

Turning away from the wonderful view behind us, I glanced at her with undisguised affection.

'Come on let's walk to the castle. Then we can get some food somewhere, by which time I will have come up with some amazing plan.'

She managed a cheerful smile at last and slipping down from the sea wall she took my hand.

Of course the amazing plan I had promised never emerged.
I hardly expected it to.
We had a light lunch in a restaurant close to the cathedral, an ancient and magnificent edifice that was just a short walk from the edge of the harbour. Afterwards, almost on impulse, we stepped inside and sat for a while on one of the polished wooden pews, enjoying the pristine silence and the wonderful architecture of the vaulted ceiling hovering above us, the

construction of which seemed almost impossible to achieve, even with today's technology.

When we spoke it was in hushed whispers, perhaps out of some respect for the sanctity of the place, because there was certainly no one to overhear us.

'It's lovely isn't it Harry, so peaceful.'

Lucia's lips were close to my ear as she uttered the words.

'It certainly is love. Makes you wonder if perhaps there is a God after all.'

'Yeah, maybe carino, __maybe.'

The second trip to the cayos was uneventful.

A clear run to the isolated set of islands just off of the mainland coast, and a new location, where we quickly carried the cases of weapons a short distance into the trees and covered them over.

I set the beacon and in less than an hour we were on our way back to Havana.

Shortly afterwards I was notified of the third and hopefully final voyage to the furthest western point of the long narrow island of Cuba.

Chapter___

The third gun-running trip to the western end of the island was confirmed just three weeks later.

I informed the CIA agent, or whatever he was, via the coded telephone link, a mere hour or so before we left giving him the set coordinates of our destination, and we set off in the boat at just before five in the morning.

This time I had a new companion, although, very much like the previous guy, he was a man of few words, which in a way was a relief I suppose.

We had a job to do and that was it, the sole extent of our temporary union.

He gave his name as Carlos during the brief exchange as we prepared for the journey and then cast off.

The man glanced at a heavy stainless steel watch as we left the narrow inlet to the harbour, turning directly west as soon as we were in open water.

He was dressed in black jeans and a dark waterproof jacket over a black tee shirt. Around his neck on a heavy gold chain was a gold crucifix, the only relief to his somewhat sombre attire.

Continuing westward, we took turns at the wheel and as the sun dipped below the horizon we arrived at our destination in good time, thanks to a placid sea with hardly a breeze to speak of.

It was a different island location to those of previous trips and motoring cautiously into one of the many inlets we moored up against the dense undergrowth of stunted trees and bushes, and began at once unloading our cargo of weapons with the aid of dim light from a couple of gas lamps.

Barely a word passed between me and the other man as we struggled with the heavy crates. The sole object was to get done and get out as quickly as possible, which is exactly what we did.

The crates were covered with tarpaulins, the radio beacon was set and in what seemed no time at all we were casting off again and heading out slowly into the open sea.

With no moon, everywhere around us was now in almost total darkness, relieved only by the spectral light of countless stars.

Behind us and further to the north I could see faint navigation lights in the distance. Was it the Americans waiting to check on the cargo, which we had left behind? Who could say and neither did I care as we headed back towards Havana at full speed.

My job was hopefully completed, or at least part of it was.

After an hour I left the man, Carlos, at the helm and went below to make some coffee for both of us.

Lucia had given me a mountain of food to take on the trip and I carried a bag of sandwiches up on deck together with two mugs of black coffee.

'How's it going?'

I asked him in my less than perfect Spanish.

'Bien!'

Was his sole response, staring directly ahead his hand resting loosely on the wheel. The faint light from the control panel reflected from the gold crucifix clearly displayed over his black tee shirt.

'You religious Carlos?'

I asked, for no other reason than something to say.

'Si!'

That was his sole response, and there seemed to be no point in pursuing a matter that was of no particular interest to me anyway.

'No sign of any shipping?'

I added.

'Nada.'

'Good. __Nobody's interested in us now anyway.'

I hardly expected a detailed answer, and surely enough I didn't get one.

He sipped at the coffee, standing the mug on the wide shelf below the windscreen.
'Sandwich?'
I asked.
Without answering he thrust his hand inside the bag that I was holding out to him.
'You're welcome!'
I murmured in English.
If he understood he showed no indication.
"Well fuck you then!"
I thought to myself. The man was certainly less than friendly.
But so what! In a few hours we would be back in Havana and hopefully our brief partnership would be over.
The mooring ropes were still in an untidy pile on the decks at the bow and stern, and it seemed a good moment to secure them properly.
After a few minutes I returned to the wheelhouse and picking up the mug of coffee I drained it. Rummaging in the plastic bag I pulled out a sandwich and heaved myself up into the elevated chair next to the one occupied by mister talkative!
He was still obviously still in no mood for casual conversation and I chewed away at the sandwich in silence, staring out ahead into the darkness.
After ten minutes I could feel my eyelids drooping and was suddenly overcome with tiredness. It had been a long day and now seemed a good moment to get some sleep for an hour

'I'm going below to get some rest Carlos.'
I said to my uncommunicative companion.
'Wake me up in a couple of hours and I'll take over for a while.'
He nodded, but said nothing.
"Miserable bastard!"
Again the remark was addressed to myself as I trotted down the steps to the cabin below.
Anyway who cares? In another few hours we would be back in port and with any luck that would be the last I saw of him.
I closed the narrow door to the forward sleeping accommodation, and almost fell onto one of the bunks.
In seconds I was out for the count!

Drifting slowly back into consciousness, and still only half awake I turned over slowly to glance at my watch.
I had been asleep for almost five hours.
My head was pounding and there was a vile taste in my mouth. Closing my eyes I lay back again as jumbled thoughts drifted through my mind. How had I managed to sleep for so long, perhaps I was more tired than I thought.
Then, like a juggernaut, it hit me, the sudden stark realization.

There was no engine noise, no movement of the boat in the water, no sound of any kind.
I froze for a moment and then rolled out of the tiny bunk bed.
Still drowsy with sleep, I fumbled in the dark for my shoes.
I moved slowly across the cramped forward accommodation, and opened the door carefully to the main cabin.
It was in complete darkness, although there was a glow of light from the upper deck through the open hatchway. I called out.
'Carlos!'
No response, so I called again.
'Carlos, where the bloody hell are you!'
Still no sound.
It was the eerie dead silence more than anything that induced a fearful apprehension, even more so than on the night when Mamen had died, and I had been confronted by the American spook for the first time.
This was stranger somehow and even more frightening.
I wanted to retreat back into the small bunk-room and close the door, but this of course was not an option.
I forced myself to fumble my way across the main cabin and take the short flight of steps up to the rear deck.
Outside it was still pitch black, but from the single light that glowed from the wheel-house above, it was easy enough to see that the vessel was moored against a jetty, but that was all. There was no indication of where it might be or even where it led too.
There was no other sign of life, or indeed of land, just total darkness in addition to the total silence.
The artificial light above me obscured any possible sight of anything beyond the tight circle of illumination around the boat.
If I turned it off I might have a better idea of where we were.
I climbed the steps to the navigation area and was instantly shocked to the core of my heart.

The man Carlos lay on his back, slumped on the decking on the starboard side of the wheel-house, one leg twisted under the other. There was a large jagged hole in the centre of his forehead, and another in the centre of his face. His features were virtually obliterated, and obscured by a vast amount of blood.

From what little I knew about such things I presumed it to be the exit wounds of bullets, although there was no way I was going to investigate further.

Feeling weak at the knees and with rising nausea I leaned over the opposite side of the boat and vomited profusely.

I turned back after a minute or so wiping my mouth on the sleeve of my waterproof jacket and with some difficulty, pulled myself up onto one of the two metal chairs bolted to the deck in front of the controls, staring down in disbelief at the corpse lying on the deck in front of me.

On its crumpled chain the crucifix lay in the centre of his chest as though in the performance of some final bizarre benediction.

I was unable, for a minute or so, to move, or for that matter even to think. What the fuck was going on! What in God's name had happened while I was sleeping!

I now noticed that part of the windscreen on the right hand side was a web of fractured lines in the glass with a small hole in the centre, the whole of which was sprayed deep red. To my horror I also realized that the controls and part of the bulwark were also drenched in blood. It was as though someone had thrown a pot of red paint over the whole area.

My hands felt damp and glancing at them I could see that they were also covered in blood from the seats.

Without thinking I wiped my hands on my jacket.

Cautiously, perhaps out of fear of being seen, I reached across to the bank of controls and switched off the light above my head.

Getting up slowly from the seat I leaned over the port side again, my eyes slowly getting accustomed to the dark.

In the dim starlight I could see that the wooden jetty ran to a rocky shoreline no more that ten metres away. At the end of the jetty there was a flat piece of land, a clearing used perhaps for parking vehicles. From this a rough track led away from the clearing, disappearing into a dark huddle of hills, and that was it. No sign of humanity, no buildings, no waiting vehicles, nothing!

Nothing that could clearly be seen anyway because of the almost total darkness.

In the complete silence and stillness it felt like being stranded on the moon, except for the fact that I was surrounded by water and was breathing air.

Gingerly I switched on the light again and stared down at the dead body of the man who I had barely known, the large hideous wounds to his face once more turning my stomach.

So what the hell now?

I forced myself to think, to consider what to do next.

The most obvious seemed to be to get away from there as quickly as possible. Plenty of time for thinking properly once I was at sea and heading back towards Havana.

I glanced quickly around the small navigation area. Apart from the vast amount of blood covering everything, nothing seemed out of place. The radio appeared to be intact, the two coffee mugs still sat on the shelf in front of the windscreen next to the bag of sandwiches, the keys to the ignition were still hanging from the control board, in fact the only anomaly was the dead body lying in front of me.

The huge gruesome pool of blood and gore around his head had run in rivulets across the decking, and I realized to my horror that I had unwittingly been walking in It, there were a number of my footprints clearly visible on the mahogany planks, to my further and utter revulsion.

So now what? I could hardly clean it up, there wasn't time, not if I was to get away from this place without any more delay.

The grotesque sight of his corpse and the terrible injuries to his face were too much to bear. Dragging off my waterproof jacket, I covered the upper part of his body.

Then I climbed into the high backed stool in front of the wheel and reached a hand towards the ignition key.

I hesitated just in time. The boat would be tied up, __of course it would! I raced down the steps again to the lower deck and jumped over onto the jetty.

Each one in turn I freed the moorings fore and aft, throwing the lines back on board. As the boat began to drift away from the jetty I leapt over the side onto the deck and then up again to the elevated position of the wheelhouse.

Now without waiting another moment I took the seat and started the engine. The noise as it turned over sluggishly and then caught with a roar made me cringe inside. If there *was* anyone in the vicinity they would surely now be alerted.

Without waiting to find out I thrust the gear-box into reverse and gunned the engine. The boat lurched backwards under the sudden power, out into clearer water. After a few more seconds I put the control into neutral and spun the wheel hard to starboard, then I engaged the forward gear and pushed the throttle as far as it would go.

The boat almost leapt out of the water as it surged forward.

Switching off the light above me again I turned and glanced quickly behind into the darkness.

Still no sign of life! No shouts of warning, no blazing lights, no gun-shots, no bullets flashing past me into the night.

I spun round to face the windscreen, concentrating now on what lie ahead. The boat appeared to be in a small sheltered bay with a narrow opening directly in front that was just visible in the faint light from the stars.

I headed straight towards it.

Turning the boat to the east, I glanced at the sat-nav, and set the course for Havana.

The steady noise of the engine and the fluorescent glow from the instruments on the control panel felt somehow comforting, and I started to relax, if only slightly.

The foul, sticky mess on my hands and on the helm was too much to bear and I raced down the steps into the main cabin found a towel and soaked it in water. Rinsing my hands under the tap I went topside again and wiped the steering wheel and the seat as best as I could.

Sitting down again I attempted to make some sense of what had happened. Had the boat been intercepted and taken over? Or perhaps the dead man, Carlos, had already made some kind of plan, a pre-arranged strategy to arrive at the deserted location, but for what reason? And, most of all, why was he dead?

I could make no sense of any of it. Now I was on my way back to the port with a corpse on board, who or which had quite obviously been murdered. This was the second time in almost a year that I found myself in a similar position, when the two American agents had been shot. At least that was clear-cut and Lucia had been with me to corroborate the bizarre story. Now it was just me and a dead body and a situation, which I couldn't possibly explain.

I heaved a deep sigh of regret, or perhaps desperation would be a better word.

So now what? Should I call Lucia or perhaps Raul? It was two in the morning, so not a good time.

I decided to postpone that decision, give myself more time to think.

It occurred to me momentarily that I could simply dump the body overboard and clean up the mess. No, not a good idea! Then I would have to explain the man's absence, which would be complicated to say the least. I dismissed the thought almost as soon as it entered my mind.

The question became more complex the more I thought about it.

I had perhaps five hours before I would be back in Havana and as the time passed and I considered my predicament, there seemed to be no other solution than to relate the facts as I saw them.

As the boat ploughed onwards, an idea occurred to me.
The broad shelf in front of the windscreen doubled as a chart table with a shallow drawer beneath it to hold maps and other navigation equipment. Leaving the steering wheel for a minute or so I pulled out a map of the area. It seemed impossible within an hour or two to calculate exactly the position of the small bay I had just left, simply because I had been asleep for four hours, but I made the effort anyway.
A small spot-lamp fixed to the shelf served to illuminate the charts. I switched it on and began tracing the coastline.
The sat-nav gave an accurate reading of my current position and with the reasonable assumption that I had been at sea for just over an hour and with the vessel making about fifteen knots, I could perhaps estimate the position of the small inlet.
On the chart I marked my present position with a pencil and rummaging in the drawer again I found a ruler and measured what I thought was a fair estimate of the distance I had travelled since leaving the bay, marking the position again.
Sure enough, within a kilometer or so I located a small natural harbour that seemed not too dissimilar from the one I had just left, There was precious little detail on the map but it appeared to be close to a small town, or perhaps pueblo would be a better description, no more than a few kilometres inland.
No, I couldn't be sure, it was one amongst fifty natural inlets along that section of coast, but I circled the bay clearly and after staring at the location again for a few moments I switched off the lamp and took the seat in front of the helm again.
There seemed little else that I could do except push on towards the port of Havana. I resolved to contact Raul as soon as I got closer to the harbour, tell him the story exactly as it had occurred and hope for the best.

Dawn was beginning to break in a spectacular red glow that blended seamlessly with a clear cobalt blue sky, however I had only a brief few minutes to enjoy the wonders of nature because now I could see the familiar shape of the lighthouse on the edge of the coastline with its intermittent beam sweeping across the sea.
It was time to get in touch with Raul.
I dialed his home number on the radio and waited.
'Harry! Are you back now amigo?'

His familiar accented voice burst from the ear-piece of the phone.
'Not quite Raul, another hour maybe.'
'You're a little late my friend.'
'Yeah, there's a reason for that__'
'How did it go?'
He interrupted.
'Good question! We delived the er, merchandise, but there is a problem Raul.'
'A problem?'
'Yeah erm,'
I hesitated.
'__Carlos is dead. He's been shot!'
'What!'
'I don't know what happened, or how it happened Raul and that's the truth.'
There was a long silence.
'Raul!'
'Where is Carlos now Harry, I mean his body.'
'On the boat.'
'I see.'
Another silence.
'Where are you amigo?'
'About, I don't know, twenty kilometres from port, I mean Havana of course.'
'Ok. Cut your engine and wait! I'll be there as soon as I can.'
The radio link went dead.
I did as he said and the boat slowed quickly and was soon wallowing in the sea in a light swell.
What now?
The most obvious thing seemed to be to make some coffee so that's what I did.
I glanced at the corpse, the top half covered with my blood stained jacket and I shuddered as I took the steps to the lower deck.
In revulsion I turned away and hurried down to the main cabin.

It could have been little more than an hour when I saw a boat in the distance. It was approaching from the direction of the port and when it drew nearer it was plain that it was a large coastguard launch.
I stood on the after deck until it came alongside.
Raul with several other men was standing on the prow of the boat staring down at me over the rail. It drew nearer and I took lines from the crew and

tied up securely. Then Raul climbed down a short ladder and jumped down onto the deck.

'Hola Harry. Where is the body?'
I pointed up to the wheelhouse.
In seconds there were three other men in uniform on the boat together with a man in plain clothes, a doctor quite possibly.
Turning to them Raul spoke in rapid Spanish, of which I understood very little.
The four of them took the steps at once to the navigation area. 'What happened Harry?'
Raul asked as the men began to examine the corpse, taking photographs of the atrocity from every angle
'I don't know Raul, and that's the truth!'
I explained everything up until I woke up in the bunk and came up on deck to find the body of the man Carlos.
'So where was this place where the boat was moored? Do you have any idea Harry?'
'No! And I didn't hang around to find out. I got away from there as quickly as possible. However Raul I think I might have located it on the map. I'll show you.'
I started towards the short flight of steps, but felt a restraining hand on my arm.
'It's ok Harry, one of the men will bring it.'
Raul called up to one of the officers and the chart was brought down and handed to him.
I pointed out the estimated position.
'That's where I *think* it was, but I can't be sure. I don't suppose you'll find anything there, but I guess you can check it out.'
Raul looked carefully at the map and nodded slowly.
'Yes we will.'
At that point one of the uniformed men came down the steps and approached us. He spoke briefly to Raul, which again I barely understood. He nodded quickly and turned to me.
'Did you move the body?'
He asked.
'No. I didn't even touch it! Apart that is, from throwing my coat over his face.'
'Ok, it doesn't matter. The man was shot in the back of the head.'
'Right, that's what it looked like.'
'And you heard nothing Harry?'
'Not a thing! __I've told you everything I know Raul.'

'Yes I believe you.'
'I mean I slept for almost five hours! It was as though I'd been drugged.'
'By who?'
'Who knows Raul, by this Carlos bloke maybe, who else? I really have no idea!'
He pondered for a second and took out his cigarettes.'
'A real mystery then!'
He murmured as he lit up.
'Yeah, __not to say bloody terrifying Raul.'
He smiled.
'I'm sure it was my friend.'
'Who was this guy anyway? Carlos I mean.'
'He works for the government. I don't know exactly what he does, or rather what he did. There will be an investigation of course and you may be asked the same questions, but I wouldn't be worried too much Harry.'
He gave me a reassuring glance.
'There is a mystery here, but we will get to the bottom of it.'
I felt a sense of relief. Raul knew that I had absolutely no motive for killing the man and perhaps he also knew that I was incapable of such an act.
'So what happens now?'
I asked him.
'We shall get the body onto our boat, clean up the evidence and that will be that.'
'Just like that!'
'Yes. We have all the information we need, so now I will talk to the authorities later on and explain to them what you have told me.'
'Then I suppose I'll be languishing in a Cuban jail until this is sorted.'
I commented sourly.
He laughed at once.
'That's not going to happen Harry, trust me.'
'Well, if you say so. What about this location I showed you on the map?'
'We're going to look for it now. Would you like to come with us?'
'Not really. That place gives me the willies!'
'The what?'
'Nothing. It's er, __an expression.'
'Ok, so these men will clean up for you, then you can make your way back to port and I'll be in touch with you soon.'
He glanced at my clothing that I now realized were stained in numerous places with blood.
'We'll give you some fresh clothes Harry. Put those in a bag and give them too us, then you had better clean yourself up.'

The body, now in a zip-up canvas bag, was lifted onto the other boat, and while I took a quick shower below deck and put on a change of clothes, several crewmembers from the other ship scrubbed the upper part of the boat and washed it down with high-pressure hoses.
Then, in what seemed no time at all, the lines were released and the police launch set off westward. Raul gave me a final wave from the rear deck.
'Don't worry Harry about this, I'll see you soon.'
He called out.

'Don't worry! __Bloody hell, it seemed that now I was in even deeper crap than before, in spite of Raul's assurances.
I watched the police boat as it surged away into the distance then slowly I mounted the flight of steps to the steering area and started the engine.
Just over an hour later I was tying up the boat at its mooring point in the bay of Havana.
I went below deck, found a bottle of Barcardi and poured a good dose into a glass, then I sat down at the table and took a strong sip as I tried without success to figure out what could have happened.
I felt desperately tired and the temptation to crawl back into the tiny bunk and cover myself with a blanket was overwhelming.
I resisted however and finishing off the rum I climbed wearily up to the rear deck again.
Locking up the boat I climbed ashore.
I had intended to walk back to the apartment, which was easy walking distance from the harbour, but instead I caught a cab.
It was late morning when I let myself into the apartment building.

Lucia had left me a note on the kitchen table.

"You late Harry, I was worryed, but then Raul call me to say that you were on you way back, so thanks to God!
It's nine thirdy now and I have to leafe for the hospital. (Just routine stuff!)
I see you soon carino.

All my love.

L.

I smiled as I read it. She had spelt 'worried' the same way she always pronounced it, in spite of my numerous attempts to educate her.
I had missed her by just over half an hour.

In that moment I longed to hold her close, to bury my face against the soft skin of her neck and to stroke her thick dark hair.

For a second or so I forgot all about the dramatic, not to say disastrous events of a mere few hours before.

The memory returned quickly enough however and with it the mystery of why!

I decided almost at once to get a taxi to the hospital and meet her there. Walking directly into the bathroom, I stripped off and glanced at myself in the mirror. Then for the second time that morning I took a hot shower, ran a comb quickly through my hair and as an afterthought, brushed my teeth. The smell of rum would still be on my breath and I certainly didn't want that!

I pulled on fresh clothes, picked up my keys and wallet and I was ready.

I waited for Lucia at the maternity department of the hospital and in less than half an hour she emerged from a doorway in deep conversation with a woman in a white coat.

The woman smiled, put a reassuring hand on Lucia's arm and then turned back into the consulting room. I stood up and she saw me almost at once, giving me a broad joyful grin.

She hurried across the waiting room and threw her arms around me planting a kiss on my cheek.

'Harry! Are you ok? I was so worried!'

'Sure no problem, but what about you? How did it go?'

'Fine Harry, everything ok __an' i's a boy!'

'A *boy* Lucia!' I remarked almost in disbelief.

My heart jumped and I felt an instant sense of elation, my current problems forgotten momentarily.

It was a boy, but if she had said it was a girl no doubt I would have felt the same reaction. Perhaps the defining statement gave the whole question of Lucia's pregnancy a sort of new reality somehow that hadn't quite registered before.

Whatever it was I felt a sense of sheer happiness.

She stared up at me with those wonderful brown eyes and once again I was completely swept away.

'Lucia that's wonderful sweetheart! Lets get out of here, I need a drink now!'

'I can't drink Harry.'

'No I'm forgetting. A drink of something though, come on lets go!'

We stopped at the first bar we came to and Lucia had some orange juice while I got a large whiskey.
'I's not like you to drink whiskey carino!'
She commented, with a look that was mildly humourous rather than critical.
'Special occasion love! __And everything's ok yes? I mean__'
'Sure, like I say! Nothin' to worry about.'
She looked at me seriously.
'But you Harry! Why you so late geddin' back? I was really worried about you.'
Suddenly I was back to earth with a jarring thump.
I couldn't make something up. Lucia knew me better than anyone and was not easily fooled. Better just to tell her the whole story however reluctant I felt, and in what should have been a special moment.
I told her the whole story, leaving out nothing and she listened in horror as I explained what had happened to the man who had accompanied me, and then with rapt attention as I explained how Raul had met me at sea in the coast guard vessel.
'He said nothing to me about this carino!'
'No I expect not. __Understandably I suppose.'
'I knew something was wrong Harry, as soon as I saw you!'
I grinned ruefully.
'You know me better than I know myself sweetheart.'
'But this is terrible Harry!'
'It certainly is. Raul told me not to worry, but__'
'The poor guy, what was his name?'
'Carlos, that's what he said anyway, but who knows?'
'An' you didn' hear nuthin?'
'No, I was out of it, totally! It was as though I'd been drugged.'
'But by who Harry?'
'Y' got me there honey!'
'An' you think you know where this place is?'
'Can't be sure, but it's as near as I can figure out.
Raul said he was going to search the area. Even if he finds it, it doesn't prove very much.'
'No I guess not carino.'
'The point is Lucia, I think that this guy was working for Cuban intelligence, so they're going to be asking me a lot of questions.
I was the last one to see him alive remember!'
She gave me a gentle smile.
'Harry you couldn't kill anyone.'
'Let's hope they see it that way!'

I suddenly felt low and very depressed. She must have sensed this and took my hand tightly in hers.

'Raul will speak for you Harry. He is a powerful man to have as a frien' and he also knows everythin' about this gun-runnin' game that is being played out. I's not your fault! __Any of this carino!'

I let out a sigh and threw back the rest of the whiskey.

'No I suppose you're right love. We'll just have to wait and see what happens now.'

She pulled me closer and put her lips close to my ear.

'I tell you what 'appens now hombre. We go back to the apartment an' I make love to you, how does that sound?'

'That's a good idea Lucia. I could be banged up for some time!'

It was a total and wonderful diversion, and for an hour, that in Lucia's arms seemed timeless, I forgot about everything else. Hearing her soft urgent cries and feeling the intense movement of her body pressing against me, engulfing us both in a compelling mutual rapture.

In the warm afternoon air, cooled only slightly by the leisurely spin of the ceiling fan, we lay next to each other in total peace, the incidental and intermittent sounds from the paseo floating up through the open window. In seconds we were both asleep.

At four in the afternoon I was woken by the sound of the phone.

It was Raul and in a split second I was sitting up on the edge of the bed, the instrument pressed against my ear, while Lucia stirred lazily behind me.

'Harry! Good, you're at home. Is it possible to call on you now at the apartment?'

'How soon is 'now' Raul, I've only just woken up!'

'Tranquilo my friend!'

There was distinct humour in his tone.

'Is half an hour long enough for you to recover from your siesta?'

'Er, yeah sure Raul. We'll see you soon then.'

I hung up.

'Wha' does he want carino?'

Lucia murmured sleepily.

'Well that's probably easy to guess! He'll be here in thirty minutes!'

'Thirdy minutes! Oh shit!'

She remarked, sitting up at once, the sheet falling away from her beautiful firm breasts that were even more prominent now because of her condition.

'I better get tidied up, __an' I need a shower.'

I smiled at her.

'So do I!'

'Ok, but me first chico!'
With an excited squeal she raced to the bathroom with me in close pursuit of her naked body.

Half an hour later the ancient electric door-bell rang out with its nerve shattering racket that was more than sufficient to wake the dead, and I made yet another mental resolution to get it changed. Lucia answered it, there were brief murmured greetings and then Raul appeared in the doorway of the lounge.
I got to my feet at once, nervous without knowing exactly why.
'Raul, come in, please. Can we get you a drink?'
'Sure, a beer Harry, thanks.'
Lucia, who was directly behind him, went off on cue to the kitchen.
'Have a seat Raul.'
Still unaccountably nervous I asked him the question already poised in my mind.
'Did you find the place? The bay, the mooring point I mean?'
He dropped into an armchair.
'No Harry we didn't find it!'
'Oh right, well it was a bit of a long shot I suppose.'
'We covered about ten kilometers along the coast, but there was nothing. __Nothing that we could see anyway.'
'No. Like I said, it was just a rough guess really.'
I glanced at him.
'You do believe the story though? My story I mean!'
'Yes. I don't have one good reason not to. __And as you said yourself if we had located the place it's unlikely to provide us with any evidence.'
'So what now Raul?'
'So now __thanks Lucia.'
He took the can of beer from Lucia's outstretched hand.
'So now I will contact the authorities and give them my report.
The point is Harry they know you were both working together and that you had absolutely no motive at all to take his life.
Together with my recommendation, this should leave you completely in the clear.'
He popped the lid of the can and took a sip.
'The other thing that occurred to me during our search was that the people, the government group that the man Carlos worked for, may know something about this. If they do it's unlikely that they will share such information with me, an ordinary cop.'
'No maybe you're right Raul. Who knows what these bloody people get up to.'

'So as I said before I don't think you need to worry too much. If they want to talk to you, I shall insist that I'm there to support your story.'
'Thanks Raul'

He broke into his usual broad grin and took a long pull from the can.
'I've got to say that your wife looks very beautiful Harry, this child bearing condition seems to agree with her!'
Now it was Lucia's turn to smile.
'So far Raul. No sickness yet, well no' much anyway, an' no' much evidence that I am embarazarda!'
She ran a hand over her smoothly rounded belly.
'In a month or two maybe, then I start to make this man's life a misery!'
She put her arm around my waist as she spoke.
'An' I's gonna be a boy Raul.'
'A boy! That's wonderful! Felicidades to both of you.'
With another long gulp he finished the beer.
'Ok! So, I must leave you now. Like I say don't worry about this Harry. I will let you know what's happening.'
He stood up.
'Thanks for the beer. __And visit us soon at my house yes!'
'We will Raul, that's a promise.'
I took his proffered hand and walked him to the door.
'Adios amigo. I'll see you soon.'
He remarked with another reassuring smile. Then he was gone.
I waited as I listened to the echoing sound of his footsteps on the wide staircase and then the sound of the door on the lower level as it opened and then closed again, then I pushed the door to the apartment slowly until the lock clicked and walked back thoughtfully to the living room.

'What's up Harry?'
Lucia asked as I slumped into a chair.
'Nothing love.'
'Don' tell me nothing chico, I know when you got somethin' on your mind.'
'No it's nothing love, just__'
I shrugged.
'Jus' what? Come on Harry, you' thinkin' about somethin'!'
'Yes I suppose I was, __I mean maybe it is something, or maybe I've got it wrong.'
'So?'
She looked at me expectantly.
'I don't think he's being truthful!'

'You mean Raul!'
'Yes love.'
'Harry, Raul is a good man, why would he lie to you?'
'I don't know. I'm not even sure that he is.'
'Carino, you' talkin' roun' in circles!'
'I know Lucia, I know I am.'
She seemed about to interrupt again.
'Look I know it was just a guess ok. I can't really be sure where this bay, or this inlet or whatever, I mean where it's located exactly. The place where it seems to me at least that Carlos was most probably killed. I searched on the chart and measured it as near as I could, but__'
I hesitated again.
'But what Harry? You got it wrong, an' tha's all!'
'But *did* I get it wrong? Ok it was dark, *very* dark in fact. The thing is I just have a feeling in my bones that it was the right location.
It matched the position on the map, ok, almost matched and __well as I said, I just have this gut feeling somehow.
'Carino you heard what Raul said, he searched the coastline for ten kilometres!'
'I know what he said. I'm just __ I don't know.'
'A bit confused maybe Harry?'
'No I'm not confused Lucia, I'm__'
I pushed myself up out of the chair and walking over to the window, stared down at the peaceful avenue below with its double line of trees, at pedestrians taking a leisurely stroll along the marble paved area at the centre.
Some dancers were out again and, detached for a moment, I watched them in their precise rhythmic movements to the subdued sound of salsa music.
'Something isn't right somehow, I'm sure of it.'
I murmured, turning back to face her.
It was her turn to shrug her shoulders.
'Ok, but what can you do about it?'
Her question remained unanswered as, once again in my head, I went through the events of the previous night.
'I'll tell you what I'm going to do, I'm going back there tomorrow and I'm going to find this bloody place!'
Lucia protested at once.
'Harry no! Tha's loco carino. Even if you find it, what are you gonna do then?'
'I don't know. Yes maybe it is crazy, but I want to prove to Raul that the place exits!'

'He believes your story honey, so why do you *care*. That coasta has a thousand places like you describe and I believe Raul when he say tha' they couldn' find it. Why would he lie Harry?'
'I don't know if he is lying, or indeed why he should lie. Maybe he's right, maybe they did search, who can say for certain. I just know I have to find it, that's all Lucia. I'm leaving on the boat tomorrow!'
'Then I'm coming with you.'
'Absolutely not! No way Lucia! Apart from the fact that you've got the little one to care about now I'm not going to put you in harm's way.'
'Don' be crazy Harry. You said yourself that the place was deserted. That there was nothing there to see.'
'I don't care. You're not coming and that's it!'
'Don' argue with me hombre! We are going together or you' not going at all. __Claro!'
She gazed at me with that look that she had and staring back at her I knew that I couldn't win. If Lucia made her mind up about something then that was that. She was nothing if not strong-willed, maybe it was one of the reasons I cared about her so much.
My shoulders slumped forward, not physically exactly, but certainly in some kind of subliminal resignation. There was no point in starting a row, which I knew I would lose.
I'm sure I've mentioned already that Lucia was pretty bright.
To be fair, there was no logical reason why she shouldn't come with me on a trip that was hardly fraught with any apparent danger, so there was no point in arguing. Instead I smiled at her.

'Ok love, no reason why you shouldn't, I was just __I don't know, being protective I suppose.'
She walked across and put her arms around me.
'I love you Harry!'
'I know you do, and I love you sweetheart.'
I held her close, someone who was more precious to me than I could ever possibly evaluate.
'Early start tomorrow, it's at least five hours on the boat to where I think it might be.'
'Sure Harry, we leave whenever you say.'

I wasn't quite sure why I was going on this trip, or expedition, call it whatever.
Although I suppose that even if Raul was prepared to support me in whatever enquiry was going to be initiated by the Cuban authorities and

would, I was quite certain, back up my account of what had happened, I had to confirm in my own mind that this episode had actually occurred and that I hadn't, in someone else's eyes at least, dreamed up the whole story, which now, a mere twenty four hours later, might appear to have a definite element of fantasy. I had woken up on the boat in an unknown location, came up on deck in the dead of night to find a dead body and that was it! A deserted bay with a decaying wooden jetty, no buildings of any sort, no one else around, no one I could see at least and no apparent reason for the man's death.

Was it all just a bad dream? Not to me and I was determined to discover the mysterious mooring point in the middle of nowhere if it took all day and perhaps even the next.

We set out early the next morning.
I left a message with Pasqual at the café to say that we had an unexpected charter and might be away for a day or so.
I also made sure that the radio was turned off. I didn't want anyone, even Raul, to contact me and perhaps cause a premature end to the search.
It was another spectacular Caribbean sunrise, impossible to adequately describe even after having spent any length of time in that part of the world. It's one of those things that you just have to see for yourself, but when you do it will then stay in your memory forever.

The boat pushed its way happily through a light sea, with the occasional deluge of spray from a rogue wave that burst over the bow and caught by a gusting breeze drenched the windscreen, momentarily obscuring our progress until it was cleared by the wipers,
We took turns at the helm for the next five hours and arrived just after midday at more or less the position I had marked on the chart. Pulling back the throttle lever until the boat was iding slowly through the water. I scanned first the map and then the shoreline, focusing carefully with binoculars.
'Can you see anything Harry?'
Lucia asked.
'No not really! We'll have to get in a little closer. If you steer I'll keep a lookout. To be honest love it's a bit like needle in a haystack, but anyway we have to try.'
And try we did. For the next three hours we cruised back and forth at little more than a kilometre or so from the ragged coast.

We stopped our search for a short while, dropped the anchor close inshore and had a quick meal before continuing the tedious routine, widening our search area with each return trip.

By six oclock I was beginning to lose hope of ever finding the narrow entrance to the bay. Lucia was very patient and kept the boat on course close to shore calling out our position occasionally from the sat-nav.

I lowered the binoculars and turned to give her a somewhat rueful grin.

'Not having much luck are we love!'

I commented.

'Don' worry carino. If we don' find it today we try again tomorrow.'

'Yeah I suppose so. It's here somewhere Lucia, I didn't just imagine all this.'

'Of course you didn't Harry, I know that. This is a pretty deserted part of the coast, nuthin' much here excep' rocks an' a thousand little ensenadas, but we keep tryin'.'

'Ensenadas?'

'Yeah, like little sheltered places where you can tie up a boat.'

'Right! Well that's what we're looking for. __How much coast have we covered now?'

She glanced at the chart.

'Abou' fifteen kilometres!'

'Then maybe we missed it! I'm sure that it was somewhere around this area, I just have this feeling somehow.'

Lucia slowed the vessel to a walking pace.

'Will I turn the boat 'round again Harry? Like you say, maybe you missed it!'

'Might as well love, we've got another hour or two of daylight.'

We started back towards the east at low speed.

I felt tired now and my eyes were smarting from the constant surveillance of the coastline.

With a resigned sigh I lifted the binoculars again and began to scan the shoreline with its background of undulating hills, now divided up into ragged segments of dark shade, in contrast to similar areas illuminated in a bright orange glow by the diminishing rays of the sun that was now on its daily downward trajectory towards the horizon.

Lowering the glasses again I cleaned the eye-pieces carefully on the edge of my tee-shirt. Then I began once again to scan the shoreline a mere kilometer or two in the near distance.

Again I lowered the lenses, gazing at a remote section of land for a moment before raising them again, focusing carefully on a particular spot.

'Lucia! Head towards there!'

I pointed to where white crested waves could just about be seen breaking against a darkened outcrop of land.
Lucia turned the wheel and pointed the boat in the direction I had indicated.
Hurrying to the prow of the vessel I lifted the glasses again.
There was a break in the constantly changing line of surf. A narrow section of untroubled water no more than perhaps ten or maybe fifteen metres across.
As we drew nearer it was clear that there was an opening of some kind, a break in the rocky shoreline almost impossible to see at a distance because of the dark featureless terrain, a continual backdrop of low cliffs, strewn with jagged boulders where they met the sea.

Within a few minutes it was clear that it was an entrance to a small cove, through which soon after, Lucia carefully steered the boat.
In the clear light of early evening I could see that the narrow portal widened out into a small bay no more than a hundred metres wide. At the far end of the sheltered area of placid sea a dilapidated jetty jutted out into the crystal clear water.
In minutes we drew alongside.
'This is it love, I'm certain!'
I called up to her.
Cautiously I stepped over onto worn mildewed planks that seemed barely able to support their own weight, tying up the boat at wooden piles that also appeared to be in imminent danger of collapse.

Back on board, Lucia took the steps down to the lower deck and carefully clambered over the side and onto jetty, She immediately put her arms around me, giving me an affectionate hug.
'You were right Carino.'
She gazed up at me with a broad smile and swept her fingers briefly through my hair.
'I was, wasn't I! __ Bit worried there for a while, but there it is.'
I glanced around the small bay sheltered on two sides by steep cliffs.
'That night it was dark of course, I mean like really black, but I'm convinced that this is the place.'
As I recalled, the jetty ended on a clearing, a dusty patch of flat land from which a track led away up through a breach in the hills.
But now in the clear light of day I could see a cluster of run down wooden shacks, backing on to the cliffs and now quite obviously deserted.
'Maybe it was used for fishing at some point.'
I mumbled almost to myself.

'Maybe. So what now Harry?'
'I dunno! We could look at the map I suppose, it might indicate where we are. There must be something at the other end of that track.'

We both scrutinized large-scale charts of the area, spreading them out on the table in the lower cabin.
The bay was clearly indicated and coincided with the sat-nav reading. It was little more than a few kilometres from the position I had originally marked.
I chewed my bottom lip.
'Easy to see how Raul missed it love. Not easy to spot from a distance.'
'No, tha's for sure Harry!'
Lucia remarked, leaning across the table as she studied the maps.
'See here! This dosn' show the camino, the er__'
'The trail you mean, the pathway.'
'Yeah, but it looks like there is a pueblo abou' maybe three or four kilometres inland.'
She pointed with her finger.
'San Sebastion it says. No' much there it dosn' look like.'
'No. As you say, it's just a small village.'
I heaved a deep sigh.
'It doesn't really tell us very much, does it Lucia. And really we're still in the dark about the whole sodding thing! For instance, why would Carlos bring the boat here? He obviously intended to meet someone and then got shot for his trouble. None of it makes any sense!'
Lucia began to fold the maps.
'Let's get out of here Harry. I got a bad feelin' abou' this place!' 'Yeah so have I love. There's obviously nothing around here, no sign of life or anything else come to that! So yeah you're right, let's get going, it'll be dark in an hour.'

I released the boat from the rickety mooring and Lucia reversed the vessel out into the bay before turning and heading directly towards the break in the cliffs and out into the open sea.
I'm sure I wasn't alone in heaving a sigh of relief at leaving what was a remote and somehow ominous place.

'Well at least we found it love, and at least I proved that I'm not crazy!'
'No one say you was crazy Harry.'
'Maybe not, but it's a relief nevertheless.'
'Are you goin' to tell Raul about this?'
'I suppose so. No good reason not to tell him.'

For a while we were both silent.
With Lucia at the helm the boat surged through the water on the return journey to Havana, which I reckoned would take us all of six hours.
'Do you want a drink honey?'
I asked her.
'Sure, some tea would be nice.'
I started down towards the rear deck as daylight began to fade.
'An' somethin' to eat carino!'
She called out.
'Ok, if I can find something.'
I busied myself with heating up water and finding some mugs, searching in the bag we had bought with us for any remaining food.
While I waited for the kettle to boil I opened up the chart on the table again and glanced at the little inlet we had found, circling it with a pencil. For a long moment I was deep in thought.
I carried hot tea and the rest of the food to the upper deck and set them on the shelf in front of the controls.
From behind us there was just a faint glow from the sun, now well below the horizon. In front of us the night sky was infused with stars and a full moon, its image glittering on the surface of the sea and providing us with a clear view of our way ahead.
'Tea love! __Drink it while it's hot.'
I urged her.
Lucia reached out and picked up a mug. Blowing on the contents she sipped carefully from the edge.
'I been thinkin' Harry!'
'What about?'
'About this trip we're makin'.'
'Go on.'
'I don' think we should tell anyone about it. __No' yet anyway.'
'Well that's odd because I've been thinking exactly the same thing.'
She turned to look at me, a quick sidelong glance.
'I don' think we should say anythin', not to no one!'
'No. __I agree with you.'
'No' to Raul either.'
'Ok we won't. There's something fishy here somewhere and it would be wise to keep this to ourselves, for now at least until we can find out what the hell is going on.'
I hoisted myself up into the comfortable seat next to Lucia and settled back into the leather upholstery.
'Raul said quite clearly that he couldn't find the inlet.'
'Well we find it ok carino, __didn' we! Maybe we got lucky!'

'Yeah, maybe.'
I lapsed into thought again.
The constant rhythmic sound of the engine together with the slight roll of the vessel in the waves was mesmerizing and I soon felt my eyelids drooping.
'Honey, why don' you sleep for a while. I's been a long day for you.' Lucia remarked.
'I can wake you in a coupla' hours.'
'That's not such a bad idea. Are you ok on your own up here?'
'Sure, why not! __Get some sleep Harry.'
I made my way below and dropped into a bunk bed.
The long hours of constantly searching the coastline had taken its toll and within seconds I was dead to the world.

We arrived back in Havana at three in the morning, gliding quietly across the surface of the harbour towards the dock, tying up finally in our usual place.
Lucia was understandably dog tired by now, and outside the fenced off area of the docks we waited, huddled together on a bench seat, for a passing taxi, one of many that seemed to prowl the streets of the city at all hours of the night and day.
I paid off the cab and with my arm around Lucia's waist I helped her up the staircase to our apartment and then into our bed.
With barely a murmur she was almost instantly sound asleep.

I was up at nine o'clock the same morning and slid quietly out of bed so as not to wake Lucia.
Making myself some coffee I stood by the kitchen window staring down at the already busy paseo, barely noticing the constant and familiar movement of people and vehicles as I though about our previous day's adventure, wondering yet again why it was that Raul had not discovered the mysterious deserted inlet.
He had more resources and more men to scan the coast surely, or maybe we really had just been lucky!
My heart jumped in fright as Lucia's arms suddenly closed around my waist.
'*Jesus* you scared me love!'
I turned to look down at her lovely face smiling up at me and into those wonderful clear brown eyes.
'I'm sorry carino, I didn' mean to. __Come back to bed Harry, I need you to make love to me.'

I smiled back at once.
'Sure. Now that you're awake, what better way to start the day!'

As always we made love with what always seemed insatiable hunger and with a fierce intensity.
I came quickly and copiously inside her, with Lucia reaching her climax almost in the same moment uttering a long deep sigh, her fingertips digging painfully into my back.
We lay exhausted in each other's arms while I kissed her face and her smooth forehead, feeling the most profound love for this incredible and most beautiful woman, who I felt certain and not for the first time, was surely a gift from the Gods.

We slept for another hour or two and it was midday when I finally rolled out of bed.
'I'd better walk across to the café honey, just to see what's going on.'
I remarked as I pulled on a pair of trousers.
'Pasqual will be there Harry, don' worry abou' things.'
'Even so, I'll just look in briefly and pick up some bread for us at the same time.'
'Ok, __you' the boss!'
She said with a broad smile.
'Oh I doubt it!'
I replied and leaning over the bed I kissed her gently.
'Won't be long love.'

The café was as busy as always. Consuelo was hurrying around the tables and gave me a brief wave.
Pasqual was behind the bar serving up drinks to thirsty Americans who now seemed to gravitate to our little watering hole. Maybe word had got around.
'What would you like Harry?'
Pasqual asked cheerfully.
'Just some bread, __for a late breakfast.'
I added.
'How did the fishing go yesterday?'
'Bien, mas o menos Pasqual.'
'Did you have a good catch?'
'Couple of medium sized Marlin that was all.'
'Mmm. Were you late getting back Harry?'
He asked again, shoving a fresh baguette into a bag.
'Yeah we were a bit. Hence the late start this morning.'

"Nosey bugger." I thought, chiding myself at once. Yes, he was a bit of an old woman, a magnet for gossip and the small intrigue, but he was a good guy and was almost indispensible now as a manager.
'Someone came in earlier asking for you!'
He remarked with a conspiratorial look.
'Asking for Me?'
There was no need for me to feign surprise.
'Yeah, your friend the policeman.'
'Well he's not exactly a friend Pasqual. What did he want?'
'Just to talk with you I think. I said you were both out fishing all of yesterday and would probably need a rest this morning.'
'Well that was true anyway! I'll give him a call later. Thanks Pasqual.'
'No problem Harry, see you later.'

What did Raul want, I wondered.
Crossing the paseo I let myself into the building.
I resolved to call him as soon as we had eaten, however that wasn't necessary.
When I entered the apartment I heard voices at once. The nearest door in the narrow passageway led into the kitchen and that's where the talking was coming from.

'Buen dias Harry!'
Raul looked immaculate as always in his police chief's uniform, his peaked cap rested on the kitchen table where he was seated and he presented his usual broad smile from beneath the large, carefully trimmed mustache.
'Hi Raul, nice to see you.'
I passed the bread to Lucia and took a vacant seat opposite while she passed a cup of fresh coffee to me.
'How was the fishing amigo?'
'Oh not bad. We caught a medium sized. __They were novices, the yanks!'
'Two Harry! Lucia corrected me quickly.'
I recovered seamlessly.
'Was it, __yeah maybe it was. Hardly worth the effort though, it was a bloody long day Raul!'
'Yes, Lucia told me. Never mind Harry, you got paid, so!'
He shrugged his broad shoulders.
'You wan' more coffee Raul?'
Lucia asked him.
'Si, gracias chica!'
I interjected as she poured into his cup from the cafetierre.

'Went over to the café for some bread. Pasqual said that you'd called in there this morning Raul.'
'Yes I did, about ten o'clock. He said you had probably got back late last night so I left you both to rest.'
I smiled at him.
'Well thanks for that mate, we were too tired for anything this morning after our trip yesterday.'
Lucia, who was leaning against the stove directly behind Raul, gave me a sly grin, raising her eyebrows twice in rapid succession as she sipped from her cup.
I had to struggle to keep a straight face.
'So yeah we had a good lay-in. We needed the sleep.'
'I'm sure you did amigo. Tha's why I left you in peace.'
I took a sip of the hot coffee.
'So was it important Raul?'
'Probably my friend, although maybe it's good news.'
'Really! __Incidentally have you heard anything about erm__'
Now it was my turn for raised eyebrows.
'Yeah, tha's the main reason I'm here. You don' have to answer to the intelligence people about the death of the man on your boat, Carlos Roldan.
I spoke to them yesterday an' explain' everything.'
'I see! __Well that's a bloody relief. Raul'
'I told you not to worry, did I not! Because of all the current circumstances there can be no accusations against you.'
'Well, like I say that's really very good news.'
'I tried to call you yesterday evening on the radio to tell you, but I couldn't get a response.'
'That's because the radio is buggered Raul! __Lucia spilt a mug of tea over it.'
He laughed at once.
'These things happen amigo!'
'They certainly do. __So what with the two dumb-arsed Americans it was not a very successful day!'
'No pasa nada Harry!'
'No Raul, as you say.'
He finished his coffee and stood up.
'I must get going.'
He picked up his cap from the table.
'But before I forget, I must invite you to our home on Friday if that's ok. For dinner that is! My wife is looking forward very much to seeing you both again.'

'Well thanks again Raul, that's very kind. Of course we'll be there.'
I glanced at Lucia.
'Yes love?'
'Sure, that would be lovely Raul. Please tell thanks from us to Maria.'
'Good. Eight o'clock, __ok?'
I stood up and we shook hands warmly.
'Great Raul, and thank you __for the other business as well.'
Lucia walked him to the door. There was a brief exchange between them and then he was gone.

'He was right. That was good news for you Harry!'
Lucia remarked as she took the chair that Raul had vacated.
'I s'pose it is love. __Er, he didn't ask__'
'No Harry of course not, How could he know what we were doing? I think we are right to keep silent about this, for now anyway carino!'
'Yes I'm sure you're right.'
I bit at my bottom lip.
'It's a complete bloody mystery love, this whole business.
And we have to try and find out somehow exactly what the hell is going on!'
'How?'
I swept my hand over my head.
'*That* I don't have an answer to!'

The next few days passed quickly. Lucia wanted to get a new dress for our planned visit to Raul's house on Friday evening.
The slight bulge that contained our unborn child was not really that prominent, but her small collection of clothes were becoming uncomfortably tight. So, on her insistence, I accompanied her on the quest to find something new. We visited several stores in central Havana, and I made a supreme effort not to look bored as she tried on one item of clothing after another.
I finally had to admit that the black dress she eventually settled for made her look even more beautiful than before, if that was at all possible.
'Why don' you get something for yourself as well Harry?'
She asked me as we paid for the dress.
'Why, am I putting on weight as well?'
She smiled and pushed a finger into my belly.
'Jus' a little chico!'

I bought a new shirt, not because I particularly needed one, but more to please Lucia than anything else.
'Can I get some new shoes as well Harry?'
'Course you can, get whatever you like sweetheart!'
I remarked, pulling her close for a moment.
Our little shopping trip over with, we got a cab back to the apartment.
We had a light lunch and then a couple of hour's siesta, leaving plenty of time to get ready for our visit to Raul later that evening.

It was only the second time that I had met Raul's wife, Maria, a tall slim woman who, although attractive, had a detached, haunted look. It was plainly obvious, in spite of any attempt she might have made to conceal it, that her grief at the loss of her eldest daughter was still clearly palpable. Lucia greeted her with the utmost affection and the two women embraced for several moments as Lucia whispered a few quiet words to her.
Raul stood quietly and perhaps with a slight feeling of embarrassment, which could certainly be compared to my own.
Then.
'Come inside both of you.'
Raul announced cheerfully, closing the front door to the house.
'We need a drink now I believe.'
'Good idea Raul!'
I hastened to agree.
'Where is your young daughter? __Er, Juanita isn't it?'
'She is in her room studing for school Harry. She'll be down soon. What will you have my friend?'
He ushered us into the small room at the rear of the house.
'Whatever you're having Raul. As long as it contains alcohol!'

The dinner was a limited success, Raul's wife was, on the face of it at least, cheerful. And, with what must have been a distinct effort, quite talkative. Their daughter joined us after a while and it was sheer pleasure to listen to the young girl's intelligent and amusing anecdotes, about her school and about her friends, all held in very passable English.
'I'm surprised that you're taught the language of us dreadful capitalists in your school Juanita!'
I said to her.
'Not all capitalists are bad Harry!'
She commented.
'For instance, you are not a bad person.'
Her comment caused immediate laughter from all of us.

'I don' think so anyway, __an' neither did my sister.'
There was more laughter, if slightly subdued this time.
'So is that what she said?'
I pressed her.
'Sure! An' she said that Lucia was lucky to have you for a husband.'
Even more laughter followed her innocent, but perhaps not so naïve comment.
'Well I certainly agree with that Juanita. Your sister was obviously very observant.'
I winked at Lucia as I spoke.
'But of course I was very lucky as well!'
Raul refilled my glass with red wine.
'My daughter, as you can see Harry, is very aware, not to say outspoken.'
He commented.
'I think she will be a politician one day.'
'No papa. Politicians do not tell the truth!'
Again there was genuine mirth all round at the small girl's incisive remark.
'Ok Carino, maybe you're right.'
Her father said with quite obvious pride at his daughter's erudite comments.
'But right now Juanita it's time to say goodnight to everyone.'
'Papa no, please, it's not late, an' I don' have school tommorow!'
'But you do have basketball practice at eight o'clock carina.'
He countered.
Her mother intervened gently.
'Papa is right Juanita, you don' want to miss that, do you!'
With a reluctant good night and a special embrace for Lucia she left us, with her mother accompanying her to her room.
The three of us continued to discuss general topics, primarily about Cuba and the dire economic situation that faced the country.
On a lighter note I spoke to Raul.
'Your daughter's a good kid. Very bright as well! __How old is she Raul?'
'Nine years, __ten in a couple of months.'
He sipped reflectively from his glass.
'How the time passes so quickly Harry! It is difficult to believe it.'
There was an awkward silence, and it seemed that perhaps he was thinking about his eldest daughter. However his cheerful manner returned quickly, as soon as his wife could be heard descending the stairs.
'Another drink Harry?'
Before I could respond he had poured more wine into my glass.
'But not for you Lucia, no?'
'No gracias Raul, one glass only for me now.'

He turned to his wife as she took her seat again.
'Esta ella bien Maria? Esta durmiendo?'
'Todavia no, pero pronto pienso.'
She replied.
He stood up.
'Will you please excuse for a moment. I need a cigarette, but my wife disapproves of this inside the house, __so!'
He shrugged.
To murmured agreement he left the room, and I could hear as he let himself out into the small garden at the rear of the house.
His wife's English was limited, but she gazed after him with an expression of concern.
'I want him not to smoke these things, pero__'
She lifted her hands in an expression of resignation.
Lucia smiled and spoke with her in rapid Spanish of which I understood only a word or two. Then she turned to me.
'Maria worries, and she is right of course, but Raul is Raul and he loves his cigarettes. Maybe you can talk to him Harry?'
'*Me!* Why would he listen to me for God's sake?'
'Because you are his friend!'
'Lucia, I'm hardly his friend, now am I!'
'Maria thinks that you are!'
She glanced at me with that look that she had that defied any discussion.
'Oh all right then love, but Raul is his own man as you said yourself, __but ok, I'll do my best.'
Lucia spoke again to Raul's wife, a conversation that was impossible for me to follow.
'Sorry Carino, I was saying that they should take a holiday somewhere, an' that we could look after Juanita, for a few days at least.'
'Sure why not, no problem.'
She turned to the woman again, continuing in the same indecipherable fashion.
'He is always busy, Maria says.'
'Well he can spare a few days surely, I should think they could both do with a break after, __well you know.'
'I have said that Harry, but she say' it's no easy for him. He visit his brother earlier this week, but only for one night.'
'Oh right! I didn't know he had a brother.'
Again they spoke together for a few moments.
'Older brother. An' she couldn't go because of Juanita.'
'No I suppose not. __Look I'll speak to the man, not just about the fags, but about taking a holiday with his wife.

And you were right Lucia, of course we can look after his daughter for a while, certainly for a week at least.
Once again they engaged in rapid and lengthy conversation, but when Lucia turned to me again she had a guarded, perhaps cautionary look and fixed me with directly with her eyes.
'Maria say that you have a good plan Harry, about a vacation. She ask also if you could explain to Raul, __about his smokin' as well.'
'Well I'll certainly try love. No guarantee of success, but I will speak to him.'
'Speak to who Harry?'
Raul had suddenly appeared in the doorway.
'Oh, you weren't supposed to hear that mate! There's a bit of a conspiracy going on here.'
Raul took his seat and lifting the wine bottle he refilled his glass and mine.
'Lucia suggested that you and Maria should have a holiday somewhere.'
'I see, and what about our daughter? She has her school to attend.'
'We'll look after her for a few days. For a week if you like. It'll be a nice break for you both Raul.'
He pursed his lips and then nodded slowly.
'Yes, it is a good idea, but are you sure you don' mind caring for Juanita.'
'Sure Raul!'
Lucia interrupted.
'Of course! Your daughter an' me are good frien's now. You don' need to worry about her. She will be safe with us.'
Again he nodded thoughtfully.
'Vale! I will think about this, like you say, it's not such a bad idea.'
'Good. Sorted then Raul. So just let us know when."
'I will Harry and thanks!'
'Well it was Lucia's idea, so she can take the blame if it all goes wrong. Right love?'
I grinned at her, but her response was muted somehow.
'Sure Harry.'
She remarked quietly, turning then to our host.
'Raul, would you mind so much if we leave you now. I'm feelin' a bit tired. Maybe it was the trip yesterday, an' also this little guy in here!'
She passed a hand over her stomach.
Raul looked instantly concerned.
'No no, of course not Lucia. I will call for a taxi.'
'Are you ok love, you do look a bit weary.'
'I'm fine Harry, but like I say, jus' a bit tired.'

Raul phoned for a cab and shortly afterwards, with hasty "thank you's" and a long embrace from Maria for both of us we were quickly taking the short flight of steps down to the street and to the waiting taxi, with Raul and his wife waving us off from the open doorway.

'You ok love?'
I asked with concern as the cab pulled away.
'Sure Harry. As a matter of fact I do feel tired, but there is somethin' else!'
'Something else?'
I turned to her on the back seat, instantly curious.
'Yeah! I tell you when we get back, ok.'
'Of course love. __Are you sure you're alright, It's not that far to the hospital from here, I mean__'
She smiled and kissed me lightly.
'No Carino, we go back to the apartment, then I explain to you.'

It was quite chilly when we arrived back at the paseo.
I put my arm around her waist and Lucia leaned against me as we ascended the stairs to our apartment.
I got her seated in the corner of the sofa and covered her with a warm decorated overlay from our bed. Then I made her some tea and brought it in for her.
'That better love?'
I asked, tucking the blanket around her legs.
'Sure, I'm ok Harry, don' fuss carino.'
'I'm not fussing, I'm just making you comfortable.'
She glanced up at me.
'Give me a kiss!'
I did so at once, a long wonderful kiss, filling me with pleasure and as always the same familiar longing.
'You looked beautiful tonight Lucia!'
I remarked with a distinct lump in my throat.
'Thank you Harry, __You know that I love you carino!'
'And I love you honey.'
I straightened up and then sat next to her on the sofa, clearing my throat in a feeble attempt to quench my desire for her, a desire that was never very far beneath the surface.
I had brought a can of beer for myself and took a strong pull.
'Ok, so what was on your mind in the taxi, and also when you were talking to Maria. Or I did I imagine that?'
'Yes, well you better prepare Harry, cos' this will shock you.'

She sipped at the mug of tea.
'When I was talking to Maria about, well about taking a vacation of some kind, she mention' somethin'.'
'Mentioned what?'
She said that Raul can never get away from his work, but earlier this week he went to stay with his brother for the night.'
'Yes, so you said.'
'His brother lives further east from here, about seventy kilometres.'
'Ok, so.'
'In a village called San Sebastion Harry!'

I felt as though I had been bludgeoned and for several moments I was unable to say anything, while Lucia continued to stare at me.
'Jesus bloody *Christ!*'
I finally managed in a subdued whisper.
'Yes Harry, San Sebastion! I'm no' so good with geography, but it is the only town or pueblo in Cuba with that name I think. Certainly close to Havana.'
I was still stunned as I took in what she had said, or tried to at least.
'Are you sure about this, about the date as well?'
'Yes Harry, I got her to repeat it because I said I never heard of the place.'
'Good God! But this sort of implies__'
'Yeah it does, er, what you said.'
'I mean __ this is crazy Lucia!'
'Yes, loco, you' right Harry.'
We were both silent, and *my* mind at least was in turmoil.
'We can't say anything about this to him!'
'No carino.'
I shook my head in disbelief.
'But why? I mean if he did, __ if he was responsible in some way. __ And who knows, maybe there were others with him.'
'Maybe there was.'
I put the beer can up to my mouth and emptied it.
'I need another of these.'
I said, getting up from where I'd been sitting.
'Do you want anything?'
She shook her head and I walked back into the kitchen.

A hundred things were racing through my mind, the most predominant of which was fear, fear for both of us whether it was justified or not.

When you are confronted with a perilous situation, which it most certainly was, and about which you know absolutely nothing, except that you are deeply involved, then fear is the primary and most dominant emotion.
I took another can from the fridge and returned to where Lucia was still sitting, tucked beneath the blanket.
'Well love, this is quite a shocker.'
I dropped onto the sofa again.
'What should we do now carino?'
'I don't have a bloody clue Lucia!'
'What is clue?'
'Er, it's um __pista__ I think.'
'Yeah pista is right.'
I popped the lid of the can and took a very long drink.
'Christ, now what?'
The comment was addressed primarily to myself.
'But *why* lucia? __It just doesn't make any sense!'
'No it doesn'.'
She murmured quietly.
I turned to where she was huddled in the corner of the sofa.
'It could all just be a huge coincidence sweetheart. I can't believe that Raul of all people__'
'No Harry, neither can I!'
I heaved a deep sigh and fell back into the cushions.
'But if Raul was __ I mean if it is a coincidence it's a very strange one. For him to be a mere three kilometres away and on the same night when all of this happened__'
Again I fell silent.
'We can't be sure of this Harry.'
'No we can't be sure it's true. It's just all this sheer bloody__ accident! __if that's what it is!
And supposing I'd woken up, what then?'
I shook my head in total confusion.
'These are the facts Lucia. Raul is just a few kilometres away on the very same night that I wake up on a boat to find a dead body! Then he say's that after an extensive search he can't find the place where I said it had it all happened. What do you make of all that?'
'I know what you' sayin' Harry, it's jus'__it's Raul! He's a good man, a friend, he help' us both.'
'Yes he has.'
I could do nothing other than agree with her.
'So what are you going to do carino?'
'I know what I'd like to do, and that's put us both on a boat to England!'

She gave me one of her typical smiles, her sense of humour never far below the surface.
'So I would like England, would I Harry?'
'I doubt it love. You'd be like a fish out of water.'
'A fish outa water! __I like that carino!'
Again she grinned, amused by the ancient aphorism.
'Like I say, I doubt very much that you would. __Like England I mean.'
Again we were silent, both preoccupied by this latest piece of knowledge, or was 'bomb-shell' a better expression.
If Raul had indeed shot this man dead, or at least been involved in some way, then why, for what reason?
The dead man, Carlos was probably involved in some way in state security, which essentially I suppose is what Raul also was!
No, it made no sense.
I turned the whole thing over and over in my mind until I couldn't think straight anymore.
'Right come on love. __Bed, before I go completely nuts! We'll think about all this tomorrow.'
I stood up again and with my hand beneath her arm I lifted her gently to her feet.
'Will you fetch me some water Harry?'
'Sure. You get into bed now. It's been a tiring evening. __For both of us!'

I had difficulty getting asleep. The revelation that Lucia had made was troubling to say the least.
Could it have all been pure chance? It hardly seemed likely and if Raul in a fully equipped coastguard boat couldn't find a small inlet on the coast, and we could?
No, something was most definitely wrong somewhere.
I had actually considered confiding in Raul about our discovery, that very same evening in fact.
I was distinctly relieved now that I hadn't.'
But then I knew the guy, didn't I, or so I thought!
It seems the only thing you can be certain about in life, is that you can't be certain about anything,
I turned over in bed again and again, carefully though so as not to wake Lucia who was sleeping soundly. Eventually I must have succumbed to tiredness and the final relief of deep slumber.

We we're up fairly early the next morning after an equally early night, and, even for me, a very deep sleep.

We spoke little as I got some breakfast ready for us both, absorbed perhaps with our own thoughts.
'Is that coffee strong enough?'
I asked her.
'Sure, it's fine.'
I shoved scrambled eggs and fried tomatoes on a plate and set it front of her.
'Do you want any bacon?'
'No gracias. This is fine Harry.'
I made some toast and put this on the table as well, then I took a chair opposite her.
'You not eatin' Harry?'
'No love. Not hungry really. I'll have a bit of this toast, that will do for me.'
I sipped at my coffee.
'Harry I can't believe that Raul was responsible for this. It jus' doesn' fit somehow.'
'Well it certainly fits! No question!'
'No, I mean I jus' don' believe he do that!'
'Well the evidence is pretty conclusive, isn't it Lucia.'
She breathed out heavily.
'I suppose so, but__'
'But what love?'
'I don' know, I jus' don' believe it tha's all!'
Again we lapsed into silence.
I was inclined to agree with her on an emotional level at least, quite strongly in fact although the evidence seemed irrefutable.
'Look! Don't say anything about this, not to anyone. Until we find some answers here we keep this to ourselves, ok love.'
'Sure Harry, my lips are closed, isn' that what you say?'
She gave me a weak smile.
'Near enough honey.'

I stood up and carried my mug of coffee across to the window, staring down at the paseo.
It was just after eight o'clock, it was Saturday, and consequently there wasn't very much going on.
I could see the café across the street between a break in the trees. It was closed and Pasqual wouldn't be along to open up for another hour. It was also raining, a light drizzle that gave a watery gleam to the marble paving at the centre of the paseo.

A woman strolled past, sheltering beneath an umbrella and with a small dog on a lead that trotted happily behind her seemingly unconcerned by the saturating weather.
The dog halted suddenly and began to pee contentedly against a tree, while the woman waited patiently. The animal sniffed briefly at its byproduct and apparently satisfied continued with its morning constitutional.
A taxi passed slowly, its tyres hissing across the drenched tarmac.
Then a woman appeared on the opposite side of the paseo, walking quickly from the direction of the central part of town.
She wore an anorak, the hood pulled up over her head that was bent forward against the rain.
She ducked under the sheltering stone arches, stopped at the door to the café and pulled back the hood. Taking keys from her pocket she wrestled for a moment with the lock, entered and closed the door behind her.
Seconds later the lights came on beyond the plate glass front of the café.

'Consuelo's just turned up.'
I murmured, loud enough for Lucia to hear.
'She's early Harry!'
'Yeah. Maybe there's some clearing up to do before she opens the cafe.'
I turned from the window and walked back to the table where Lucia was still eating her breakfast.
'Have some toast carino!'
'I will, probably cold now. I'll make some more and have a bit of bacon with it. _Now I'm hungry suddenly.'
I lit the stove, put a few slices of bacon in a pan and cut some bread, slipping the pieces into the toaster.

'So what next Harry?'
'What next! _Now there's a bloody good question.'
I pondered for a moment.
'When in doubt do nothing love! And more importantly *say* nothing. That's seems to be the only workable plan at the moment.'
'S'posin' Maria mention' to Raul about wha' she say to me. I mean about visitin' his brother in San Sebastion?'
I shrugged, turning over the bacon in the frying pan.
'So what? As far as Raul is concerned we have no idea where this place is or indeed where this mysterious bay is, come to that.
At the moment that's our little secret.'
'Yeah I guess you' right Harry.'
I turned to her with what I hoped was a reassuring smile.
'Don't worry about this honey. We'll sort it out one way or another.'

'Morning Pasqual, everything ok?'
'Buenos dias Harry, sure, plenty of customers as you can see. I guess they like this place.'
'Yes, well that's good news for all of us Pasqual.'
'Do want something to drink Harry?'
'No. I've overdosed on coffee already this morning. I just dropped in to see if you need anything. __Incidentally you were here quite early this morning.'
'That was Consuelo. She wanted to get a few things straightened out before we opened.'
'Right, well I won't keep you then. If you need an extra hand then give me a call. We're not going anywhere this morning.'
'Sure thing boss!'
'How's the baby by the way?'
'Fine, todo bien!'
'Ok then, I'll see you later.'

I left the café and strolled back across the paseo towards the apartment. The pavements were still wet, and although it had stopped raining, low cloud threatened more of the same.
I had a pretty good idea why Consuelo had turned up early that day, but we were one step ahead.
I had filled the fuel tanks on the morning that Lucia and I left on our quest to find the mystery bay, and I was quite sure that Consuelo would have checked in the charter accounts book, perhaps earlier this very same morning, but I had made sure that the invoice for the diesel oil was less than we had actually taken on board.
So as far as she knew we were simply motoring around in the seas close to Havana. I had even entered names of two fictitious Americans who had chartered the boat.
It wasn't exactly comforting having a spy so close to us, and knowing that everything that we did was being noted down and passed on to the enemy, in this case the CIA. However there was nothing much we could do until this gruesome drama finally ended, whenever that would be, and at the moment there seemed to be no end in sight.

Almost two weeks passed and nothing came up to spoil our relatively peaceful lifestyle. Lucia continued with a couple more fishing charters, in spite of her condition, resisting any pleas from me to start taking it easy.
'Harry I'm ok! I wanna keep active as long as possible.'
She had remarked, then, pointing at her belly.
'This little chico here will tell me when to slow down!'
She had a point I suppose, and with the old man who lived on the other side of the harbour in Regla helping out, my concerns were probably unfounded.
I heard nothing more from the CIA spook, to my acute relief, and life in Havana continued pretty much as before, but always with the underlying threat, the spectre of the American secret service never far from my mind.

On a Saturday afternoon I got back from helping out for a few hours at the café, having enacted the usual farce for Consuelo's benefit, of "Happy families and all friends together".
Oddly enough I still found it difficult to believe what she was up to. She always came over as entirely innocent and if she wasn't then what had induced her to work for the yanks, or at least for the insidious element that had caused the death of Mamen and had then ensnared me into participating, however unwillingly, in their diabolical schemes.

Lucia had made me some late lunch and I chewed contentedly away at an excellent meal of fried chicken.
'From the campo carino! I'm not buyin' anymore of that supermarket shit, with who knows what kinda' crap they put in it.'
'It's delicious love!'
I assured her.
'We gotta start thinkin' abou' lookin' after our bodies in future. You read too much abou' what they put in our food these days, especially the Americans.'
'Well there's not much chance of American grub ending up over here love, they're trying to *starve* us all to death!'
She smiled at the flimsy humour of the comment.
'I guess you' right Harry.'
I finished my lunch with relish and pushed the plate away an inch or two.
'Excellent love! Now it's time for my siesta.'
'*Your* siesta! Listen hombre, I'm the one who suppose' to be takin' all the naps aroun' here!'
'Well unfortunately you've got far too much to do in the home my dear, what with all the cleaning and the cooking__'
I easily dodged a playful slap from the back of her hand.

'Listen Harry, before you go to bed I got somethin' to tell you. An' it's importan'!'
'Oh right. Ok love what's on your mind?'
'It's this carino. I kept thinkin' about this guy Carlos an' how he got shot in the head.'
'Yeah it was a bad business, and I'm not sure exactly how we're going to resolve this, especially as Raul__'
'No Harry, I don' think it was Raul.'
'What do mean honey? There's no doubt surely, we've been over all this.'
'I know that, but I jus' keep thinkin' about it. Raul is a good guy, I feel it inside me.'
'Well so do I love, but you can't ignore what is pretty damning evidence after all.'
'Harry I know this, an' after we went over to their place for dinner an' Maria was telling us__well I agree' with you, but then like I say I started thinkin'.'
She leaned forward over the table, her neat little chin propped up in the palm of her hand, her amazing dark hair framing her face perfectly.
It was easy to be distracted, but I responded quickly.
'Ok, so thinking about what?'
'About maybe someone else kill him, this Carlos guy!'
'Someone else! __Who then?'
'I'm not totally sure yet, but a few days ago I talk' to my aunt.'
'Your aunt!'
'Yeah, the one who lives in the same old broken down community building as Consuelo.'
'Oh that aunt. __Aunt Jill, of the bucket and well tragedy!'
'*Which* aunt? Carino wha'd are you talkin' about?'
She wrinkled her forehead.
'It's not important. __So what did she say Lucia?'
'Well I ask her about Consuelo, Jus' sort of talkin', and I ask if she see much of her recen'ly. My aunt who is er, how do you say?'
'Observant! __I was going to say nosey, but as she's a relative__'
'No you' right Harry, she's nosey. So she said that one afternoon a few weeks ago, at the same time that you was on the boat with this guy Carlos, Consuelo caught a taxi to somewhere.'
'How could she possibly know that? The exact day I mean. __Or remember it I should say.'
'Well that was luck, __like in two ways.'
Lucia had both arms crossed in front of her on the table now, and was obviously eager to relate her story.

'You see she won the lottery that very day, no' much, only five hundred bucks, but to her that was a lotta money. So she kept the lottery ticket an' she show it to me.'
'I see.'
She gave me a hundred dollars, said it was for the baby.'
She shrugged.
'I couldn' say no Harry.'
'No of course not love. It was very generous of her. So what then?'
'So then I start checkin' aroun'. There are a lotta taxis in Havana, but a lot of the drivers work together in groups and have their own regions where they work, so they don' get into arguments.
It was a lot easier than I thought to get to the driver who picked up that fare. I had the date an' the time when she left. I ask' him if he took a woman somewhere that day an' he told me to mine' my own business, which was fair. So I offered him cash to tell me.'
'How much cash?'
'It doesn't matter Harry. I paid him ok! __ Ok it was fifty bucks, but it was worth it Carino!'
She was genuinely excited now.
Guess where he took her Harry, on the same evening before you wound up in that lil' deserted bay with a dead body on board?
It was San Sebastion Harry!'

I could hardly believe what I had heard and for several moments I just stared at her.
'Are you *sure* about this Lucia! I mean__'
At a complete loss for words I continued to gaze at her.
'Sure I'm sure! What d'you think Hombre!'
'No no, I mean I'm not suggesting you've lost your marbles honey.'
'Los' my *what!*''
'Oh it means, er, loco.'
'Loco! I'm not loco Harry!'
She was indignant suddenly.
'No of course you're not love, I didn't mean that, of course I didn't! I erm, __ it's hard to believe that's all.'
'No' for me it ain't!'
'No, I mean yes. It's erm, __Jesus Christ!'
Again I could think of nothing to say, nothing sensible anyway and Lucia continued with her story.
'You see Harry I just don' think that Raul would do this thing! Sometimes you jus' gotta trus' people.'

'Well maybe you're right love, but have you considered that she might be colluding with Raul? Is that a possibility!'

'Tha's a big maybe Harry, an' I don' think so. Like I said I trus' Raul, but I would never trus' that bitch, not ever. We know she' been sneakin' aroun' in our business anyway, an' now this!'

I drew a deep breath.

'Yes I must admit, it does seem pretty convincing.'

I had no idea what to do or to say next.

Why in God's name would Consuelo take a cab to a remote pueblo that was almost walking distance from the place where the unfortunate man Carlos had died.

It seemed overwhelmingly obvious that she was involved in some way. In addition to all that, Raul had already told us of his suspicions about her activities.

'I can't believe that you did all of this detective work Lucia. Why didn't you tell me?'

Because I could'n be sure carino. I spoke to my aunt two days ago. Then I had to track down the cab driver, which was this mornin'. __So *now* I'm tellin' you!'

'Bloody hell!'

I shook my head in exasperation.

"So now what? We can't go to Raul in case they *are* in this together, which, ok, seems highly unlikely, but the coincidence of them both being in the same place at the same time is overwhelming Lucia.'

'I don't care Harry. I jus' don't believe that Raul is tied up in this. Before, maybe! But now.'

Now it was her turn to shake her head and my instinct if nothing else told me she could be right. Maybe he did have a brother in San Sebastion, his wife had said as much and quite innocently.

Maybe that's all it was, he was just visiting the man and that was it!

'So what do we do? Do you want to tell Raul about this new situation?'

'Yes Harry.'

I thought about all she had said, Perhaps she was right, but if she wasn't then what of the consequences.

'Look I think we should keep this to ourselves love. At least until we know more about it. There are risks here!'

'But Harry__'

She began to protest.

'No love! __Look, like you I'm inclined to trust Raul, particularly after everything he has done for me, __ for us really, but you can never really know someone, I mean completely.
'You know me Harry!'
Her frankness, the look in her eyes as she stared at me was irrefutable.
'Yes I do honey. Beyond any question!'
She reached her hand across the table and gripped mine for a moment.
'So what do we do then Harry?'
'Nothing! For the moment anyway. Let's just see what happens.'
'If you say so carino.'
'We have nothing to lose sweetheart, so let's just wait.'

A day later I heard from the nameless American, the spook who worked for some unspecified agency or another.
Who could say which one of those shady organizations that according to the U.S., protect the world from evil elements that, given the chance, would destroy the God given rights of democracy and freedom.
Well, that was their well-publicized version anyway!
I suppose they have a point. There are certainly a number of evil regimes out there in the world, always have been always will be! And maybe confronting such threat requires a ruthless approach.
Fighting evil with evil.
Not much of a legacy for the human race, but maybe the human race gets what it deserves!

During my time in England when everything seemed so clear-cut, when my naivety was monumental and my lack of curiosity lamentable, it had always seemed that America was the sentinel of a free and egalitarian world. However, after a year of living in Cuba my opinions had changed somewhat.
I was no communist that was certain. The previous totalitarian regimes in Russia and Eastern Europe had failed miserably, and at enormous cost to the poor buggers that had to live under the tyranny of the so-called socialist states.
I was no fan of Castro either, as courageous as he undoubtedly was, and I felt also that unless he changed his entrenched ways Cuba would also be doomed.
That was my partially informed opinion anyway.
Living in another country, one that was impoverished and subjected to outside forces that were causing economic turmoil, has a way of opening

your eyes to the frailties of the human condition, and to the unpleasant individuals that seek to exploit them.
Maybe I was growing up at last!

The agency man had called me at the apartment and I left at once, making the short walk to the nearest phone box. Using the usual code for North America the man was on the line in seconds, and no time was wasted on preliminaries.
'Ok Burgess you held up your end of the deal, part of it anyway.'
'So now what?'
'You know well enough now what!
I want the name of the spy, someone who is working for the communists in that shit-hole country you're currently living in.
This, as you well know, is part of the deal.'
'And that's going to be easy is it?'
'Don't be smart with me Burgess. I didn't say it would be easy, which is why I've given you time to come up with something. You can consider this call as a progress check.'
'Well you've already shot one undercover agent!
On my boat and quite recently if you recall.'
'I don't know what you're talking about.'
'This man Carlos Roldan! Who was he working for?'
'I still don't know what you're talking about Burgess!
Anyhow it's none of your business so don't get involved!
He hesitated.
Yeah, so as I was saying you still need to deliver on the original part of the deal.'
'I didn't actually know who this guy Roldan was, what his role was I mean. Thanks for confirming that!'
There was a silence and I could almost smell his anger.
'I already told you what would happen if you fuck with me. I don't think I need to make that any clearer. I'm a patient man Burgess but don't try me.'
'Listen, you know my situation here. Even if I *can* locate someone it's going to take a lot of time.'
'Sure, like I say I understand that. Just keep your eye on the ball. If anything at all comes up you call me, like yesterday! Have you got that?'
'Yes.'
'Ok. __I been told that the bug we put on your place no longer functions.'
'No. A friend of mine discovered it and very kindly removed it.'
'We guessed that. You seem to be cozying up to the Cuban police quite a lot just lately.'

'I explained all this to you before. You murdered the man's daughter remember, who happened to be a good friend of my wife, and as she was on my boat at the time, I felt obliged, and still do, to show the man some sympathy and yes, friendship. If you have a problem with that well I suggest you live with it.'
'We didn't kill her, it was an accident. According to what you've said, that's all he knows isn't it?'
'That's exactly what I told him. If I had told him the truth, then the U.S. government would be facing a very embarrassing international situation.'
'I doubt it Harry. Even if the U.S. government knew anything about this little event, they wouldn't give a shit!'
'Maybe you're right at that.'
'Ok then. Well I enjoyed our little talk Harry__'
'I can't say that I did.'
'Just make sure you stay on the same page that we're currently reading from. __Keep in touch Harry.'
The line went dead.

The man was an obnoxious bastard and that was a fact.
Such people have the potential to destroy any faith in human nature. I felt a deep sense of depression as I hung the receiver back on its cradle and turned to walk back up the paseo to the apartment.
What motivates such people I wondered. Perhaps it was their comfortable, well paid lifestyle, or perhaps they really did believe in the American dream, whatever that was!
I suddenly pictured him and his ideal family turning up in their best clothes at a white painted church on a Sunday morning, in some sedate town in middle America, listening to the comforting platitudes of a parson's sermon.
Yes, maybe he did believe, even as he plotted his diabolical schemes of connivance, murder, and God only knows what else.

I was shaken from my thoughts by two middle-aged, overdressed women who had approached without my noticing.
'Excuse me sir!'
One of them said.
'You're the English guy that has that little Café just along the street from here, am I right?'
I managed a smile.
'Er, yes I am madam.'
'Well we simply love that little place!'
She gushed, her bright red lips formed in an over-friendly smile.

'I'm pleased to here it__'
'We come over here from Miami every three months or so, this town is so quaint, all these old buildings. Such a pity the communists got hold of it. Oh dear, I hope I'm not talking out of turn here, I mean you're not an informant or anything are you?'
Another forced, and now uncertain lipsticked smile.
'No of course not, I__'
'Oh I didn't think so.'
She turned to her companion.
'Annie, do you think this man is a Russian spy?'
'Don't be silly Margie', he's English.'
'Oh I'm just joking really sir.'
'I'm sure you are__'
'My husband loves the neat little bar you have there as well. As a matter of fact you keep his favourite Bourbon.'
With an effort I managed a cheerful response.
'I'm pleased to hear it. Does your husband like fishing as well.'
Her face fell in surprise and the smile vanished.
'Fishing! __Well now I don't think so__'
'I ask because I run Marlin charters. We have a lot of Americans as clients.'
'Oh really__'
'Yes. __Look, take this just in case.'
I pulled out my wallet and handed her a business card.
'It's good fun!'
I gave her a broad grin and lifted my eyebrows briefly.
'You never know till you try it!'
'Oh well thank you mister er.__'
I began to move off.
'Perhaps I shall see you in the café at some time. Enjoy your stay in Havana ladies.'
I turned and walked off along the paseo, leaving two bewildered looking women standing there, with one of them holding my card, which she seemed not quite sure what to do with.
My liking for Americans that day was definitely in decline, even if temporary.

I had received a number of letters from my mother in England during the year I had spent living in Havana.

They were backdated somewhat because of the deplorable postal system in Cuba, and most probably there were letters that had gone permanently astray.

I had replied, to those letters that I received anyway, simply saying that I was well, I had a job working in a bar and I was happy, which I was sure was her primary concern.

Beyond that I said very little, and obviously nothing at all concerning my numerous adventures, and my unfortunate involvement with the American secret service. That would have been more than sufficient to induce a heart attack, probably for both of my parents.

Neither did I mention Lucia and the imminent birth of our child, pretty much for the same reason.

I could have given her our telephone number, but after short consideration, I thought better of it!

If Lucia had answered a call, __well, there is no need to enlarge on that possibility.

I made the excuse that it was almost impossible to have a telephone connected, which in fact wasn't far from the truth, unless of course you knew the right people, which Lucia always did!

In spite of my mother's entreaties to me to return, if even for a short break, I had declined, making various excuses.

In any event, with the current situation regarding the nasty creature, the American spook who had forcefully drawn me into his insidious schemes, I was sure that I wouldn't be allowed to leave the country anyway until I had fulfilled my task, and God only knew when that would be.

When I reflected on the quiet almost sedentary lifestyle I had once lived in England, it was hard, if not impossible to believe how much my life had changed.

For the better? __Without question, despite all the current difficulties!

After all, I had met Lucia and she was everything I could ever have hoped for.

At some point of course I would tell my parents about our relationship and about our child, and no doubt we would eventually return to the UK, if only for a short stay.

I loved this country, which I had visited purely by accident and had now chosen to live, and the mere thought of going back to England was an anathema for me. In spite of the current demands by the American spook I knew that I could never now through choice, return permanently to the place of my birth.

I had a surprise call from Raul, which turned out to be surprising in more ways than one.
'Raul! How are you?'
'Not so bad Harry. Look, I have a few things to tell you, can we meet today?'
'Sure, why not, but what time?'
'I don' care, you decide.'
'Ok, one o'clock.'
'Do you know the Parque Fraternidad?'
'Of course.'
'Good, I'll meet you there at one. Bye Harry.'

So what was this all about, I wondered.
I knew the park very well, close to the Capital building.
A nice place, lots of trees, lots of grass, reminded me in many ways of Hyde park, except for the heat of course and the odd palm tree dotted about amongst the more familiar arboreal varieties. Lucia and I had enjoyed, many evening and weekend strolls there, as it was just a short walking distance from the apartment.

I met up with Raul, who was dressed uncharacteristically in light beige trousers and a colourful shirt.
'Hello mate! Day off, or did you get fired?'
'No Harry I am trying to look inconspicuous!'
He remarked with his usual broad smile.
'Not in that shirt surely!'
'It was a gift from Maria, I'm not entirely sure about it!
'I'm not entirely surprised! __How is your wife?'
His tone changed
'Just the same Harry.'
'Yes, silly question. Incidentally, thank you for your hospitality, we enjoyed ourselves immensely.'
'I hoped it was ok, I mean, __well you know what I mean my friend!'
'It was most enjoyable Raul, for both of us.'
'Good, I hoped for as much.'
He took out his cigarettes and lit one.
Remembering my promise to his wife, this did not seem to be the best time to lecture him on the habit.
'So, what did you want to tell me Raul?'
'Couple of things amigo. First, we both know that the chica who works for you is probably also working for our American "friends".'

'Yes I know. Hard to believe but there it is.'
'It's probably for money Harry, it usually is. People in Cuba are generally quite poor.'
'Yes I suppose so, but still difficult to believe anyway.'
He drew deeply on his cigarette, taking time before he released a long plume of smoke that dissipated slowly in the still warm air.
'I have some news about the man who died on your boat. Well, some old news really.'
'Go on.'
'I have an elder brother who lives in a small village some distance from here. It's called San Sebastion. Maria mentioned it to you I believe when you came to the house.'
'Um, she might have done.'
I made a good cover-up, or so I hoped.
'My brother was also in the police, but is retired now.'
'Right ok.'
'Sits around playing cards and drinking beer with his friends these days. I tell him he should exercise, but__'
He shrugged his shoulders.
'Maybe I will end up the same way.'
'You're not ready to retire yet, surely Raul.'
'In another six years maybe amigo.'

A pretty girl was approaching on the stone clad pathway where we were sitting together on a park bench.
She had a dog on a lead that trotted confidently in front of her on the uneven flagstones as though proud, and justly so, of his shapely escort.
Both Raul and I glanced appreciatively at the young woman as she passed.
'Anyway Harry I will get to the point.
'I visited San Sebastion on the night that you were returning from delivering the weapons to one of the cayos.
'Oh right, __ to see your brother I presume.'
'No that wasn't the reason. San Sebastion is only about three kilometres from the small inlet where you found yourself on the night that the man Carlos was shot.'
'I see, well I wouldn't know that Raul.'
He looked at me steadily before continuing.
I felt guilty with myself for lying, or at least for not disclosing what we had found on our recent trip.
Lucia and I had agreed on the plan to say nothing to anyone about our discovery, a plan that still seemed perfectly reasonable.
'I had good reason to make this journey Harry.'

'Ok, I'm sure you did.'
'We had a tip-off, as the Americans would say, a late tip-off unfortunately. It seemed that a woman had left for that very same pueblo on the evening before Carlos was killed. The woman was Consuelo, who we both know very well of course.'
'Consuelo!'
Once again I feigned surprise, although feeling equally guilty for doing so.
'Yes Harry! I left at once with a couple of men, but of course we had no idea why she had made this trip. It just seemed unusual and because of our suspicions about her, I decided that we should follow her, which we did although we were two hours behind.
When we arrived we had no idea where she could be or how we could locate her. However I met up with my brother in his favourite bar and asked him if he had possibly seen her arrive.
It was a long-shot, yet another gringo expression I'm afraid, luckily one of my brother's friends had noticed a taxi from Havana. It had pulled up close to the bar and was carrying a woman.
We were very lucky that the man had seen her. He said that when she got out of the taxi she walked off towards the church, but before she reached it she then took a turning off from the single main street.
This pueblo is very small Harry, and as a consequence everyone who lives there knows exactly where every road leads.
Apparently the turning she took, no more than an unmade road, just a dirt track really, led to a small bay that was once used for fishing, but had been abandoned many years ago. It could only be the same place where Carlos moored your boat on that fateful night.'
He paused to catch his breath and perhaps for me to catch mine before I intervened.
'So you knew about this little inlet then, __all along Raul!'
'Yes my friend.'
'But you told us__'
'Yes Harry, I did tell you. It was a lie because I didn't want you to become involved any further in this matter.'
'Yes I see.'
I waited while he lit another cigarette.
'It was to protect you both. No other reason Harry.'
I nodded.
'Ok Raul, I can see that.'
'And you lied to me as well Harry.'
There was no look of resentment or even disappointment when he spoke, and he was smiling again.
'Not lied exactly Raul, just sparing about revealing what little we knew.'

'Sure, and I understand your motives for this, you and Lucia. You couldn' be sure if it was me or Consuelo, am I right?'

'Yes you are right, we couldn't quite be sure, which is why we kept some things to ourselves.'

'And you both went off to find the bahia for yourselves.'

'How the bloody hell could you know that Raul?'

'I didn' know until now amigo. I thought that you would, but I couldn' be certain. A guard at the docks said that you both left the port in early morning a few weeks ago. He said that there were just two of you on the boat so it didn' seem likely that it was a fishing charter.'

Now it was my turn to release a short laugh.

'Well no one can say you're not good at your job Raul!'

'Police work is no more than routine Harry. Being observant, taking note of everything, an' then putting two and two together, isn't that what you English say?'

'Yes that's exactly what we say!'

There was no question that my liking for the man increased every time that we met, and for a moment I felt regret that I hadn't trusted him. Lucia's instinct it seemed had been correct.

'Ok, so you think it was her that shot Carlos!'

'It seems pretty certain does it not amigo!'

'Right so now what? In spite of everything you've told me she is still just a suspect.'

'I haven't quite finished the story amigo. At the time we didn't know what she was planning. Maybe she had arranged to meet her Yankee employers, we couldn't be sure.

If we had just turned up at the bahia, it could have been like three dumb Cuban cops turning up at the wrong place and at the wrong time. If we *had* done that, an' If it *was* the yanks then maybe I wouldn't be talking to you now. These people don't fuck around!'

'As I know only too well Raul.'

'Yes indeed my friend.'

'So what did you do?'

'We waited until she returned, perhaps an hour later. My brother got a young muchacho to watch out for her and tell us when she got back. It was fairly late by then of course.'

'Where were you while all this was going on.'

'In the bar with my brother, drinkin' beer.'

'What three men in police uniform! That was a bit, well __obvious, wasn't it Raul?'

'Be sensible Harry! I was dressed as I am now.'

He grinned.
'Ok with a different shirt, an' my colleagues as well.'
'No sorry, I wasn't thinking straight. __So then?'
'Afterwards the boy came into the bar, like I say, it was quite late by then. He said that she had returned and was waiting outside the church__'
'For absolution maybe!'
Raul laughed at once.
'Yeah maybe! So we waited. Eventually a taxi came an' picked her up, an' we know it took her back to Havana.'
'Go on.'
'So then we drove the car down to the bahia. Your boat was tied up at the jetty with jus' the light in the wheelhouse.'
'Jesus *Christ* Raul! So you went on board and found the body.'
'Exactly amigo!'
'He looked completely calm as he lit another cigarette.'
'So__'
'Yes Harry you were asleep, or probably drugged is my guess.'
'Drugged!'
'Sure. We are still waiting for the analysis on the coffee mugs that we found on your boat. __In Cuba these things take time.'
He lifted his shoulders casually.
'So yeah, it would seem so. I believe that the only reason why Carlos brought your vessel into that small inlet was because he intended to meet with someone. Possibly he knew it was Consuelo, or possibly not. She, or perhaps someone else arranged the meeting place quite probably with the excuse of passing on information about something.
We know that the man worked for Cuban intelligence and it would have been an ideal place to meet and discuss whatever it was.'
'While I was sleeping peacefully!'
I remarked.
'It looks that way!'
I shook my head ruefully.
'Not your fault Harry!'
'No it certainly wasn't.'
Raul coughed several times and then drew deeply on his cigarette, which seemed to act as a balm.
'So, to continue my friend! We backed off up the track in the car keeping out of sight. It was dark of course, we could see you but you couldn' possibly see us.'
'But why didn't you__'

'Wake you up? No! Not a good idea. I still didn't know what was going on Harry, you gotta remember. I'm still not quite sure even now. So we waited.
Maybe someone else would come, I didn' think so, but maybe.
I had called for back-up from the police in San Sebastion and If someone else had come along, maybe in a boat then we would have been ready for them.
We waited until you came up on deck, until you, very wisely, decided to get out of there pronto and then we returned to Havana.'
'Fucking hell Raul!'
'Yes, exactly. __I am sorry amigo.'

It wasn't easy to take this all in, and I sat in silence for some time as I considered what Raul had said.
The attractive young woman with the dog passed by again in the opposite direction, although this time I barely noticed her.

'So you don't know why this guy was shot.'
'Not yet we don't, but it seems a safe bet that it was Consuelo who took care of him.'
'So why didn't you arrest her?'
'There are two reasons Harry. First of all there is no smoking gun.
I am certain she is guilty, but she is pretty smart. If we had arrested her and couldn't find a weapon we would look pretty stupid. My guess is she got rid of it as soon as she killed him, threw it in the bahia maybe.
So that leads us to the second reason.
She doesn't know for sure that we are on to her. Maybe she suspects, but she doesn't know!
We want to keep it that way, because I want to discover who is paying her. I want to catch whoever is behind all this.'
'That's a tall order Raul. It's quite possible that whoever it is has never put a foot on Cuban soil.'
'The American did. __And quite recently Harry if you remember.'
'Yes that's true enough.'
'She is jus' a small cog in a very big machine Harry. We could take her in on suspicion and maybe prove a case of some kind, but the yanks would jus' shrug their shoulders an' deny everything.
__So we wait.'
'Yes I see your point Raul.'

I leaned back on the bench and stared around at the peaceful scene of the park, where children were playing and couples were strolling together beneath the plentiful dark green shade of numerous trees.

It was hard to believe why all these conspiracies should be taking place in such a beautiful, and apparently peaceful town, a place that I was gradually growing to love.

What could America hope to gain by their interventions now that the dissolved communist states in the east of Europe were surely no longer a threat, or indeed a serious influence in the Caribbean?

I remembered what Raul had once said about a possible return to the corrupt days of Batista and how strongly he was opposed to any such influence by the U.S.

I could do nothing other than agree with him.

'You ok Harry?'
'Yes I'm ok, just thinking. Look Raul if there is anything I can do to help in any way at all, you only have to ask.'
'Thank you amigo.'
'I'm sorry I didn't trust you.'
'Don't worry about it Harry. An' if I need your help I will ask, but we're doing ok right now as a matter of fact, however I will remember what you have said.'

We both got to our feet at the same moment, intuitively perhaps, grasping hands briefly.

'Watch out for the waitress Harry!'
He remarked with his usual mustachioed grin.
'I certainly intend to. Keep in touch Raul.'

It was a peaceful month or two that followed.
I spent time helping out in the café while Lucia took on a couple of additional charters before finally calling it a day, much to my relief!
The evidence of her pregnancy was now well pronounced.
The thing was that it seemed to enhance her already considerable beauty, certainly in my eyes at least.
She seemed supremely happy, even ecstatic and entirely overwhelmed by the impending birth of our son, as indeed was I.
It was nothing like I had expected, or indeed, as she confessed to me, what she had expected. She seemed somehow to bloom as the day of the birth grew closer, and, if it was possible, our relationship, no, wrong word, our devotion to each other increased even more.

We took our regular walks down to the sea wall at Malecon, albeit at a slower pace, until eventually even this exercise ceased altogether, and Lucia was pretty much confined to our apartment, with just the occasional visit to a café' or, on her insistence, to a local grocery store.
Yes everything seemed fine, however I wasn't exactly complacent, with the recent memory of everything that had happened.
I knew that I couldn't afford to be because I was no closer to finding and exposing a Cuban undercover agent and I was hardly confidant that I could. One thing was certain, sooner or later the American would be back for his pound of flesh.
It was a constant concern for me, although I barely talked about it with Lucia, however the matter was eventually resolved in a way that I could never have predicted.

The café became even more popular particularly with foreign tourists. Lucia suggested that we open a second and perhaps larger restaurant, which I suppose was not a bad idea although it would mean more work and of course there was the problem of finding extra staff.
I was less enthusiastic than Lucia about the project. We certainly didn't need the money, however if that was what she wanted then I would support her all the way, but not until after the birth of our son, __*well* after in fact.
I felt that in the following months there would be more than enough to occupy both of us. Certainly the charters would have to stop and in fact I wasn't even sure that they could restart with Lucia essentially playing the major role in running the business.
There was no point in agonizing over such things now and I chided myself for doing so. One day at a time seemed to be the best policy.

I was sitting at home with Lucia watching a dreadful television programme, a South American sitcom, far worse than any similar English versions, however Lucia was addicted for reasons beyond my comprehension.
She always insisted that I sit next to her during the awful and apparently endless drama, if it was only to huddle herself against me, and for me to pass squares of tissue to her from a Kleenex box.
It was during a particularly tense moment in the episode that the doorbell rang.
'Shit!'

I murmured irritably, although it meant a brief respite from the utter nonsense on the screen.
'Who the bloody hell could it be at this late hour!'
Lucia shushed me loudly.
'An' close the *door* after you Harry!'
She added in a fierce whisper as I got to my feet.
I pressed the buzzer to open the main door at street level and walked out onto the elevated landing.
It was Raul who entered, dressed in his police uniform. He glanced upwards briefly and then took the stairs two at a time.

'Raul you're late, what's up?'
'I want you to come with me Harry, there is something you should see!'
In a second he was standing in front of me with an expression on his face that I had never seen before.
'What, you mean *now?*'
'Yes now!'
'Bloody hell!'
I muttered in annoyance.
'Ok, let me find some shoes and I'll be with you.'
I walked back inside and quietly opened the door to the living room.
'Lucia!'
I whispered.
'I have to go out with Raul for a few minutes. Ok? I shan't be too long__'
'Ok, go go!'
She waved her fingers at me dismissively without turning her head from the on-screen melodrama, that now appeared to have reached fever pitch.
I was about to leave her to her soap-opera when she called out briefly in a loud whisper.
'An' Harry! Ask Raul if he can do somethin' abou' this bloody phone!
__I's been out for nearly two weeks now!'
'I willl love. Promise!'
I whispered back.
Then I crept out closing the door carefully behind me.
Finding some shoes quickly, I left the apartment.

'What's this all about Raul?'
I asked, following his rapid descent on the stairs.
'You will see Harry.'
Outside on the paseo a police car was waiting with its engine running.
Raul opened the rear door.
'Get in!'

I did so, in some trepidation, with Raul following behind me.
As soon as we were seated the door was slammed shut and the car roared off along the paseo.
'Where the hell are we going Raul?'
'To Regla. There is nothing for you to worry about Harry, but its important, trust me.'
Not another word was spoken as we sped along the half deserted street towards the harbour.
Then the driver turned left along the perimeter road where I could see the light from street lamps glistening brightly on the surface of the water. The car careered onwards, the emergency lights on the roof flashing, inducing a sense of some sort of urgency.
Then we were entering the tunnel that led underneath the harbour to Regla. When we emerged the car barely reducing speed, as it turned into a maze of rundown streets with a few dimly lit apartment blocks and numerous disused warehouses.
Turning right suddenly with a screech of tyres the car slowed rapidly and then turned again through the open doors of what looked like a large garage perhaps for lorries or buses, a rusting hulk of a building that had seen far better days. The noise of the tyres as the car braked hard, echoed from a lofty corrugated ceiling.
Raul turned to me and spoke quietly.
'Harry I believe that your problems may be over!'
'Well that's a bloody relief! I was__'
'*Listen* Harry! Listen carefully. We are getting out of the car and I want you to see something. There are two bodies, quite dead. You know both of these people I believe and I want you to identify them. This is important Harry, so have your wits about you, an' don say anything unless I ask you ok!'
'Er, sure, I mean, of course.'
I was distinctly nervous now.
The door on my side of the car was opened by a policeman and I got out gingerly, glancing around the large enclosed space that was in darkness except for the headlights of three other police cars and an ambulance. Maybe a dozen people, police and medics stood around in complete silence.
Perhaps ten meters away in the circle of light I could see a motionless body lying on the cracked concrete floor, and only a few metres from that, what appeared to be a second body, which was covered by a blanket.
'Look at each of them Harry. Tell me who they are!'
Raul said quietly. He was now standing just behind me.'
'Ok, but__'

I began.
'Just look Harry that's all. I want you to identify the two bodies.'
I could feel his hand pressing gently in my back, urging me closer.
I walked across to the nearest, the corpse that had been covered over.
Raul walked past me, crouched down and pulled back the blanket to reveal just the head and shoulders of a woman.
She lay on her back and her eyes were closed, almost as though she was sleeping. There was a small neat hole in the very centre of her forehead with just the merest trickle of blood that ran upwards into her dark hair.
I turned my head to one side, and when I focused on her face It was with profound shock because I knew her immediately.
'My God! *Consuelo!* Jesus *Christ* Raul__'
'Her apellido Harry, her last name please?'
'Jimenez, her last name is Jimenez!'
It was then that I noticed the large pool of blood that had formed on the floor around her head, almost like a halo.
I raised a hand slowly and covered my mouth.
'You gonna vomit Harry?'
Raul asked, looking up at me.
'I don't think so!'
He pulled the blanket back, carefully covering her face again, then he stood up.
'So then now look at the man, then we can get out of here.'
I walked across slowly and glanced down at the second corpse spread out on the concrete. I recognized him at once.
Both sides of the casual zipper jacket he wore lay spread apart. He had at least four bullet wounds to his body and a copious amount of blood had spread across his torso.
A shoulder holster was clearly visible tucked beneath his left arm, and in his right hand a pistol was held loosely in his fingers.
I stared down at the body for several moments.
'I know who it is and I think maybe you do as well Raul! But I don't know his name.'
'Ok, so for the record, say who you think it is!'
'It's the bastard who intercepted our boat when we were returning from the cayos, some weeks back, or is it months. It's the man that set me up to__
Well you already know how he set me up! He's also the man that killed your daughter, or at least ordered her death. __American. Works for one of their agencies. __I presume so anyway, but of course I don't know which one.'
'Ok, so now we can leave.'
He took my arm, as a friend rather than a cop, and led me back to the car.

Inside on the back seat I threw my head back onto the head-rest.
Raul got in the other side next to me.
'You gonna be sick Harry?'
'No, it's passed.'
He turned to the driver
'Ok Sanchez vamos! Regreso a la estacion!'
The man reversed, turned the car around and pulled away slowly through the open double doors.

The drive back to Havana and the police station was taken at a leisurely pace and the flashing red and blue lights had been switched off.
'Consuelo dead! __What the bloody hell is going on Raul?'
'I will explain everything when we get back to the station.'
He said quietly, then he fell silent and there seemed little point in asking anything further.
The car pulled up outside the police station and we both got out. Raul spoke briefly to the driver and then I followed him through the entrance.

'Sit down Harry.'
We were in his office and I did as he said, taking one of the chairs in front of his desk.
'I believe you need a drink, an' so do I.'
He took a bottle and two small glasses from the bottom drawer of his desk.
'Only whiskey I'm afraid, it's all I have.'
'As long as it's got alcohol it will do.'
I remarked with a poor attempt at a grin.
He filled both glasses and pushed one across the desk.
I took a gulp, the strong aroma rushing instantly up into my nose and my throat, causing me to cough slightly.
'Better Harry?'
'Not much. __Consuelo though, I can't believe it. I mean I know she was spying and__'
I slumped backwards into the chair.
'But she was quite young, thirty maybe__'
'Don't cry any tears for her Harry, you don' know about her!'
'Maybe not. __Look I've got to get back, Lucia, she'll be wondering!'
'She'll be ok Harry, for ten more minutes. I'll give you a ride back when we finish.'

As though through providence the phone on Raul's desk rang out suddenly.

He picked up the receiver, mumbled an acknowledgement and listened for a moment before passing it across to me, his hand clamped over the mouthpiece.
'It's your wife! __We're jus' havin' a drink ok!'
He whispered.
I took the phone and held it to my ear.
'Harry, where are you?'
'It's ok love I'm with Raul, we're having a quick one. Where're you calling from?'
'A neighbour's apartment. *Her* phone's workin' ok, so why not ours?'
'I don't know love, maybe she's got a thing going with the telephone guy!'
She raised her voice in obvious annoyance.
'So what! __I should do the *same* Harry!'
'Oh come on honey, I've done the best I can! As always it's this bloody Cuban bureaucracy.'
'So a quick one you say, I s'pos' that means a quick drink! __What does Raul want?'
She sounded even more irritable now.'
'I'm not quite sure yet. Look don't worry I'll be home soon, bye honey.'
'Harry__'
'Don't worry love I won't be long.'
I handed the phone back to Raul. He spoke briefly to her, restated my own assurance that I would be home shortly, and then hung up.
I sipped again at the whisky.
'Can you do something about this bloody phone of ours Raul, It's driving me nuts.'
'I'll make a call my friend. It will be back in a day or two, I guarantee!'
'Ok so where were we?'
I thought for a moment, catching up to where we had left off.
'Right, so what was all that about then Raul. They couldn't have shot each other surely, that hardly seems possible!'
The inevitable packet of fags came out and he lit up with obvious pleasure.
'I will explain everything to you Harry.
It seems that the man, who we know she called 'Gary', not his real name I suspect, was her contact, or one of them at least.'
'The spook, the undercover for the Yanks!'
'Exactly. We knew that she was meeting someone tonight because, as you know, her apartment was wired and the phone was bugged.'
'He would have suspected that surely Raul, the man isn't daft!'
'No my friend he isn't. If they spoke about a meeting place then she would probably have used a phone box as you do.

However we knew she had made a call earlier today and ordered a cab for six this evening. I alerted our man in the Taxi business and he said that she had asked to be taken to Regla.

Now why Regla? There's nuthin' there but slums an' old warehouses, like the one you visited tonight.'

'I know, I've been there a few times! __Ok, so they met up!'

'Yes they did Harry. Risky for him coming to Cuba, but that is what happened.'

'Well he's done it before as you know, quite recently in fact. Who can say how many times he's taken the same risk. The man is an arrogant bastard, or *was* I should say. __He obviously believed he could walk on water. Not any more though!'

'No, that's for sure!'

'Right, so who shot who, and then who shot the other one?'

'I'm getting to that. First of all I will repeat what I told you earlier. I believe that you are 'off the hook' as the Yankees would say. I have been planning this for some time now Harry.'

'Planning what?'

'First of all to get you out of danger, you and your wife! I know you were dragged into this situation through no fault of your own, and if I am to be completely honest, it was partly my daughter who was responsible.'

'Raul, I know she had her political motives, I've never criticized her for that.'

'I know you haven't__'

'I mean I didn't agree with her, or with Lucia come to that, but I understood her reasons, perhaps more now than before. Since I arrived I've learned quite a lot about the U.S. role here in Cuba and in Central America, things I never knew about when I lived in my safe cozy British environment. It's been something of an education coming to this part of the world.'

I sipped at the whiskey again and pushed my glass across the desk for a refill.

'When I look back I hardly feel as though I'm the same person.'

'Experience changes us all Harry.'

He smiled as a close friend might, and I lifted my eyebrows.

'Yeah maybe it does mate.'

He reached for another cigarette.

'You smoke to many of those Raul!'

I looked at him squarely.

'I know that. __My wife has spoken with you about this, am I right?'

'Well um__'

'I thought so. An' she is right of course, you both are, but__'

He lifted his full shoulders briefly.
'I doubt if I could stop now even if I wanted to.'
I waited while he lit up again.
'So now I will explain everything to you Harry, it's quite a long story I'm afraid.'
I laughed.
'Well you'd better get on with it before Lucia gets on the phone again. Then we're both in trouble!'
'It's not easy to tell Harry, but you must hear this.
Ok, so first of all, it was the American who shot Consuelo!'
'Yes I presumed that.'
'We were too late to prevent it I'm afraid, by just a minute or so probably. I don't know what the meeting between them was about, but I knew that she was apparently working for both sides. Loyal to who I didn't know, and in fact I'm still not sure. My belief is that he discovered she was maybe double-dealing them and decided to put her out of the picture just to be safe.
Anyhow, shortly after we got there we drove straight into the warehouse and I saw her body at once.
The Yankee spy was caught in the headlights an' just put his hands up calmly an' with a big smile, still holdin' his gun
Maybe he thought that the U.S. cavalry would soon be riding into town to rescue him one way or another, an' who knows maybe he was right.
So I got out of the car and shot him in the chest four times!'
'Jesus Christ!'
'Yeah, that's what happened Harry. __And now I know for sure after you identified the dead man, that it was he that killed my daughter, so I don't feel too bad about shooting the bastard.
I was always against this crazy, loco adventure, running weapons to the cayo's, but I never thought that either you or Lucia, or indeed Mamen, were in any real danger. Recently we learned for sure that the Americans wanted the arms to be delivered, so that they could catch the rebels from whichever country in Central American, who came to collect them. In which case it didn't seem to be in their interest to shoot the delivery guy!'
'But if you knew all this then why the hell did you allow the delivery of these weapons to go ahead? I'm not with you Raul!'
'No I guess not. It's all part of er, somethin' I can't tell you about right now. What I *didn't* know Harry, was that your boat would be stopped and my daughter would be killed. __Also that you would be dragged into this fuckin' mess! I never expected that.
It seems that Mamen was dispensable. Knowing that she would never agree to be involved in their schemes, they jus' killed her! __Perhaps also

350

as an example for you, so that you would take them very seriously when they told you what they had in mind.'

'Yes I see what you mean. So where does Consuelo come in to all this? I'm still not clear.'

'Consuelo I told you about previously Harry. We are sure now that she was an agent for the Americans, CIA or whatever. What she did for them is not entirely clear. We think maybe it was she who told them about our plan to ship arms to the cayos on the western tip of Cuba. Later on Carlos Roldan discovered this. Or maybe it was Roldan who told the woman. Again we are not entirely certain. We knew some business or other was going on between them, but not the detail. __You have to remember Harry, I'm a simple policeman and I don't always know what Cuban intelligence are planning. It's not an unusual situation!'

'No I guess not! __But you can't be serious Raul! __*Carlos!* He worked for Cuban intelligence, you said so yourself for God's sake!'

'Yes he did. He also worked for the Yankees, the classic double agent, except that he was dedicated to the cause and to Castro.'

'So why didn't Carlos tell the Cuban security service that the Americans now knew about the plan to plant weapons?'

'He did of course, but by then it was too late to do anything. You and my daughter were already returning from the cayos, and as I said to you, I never expected, __nobody did, what was going to happen that night!'

'My God I can't take all this in, it's like a bloody bad dream!'

'That's how it is Harry. Hard to believe? __Sure it was!'

I stared unseeing out of the darkened window of Rauls office as I tried desperately to get my mind around everything he had said.

'So you knew right from the start about all this! From the moment I called you in that little town after I had managed to row ashore in that ridiculous emergency dinghy!'

'Not everything, of course not Harry, what do think!

If I had known that my daughter, both of you in fact, were in danger! __No my friend, nobody knew what the Yanks were going to do, maybe not even Consuelo.'

'But I gave you a cock and bull story when we met in that little town near the beach where I rowed ashore!'

'At first you did yes.'

'And if I hadn't told you what really happened, what then Raul?'

'But you *did* Harry, and that's all that matters. This is one of the reasons why I have trust in you.'

I leaned forward wearily in my chair.

'Fuck!'
I murmured the expletive under my breath.
'So why did she murder Carlos?'
'We believe because she discovered his true allegiance to the Cuban cause, we can't be sure, but that seems most likely.'
'But this man Carlos would have told you earlier surely, of what he thought at least that she might be up to?'
'Harry of *course* we knew about her, for some time now, but she was more valuable to us as a conduit for mis-information. That's simple enough isn't it?'
'Too simple for me it seems.'
'No Harry, you are an intelligent man. Remember that it was you who suspected that she was checking on every trip you made on your boat, but you couldn't possibly know everything that was going on. Certainly that she was going to shoot Roldan's brains out, even we didn't know that!'
'Well you're certainly right about that Raul!'
I shook my head slowly as I struggled to come to terms with what I had just heard.
'Lucia will be worrying where I am.'
I murmured absently.
'She'll be ok Harry. Here__have another drink.'
He poured more whiskey into my glass.
'I'm still confused, about what happened in that garage or warehouse or whatever.'
'Ok I will explain Harry. We were just a short distance behind the taxi that took the Jimenez woman to Regla.
As soon as it dropped her at the warehouse the taxi left. We waited outside for a few minutes and called for more police support. Remember, we had no idea what was going on or what to expect.
Then we heard a gunshot. Immediately we drove straight inside through the open doors. They had no chance, or rather the American had none. He was like a rabbit caught in the headlights, or a rat in a trap, tha's a better analogy.
I saw the woman's body with him standing over it. It was quite a drama scene, __but this time with the smokin' gun!
As I already told you, I got out of the car and shot him four times.'
Raul broke off for a moment, fumbling in the pack for another cigarette.
'Yeah, he didn' expect that, he had put his hands up thinkin' he would jus' get arrested, an' then the Americans would have come along an' saved his ass almost certainly! __But I wasn' gonna let that happen, not after what he did!'
Once again he paused, drawing slowly on his cigarette.

'So yes, that's the truth Harry! Sometimes we must do unpleasant things simply because there is no alternative. But like I say, I don't feel too bad about it.'
'No I'll bet you don't.'
I murmured quietly.
He shrugged his shoulders nonchalantly.
'The CIA will demand to know what happened, an' of course we will cooperate with them, to one extent at least. We will return the body of the American, but not the woman, not Consuelo. She was Cuban and will remain in Cuba. They will want to know everything tha' happen', an' of course we will tell them everything.
We will provide photographs so they can see her body and his, and they can know that she was shot by their own agent, who, we shall make it clear, was in this country illegally!'
'So what about him? The CIA bloke or whatever he was.'
'We will say that we suspected her treason, and her activities with the US secret service and that was the reason we followed her to Regla. Maybe the guy thought she had betrayed him, an' this was the reason he shot her. Of course we had no idea exactly what was going on. The man shot at us and we returned fire. Simple as that Harry.
That's our official story anyway.'
'I see.'
I recalled the blood drenched corpse of the man lying on the floor of the warehouse, but it was the body of Consuelo with the neat bullet hole in her temple, lying in a pool of her own blood that precipitated sudden, unexpected nausea.
'Now I think I *am* going to be sick!'
I murmured quietly.
He pointed to a door at the rear of the office.
'There is a wash-room. Try not to make a mess Harry.'
He added a dry smile.

I had hoped to make a dignified approach to the toilet, but I could feel my stomach rising to my throat and it ended in a hurried dash.

When I returned a few minutes later the man I was looking at now hardly seemed to be the same person.
He was of course, he looked no different than before.
The same dark wavy hair, the mustache, the immaculate olive green uniform, the usual cigarette stuck between his fingers, but he was not the same man, not to me at least.

'I'm sorry about that.'
I remarked, feeling slightly weak at the knees as I took my seat again.
'There's no mess incidentally, unpleasant smell I'm afraid, but I opened the window.'
'Harry I wasn't serious about that, it doesn't matter my friend, the cleaner will take care of it all tomorrow.'
Curiously somehow he was smiling his familiar smile.
Same smile, different person somehow.
'Raul I had better get back, Lucia worries.'
'There is much more to tell you amigo.'
'Maybe, but I've had more than enough for one night.'
He shrugged again, a brief inconsequential movement.
'Another time then my friend, but you must hear it all nevertheless, and soon. This is effectively the end of your difficulties with the Americans, but you still need to understand why!'
I downed the remains of the whiskey and stood up.
'Well that's something at least I suppose, but right now I need to get back to my wife.'
'You can't say anything to her Harry, about this, or indeed to anyone. Not yet anyway.'
He put his head on one side, as he seemed to consider.
'Ok, about Consuelo maybe, buy nothin' else. Ok Harry!'
I nodded.
'Sure. __If you say so.'
'I am being cautious because the next few days are crucial and the less anyone knows the better it will be.'
'Ok, if you say so I won't. __So I'll see you soon I suppose Raul.'
There seemed to be some element of regret now, both in his manner and also in the policeman's expression.
Perhaps it was remorse of some kind, maybe the spook deserved what he got, but at that moment I didn't care any more.
'Good night Raul.'
'Buenas noches Harry. We must speak together soon!'
I turned and left his office closing the door quietly behind me.

'You were a long time carino!'
Lucia had put her arms around me and then kissed my cheek as soon as I got back to the apartment.
'Yeah sorry love.'
'An' you' look a bit strange. __I can smell whiskey as well!'
'Well, just had a couple love, I did tell you.'

'Bu' whiskey Harry! You don' usually drink whiskey! __Anyway, what did Raul want?'
'Well here's the thing love, I'd better tell you now I suppose.'
I took a deep breath.
'Consuelo's been found dead, __also with some guy as well.'
'*Dead!* __Consuelo!'
She was obviously shocked. No surprise there I suppose.
'But *how* Harry?'
'Shot, both of them!'
I knew that she had no liking at all for Consuelo, but her grief was clearly apparent.
'My God, that's terrible Harry!'
'Yes it is. That's why Raul came round here. He wanted an independent identification. Afterwards he took me to a bar perhaps to calm me down a bit, because I certainly needed it! __Anyway, I threw up in the lavatory, hence the nasty smell.'
She took my hand and drew me towards the sofa where we both sat close to each other.
'How awful Harry, for you I mean. __An' for her of course. I didn' like her, but__'
She let out a deep sigh.
'Where was this, where did it happen?'
'Oh some dump in Regla, __an old warehouse.'
'An' the man?'
'Don't know who he was. He was lying a few metres away, half a dozen bullets in him!'
She raised a hand to her mouth.
'But why carino?'
'No idea! __If Raul knew he certainly wasn't going to tell me. Understandably I guess.'
'No I s'pose not.'
She murmured quietly.
'Oh Harry it mus' have been terrible for you to see her like that!'
'It was, __*bloody* terrible! These things happen love, I just wish I hadn't seen it that's all.'
She ran her long fingers slowly through my hair.
'Poor Harry, I's one thing after 'nother for you!'
I grinned sheepishly.
Well I've certainly had an interesting year and a half since I arrived in Cuba, and *that's* a fact!'
'You don' regret though baby?'
Her brown eyes looked directly into mine.

'Oh Lucia, sweetheart, are you serious? I met you didn't I! What more could I ask for!'
I put my around her and kissed her gently.
'You're my world Lucia, you must know that!'
'I do know it Harry, an' I love you very much!'
Again I gave a weary smile.
'Lucia I promised him I would say nothing to you about this, ok!'
'Sure baby, I will keep a zip on it.'
'Good! __Well come on then, let's go to bed love, I'm worn out.'
'Sure, but you' better brush you' teeth firs' cos' you stink!'
She stood up and took my hand.
'Come on English guy, doucha then bed!'

The next morning I made an early, not to say reluctant appearance at the café. In spite of what Raul had said to me about maintaining secrecy, I intended to break the news to Pasqual about Consuelo's death. I wouldn't say anymore than I had said to Lucia, but it seemed deceitful not to at least tell the man that she had been killed.
There was no need to say any more than that, and if he asked me I would simply say that I knew nothing other than what I had been told officially by the police.
Nobody could argue with that not even Raul.
The Café was virtually empty with only a few customers taking an early breakfast.
Pasqual was seated behind the bar sipping at coffee and reading a newspaper.
'Harry! Good morning.'
He said brightly, folding the newspaper and shoving it beneath the bar.
'Buenos dias Pasqual. Everything ok.'
'Sure, everything is fine. Consuelo is a bit late, but we're not too busy so__'
He spread his hands expressively.
'Family ok Pasqual?'
I asked, delaying the dreaded announcement if only for a minute or more.
'They're good Harry. The baby is fine, never wakes up now during the night, an' thank God for that.'
He continued before I could say anything.
'An' how is you're lovely wife Harry? Won't be to long now eh!'
'No erm, quite exciting really.'
'Sure, then you have your hands full senor, make no mistake.'

'Yes I expect so. __Pasqual look, I have some bad news, well, terrible news really.'

His expression altered at once, but before he could respond I ploughed ahead.

'It's Consuelo. I spoke to the police last night, they actually came to the apartment.

It's pretty grim I'm afraid, so, __fact is she's been found dead!'

He stared at me in disbelief.

'*What!* You can't be serious Harry, surely not!'

'Yes er, I am serious I'm sorry to say, it's dreadful news and__'

'But *how* boss? How did she die, this is so terrible!'

'I don't know Pasqual. I got another call this morning, but that's the only information I have. I expect to see Raul at some point today, perhaps he will have more detail. I hope so anyway, this is a shock for all of us.'

He looked distraught, which was hardly surprising really. They had both got on well, both working together in the café and as far as I knew, on a social basis.

'I'm sorry to break the news to you like this, there's no easy way to tell you.'

I continued, if only to break the heavy silence.

'She had relatives I presume?'

'Just her mother, her father died some years ago. No siblings.'

'Right.'

I murmured awkwardly.

At that point two more women customers entered behind where I was sitting, and for a moment Raul became the consummate café manager again.

'Buenos dias. Le gustaria desayunar senoras?'

He asked them with a cheerful smile

The two women giggled nervously.

'I'm sorry senor, I'm afraid our Spanish isn't all that good.'

One of them twittered. I recognized the voice at once but said nothing and remained hunched over the bar.

'Would you like breakfast ladies?'

'No er, just some coffee please.'

'Then find yourselves a table and we will attend to you at once.'

He rapped on the half open hatch to the kitchen.

And called through the opening.

'Dos clientes mas Jose! Pronto.'

His cheerful expression evaporated as quickly as it had appeared as he turned to me again, slipping onto the stool behind the bar.

'I will go to her mother as soon as I can Harry.'

'Sure, __that's not going to be an easy job!'
'No, but I must tell her senor.'
'If you want to go now I'll look after things here Pasqual.'
'I's ok, I'll wait 'til Consu__'
He realized his perfectly excusable error at once.'
'Tha' was so stupid!'
'No of course it wasn't Pasqual! Look you go off now and speak with her mother. I'm pretty sure the police will have visited her already, but__'
'She will be devastated Harry!'
'Yes she will, so get going and take your time.'
He nodded and retrieving his jacket he pulled it on over his white shirt.
'I'll be about an hour.'
He said almost apologetically.
'Like I said Pasqual, take your time!'

When he had left I called through into the kitchen.
'It's alright Jose, I'll take care of this.'
I set two large cups under the vast chrome plated machine and pushed a switch.
Then I set a tray on the bar and laid two saucers on it with paper sachets of sugar and a few wrapped biscuits.
When the coffee was ready I carried the tray across to the two women. It was with a degree of reluctance because I sensed what was coming.

'Well hello again, do you remember us sir!'
The lipsticked woman, her hair neatly permed, was dressed in an equally flowery outfit as the last time I had seen her and her companion in the paseo.
'How could I possibly forget two nice ladies such as your selves!'
I had to force a smile as I spoke.
'Oh well now that is nice! That's what we need isn't it Annie, compliments from handsome young men, we sure as hell don't get them at home!'
Her companion glanced up at me.
'I don't suppose you have any apple cake or somethin' similar do you?'
'Apple pie madam! Very good indeed, with just a touch of cinnamon.'
She looked uncertain.
'I'll bring you a piece. If you don't like it we won't charge you.'
She brightened at once.
'Oh well that's very considerate of you. Ok then I'll try some!'

I stuck my head through the opening to the kitchen and passed the woman's order to the waiter.

'Can you take it across to the lady Jose? And watch out, I think they're on the prowl!'

He grinned.

'I'll take care of them Harry!'

I returned behind the bar and started clearing away some plates.

The glass door to the café swung open and I looked up at once.

Normally I would have been pleased to see Raul, but today was different.

'Good morning Harry.'

'Morning Raul, Buenos dias. What will you have?'

'Nothing. I was hoping we could continue our discussion.'

'That's a bit difficult at the moment Raul. Pasqual isn't here. He's gone to see Consuelo's mother.'

He glanced at me with that all-seeing way that he had, and I guess he knew that I was in no mood to talk with him.

'There are some things you still need to know my friend, things I must explain, maybe not now, but soon Harry.'

'Ok later then, but I'm not sure when I can get away, __we're a bit short-staffed at the moment.'

One glance at him told me that my heavy sarcasm had been noted, he nodded slowly, and lowered his voice.

'Whatever you may think Harry, these things had to happen. You will understand more after we talk!'

He didn't wait for a response, but turned and walked out of the café. I watched as he climbed into the waiting police car outside, which was then driven off at once.

'Fuck it!'

I mouthed to myself as I continued tidying up things that didn't need tidying up.

Why was I so unsettled, although not the right word perhaps.

Angry? Maybe. But with who? Raul? His chilling account of shooting the American agent was certainly deeply disturbing.

I had never killed anyone and the very thought was repugnant, but then my daughter hadn't been ruthlessly murdered, and yes, maybe through collusion between the two people recently deceased.

I knew that the American agent was certainly responsible and I actually believed Raul when he said that Consuelo might also have been instrumental in her death.

No amount of reasoning made me feel any better however, or more resigned to the fact that the policeman had perhaps done what was necessary.

I was more angry with myself really, or though I didn't know why, which was absurd.

The two American women got up from their table and prepared to leave. I knew that I would have to be pleasant to them, which I was in no mood for at all.
'Enjoy your coffee ladies?'
'It was fine!'
The woman I remembered as 'Margie' remarked, rummaging in her purse.
'And the apple pie?'
'It was delicious, I'll be coming back for more!'
Her friend gushed.
'I'm pleased to here it. We look forward to seeing you again.'
They paid and left, and I returned to my immoderate frame of mind.

Pasqual returned after an hour or so.
'What happened?'
I asked him at once.
'It was pretty bad Harry. She knew because the police went there early this morning, but__'
He looked genuinely upset, and I made him some coffee at once and set it in front of him as he took one of the stools on the opposite side of the bar.
'Do you want a drink with that, a glass of rum maybe?'
He shook his head.
'I couldn' console her Harry. Consuelo was her only daughter.'
'No, it's erm, pretty bloody awful.'
'She was shot Harry!'
'Shot!'
I feigned surprise of course, which wasn't easy, and I felt badly about doing so.
'This is what the police told her.'
'I see, shot? That's terrible Pasqual.'
I replied, easing myself further into the lie.
'Did they say why? I mean__'
'No. Just that she'd been shot.'
'I expect more facts will emerge at some point. There will be an inquest of course.'
'Yes I guess so Harry.'
He said glumly.
His distress was obvious and I felt even worse for lying to the man, although I had little choice in the matter.
'So!'
I continued.

'She will certainly be missed around here. She was very good at her job and very popular with the regular customers as well.'
'But not with your wife Harry.'
He looked up as he spoke.
'No, hold on Pasqual, that was a personal thing!'
I responded defensively.
'And it was resolved if you remember. Lucia and Consuelo talked about this and she was reinstated.'
'I know that boss, I'm sorry. I jus' feel really bad about everything.'
Relenting at once, I reached across and put my hand on his shoulder for a moment.
'Look, take the day off, I'll manage here and Lucia won't mind putting in an hour or two.'
'I can't do that. This is my work, I will be ok Harry.'
He finished his coffee and carried his cup around to the other side of the bar.
'It's better if I just get on with it now.'
I couldn't argue with the man. He took a genuine pride in what he did and I didn't want to undermine that.
'Ok Pasqual, then I'll leave you to it. If you need anything I'll be in the apartment.'

I left him then and strolled back across the paseo to our home.
My intemperate mood persisted and I still felt uncertain about everything and about what I should do next.
At some point I knew I would have to talk to Raul, but at that moment I didn't want to talk to anyone.

Lucia had just taken a bath when I walked in and she was wearing a dressing gown that barely covered her now prominent belly.
'Hi carino!'
She greeted me brightly. She was sat in the kitchen holding a towel, a glass of orange juice on the table in front of her.
'You' jus' in time! __Dry my hair for me will you baby.'
She handed me the towel and I proceeded to rub her abundant dark tresses vigourously.
'I think maybe I should get it cut short, wha' d'you think Harry?'
'If you do I'll leave you!'
I remarked, forcing a smile.'
'It will jus' be easier when the baby comes chico, tha's what I was thinkin'.'
'This beautiful hair stays exactly where it is Lucia!'

She laughed at once, that lovely and so familiar sound that as always warmed my heart, even now in spite of my current mood.
'You' the boss Harry! __Everythin' ok with the café?'
'Not really love. I told Pasqual about Consuelo!'
'That mus' have been difficult.'
'It certainly wasn't easy. Anyway he asked if he could take an hour off and go to see her mother.'
She was silent for a moment before she spoke.
'I's a bad thing Harry!'
'It's certainly that all right.'
'Did you tell him__'
'No I didn't! Just that she was found dead, I don't want to seem to be too involved, you know what he's like, he's a bit of a gossip. It will be around the town in no time.
Anyway it seems that her mother told him how she had died, the police visited her this morning apparently and they obviously gave her more detail.
He was pretty upset about it when he got back.'
'Yeah I'm sure he was.'
She responded quietly.
I finished drying her hair and she handed me a hairbrush.
It was always a pleasurable experience for me, drawing a brush slowly through her dark curls until they resumed their lustrous shape, until they gleamed with an ebony sheen.
'Wha'd are you gonna do Harry?'
'I don't know sweetheart, short answer!
Raul called in after Pasqual had left.'
'Wha' does he want now?'
'To talk he said.'
'Abou' what?'
'I dunno! I was busy and said we would have to speak later.'
Again she fell silent and I continued to brush her hair gently into its natural shape.
'There!'
I laid the brush on the table.
'Now I'm going to make myself a drink.
D'you want some breakfast love?'
'I had some already. __Harry wha's goin' on?'
'What do you mean?'
'I know you carino, I know you' moods, somethin's up with you!'
I walked across to the stove and put a light under the kettle.
'Harry?'

'Oh shit!'
I muttered bad-temperedly.
'Talk to me carino, I'm you' wife!'
With a deep sigh I turned and sat in the chair opposite her, avoiding her eyes.
'Lucia, Raul told me some more things last night, but I swore to him that I would say nothing, not even to you. It's for your own safety Lucia. He didn't explain everything, but he did say that it's of great importance.'
'What really happened last night in Regla Harry?'
'Honey I can't tell you. You must trust me. He will be contacting me very soon, I'm sure of that. So maybe after I talk to him__'
She looked, I don't know, disappointed, probably with me, but I had promised Raul I would say nothing and I was sure that he had good reason for asking.

At that same moment the doorbell rang out, startling us both.
'Don't answer it!'
I said at once.
'Why not?'
'Because it's probably Raul.'
'Harry wha's *wrong* with you!'
She got to her feet with some effort and walked out into the hallway, she had pressed the intercom and I could hear her voice clearly, echoing back down the corridor.
'Yes?__Hi Raul!__Yes he's here.'
She called out to me and reluctantly I followed to where she was leaning against the entrance door, her arm outstretched, dangling the receiver in her fingers.
'I's for *you* carino!'
She announced loudly, and that 'no nonsense' look was not to be defied. Reluctantly I took the receiver from her hand.
'Yes Raul.'
I said bluntly.
She continued glaring at me, both arms raised in question, her shoulders hunched towards her neck.
'Harry, talk properly to him!'
She mouthed the words silently.
'Yes.__er, ok.__What *now!*__But you said__Ok Raul, if that's what you want!__Ok, half an hour.'
I hung the receiver back on its cradle.
'Harry what's up with you!'
She was staring at me angrily.

'Lucia please be quiet, you don't understand.'
'Don' tell me to be quiet! Raul is a good friend to both of us!'
I walked back into the kitchen and slumped onto the chair putting my head in my hands.
'Harry?'
'Lucia you don't know what's going on. He said he will be back in thirty minutes to pick us up, then maybe you will understand!'
'All this fuckin' mystery! Why can't you jus' tell me!'
I looked up at her slowly.
'Because he asked me not to, that's why. Maybe it was for your protection I don't know, but I wasn't going to take any chances!'
She stared at me angrily, but said nothing.
Eventually I broke the silence.
'He's coming back in half an hour.'
I said.
Still she said nothing.
'Lucia__'
'If he's comin' back then maybe I shou' get dressed.'
She stood up again, but before leaving the room she turned to me.
'An' as a matter of fact Harry, when are you gonna do somethin' abou' this *bloody phon'*?'
I flinched, but before I could make a defensive response she had flounced out.
In the bedroom I could hear drawers being open and closed noisily, doors to the wardrobe being slammed.
I put my head in my hands again, wondering what the hell I had done to deserve it all.
I was still languishing in self-pity when she came back into the kitchen. Even simply clothed in a loose fitting dress and with the lightest touch of make-up, and wearing a thin gold pendant necklace that I had bought for her last birthday, she looked quite extraordinarily beautiful
I looked up at her longingly.
'Lucia, look love__'
She came up to me at once and putting her hands on each side of my face she pressed my head gently against her belly.
'Harry I'm so sorry carino. This pregnan' thing makes me crazy sometimes. I know you always do the bes' for me an' I love you for that! Forgive me Harry!'
I stood up and kissed her.
'For what? This bloody business is driving both of us crazy. Anyway let's see what Raul has to say when he gets here.'
'Ok, but be nice to him Harry. I's no' his fault, no more than I's yours.'

I gave a resigned sigh.
'All right love. Like I say, lets see what's on his mind!'

Shortly afterwards the doorbell blasted out its heart-stopping sound again and I reminded myself yet again to get it changed for something a little less noisy.
I opened the door to Raul. He was still in his uniform and his face held an expression that revealed nothing at all.
'Hello Raul.'
I greeted him politely.
'Is your wife here?'
'Yes she is.'
'Then come with me both of you, there is much to explain!'
'Come, where to?'
'Just come Harry. What do you think? __That I'm going to throw you both in jail?'
'No of course not__'
'Then come!'
Lucia was already behind me carrying her handbag.
'Hello Raul, how is Maria?'
'She is ok Lucia.'
'Right then Harry, le's go!'
She took my arm firmly.

Outside a police car was parked with no one else inside.
Lucia and I climbed into the back and Raul got behind the wheel.
'Where are we going Raul?'
I asked as he pulled away into the light traffic.
'Malecon, just down to the waterfront. It's peaceful there, not many people about and we can talk in private. It's unlikely that the gringos have wired your apartment again, but better not to take chances.'
We all fell silent, even Lucia. Normally she would have been chattering away happily, but I had the feeling that she was now slowly becoming aware of the situation if not the detail.
Nothing more was said until the car drew to the side of the road at Malecon next to the sea wall. It was another fine day with just a few clouds floating across the sky, providing occasional shade from the hot sun.
'Let's er, sit near the break-water.'
Raul said taking the keys from the ignition.
'I come here quite a lot, it's a good place to think, an' the vista is of course hard to beat!'

I could hardly argue with him, because for the same reason Lucia and I regularly took a stroll, further east towards the Castillo, along the wide pavement that always seemed in constant need of repair.

We all got out. Raul tossed his cap onto the drivers seat, locked the car and we sat together on a long bench facing the sea, the surface of which was stirred up into white tipped waves by a steady breeze blowing south from the gulf.

Raul was the first to speak.

'Are you in a better mood now Harry?'

'That depends on what you have to tell us.'

He nodded in apparent acquiescence.

'I understand how you feel, but my job is not an easy one, and as I said to you, sometimes it is necessary to do things that are __disagreeable!'

'That's one way of putting it.'

I sensed at least that he was perhaps losing patience, but maybe I was wrong.

'I presume that you've said nothing about this to anyone.'

'I told Lucia that I was taken to Regla last night to identify Consuelo's body, and I also told Pasqual this morning, but that's all, nothing else!'

Again he nodded slowly.

'Ok.'

Then he turned to Lucia.

'Lucia some things have happened recently that may shock you, but part of my plan has always been to protect you both from a situation that was not of your making. I'm sure you know what I'm talking about.'

'Yes Raul, sure I know.'

She answered quietly, and he continued

'As I explained to your husband, I now believe that he will no longer be threatened by the Americans, or more accurately by their malevolent security services.'

'I didn' know that.'

'No, I suppose the less you know about any of this the better and safer it will be for you.

You know of course that Consuelo was killed. We believe, __no we are quite certain that she was shot by the same man who 'enlisted' Harry in his pernicious schemes. It was his gun that was used in the murder.'

I listened in silence. Remembering what he had said to me, it seemed to be the sensible thing to do.

'On information, we had followed her to Regla and heard the shot as we arrived. Of course we deployed at once inside the warehouse. He was caught red-handed with Consuelo apparently dead on the floor in front of him. And so I shot him!'

'Do you mean killed?'
Lucia asked in a subdued voice.
'Yes. He was holding a gun and I fired several times. There was no choice, not that I regret his death even for one moment.'
'No I guess not. It was the same man that murdered Mamen, isn' that right Raul.'
'Yes he did. It wasn't a question of revenge Lucia. He was ordered to lay down his weapon, but obviously thought he could shoot it out. That was a mistake.'
He paused and took out his cigarettes, staring across at the expanse of blue sea.
'Now! His employers will soon be asking questions. He probably wasn't alone, but my view is that whoever was with him decided to make an early escape, a wise choice for them, because within five minutes after we arrived we had the warehouse covered on all sides.'
He lit his cigarette and leaned back on the bench seat.
'However the pressure will soon be on from the CIA, or whoever is behind all this. They may contact us, which seems unlikely given the clandestine nature of the intrusion, but if they do then of course we will respond. I will be very surprised if they make a complaint directly to our government over this. It is an embarrassment for them as they have been caught with their pants down! __ But who knows? Only now we have the advantage.
Our immediate response will be of course that a man, believed to be an American, entered our country illegally and shot to death a Cuban citizen. Simple as that!'
'Did he have identification on him?'
I asked.
'Of course not Harry! If we do hear from the Yanks I think it will be on an informal level and we will of course offer full co-operation. We will send photographs of the scene, and of the woman he murdered and incontrovertible evidence of the incident. If they want the man's body returned then they are welcome.'
He smiled astutely and spread his arms apart.
'After all we have nothing to hide here!'
I intervened at once.
'But surely Raul, they will question how it was that you and your men happened to be at the warehouse at the precise moment of their meeting?'
'Of course they will! And of course they will know a great deal more than that.
Our official line will be that it was a routine patrol and that we heard the single shot and responded!'
'Yes I suppose so, no one can argue with that.'

I pondered for a moment.

'But I still don't understand why he would have shot Consuelo? She was working for them for God's sake!'

'Ah, so now you ask the pertinent question. He shot her because he discovered that she was a double agent working for the Cuban authorities.'

'How the hell will you prove that?'

'*You* will have proved it Harry!'

'*Me!* You can't be serious surely! __What the hell do I know?'

'I am *completely* serious my friend. This is what I wanted to talk with you about. __To explain to you.'

He paused briefly.

'It was you who will have told the American that Consuelo was spying for both sides, but was in fact a loyal Cuban. We know that she murdered Carlos Roldan on your boat, and the reason for this was because she discovered that he was working exclusively for the Americans, or at least so they believe.

In fact as I explained to you before, Carlos was dedicated to the Cuban cause and this is the real reason why she shot him.'

'Ok I think I see now what you're getting at Raul, but the problem is that I never knew much about any of this, and not until very recently, like yesterday. So how could I have possibly conveyed this information to the American and to whoever he is working for?'

'But you did Harry! __Or should I say we did!

You sent him a full report on all these things a week ago. A detailed account, which you wrote, and in which you said that it was she, Consuelo, who had murdered Carlos Roldan.

Obviously the woman would have suspected his real allegiance to the Cuban intelligence service, and decided to take care of him, which she did. Who knows, maybe she thought that he was on to her, maybe she was hoping for an extra bonus of some kind from the Yanks, who can say for sure. But you of course believed that Carlos was loyal only to the Americans.'

'Really, and how the bloody hell did I know that?'

'Because I told you so on good authority, and to be wary of him because I knew he would be accompanying you on the gun-running venture.'

'My God, this is difficult to take in Raul. You just said you knew without question that Carlos was really a Cuban patriot.'

'Of course I knew! But what I didn't know was that this woman was going to shoot him dead.'

'Er, no, I suppose not!'

'There is no suppose Harry! Roldan's death was tragic. I didn't like him much, but he was a good Cuban and hated the Americans and what they have done to our country.'
'But they will see him as a martyr for the U.S. surely.'
'Sure they will. That is the whole idea Harry, but we know the truth, and at least he died in a good cause.'
'That sounds pretty callous Raul.'
'Maybe amigo. But I think he would be pleased to know that, and also that this woman's treachery, __to you as well don' forget, was her eventual downfall.'

I could hardly believe what I had just heard.
'Raul this is complete nonsense, a total fabrication!'
He smiled the Machiavellian smile again.
'Of course it is Harry!'
'I mean to begin with, why the hell would they believe that you, a chief of police would confide such matters to me. I mean secret information.'
'That is not as difficult to believe as you may think Harry. Firstly you tried valiantly to save my daughter when, as you related to me, your first boat, the 'Lucy' was cut in two by a ship in the dead of night.
From that moment we became good friends, which is still true I hope. Not only because of that, you had also gained my confidence by agreeing to run guns for Cuba. There was also an earlier event, which will convince the Americans even further.'
'Which earlier event?'
I was distinctly nervous, simply because I had no idea what was coming next.
'Do you remember when you first started your charter business and you took two Americans out fishing close to the peninsular of Varadero?'
'The two blokes who got shot you mean. How could I forget that! If it wasn't for Lucia I wouldn't be talking to you now.'
'Exactly so. Only it didn't quite happen that way, not according to the record.'
'What does that mean?'
'It means this Harry. We have suspected that the woman Consuelo has been acting for the Americans for almost two years now, before you arrived in Cuba in fact.
When you returned with the two corpses on board it gave me an idea, the germ of an idea at least.
We decided to return the two bodies to the Americans and explained that they had been shot by one person who was driving a fast motor boat and then immediately afterwards made an escape.'

'But Raul__'
'Wait harry! Let me finish. __An autopsy was of course performed, the bullets were removed from the two corpses by the pathologist and his report registered. Afterwards the bullets were placed in a secure container and returned together with the bodies to the United States.
We made no claim as to who they were, simply that they were American citizens who had been killed by a person unknown during a fishing trip. No mention was made at the time that it was your boat that was used.
We made an official statement and said that the owners of the vessel were above any suspicion, and had narrowly escaped being shot themselves.
They then immediately turned over the bodies to the Cuban authorities, __which of course you did!'
He paused to light a second cigarette.
'When we searched the apartment of this woman Consuelo some time back, __you remember that Harry?'
'Yes of course I remember.'
'One of the things we found was a gun. The same weapon which was used to kill the two Americans.'
'That's impossible. The boat that attacked us was sunk, together with the two men on board.'
'Was it Harry? We don't have a record of that.'
'I don't understand. You're not making any sense Raul!'
I glanced at Lucia, expecting her to make a comment, but she was simply staring in silence at the policeman.
'Lucia?'
I prompted her.
'I think we shou' jus' listen Harry!'
She remarked quietly.
Raul continued with his fantastic story, which I was slowly beginning to realize was exactly that.
'The markings of the bullets found in the bodies of the two men matched exactly with a bullet, which we fired from the gun, a type widely used by operatives for American intelligence. Her prints, Consuelo's prints, were found clearly on the weapon. This gun has now been sent to the American authorities, but not before it was photographed and all the evidence carefully documented.'
So you can see that she was clearly implicated.'
'Yes, I'm beginning to see quite a lot Raul.'
'Good. I was hoping that you would my friend.'
He smiled craftily.
'Then, some weeks after the incident, you went to see the man Alberto in Regla.'

'I did?'

'Yes, he remembers it clearly. He asked you to visit him because he had found some information, some important manuals relating to the maintenance of the engine on your fishing boat, which he said you could collect from him.'

'I don't remember that.'

'Oh I expect that you will Harry, it's just a brief and temporary memory lapse on your part.

When you visited him on his new motor cruiser, where as you know he now lives, you noticed a smaller boat moored nearby, quite a new one and with a large outboard motor. You recognized the vessel almost at once. It was very similar if not the same as the vessel that was used when the two Americans were assassinated during the fishing trip, which you and your wife had organized.

You asked Alberto about the craft and he told you that it was his, and that he rented it out occasionally to fishermen.

You asked him if you could look it over in case it might have a similar use for you with any potential clients in the future.

He agreed at once of course, why would he not. And so while he was getting some beers for you both and perhaps something to eat, you went aboard for a quick look around. Purely by chance you found some cartridge cases in the scuppers, because this is what you were really searching for and was lucky enough to find.

Before Alberto came back on the deck of his cruiser you pocketed these, and then joined him again on his boat.'

'Yes I see, that *was* a bit of luck, although I'm still struggling to remember all this.'

'You will Harry, trust me. __You will.

Then you asked the man if he had rented it out recently. He responded that, yes, because of it's moderate size and high power that it had proved quite popular. You then asked him if he had rented it out to a woman in recent weeks. He thought that possibly he had, and was able to confirm this by referring to a log-book that he kept where the names of people that had used the boat were clearly documented. No signatures of course in case the tax authorities became curious. It was simply a personal record for his own use.

He ran through the names and sure enough the woman's was listed, Consuelo Jimenez. Also the date when she had taken it out on charter.'

'Right, well that's quite a story Raul! __And Alberto remembers all this quite clearly does he?'

'As clearly as if it had happened yesterday Harry.'

'Ok, I get it. __But when Lucia and I made a written statement to the police, after we returned to Havana with the two dead Americans on board, we said in our statement that we had been attacked by two men who killed the Yanks and then fired at me.'
'We don't have a record of that statement Harry!
Your signed account simply says that a solitary woman approached the 'Lucy' in a small boat, asking if you had had any luck with the Marlin. She drew alongside, pulled out a gun and shot the two Americans, then she took a shot at you. If it had not been for your wife's quick thinking in maneuvering your vessel, you might well be dead as well!
Then, obviously thinking better of it, the woman made her escape.'
'But for God's sake Raul, I would have *seen* her and Lucia would have as well. Later on when she came to me for a job I would have recognized her at once!'
'But the woman wore dark glasses, a woolen hat pulled down over her long blond hair, you noticed that but nothing else because she was firing a gun at you.
Consuelo had dark hair if you recall, isn't that right Harry?'
'Yes I suppose it is, __I mean of course it is!'
'Exactly my friend! __After all this you brought the information to me, which was further proof that she was really a Cuban agent. In doing so you had earned my trust and my confidence. Do you see now Harry?'
'Yes I certainly do! __I have to say that it's a fascinating tale Raul, it would make a very good movie!'
Rauls expression changed at once and he became serious.
'It will also quite possibly save your life Harry!'
Suddenly I felt Lucia's hand on my thigh.
'Harry, it is a good story, an' some of it is true Carino. Maybe Raul is right. It get's you off the hook like he said!'
'Yes, yes maybe he is at that.'
I said quietly.
'I have a feeling that there is more to tell Raul, am I correct?'
'There is. __You sent your report about everythin' recently, together with a copy of your signed official police statement about the first event, the incident on the 'Lucy'.
You sent it to the Americans at the address which they gave you.'
'How did I do that? Surely not via a post office in Havana.'
'That would have been reckless Harry. No, you know exactly where I mean, at the place where the American told you to leave any messages, an edificio, a building on Calle San Rafael. Apartment number seven, post box number seven. Easy to remember!'
'How could you possibly know that?'

'It's not important.
All this information was sent just over a week ago. In addition to this, your belief that it was Consuelo who shot Carlos Roldan on your boat! The same man who, she had quite possibly suggested previously to the Americans, was in fact a Cuban agent.
But she killed him because she discovered he was working solely for an American covert group! This is your clear message to them. You knew that we had followed her to San Sebastion, and also that we were too late to prevent the man's death.
Don't tell me you forgot that as well Harry!'
A smile crept back on his lips.
'He was both, as we know. A double agent, it was a dangerous game for him and it cost him his life!
The Yanks however will see only that she had killed their man.'
'I don't get all this?'
'You're not trying Harry! The Americans believed that Roldan was spying for them. He has been feeding them shit for years with the occasional cherry on top, like the regular gun-running trips.'
'But they knew about those anyway!'
'Sure they did, but Roldan didn't know that, or so the Yankees thought! As far as they were concerned he was simply confirming information they already possessed! So when they know, from the information you sent to them, that this woman shot him they can only draw one conclusion.
As they will now see it, having received the detailed report that you sent to them, she has killed three of their people, and when they realize that their own man shot her through the head they will presume that he must have discovered this, and this was the reason for their meeting, __and her assassination!'
'He might have had another reason for contacting her.'
'Maybe he did Harry, who can say? So why then would he kill her?'
He paused for a few moments, no doubt to allow it all to sink in.
'So do you see everything clearly now Harry?'

I turned to stare out at the sea, utterly bewildered and unaccountably depressed by everything I had heard.
I felt Lucia move closer to me, then her arm around my shoulder, holding me tightly.

'So I have framed her then __Consuelo, __or rather you have!
I hate to use that horrible American expression, but__'
The words dried up suddenly.
'Yes Harry, that's exactly what has happened.'

I paused to draw a deep breath.
'This is diabolical Raul! __All of it!'
'Maybe, but this is the world we live in my friend.'
'But it's a complete fabrication, about Roldan and Consuelo, about everything!'
'Yes it is. But they are both deceased now Harry, so does it matter?'
For a moment or so I was lost.
'Consuelo worked for us at the café. I never thought even for a moment that__'
Again I could find no words.
'I mean I liked her, sort of. How the hell could she__'
'Don' feel sorry for her! It was you, was it not, who discovered that she was probably going through your accounts to find out when you were planning any long boat trips, you know this Harry!'
'Yes. __Suspected anyway, it wasn't easy to believe.'
'She was a traitor! She was a threat, both to you and to Lucia. She probably was also paid a great deal to betray her country, maybe into some bank in Miami. Perhaps she planned to escape there when this was all over. No, I don' feel sorry for her my friend, she only cared about herself.'
He dropped the butt of his cigarette on the pavement and pressed his boot on it, twisting it back and forth.
'This is the way it is Harry whether we like it or not!
The Americans have much to answer for, an' not only on this little island of ours!
I told you before amigo, I am no communist, but the best chance we have here is to be independent and to shape our own society and our own future without the 'help' of the self appointed guardians of the free world.'
I turned to him again, perhaps more resolute now than ever before.
'Yes, you could be right Raul.'
I reached up and covered Lucia's hand with my own.
She had hardly spoken, but perhaps she felt that there was nothing to say.

'Raul there seem to be a couple of holes in all this, which I'm sure you can explain. To begin with, the gun that was used to shoot the two Americans! That was lost in deep water together with the people who really shot them, along with their boat.'
He gave a slight nod.
'I will explain. When the autopsy was carried out, the bullets that were removed from the bodies were replaced with others.'
'I see.'
'We have to be as devious as our enemies Harry!'

'I suppose so. __And I presume these were from the gun that you found in her apartment?'
'We never actually found a gun!'
'But her prints surely__'
'That isn't difficult is it? __We have her body you must remember.'
'Yes I see, I get it now.'
He sat upright and pushed the cigarette packet into a pocket of his uniform.
'Is there anything else you want to ask me?'
'Yes there is. Something I don't understand.'
'Which is?'
He responded calmly.
'As soon as the American spook had received my so-called account of all these things, he would have contacted me at once as a matter of urgency!'
'And how would he do that Harry, at such short notice?'
'He would have telephoned me of course as he always__'
I stopped short, because the penny had finally dropped.
'Any other questions Harry?
'No I don't think so Raul.'
Lucia remained resolutely silent.
'Ok then. So now I will drop you at your home, then I too will return to my house. I promised Maria I would be early today.'
He stood up, a cue for us both to follow suit.
'I know this has been a bad time for both of you, entirely undeserved. However you have now provided the Yanks with strong evidence that the woman Consuelo was in fact a Cuban agent. You have done what they asked, and I think that you are now 'out of the woods'. __Is that the correct expression amigo?'
'Yes it is, and I guess I must thank you for what you've done.'
He grinned at me.
'Your gratitude overwhelms me my friend!'
'I'm sorry, no of course. No one could have done better Raul. How you ever dreamed up such a plan is beyond me and as you say, it looks like it puts us in the clear. I'm sure you understand that I er, __what I mean is both of us are astonished by what you've told us. It will take us a while to__I don't know, come to terms with it all I suppose.'
Lucia broke in at once.
'Thank you so much Raul! __Gracias muchisimo!
I's like you say, a big shock for me an' for Harry, so we need to think some more about all this.'
'Of course.'
He rummaged for his keys and we walked back towards the car.

He unlocked it and Lucia climbed into the back. He closed the door and we both walked around to the other side of the car.
'Say nothing more to her about this Harry, it will be better.'
He said in a low voice.
'No I think you're right. I won't say a thing Raul.'
He opened the opposite rear door and I got in as he took the driving seat. From the front passenger seat he took a large sealed envelope and passed it to me.
'Everything is here that has been passed to the spooks in the U.S.! Keep it safe Harry. It's better if you destroy it after you have read it all very carefully. I feel certain that the Americans will contact you at some point, and you may have to explain some things to them. __Incidentally!'
He added with a broad smile.
'You will find that your telephone is working now!'

The revelation had left Lucia and I in a state of total confusion and, had it not been Raul relating it all to us, it would have included total disbelief. As diabolical and convoluted as it all was, it appeared that he had thought of everything.

Raul had dropped us both at the apartment and we sat together next to each other on the sofa saying very little, utterly preoccupied as we were with what we had heard.
'Harry, it seems that Raul has fine'ly solved you' problem with this American guy! __Tha's *good* isn't it carino?'
I heaved a sigh.
'The dead American you mean! Yes I suppose so honey, but I've got a nasty feeling about all this.
With all this mayhem the Yanks will want some kind of confirmation about what happened.'
'But you did wha' they ask you for Harry!'
'Yes I know, it looks that way, but I'll be very surprised if some bastard from the CIA, or whatever, doesn't contact me, just as Raul said.'
On impulse I reached across for the telephone on a side table
'We shall have to wait and see I suppose.'
I pressed the call button.
'It's working now.'
I said quietly.
Switching the device off again I returned it to the cradle.

I was right in my assumption!
A day or so later I received a call at the café.
The place was busy and I had been helping out again as we hadn't found a replacement for Consuelo.
It was a man's voice, American, someone I didn't recognize.
'Harry Burgess?'
'Yes it is, can I help you?'
'We've been trying to reach you.'
'On this number? __I'm not often here, not until recently anyway.'
'And also on your home line!'
'Ah yes. It's back on now at last. It was out of order, for more than two weeks in fact. Not unusual in this country.'
'Yeah that's what we thought.'
'So how can I help you?'
'Ring me back on the Vermont number, __you know the drill.'
The line went dead.
I froze inside. The old fears returned and I had to take one of the bar stools as my legs quite suddenly had difficulty in supporting my body.
Pasqual was whizzing past carrying a tray and glanced at me.
'You ok Harry?"
'Yeah fine, just taking a break.'
There were a lot of customers and I felt almost guilty at having to explain to the man.
I waited until he had returned from the outside tables.
'Pasqual, erm, look I have to get back to the apartment for a moment, just give me ten minutes ok.'
He smiled, but there was an expression of obvious forbearance in his face.
'Sure, ten minutes is ok Harry.'
It felt, oddly enough, as though I was the waiter being castigated by the boss!
Grabbing at my jacket I left at once, walking at a pace along the paseo until I reached the phone booth that I normally used.
Picking up the receiver and pressing in a few coins, I dialed the number.

It was answered at once and there was the usual brief delay until the connection was made.
'Burgess?'
'Yes.'
'We got your report.'
'Ok.'

'You know what's happened of course!'
'Only that the girl who used to work for me has been shot dead, for which I suppose I'm ultimately responsible, bearing in mind the information I sent to you. I shall have to live with it I suppose, but it's not a particularly nice feeling.'
'No maybe not.'
'Where is the man I usually speak with, is he er, busy with something else? I never knew what his name was, perhaps you can help me there.'
'We'll get to that. I need to talk with you Burgess, face to face.'
'I had a feeling you might say that. Look I've done everything that's been asked of me by whatever his name was! Now I want some bloody peace! My wife is about to give birth and I want some assurances__'
'What kind of assurances?'
'The man's voice was smooth and controlled and I had the ridiculous notion that he was actually reading my mind.
'Listen, you know exactly what I mean. I've been living a bloody nightmare for months now. I've done what you wanted. So why can't me and my family just be *fucking* left alone!'
'There was a lighter tone now in his voice.'
'No one said otherwise Harry. You did your job and we just want a quick debriefing, just to make sure that everything fits.'
Again the icy hand of fear gripped my heart. Did he know something that I didn't? Almost certainly, but I had no choice but to bluff it out, and anger seemed like the best camouflage.
'So what do you want?'
I retorted brazenly, and with as much bravado as I could muster.
'Just to talk and make sure that we're clear on everything, that's all Harry. What have you got to fear?'
'From past experience with you guys, just about everything! __So meet up where?'
'You take your boat out a few miles from shore, we'll get together and talk with you there.'
'You can't be serious. I've lost one boat already to you people! Only I suspect that I'll be on this one when it sinks without trace! You can't have individuals like me hanging around with possible stories to tell, now can you!'
'My predecessor made a deal with you and we'll keep to it.'
'Really! Why don't I feel too confident about that! Look I've done everything that he asked. I've risked my life making three trips to the western cayos__'
'Your life was never in danger Harry.'

'So *you* say! In addition I've shopped the woman who used to work for me, not that I'm too concerned about that if I'm to be really honest. She was playing a dangerous game, which she lost.
I know for a fact that she was spying on us as well, so if I'm to be honest, I have as much sympathy for her as I do with you and your colleague. Who are you anyway? NSA, CIA, your reputation certainly precedes you in this nasty world we live in.'
'Do you know who killed her Harry?'
'My guess would be your nice friend, who doesn't seem to want to talk to me now, not that I shall lose any sleep over that!'
The phone stared to beep.
'Hold on for a second.'
I murmured, pressing some more coins into the slot.
'Yes, so the answer is no, I will not be taking my boat out to meet you in a prearranged location. That would be pretty dumb, even for me! I suggest you come over to Havana, and we can talk here. I'll buy you lunch, chilli and beans and all the lousy Cuban beer you can drink.'
'Coming to Havana is not so easy at the moment Harry.'
'No I'll bet it isn't! The police will want to know who killed this woman for a start. Who knows, maybe they have already some ideas there!'
'So how do we do this?'
'I don't know, neither do I care!'
It felt very satisfying, telling this man effectively to fuck off! However, that feeling didn't last for very long.
'Burgess, you and I are going to get together very soon whether you like it or not. Don't believe for one moment that you are safe, tucked away in that little shit-hole island. Now I'm willing to listen to any ideas you may have as to how we bring this off.'
His threat was clear, and I had no doubt that he would be able to carry out just about anything that he might suggest.
Once again the fear was creeping up on me.'
'Ok look, I don't trust you and you don't trust me. There is no person here that I can confide in over this, but I will try to come up with something, somewhere we can meet where I will feel safe.'
'Ok, that seems reasonable enough only be careful Harry, don't say too much, not to anyone!'
'I'm not that fucking daft!'
'Good. Call me tomorrow morning!'
The line went dead.
It wasn't a request, and I knew it.
'Fuck it!' I mumbled to myself as I hung up the phone.
Why did they want to talk to me, what the hell did I know?

Or though of course I knew the answer to that. It was exactly as Raul had predicted.
It was difficult however, to know where I could meet with the man, and I had no idea how I was going to come up with an answer.

I hurried back to the café feeling slightly guilty at my short absence.
The place was still packed and I spent the next three hours carrying dishes to tables or serving drinks at the bar.
I knew that I had to find someone to take Consuelo's place and soon, and recalling how efficient she had been I also knew that it wasn't going to be easy.
For a moment or so I felt a short stab of guilt as I thought about her. Was I responsible for her death? Maybe not directly, but that didn't help much and the feeling of some blame at least persisted. Whatever she had done It was the fruitless waste of a young life, that's how I saw it.
Yes Raul was right, she was a traitor and also maybe an accomplice to murder as well as an assassin, if I was to believe his account of what happened to Carlos Roldan, and I had no reason at all not to. But had she been a threat to Lucia and I by informing the Yanks about the gun-running activities?
I wasn't sure. Certainly she was culpable for Mamens death, another wasted young life, entirely undeserved.
Whatever I may have thought, her brutal demise still left a very unpleasant taste in my mouth, and the same sense of at least partial guilt for her death still lingered.
And of course there was Raul!
I understood his reasons for despising Consuelo, he had lost his eldest daughter and yes, she had played a part in that. In addition there seemed no doubt that she had been a definite threat to the Cuban nation.

I shook my head, still engrossed in my thoughts as I set two drinks on the bar for two elderly Americans.
'Is this whiskey?'
One of them asked me with a dubious look.
'Whiskey? __Er no, I mean yes, I'm very sorry, you asked me for Bourbon didn't you. My mistake sir.'
I quickly filled two more glasses for them and set them down on coasters in front of them.
'Quite busy today, hence the er, __anyway, doubles for you two gentlemen at the price of singles!'
I presented them both with a friendly smile.
Pasqual bustled past again, balancing four plates of food effortlessly.

'Everything ok Harry?'
He called out cheerfully.

'Christ what a day!'
I commented wearily when I had let myself into the apartment and Lucia had greeted me at once with a lovely kiss.
'Waitin' at tables isn' really your thing is it Harry! __You want somethin' to eat?'
'Later maybe love. A stiff drink is what I need right now.'
I almost fell into the comfortable sofa and kicked off my shoes.
'You ok honey I asked her?'
'Sure!'
She smiled at me warmly, stroking her large belly with both hands.
'Won't be long now chico!'
'No. __You look wonderful Lucia!'
Her pleasure at my comment was obvious.
'Tha' was a nice thing to say Harry!'
I gazed at her.
'I thought you said I wouldn't fancy you when you got fat!'
'Well I didn' think you would. __You' not jus' sayin' that are you carino?'
She sat next to me and put a hand on my face as I turned to her.
'No love, I'm not just saying it. You're more beautiful now than I ever thought was possible.'
She rested her head on my shoulder and put her arm around me, holding me close.
'I love you Harry!'
'And I love you sweetheart. __Er, what about that drink.'
She sat up again.
'Oh so now I get it! You don' wanna talk to me you jus' wanna a drink is that it!'
I grinned at her and pulled her into my arms.
'Don't be daft! The drink can wait.'
It felt so good holding her close to me, the scent of her body, her soft hair against my face, and for a while I forgot about everything else as we embraced each other in silence.

'How did it go Harry, in the café?'
'Oh ok I guess. __So busy love, you wouldn't believe it! Packed out again!'
'Well tha's good isn' it carino!'
'I suppose so, but we have got to get some more staff, and soon.'

'To replace her, to replace Consuelo.'
'Yes.'
We were silent again.
'It was a terrible thing Harry!'
She remarked suddenly.
'Yeah. Yes it was. I still feel very bad about it.'
'It wasn' your fault baby.'
'Maybe not, but that doesn't help much.'
Right now seemed to be a good moment to tell her about the call I had received from the American, and that's what I did.

'*What!* But you did everthin' carino. Everythin' they ask' you!'
'Well, he just said that they wanted to, __I don't know, compare notes I suppose, grill me about exactly what happened I expect. Raul said this could happen!'
'You can't meet him like the way he said Harry!'
'I'm not going to, trust me on that! __But he's insisting that we have this discussion.'
'So tell him to come to Havana an' talk!'
'I did, but he said the heat is on at the moment, and he's probably right. The police, Cuban immigration, they will all be on the alert after what's happened.'
But Harry, you can get Raul to set somethin' up. You know he would do that!'
'I'm sure he would love, but don't you think the CIA would be just a little bit suspicious about that?'
'Yeah sure, I'm no' thinkin' straight.'
'Neither am I at the moment.'
I let out a long breath of air.
'It's like out of the frying pan and into the fire!'
I said refectively.
'Out of the *what?*'
She looked at me in bewilderment.
'Oh it's just another silly English expression, it means going from one problem to an even bigger one. Mildly ironic really because I used to be in the business once in England.
'What business?'
Again she looked at me quizzically.
'Oh, frying pans! __I worked for a company that made cooking utensils, you know, things for the kitchen.'
'You used to *make* frying pans?'

'No, nothing so complicated. I worked in the office. Seems like a thousand years ago now.'
'Why you tell me all this Harry'
She still looked confused and I had to smile.
'I don't know really. I wish that I hadn't now!'
She tweaked my nose and then eased herself up out of the sofa.
'I get you a drink now carino, I think you need it!'

The obvious thing to do was speak to Raul of course. If he didn't have any ideas then nobody did.
I meet him early the next morning in the same untidy dump of a café near the fruit market. The place that served the best paella that I had ever tasted. This time it was just coffee and a long discussion.

'I thought this might happen Harry. They want to compare notes. Make sure they're not being screwed!'
'Yes I'm sure of that.'

'So!'
He stroked his chin, deep in thought for a moment.
'Look, think of it like this. There is obviously no trust between you. Before, he could have slipped into Havana no problem, but not any longer. This whole business will have caused a real stir at Langley, and most probably in the U.S. administration.
For us it has been a significant propaganda coup!
An American undercover operative has shot dead an innocent Cuban woman, a heroine, very much like my daughter in fact, except that Mamen was a real heroine!'
'She certainly was.'
I agreed.
'Ok, so together with all the other events of the recent covert intervention by the C.I.A. the U.S. are most definitely on the back-foot right now!
Don't say too much about the guy we shot dead ok! You saw him lying on the floor obviously and you recognized him, but that's it! You didn't say that you knew him, not to me or too anyone else, is that clear? __It's important amigo!'
'Yes, very clear Raul.'
Good. So this will be the plan Harry.'

I phoned the number in Vermont later that morning.
It was the same guy I had spoken to the previous day.
'Burgess! What have you got for me.'
'Look you know my name, but I don't know yours. I mean what do I call you? __Pete, Tom, Boris?'
'Don't be smart Harry, it's not going to win you a cigar, and I don't have time for it! So were do we meet.'
'Just you?'
'Yes just me.'
'You just want to talk is that right?'
'Just to talk.'
'Ok so this is what happens. There is a small inlet, a bay really that used to be used for commercial fishing. It's about sixty kilometres along the coast, west of Havana.'
I gave him the coordinates.
'You don't know this place, unless Carlos Roldan told you about it.'
'Who's he?'
'Your Cuban informant, now deceased!'
'I don't know who you're talking about!'
'Now who's taking the piss? Look, he came with me on two occasions to drop the bloody weapons in the cayos, I was warned that he was working for you people and to watch out for him.'
'Warned by who?'
'That's not important.'
'Your police chief pal, right?'
'Are you going to listen or not?'
Brief silence.
'Ok go ahead.'
'The only way you can get there is by boat. When you enter the bay you will see an old wooden jetty, it's falling to pieces so watch your step. The boat drops you there and then backs up into the centre of the bay. There is a pathway that leads up through the hills. Start walking and I'll pick you up.'
'And the Cuban police will be waiting for me, right!'
'Don't be stupid. Why would I let the police know that I'm having a secret meeting with the CIA. We could both be sharing the same cell, __if we were lucky that is. You blokes are not very popular at the moment, that's assuming you ever were!
So that's the plan! __Remember, just you! If anyone else gets off that boat I will know and I'll be on my way back to Havana before you can walk ten yards.'
'Ok so when does this happen?'

'Now.'
'Don't be crazy Burgess, it will take me at least a day to get to the region.'
'Oh I doubt that very much. My guess is that you're very close to Cuba. On a coastguard boat maybe. With the resources at your disposal it shouldn't be too difficult.
I shall be waiting. If you're not there in four hours I'm off!'
'Now look Harry__'
'Yes or no?'
Another silence, longer this time.
'Ok, four hours.'
The line went dead.

I set off towards San Sebastion at once. It was only an hour's drive to the tiny village, and after making an elaborate fabricated excuse to Lucia, there seemed no point in hanging around.
A couple of Raul's men had concealed themselves on the hillside around the bay to advise me if the spook decided to get up to any monkey business, and we were all set.
Half an hour before the appointed time a large powerful motor yacht pulled into the bay through the narrow inlet.
It idled slowly towards the ramshackle jetty, and as soon as it pulled alongside a man jumped over the side onto the landing.
At once, the vessel had reversed into the middle of the bay and dropped anchor. Without looking back the solitary figure began to walk quickly towards the pathway.
A large number of police had followed me from Havana, keeping well out of sight.
'If they make any stupid decisions, like sending more men ashore.'
Raul had said.
'Then it will be like the Bay of Pigs all over again, but on a smaller scale!'

I was waiting alone in an old Buick, just over the brow of the hill, a couple of hundred metres further along the rough car track, and I saw the man approaching in the rearview mirror.
Then he was at the passenger side, pulling at the door handle.
He got in quickly as it had started to rain again, slamming the car door.
He was medium height, casually dressed in sneakers, jeans and a leather jacket.
'You forgot your umbrella!'
I remarked drily.
He turned to me with a humourless expression.
'Ok, so let's get down to it Harry.'

'Not here, just in case your mates decide to join us!'
I started the engine.
He didn't look anything like a secret service man, but then what do secret service men look like.
He had thinning hair, he was around fifty I guessed and looked slightly overweight.
'Where are we going?'
He asked.
'There's a small town, a pueblo really, about a mile or so further on. We can find a bar and have a more or less civilized conversation.'
'I put the car in gear and we began bumping our way along the unmade road.
'Where'd you get the Buick?'
'It's borrowed. I don't have a car.'
Again he turned to me with a look that could easily be interpreted as mild distain.
'How the *fuck* did you end up in a tin-pot dump like Cuba Harry?'
'Your colleague asked me the same question.'
'Did he now!'
'Yes. __Your deceased colleague I should say!'
'How did you know he was deceased, as you put it? You didn't mention that before.'
'Didn't I! Well perhaps you can tell me more.
I saw his body shortly after he was shot dead by the police.'
'D'you wanna explain that Harry?'
'Sure, why not. I was taken to an old warehouse in Regla, other side of the bay. Your __'friend' was laying on the floor, dead as a doornail!
And quite close to him a woman, She'd been shot through the head.'
'Why were *you* taken there?'
'Well I expect you can figure out the answer to that. I was asked to identify her, she worked for me in my café, __waitress, __bloody good one too!'
'Why would I know that?'
'Oh come on, leave out the game playing! If your mate knew her, then *you* knew her!'
'How were you aware that he knew her? __My 'mate' as you call him.'
'Now really, this is getting very silly! __Because he shot her! It was in all the local papers, and anyway I recognized him as soon as I saw the body, although obviously I didn't say anything. Not to the police, not to my wife, not to anyone.
Later on the police confirmed that he was the man that had killed her. Incontrovertible evidence so I was told.'
'By your friend you mean, the chief of police?

'Ok, yes, he did tell me, and he *is* my friend! There's no mystery about that.'
'So why did he shoot her, assuming that he did?'
'How the fuck should I know! I can only guess.'
The small village was coming into sight now in the near distance, and the man was silent for a moment.
'So back to my first question. __What the fuck are you doing here in this communist backwater Harry?'
'Living my life, and enjoying every minute. __Or at least I was until the CIA turned up!'
'Then you should have stayed out of trouble, am I right?'
I heaved a long sigh.
'Yes, yes maybe you are.'
I was back on a tarmac road again and slowed the car as we approached the junction with the single main road that ran through the village. I turned left towards the church and pulled up on the right outside the bar, which Raul had told me about earlier.
His brother would be inside, he had said, playing cards with his friends, although I had no idea what his brother looked like.

'Right this is it. You can probably get food if you want, but as I've never eaten here before I'm afraid I can't recommend it.'
In fact I've never been in the place before, or to this run down little dump of a town either, which is why I chose it.'
We both got out of the car and went inside.
Two men sat on stools at the bar and five more were seated at a table in the centre playing cards. The far end of the room was deserted, as Raul said it would be, and we took one of the empty tables.
'Do you want a beer?'
I asked the man.
'They got Budweiser?'
'Now be sensible, there's an embargo, remember?'
'What about Whiskey.'
'I'll ask him.'
I replied as the elderly barman came across to us.

'So, where were we?'
The man began.
'Don't you have a name?'
I asked.
'Ok, it's George, happy now?'
'I will be when this conversation is over.'

He ignored the comment as though it had never been made.
'Getting back to this woman. __Why do you think she was shot?'
'You already asked me that.'
'I didn't get a proper answer.'
'Well it's the only one I know. __She worked for me, that's it!'
'What if I said she also worked for Cuban intelligence!'
I pulled a face and shrugged.
'I wouldn't have said she was the type.'
He didn't reply, but stared at me with iron intensity.
His eyes, I now noticed, had that particular determined shrewdness that I had seen in the face of his dead colleague on the two occasions I had ever seen him. __Alive that is!
'You sent us a full account of what's been going on here recently.'
'I did? I don't know what you mean!'
'Are you playing cat and mouse with me Harry?'
'If I sent you a letter of some kind it must have had an address on it surely!'
'What are you playing at__'
'The address! What was it?'
'Vermont!'
'That was it, nothing else, no number, no street name?'
'No.'
'Ok, so I couldn't have sent it to you by regular post, now could I!'
'Right ok, I see where this is going now.'
'Do you, then you can tell me where it was posted can't you!'
'It was some broken down tenement on Calle San Rafael, apartment seven, post box, same number.'
'Ok. I'm sure you can understand my caution.'
He nodded almost imperceptibly.

'Right. So this woman, Consuelo Jimenez! What's the story with her?'
'Well initially I was quite sure she was working for some outside intelligence group, meaning you.'
'What made you think that?'
'I'll get to that later.'
'Ok then, so now tell me about this guy Roldan?'
'I already have. He was with me on the last occasion when I made the trip to the cayos.'
'You said that he worked for us.'
'I was told that he did, and to be wary. Although if he did work for you it was unlikely that he would be a threat to me, in view of the fact that I was running errands for you.'

'So what happened to him?'
'He was shot to death on my boat!
Straight through the back of the head, two bullets, very messy indeed!'
'Where was this?'
'Like I told you. __And in the very same location where you were dropped off half an hour ago.'
'Where were you when this happened?'
'Asleep below deck! Drugged, so I was told later, could only have been by this bloke Carlos.'
'Why?'
'I dunno! All I can think is that he had arranged a meeting with someone that he didn't want me to know about, and that same someone shot him through the back of the head, __twice!'
When I finally came up on deck, well __ it was a pretty grim sight. There was blood everywhere! Over the controls, the seats, over the windscreen, part of which was splintered because one of the bullets must have passed straight through his head and made a neat hole in the glass. I was pretty groggy, still not quite awake, and after seeing all that carnage, suddenly very nauseous. I leaned over the side of the boat and threw up.'
'Where was the body?'
He was on his back on the floor and his face__'
I hesitated.
'His face was virtually obliterated, a hideous sight. I'd never seen anything like it before.'
'And it was him, it was Carlos Roldan?'
'Well it certainly wasn't Fidel Castro, or the Archbishop of Canterbury! __Of course it was him! Ok his face__'
Again I hesitated as I recalled the terrible damage caused by the gun-shots, the image still vivid even after several months
'But yeah, same clothes same hair. Who else could it have been?'
'Ok so what then?'
'So then I got the fuck out of there! I had no idea what was going on or whether I might be next. The body, fortunately, was laying on the starboard side of the wheelhouse, so I had no problem getting to the controls.
I threw a cover over the top half and what was left of his face, my waterproof coat in fact, after that I made a run for it as quickly as I damn well could!'
'There was no sign of anyone, no cars, no other boats.'
'No, none that I could see anyway. Like I said it was very dark that night, no moon, and I had no intention of searching around.

You have to understand. __I'd led a sheltered life up to that moment, and this was__'
I shook my head as I recalled the scene yet again.
He said nothing for a while.
I picked up my bottle of beer and drained it.
'So what about the woman?'
He asked.
'Yes her! __It seemed that she, Consuelo, had arrived earlier by taxi in this very same town. She paid off the cab and then took the turning off from the main street, a road that only led in one direction, in fact the same road we've just left.'
'And who noticed this inconsequential event?'
'Couple of old guys who were sitting outside this bar, it was quite late apparently, but they noticed her clearly enough.
Then some young boy turned up, who I was told later had been assigned to look out for her in case she came back, which she did.
Then a cab picked her up outside the church and she left.
Shortly after that, the chief of police turned up in the town with half a dozen men. Too late to do anything of course.'
He nodded thoughtfully.
'You know I'm intrigued Harry. How did your friend the police chief know that it was this woman, Consuelo?'
'Easy! The young boy described her and also the two men who had been sitting outside here having a drink. In addition to that the cab company that took her call had told the police. It was the same driver who had taken her to San Sebastion earlier on. The problem was that he hadn't said anything until he got back to Havana, so they couldn't get here in time to discover what she was up to and to perhaps intervene.'
He nodded.
'Ok, go on with the story. At that point the cops now believed that she was employed by an outside agency, is that right.'
'Employed by *you,* you mean! __You don't need to be coy George!'
Yes they were sure of it and they had her under surveillance.
'So who shot him? Who shot Roldan?'
'I didn't know any of this at the time, but when I got the full story later on it was quite obvious that it was the woman Consuelo.'
'Who told you it was her?'
'The police of course.'
'You mean your amigo!'
'If you like.'
He frowned.

'Why would he tell you something like that? Why would he confide in you?'

'Why not! In the first place I was running arms for the Cubans, and quite possibly risking my life by doing so. And if you remember, he believed that I had tried to save his daughter! He told me about the waitress because he wasn't sure if she might have been a threat to me and indeed to my wife!'

'How so?'

I looked at him indignantly.

'What do you *mean* 'how so'! She'd bumped off one bloke who was carrying arms for the rebels in Central America, how was I to know that I wouldn't be next! This was all *your* idea don't forget!'

'She could have taken care of you on the boat along with Roldan.'

'Maybe she didn't know I was there. I was tucked up in my bunk sound asleep if you remember. Anyway who knows, maybe she did! __Later on I discovered the real reason why she hadn't put a bullet in my head!'

'And why was that?'

'Jesus, why do I have to spell this all out! Because she was a bloody Cuban agent, that's why!'

Again he gave a perceptible nod.

'So did the cop, this guy Raul, know who she was working for?'

'No, not at first. The Cuban security people don't share information with the regular police. And perhaps they didn't know what she was up to either at that time.'

'Someone must have known!'

'Absolutely!'

I gave him a hostile smirk.

'You should know all about this kind of thing. The non-dissemination of information I mean! Not with the police, the FBI or even amongst yourselves! __Am I right?'

Once again my caustic sarcasm simply rolled off his back.

'So how did this guy, your policeman friend, know it was her who shot Roldan?'

'Because initially he didn't know for certain who she was working for, so he had her followed everywhere! When she suddenly took a cab to this town, where we are currently sitting having a friendly drink, she was followed again as I just explained, only he was two hours too late to do anything. __But the circumstances of her being here at the same time that Roldan was killed were pretty overwhelming.'

'Yeah I see what you mean.'

He was thoughtful and said nothing for a full minute.

'Can you get me another scotch, my Spanish ain't that good.'
'Just wave at him and point at the glasses. __It looks like he's got bugger all else to do anyway!'
After a while the old barman brought us two more drinks and then left us again.
'So what made you think eventually that this waitress, Consuelo Jimenez, was in reality a Cuban agent?'
'Yes, well first off it seems certain that she murdered Roldan. I told you all this, it's all in the letter I sent you.
'I just want to get it straight, that's all Harry!'
'Ok. __Roldan was your man, so she shot him. That seems pretty clear. He worked in some government department or other in Havana, I never knew what he did exactly, but suddenly he's making the nighttime run with me to the cayos! Now why was that? I think you probably know the answer! Secondly I discovered some time ago that she had killed two Americans who my wife and I had taken out fishing.
I didn't know who they really were until quite recently in fact.
You have all the information on that as well, no point in going over it again.'
'Humour me.'
I let out a weary sigh.
'Ok. I had visited the old man in Regla who had sold us our first vessel. He told me that he'd come across some engine maintenance manuals for the boat and I went over there to collect them. Just by chance really I discovered the speed-boat she had used. __Or at least very much like it!'
I reached into my pocket and took out a small plastic bag with two empty cartridge cases inside, laying it in front of him.
'I found these on the boat that she'd hired. They should be the same calibre as the gun she used, the same weapon that was found in her apartment when the police searched it.
It was the weapon that was sent to you by the Cuban police, part of their proof that she was working for you, or at least so they believed at the time. American manufacture, same type you guys use, and her prints were all over it. It was pretty flimsy proof in itself, and they knew that. __So if these cartridges match__'
I raised my hands to make the point.'
'If they're different, then she used another weapon, but I'm fairly sure that they're from the same gun.'
He picked up the bag, glancing at it for a second.
'Ok, so why didn't you give these to the police?'
'I did. They asked me to pass them on to you!'
I grinned broadly at him.

'Are you being smart Harry?'
'Just trying to inject a little humour that's all. __Come on for God's sake, obviously nobody knows that I'm here, otherwise you would be in a Cuban jail by now, and I'd be in the next bloody cell!'
He folded the bag carefully and shoved it into his pocket.
'You say that you knew who the two men were who were shot.'
'That's right! They were your guys!'
'How did you know that? __Assuming they were as you say!'
'They had false passports and the Cuban authorities had their mugshots, it seems they'd made quite a few previous visits to Havana, ostensibly to catch marlin, only these blokes were no fishermen, __even I knew that. __So what were they doing on our boat I wonder?'
'It's not important!'
I pulled a face and shrugged indifferently.
'Fair enough.'
'Ok so who told you all this Harry!'
'Who do you think?'
He was silent again, but never took his eyes from mine.
I had no difficulty keeping a deadpan expression because everything I had said about the two Americans was true, or at least close to the truth.
'They were your men, __am I right?'
I said to him.
'Yeah they were. No one of any significance just surveillance guys, foot soldiers really.'
'I see. And dispensable I suppose.'
When I spoke it was with genuine distaste.
He looked at me as though I had just got off the banana boat, shaking his head slowly as he spoke.
'Harry, you really don't know a fuckin' thing do you!'
'I'm relieved to hear that. I prefer a simple life, which I had before you lot came along. __Any more questions?'
He drained his whiskey glass.
'No, I think that about ties it up.'
'What happened to the last lot of weapons I dropped off? You blokes seem to lose track of those deliveries pretty easily!'
'You don't need to know the answer to that!'
I shrugged.
'Fine! __Ok so, now let me ask *you* a question.
I've done everything that your nasty friend asked me to do! So now you can keep your end of *his* bargain!
I want to be left alone, I want my family left alone, is that clear enough!'
'Well now I'm gonna have to sleep on that one Harry.'

With a cynical smile on his lips he started to get up from his chair.
'No don't leave yet George I have something more to say that will interest you.'
I presented him with a winning smile and beckoned for him to sit down again. Which he did, with an expression of little more than mild curiosity.
'Let me get you another drink.'
I beckoned to the barman, before continuing.
'Now the thing is that I wouldn't trust you bastards further than I could piss, so let me explain the situation.
I paused as the man behind the bar brought over a single glass of whiskey, setting it down on the table in front of my companion.

'You should listen very carefully now George, __assuming that is your name. First of all our conversation over the last half hour or so has been recorded, not just here, but as soon as I picked you up. Second, and more importantly, all the events relating to American clandestine intervention in Cuba over the past many months has also been carefully documented. You know this is true because you have the copy, which I sent to you recently.
I said earlier that news of the shooting in Regla was in all the papers in Havana. That was also true and very easy for you to check. However there was no detail, meaning that the authorities of course suspect the covert activities of the organization that employs you, but that's all they know, they have no real proof to connect the murder so they can't print it!
If you continue to put pressure on me, or decide to write me out of this little saga, along with my wife, then all the detailed information which I still have will be passed on to the authorities here in Cuba and also to the U.N.!
This will be very embarrassing for your country and for your administration.
The world will know exactly what the CIA, or whatever you call yourselves, gets up to, __well the rest of the world knows pretty much already what you get up to, but the authorities here will be presented with a complete file of evidence on your recent activities.'
'I get it! __And in doing so incriminate yourself Burgess! The Cuban authorities won't exactly be very happy with you for keeping such information under your hat!'
'Well, that won't matter very much if I'm dead, now will it!'
I paused briefly.
'So I'm not asking for an awful lot really, am I George!'

There seemed to be no point in saying anything further and I sat in silence as I waited for his response.

If the man felt compromised in any way, it certainly didn't show in his face. If anything his expression was one of mild diversion.

He stood up again.

'Interesting discussion Harry!'

'I hope it was. __So now you can fuck off can't you! And I can get on with my life. I've done everything that you asked, so maybe now I can be left in peace.

You've got to ask yourself the question George, or whatever your bloody name is, am I really worth all the potential inconvenience!'

He stared at me for a moment in silence.

'Ok Harry! __So can we leave now?'

'Sure, why not.'

I got to my feet, left some money on the table to cover the drinks and followed the man to the door.

As I passed the table where the five men were still playing cards, one of them glanced up at me, winked and then went back to his game.

Outside in the street there was still a slight drizzle. We both climbed into the old Buick, and I started the engine.

On the short drive back to the coast he spoke up again.

'What happened after you left the bay and returned to Havana?'

'I contacted my friend, as you like to refer to him, by ship-to-shore and told him what had happened.

I was met by a coast guard boat, about fifteen kilometers outside of the port. He came on board with half a dozen men and I explained everything that had happened. Of course it seemed, to me at least that I was the only suspect, and quite honestly I was shitting in my pants. Of course I didn't know at the time that he knew pretty much everything that had gone on, like who shot Roldan, although he never said anything. Not until later that is.

Anyway they took the corpse off in a body bag and cleaned up the mess. They also took the coffee mug that I'd been drinking from. Later on they confirmed that there were traces of something in it to put me out for a few hours. And that was it.'

'Ok.' He remarked simply and fell silent again

The motor yacht was still in the centre of the bay when I reached the brow of the hill. I drove down to the clearing in front of the abandoned fish

sheds and the man got out, turning up the collar of his jacket against the light but persistent rain.
Then he ducked his head through the open car door.
'It's unlikely that we'll meet again Harry.'
'I won't pretend that's not a profound relief.'
I remarked quietly.
He slammed the door, and as I turned the car around I saw that the large vessel had pulled up the anchor and was already approaching the jetty.
I put my foot down and accelerated the old American sedan back up the slight gradient towards San Sebastion.

I really had recorded everything that had been said to the spook using the device that Raul had provided me with.
In his office in central Havana we both listened to the conversation with intense concentration to make sure I hadn't seriously deviated from the script.

'Ok! Good Harry, well done!'
Raul remarked after we had heard the tape for the third time.
'So what do you think, am I in the clear?'
'Yes, I would say so amigo. There doesn't seem to be good reason why they would trouble you again. The threat of revealing their corrupt activities to the United Nations is a very strong defense.'
'But *you* could Raul, __go to the U.N. I mean. They murdered your daughter, so who could blame you for telling exactly what happened. __I hope you don't of course, but__'
I shrugged briefly, to complete what I was hinting at.
'That's true, but naturally we will not! This political advantage for my country is too valuable to sacrifice for mere personal retribution.
And what good would it do I wonder Harry. The Americans will deny everything as they always do, there will be some minor embarrassment of course, some diplomatic protest on both sides, but things will continue no doubt as before.
The real case Harry, is that the CIA is now compromised. They know that we know, and for us that is a strong position. So no. We will keep this 'under our hats' as the Yanks would say.
He gave his usual broad, friendly grin.
'There are other matters involved here which I cannot possibly reveal to you, and it's better anyway that you don't know.

Perhaps in the near future you will understand what this has all been about.'

He leaned back in his chair and out came the cigarettes.

He lit one slowly and with obvious relish.

'Well Raul.'

I commented with a smile.

'If the CIA don't get me then your cigarettes certainly will!'

He laughed at once and leaned forward to stub it out.

'Raul don't be daft, it was a joke!'

'No my friend, you are right. I smoke to many of these things.'

He looked up at me.

'How is Lucia?'

'She fine Raul. Won't be long now.'

'No my friend, __then your troubles really begin!'

'Yeah. __God I can't believe it! Just over a year ago I was getting on a cruise liner in southern England. So much has happened since then, it's hard to believe.'

He relaxed back into his chair again, propping his boots on an open drawer of his desk.

'Are you going back to the UK Harry?'

'Well I suppose I must at some point, to see my parents.'

'You don' miss it, England?'

'No, not for a second! I will go back when the baby is old enough, maybe in a year. I don't quite know what my parents will say when I turn up on their doorstep with a beautiful Cuban woman and a new son.'

'They will welcome you all, I am sure of it!'

'I hope you're right, but you don't know my old man!'

'Your father?'

'Yes. __Well anyway, we'll see.'

He reached for his cigarettes again and then tossed them back on the desk.

'How is business with your café?'

'Great! We're thinking about opening another. __After the baby is born of course and I've got Lucia back to work again!'

He chuckled softly.

'Tha's the idea Harry, otherwise they sit in fron' of the television all day an' get fat!'

'You're right there mate!'

I got up slowly from where I'd been sitting and walked across to the window. To the left in the foreground there was the pristine white dome of the capital building and beyond in the distance the equally pristine, deep blue of the Caribbean.

For several seconds I stared out at the bright, sunlit scene, realizing, not for the first time, why I had chosen to make this country my home, and why I could never return to England.

'I suppose I'd better get going Raul.'
'Lucia knows you're here?'
'Yes, but she doesn't know why.'
I turned to him.
'There's one thing I don't understand Raul. Why were those two yanks killed on my boat?'
'That's easy Harry. The men that shot them, they had Spanish accents of course, you noticed that, but they certainly were not Cuban. And they were hanging around a small, uninhabited island!
So where were they from? Nicaragua maybe, Honduras?
One of those countries. __I'll leave you to figure that one out Harry,'
He was smiling as he spoke.
I turned and picked up the casual jacket from the back of the chair where I'd been sitting.
Walking across to his desk I offered my hand to the police chief.
'Hasta luego Raul.'
'Bye Harry. __See you soon, yeah.'

Our son was born one month later.
It was a quick, easy birth, or at least so I was told by the doctor and also by Lucia.
For me it was a traumatic event, and at one point I was close to passing out.
The tiny infant was healthy and seemed to me to be quite beautiful, although that was I suppose the common reaction of most expectant fathers.
At the moment he was born he cried for just a few seconds, but then settled into his mother's arms, with what looked to me anyway very much like a happy smile.
At home the next day I ran around like a chicken without a head, not knowing quite what to do. Fortunately at least one of Lucia's small group of friends were generally present to take care of matters of which I knew nothing about. In fact there was a constant flow of visitors to the apartment over the next week or two.
Raul's wife and young daughter called in almost every day.

Pasqual's wife as well, who brought her own young baby along with her, and was immensely helpful.

It was a brief but happy time, and gradually I got used to the extraordinary fact that we had a new child, a son, our son!

My overwhelming memories of that brief period were how beautiful and happy Lucia looked, and perhaps incidentally, the smell of babies milk. It's funny, the things that stick in your mind.

The memory of the recent drama was slow to fade, and at night I woke suddenly, sometimes in a cold sweat after enduring nightmares of what might have happened.

Lucia was often awake during those moments and perhaps she understood even without asking. She would reach out and hold me close without the need to utter a word.

We had named our son Peter. It was a sort of compromise, not exactly 'Pedro', which was Lucia's father's name, but close enough.

Three months later I had returned to the apartment after taking the baby for a stroll in his pram along the Paseo de Marti.

It was a regular pattern, which I enjoyed more than I cared to admit, although I was sure that Lucia had easily guessed at my poorly disguised pleasure.

We sat in the living room as she fed the baby while I lounged on the sofa reading the local paper, my Spanish having improved immensely, apart from the odd word which Lucia would translate for me.

'Honey, when you gonna start lookin' for a new premises for the Café?'
'Umm?'
I muttered absently.
'New premises, er, oh, plenty of time for that love!'
I turned over a page.
'No carino, we shou' start lookin' now, don' you think.'
'What's the urgency? The café is doing okay, Pasqual is on top of things, the new waitress is coping nicely, ok not as good as erm__'
I halted in mid flow.
'What I mean is, it's all going very well at the moment.'
'Harry, Cuba is gettin' popular now with the tourists. If we don' open up another place soon, someone else will! We gotta keep up with things!'

'Well that's fair enough love I suppose, but you have your hands full at the moment, and I reckon for quite a while yet.'
'I been thinkin' abou' that! We could get someone to look after Peter in a month or two, maybe jus' in the daytime.'
'Look after him! Who can you trust to do that Lucia?'
'Jumilla.'
'What!'
'The wife of Pasqual.'
'Yes I know who she is, but she has quite enough to do surely.'
'No' really Harry. I ask' her already she say' she don' mind. She tell me she could use the money.'
'Told me!'
I corrected her.
I pursed my lips dubiously as I folded the newspaper.
'Well I suppose so love, but not just yet.'
'No I say, in a coupla' months maybe.'
I released a deep breath.
'Well it's up to you Lucia. If you think she can manage, then fine.'

I knew that Lucia wanted to get back to some sort of productive work again, and I was going to be the last person to discourage her. And so a few months later Pasqual's wife started coming to the apartment on most days, for at least six hours.
While Lucia worked in the café, I took on the occasional charter with Alberto, the old guy from Regla, helping out. Or more accurately, I helped *him* out, as my expertise in fishing was still less than accomplished. However, much to my surprise I was becoming adept at looking after the engine and the auxiliary machinery on the boat, which saved us both time and money.

On the occasional Sunday morning Lucia and I took our son Peter for short trips on our boat, an excursion, which appeared to provide him with infinite joy, especially if Lucia or I managed to catch a small fish.
His expression of amazement was infinitely pleasurable to watch, as the glistening creature was pulled from the sea, struggling on the end of the line, and then finally brought over the side of the boat, flopping impotently around on the deck.
He was a lovely little kid, always with a smile, and only rarely resorting to tears.
I had never imagined or even thought about the enjoyment of having a child and watching him slowly grow and increase in his awareness.

Just the smallest things, his curiosity with his toys and his fascination with any alien object that he managed to get his hands on. His sheer determination to stand up, grasping the edge of a table or a chair with tiny fingers, as he struggled to get to his feet.

For me it provided endless entertainment, and always earned him enthusiastic applause.

Lucia was perhaps less circumspect than me, and gently challenged him when it came to learning to do simple things, to take his first steps, to begin to feed himself, and during the rare tantrum, she would wait calmly and patiently, but with a reproving eye until it was over.

It was a wonderful time, with lasting memories for both of us.

We saw Raul quite often. In the café or if he turned up on the off chance at the apartment, and occasionally when we visited him and his family at his house.

So it was no surprise when I got a phone call from him about ten months after Peter was born.

'Harry, how are you amigo?'
'Good Raul everything's fine. Lucia is really well and the boy gets bigger every day, or seems to anyway.'
'I'm glad to here it my friend. __Harry can we talk briefly?'

I didn't know why but I had an instant feeling of foreboding, accompanied by a prickling sensation at the back of my neck.
'Sure Raul, what's it about?'
'I will tell you when we meet. Do you remember the old restaurant near the market.'
Of course.'
'I don' know how busy you are__'
'I'm not! Lucia is at the café and Pasqual's wife is here, so any time you like Raul.'
'Good, is twenty minutes ok! __There is nothing to be concerned about Harry.'
Somehow his reassurance had the opposite effect.
'Ok, well I'll see you then.'

I told Jumilla that I would be out for an hour or so and would be back before four. Then I pulled on my jacket and almost ran down the stairs to the entrance door. I caught a cab at once and was outside the fruit market within ten minutes.

I crossed the narrow street, busy with porters pushing crates of fruit on barrows, and loading up lorries.
Pushing open the door to the café, I went inside.
Raul was already seated at a table and stood up at once with a brief wave of his hand.
He smiled as we shook hands, but I could tell that this was no trivial matter. Although he wore casual civilian clothes, it was clear that he was carrying the authority of his senior role in the police.
We both sat and Raul ordered beer for us both from the same young girl as before, who appeared not to have changed in the least, neither in the way she was dressed nor in her untidy hair style.
'Good to see you Harry.'
'And you. __Family ok?'
The expression on my face, my nervousness, must have easily given the game away.
'They are both well amigo. __Harry there is nothing for you to worry about here, but I want to explain some things.'
The waitress, just as sullen as I remembered, plonked bottles and two glasses on the table in front of us and left without a word.

'Some matters have occurred which I will explain, but which cannot go any further than here. The reason I tell you this is that you were deeply involved, and I feel that I owe you an explanation.
In addition my friend, you know that I trust you absolutely!'
'Well it sounds intriguing Raul, whatever it is!'
I clutched one of the bottles and took a mouthful of beer.
He lowered his voice, even though the place was virtually empty, with just a low murmur of conversation from the half dozen customers, and with the unrelenting din from the fruit market outside.
Raul filled his glass slowly as he spoke,
'Five months ago there was an attempted invasion of our country. It was on the other side of the island near Cienfuegos.'
'Cienfuegos! I know it, I've been there.'
I replied, although I might as well not have spoken.
'The invasion was repelled and with minimal losses to our forces!'
I interrupted again.
'An invasion! __Raul this is hard to believe! There was no mention of this, not in the papers, not__'
'Let me finish Harry!'
There was no need for him to raise his voice, his expression said everything, and instead of talking I listened.

'It was not a large intervention. Just a few hundred men, mostly we now know, Cuban dissidents who long for the days of Batista. There were also a small number of American undercover 'advisors', or so they call themselves.

Two small American warships were involved in the landing exercise, both of which very quickly made an exit once they realized that the game was up.'

The inevitable packet of fags came out and he lit one.

'Forgive me Harry!'

He remarked, gesturing with the cigarette.

A brief shrug was my only response, because now I was glued to the spot by his astonishing revelation.

'Our view is that they were simply __como se dice?'

He lowered a forefinger into his glass, touching the surface of his beer.

'Dipping their toes in the water?'

I suggested.

'Si, exactly! Perhaps as an exercise for a larger invasion, or maybe simultaneous invasions in different locations. Who can say? About fifty of them were killed. As many wounded and the rest of them were captured.'

'Bloody hell!'

I muttered. My mouth was dry and I took another drink from the bottle.

'We were ready for them! We knew their plans and where they were landing. __Everything! It was all over in four or five hours. Cuban troops simply overwhelmed the rebels. They had no chance!'

I was astounded to say the least by what he had said.

'But Raul, this would have been on TV, __newspapers surely, I mean around the world!'

'Yes it would my friend, __if the world knew about it.'

'If they *knew* about it! How the hell do you cover up something like that? __Five months ago you say!'

'Mas o menos! It wasn't so difficult. A deserted part of the southern coast, only a few civilians living in the area. Not so difficult to carry out Harry, and also to conceal!'

'But surely the Cuban government would have made an international protest about this. I mean this is big news! A major event!'

'Yeah! Like the 'bay of pigs', but smaller. __Sure it was Harry, but the Cuban government is getting smarter now.

They have incontrovertible evidence of the whole invasion. It was filmed extensively, documented, confessions taken and signed by the rebel leaders.'

He paused.

'They should have stayed in their fancy condo's in Miami!'
Now he smiled, but it was not a reflection of his usual cheerful demeanor, it was with overt cynicism. Something I had never seen in the man before.
'But as I say Harry, the Cuban administration is more mature now, 'streetwise' as the Yankees say. This is a major propaganda coup for us, __a lever to encourage the Americans to accept what they could never accept before. They were caught out red-handed amigo! __But with more than one smoking gun this time!
So now we can induce them to lift their trade embargo. Not to interfere in Cuban affairs, allow us to live how we want to live in our adopted socialist manner.
Sure the regime here must also change, become more liberal, and it is slowly beginning to do so. But our independence is paramount and the U.S. must understand this.'

I was speechless now.
I picked up my bottle again, but realized it was empty.
Turning my head I caught the eye of the girl behind the bar,

'Raul this is almost too fantastic to take in. I mean I still don't understand why the Cuban government hasn't made a huge protest about this. You said yourself it's a major propaganda advantage! More than that even!'
'Harry the details of the invasion have been notified to all the major powers. Russia, Britain, Europe, but secretly!
All the members of the UN Security Council now know what has happened and America will of course know that they know. However it will hopefully never need to be revealed.
It is the pragmatic result that we are looking towards, and I believe we will achieve that.'
I took a long deep breath and expelled it slowly.
The young girl brought us two more bottles and nothing more was said for a while as we both drank.

'Now Harry, this is the real reason why I am telling you all this.
We knew about this intended incursion on our country, and this is the reason why we were prepared and easily won the day against these invaders. How did we know? I will tell you my friend.
It was because of courageous people who literally risked their lives to bring this about, to make this happen!'
He was leaning forward now, lowering his voice almost to a whisper, his eyes looking directly into mine.

'The CIA, who as always were at the back of all this, had enlisted the services of people, two people really, who would provide them with details of a strategic location for the invasion.
This has been a long-term strategy about which I knew virtually nothing, at least until some months ago.
You will be surprised to know that the individual who helped set up this whole plan, and participated very successfully, was known to you, if only briefly.'
'Go on.'
I mumbled, my mouth once again as dry as a bone.
'It was Carlos Roldan!'
'Roldan! The dead bloke you mean, __the guy who Consuelo shot on my boat?'
'Yes, only she didn't shoot him Harry.'
I screwed up my forehead.
'Didn't *shoot* him! __Well then who the bloody hell did?'
'Nobody Harry.'
'What are you *talking* about Raul, you're not making any fucking sense here at all!'
'Harry, Roldan is alive!'
'*What!* __Am I *completely* fucking mad or is it you Raul!'
'Neither of us my friend.'
'I saw his *body* for Christs sake! His face was blown to *bits!* There was blood all over the fucking place! Are you telling me I imagined all that!'
'Not quite Harry! __And please keep your voice low.'
The man was entirely composed and I felt stupid, instantly regretting my outburst.
'You see amigo, what you saw was very cleverly devised and staged while you were drugged, __soundly sleeping in the cabin of your vessel.
What you saw was not Roldan's body, but an ingeniously contrived resemblance. Same height, same weight, same cloths, shoes, hair, wristwatch, same crucifix around his neck.
Impossible to tell the difference unless you really wanted to look closely, which we were pretty sure that you wouldn't.'
He must have seen clearly the expression on my face. Which was one of total disbelief, as well as profound shock.
'I'm sorry Harry, really sorry, but it was necessary my friend!
I hope you will understand that. It was never my wish to make a fool of you, or humiliate you, or perhaps more importantly to make you resent me, or maybe worse. You are an intelligent man and when you know everything I think you will understand why we went to such extremes.'
Again he paused for a moment.

'It was a pretty good image, was it not amigo? A good replica.'
Suddenly his smile, the same old familiar grin was back again.
'Well it certainly fooled me Raul!'
I spoke quietly now, still almost completely in the dark, but curious to see what lay beneath the tip of the iceberg, which I was slowly beginning to realize was so much larger that I could ever have imagined.
'Ok, right! __ So when I sailed back towards Havana, totally traumatized, and you met me, took the body away and cleaned up the blood, __was that real blood by the way?'
'Yes, but not from a human.'
I stopped to take a deep breath.
'I'm glad I didn't have anything to eat earlier, I'm feeling distinctly queezy now Raul'
'Queezy?'
'Yeah! Like I'm going to throw up!'
'And are you?'
He looked concerned.
'No, it's passing.'
I took a long pull at the beer bottle to ward off the sensation.

'So, I have a sense that there's a lot more to tell, am I right?'
'Yes Harry, a great deal more.'
'I mean if it wasn't Roldan's body that I discovered that night, then what happened to Roldan?'
'He lives near Santa Clara now with his family, and under a different name.'
'I see. But I thought he was__'
'No Harry, he was loyal to his country and took many risks over a long period of time. Without him this subterfuge could never have been achieved.'
'Good God! So Consuelo was never there that night.'
'No. Not on your boat, not in San Sebastion.'
'So your story, I mean about following her to the pueblo?'
He shook his head.
'It never happened Harry.'
'Jesus! Why is it I suddenly feel so stupid.'
'You're not stupid my friend!
You see we had to convince you of what happened Harry, or I should say what didn't happen, because we knew that at some point you would have to talk to someone from the CIA, and what you said to him that day would need to be convincing, which it was because you believed it yourself.'

'I certainly did! __ So this bloke Carlos Roldan took some pretty big chances.'
'Yes, it was a very dangerous time for him and he deserves his retirement and much more.'
'Yeah I guess he does.'

I stared out of the window at the busy chaos of porters and market traders coming and going about their day-to-day business just across the street. The normality of the scene seemed instantly far removed from the intense intrigues that Raul had been describing.

'So it all ended well then. Apart I suppose from Consuelo!'
I turned to him again.
'Who's side was she really on Raul? The story about her bumping off the two CIA agents wasn't true of course, although I thought I carried that lie off rather well!'
'Yes you did. __ They, I think, were never entirely sure about her, and your story helped to convince them that she was in fact a Cuban agent.'
'And neither were you Raul, __ sure about her I mean. Am I right?'
'Yes, I was sure about her Harry.'
I glanced up at him.
'She was also, like Carlos a loyal agent for the Cuban people.'
'What! But after everything you've told me__ No Raul this is crazy!'
'More trickery I'm afraid Harry. __ Consuelo is alive and well.'

There was a sudden throbbing in my head, and an increase in my heartbeat, which, I was quite sure would have caused any cardiologist grave concern. My vision also became impaired, very much like a migraine or at least what I imagined it to be. Whatever it was I could barely see for several moments, it was like a myriad pinpricks of light and dark that refused to form into a distinct image, and when I touched my fingers to my forehead I could feel beads of perspiration.
'You ok Harry?'
Although I couldn't see him properly, Raul was staring at me with real concern.
'Not really.'
I managed to stammer, barely recognizing my own voice.
He called out instantly to the waitress in harsh, staccato Spanish.
She must have sensed the urgency and within a moment a glass of whiskey had been set in front of me.
Raul held it up for me.

'Drink Harry! I took the glass with hands that shook. Holding it to my lips I sipped at the fiery brown liquid.
'You look very pale amigo!'
'I feel very pale!'
I responded, making a vain attempt at a grin.
'Harry you really don' look too good. I will take you to the 'ospital!'
'No! I'll sit here for a minute or two. It's all this bloody excitement!'
'I am sorry my friend. It cannot be easy for you to accept all this.'
I picked up the whiskey glass again and took another sip. Gradually my vision was beginning to clear and the pounding in my head decreased slightly.

For several minutes nothing was said, as I gradually recovered from whatever it was, the mild catatonic state that had reduced me temporarily to a non-functioning wreck.
'Do you think you need a doctor Harry?'
Raul's look of concern was genuine.
'No it's ok, I just need__'
I faltered as I tried to figure out exactly what it was that I needed.
'A holiday amigo!'
Raul responded with an attempt at a smile.
'A holiday?'
'A lot has happened over the past months Harry. Stress has odd ways of showing itself.'
'Maybe you're right. __A holiday! Yeah, not a bad idea!'

Gradually I felt my strength returning, the temporary loss of vision had cleared, although the headache persisted.
I ripped out a couple of paper napkins from the shiny metal container in the centre of the table, and wiped away the sweat on my temple.
'Sorry about that Raul. Bit of a funny turn there for a moment.'
He had beckoned to the girl for another drink and when I looked up she was staring down at me with a concerned look on her face.
'You ok hombre? You' not gonna pass out or nuthin?'
'No I'm ok now thanks, bit of a headache that's all.'
'I get you some Aspirin.'
'Well that's very kind__'
I began, but she had already returned behind the bar and was rummaging in a drawer.
'Here take three, they' no' so strong!'
When I looked up she was giving me a nice smile, and lifting my hand she dropped the white pills into my palm.

'Thanks again.'
I mumbled.
'No problem muchacho!'
She left us again and Raul gave me a knowing glance.
'You got a smile out of her amigo. I never see *that* before!'
'It's my English charm Raul! Works every time.'
His familiar grin was back again.
'Well don' let Lucia see you usin' it, or you' in big trouble my friend!'
He stared at me carefully.
'You don' look so bad now Harry.'
'No. __ Sorry about that Raul.'

I washed the Aspirin down with another sip of whiskey and gradually began to feel normal again.

'Raul the last thing I remembered you saying just now, unless I was hallucinating, was that Consuelo is still alive.
Or did I dream that?'
I looked at him directly.
'No Harry, you didn' dream!'
Brief silence.
'But Raul I saw her. __ Are you going to explain, or must I guess.
Was it like Carlos, another effigy, another fake corpse?'
'No it was her my friend! And much easier to create what was, ok I confess, another illusion!'
'But I saw her. She wasn't moving or even breathing!
'That was with the use of a simple drug that, for a short period only, sedated as well reduced breathing, providing enough time to convince you of what had happened.'
'Well you certainly did that. __ And what about the CIA man, don't tell me he's still alive!'
'No, he is quite dead I can assure you. His body was transported to the US. I told you this Harry.'
'Yes you did.'
I pondered on what he had said.
'So Raul?'
'She has now, much like Roldan, moved to a new location.
Once again I apologize to you Harry, but it was important for you to believe that they were both killed. I'm sure you understand that.'
'Yes, I do now.'
'It was vital that the Americans should swallow your story, which they did! You were the unwitting lynchpin in the plan Harry.

A foreigner who was compelled to uncover a Cuban agent and deliver him, or in this case her, to the CIA! Cuba owes you a great deal my friend.'
'Yes, you certainly do!'
I slumped back onto the worn bench seat.
'Well to start with you can bloody well get me another whiskey!'

What was I to say to Lucia?
Raul had cautioned discretion, in other words to wait, to say nothing to her, and until I had at least taken time to digest what he had said, it seemed to be the wisest thing to do.

More time had passed, three or four months.
We had opened a second and larger café, opposite the park and close to the capitol building. Finding good staff was not easy, but eventually the new enterprise was moving along smoothly.
Our son Peter was a year and two months now, having taken his first steps with a taut expression of concentration on his tiny face, a mixture of both fear and exhilaration.
With Lucia behind him, her arms outstretched in case he fell and with me enticing him forward, and finally catching him as he released a triumphant squeal of joy.
It was a wonderful and unforgettable time for the three of us.

We continued with the fishing charters as restrictions on visitors from the States gradually eased.
The old man from Regla, Alberto, proved to be invaluable.
It seemed that he had found a new impetus in his advancing years, and now eagerly invited customers on board our boat ready for another excursion into the blue Caribbean waters, with either me or Lucia at the helm.

It was decided, when Peter was eighteen months old that we should finally make the pilgrimage to England. To my parents home in northeast London.
I had phoned my mother and explained to her in tentative, and carefully chosen words what had happened in the preceding three years since I had left the UK.
No mention was made of course of the traumatic events that had entangled both Lucia and myself, most of which still remained an unspoken secret between the Cuban police chief and myself.

At some point I would explain everything to Lucia.
They were events that she couldn't possibly have imagined, much like myself at the time they had occurred.
It was on Raul's advice, and probably sound advice at that.
'Harry, these matters are so important, so vital to this country.'
He had said.
'It is not a case of deception, there are also people in government here who know nothing about these matters, it really is that classified, and that secret! Any disclosure now could cause unknown damage.
It's the old rule Harry, the less people who know, the better!
Lucia is a wonderful person, who knows that more than you and I, but knowledge of these things can be seen as an onerous and unnecessary burden on her.
So wait Harry. Let the dust settle! In a few years maybe__'

There was no need for him to complete what was a perfectly reasonable statement.

Raul drove us to the airport just outside of Havana.
He was smartly uniformed and drove a police car, so there was no problem with parking directly outside the airport entrance.
A couple of suitcases were unloaded, together with Peter's pushchair.
Once our son was carefully strapped in, Lucia embraced our driver, kissing him on each cheek.
'Hasta luego Raul! We'll see you in about a month ok, Maria has the key to the apartment so don' forget. Say my love to her an' to Juanita.'

Raul and I shook hands warmly and then almost instinctively we put our arms around each other, both of us gripping tightly for several moments.
'What can I say Raul! __Thank you for everything.'
We shook hands again.
'De nada Harry! Enjoy your trip amigo! __And take care.'

He waited until we began to enter through the glass doors of the terminal building, then with a final wave he got back into the car.
With lights flashing and the siren shrieking a brief final farewell, he drove away.

With Peter on the inside seat of the aircraft next to the window, we buckled our seat belts.
'This is the firs' time for me Harry!'
Lucia said, glancing at me anxiously.
'What! __You can't be serious!'
I remarked, with a faked expression of bemusement.
'I promise to be gentle darling.'
The comment earned me a playful dig in the ribs.
'You know wha'd I'm talkin' about muchacho! Firs' time *flyin'*!'
'Oh right! __Well you've got nothing to worry about love, because it's the first time for me as well and I've got absolutely no idea at all what's going to happen!'
'Harry!'
She retorted with clear concern.
'Oh stop worrying honey, it's a piece of cake!'
I glanced at our son.
'Look at Peter, he's as happy as a sand boy!'
He regarded us both with a twinkle in his blue eyes and a wide cheerful grin as the plane began moving towards the runway.

The aircraft suddenly surged forward with Lucia gripping tightly onto my arm with both hands. In seconds the noisy rumbling of wheels on tarmac ceased abruptly, and we were floating upwards through the air towards a brilliantly blue sky.
A quick glance through the window and there was Havana below us, in perfect miniature.
A few seconds later and there was nothing but sea, the vast expanse of the Caribbean stretching away into the distance.

We arrived in the U.K. in late afternoon at the major airport just west of London.
The sky was grey and it felt cold, even inside the airport building.
In anticipation we had brought warm coats with us, which were brought out from our cases as soon as we had collected them in the baggage hall.
We bundled our son into a colourful insulated zip-up jacket with a hood, which we pulled up over his head leaving just his small face staring out uncertainly at an unfamiliar environment.

Then it was a long wait at passport control and finally the stroll through the customs area, where we studiously avoided eye contact with the somehow intimidating presence of half a dozen officers.
Then we were pushing our way out through the revolving doors of the vast terminal building, standing for a moment as Lucia took in her first real taste and glimpse of England.
The difference for her was startling.

'I's so *cold* Harry. Is it always like this?'
She remarked, glancing up at heavy grey cloud.
'Most of the time love, except maybe for two or three weeks in the summer, you'll soon get used to it!'
She frowned.
'I don' think so carino!'

We took a taxi, the first in a rank of the familiar black cabs, familiar to me at least.
The driver was cheerful enough and helped me to load the bags and maneuver the pushchair in front of the rear seats.
Then we climbed in and were off. Driving out into the densely green countryside that surrounded both boundaries of the busy motorway.
Lucia turned her head constantly from one side to the other, taking in the unfamiliar scenery as we headed towards the capital.
'I's so *green* Harry! I mean really!'
'That's because it's always raining love!'
'Most of the time, eh Guv!'
The driver broke in cheerfully.
'Where you coming from sir, if It's not a rude question?'
'Cuba.'
I answered briefly.
'Cuba! It's all communists there isn't it guv?'
'Not all. __And the weather's very nice.'
I answered briefly again, not wishing to pursue or encourage that particular line of questioning.
'How's Tottenham getting on?'
I asked for no other reason than to steer the conversation, which I hoped would be brief.
'Not bad sir. Your team is it?'
'It was. Not easy to follow when you're living abroad.'
'Home match with Liverpool on Saturday guv.'
'I must try and get a ticket.'

'Huh! You'll be lucky, big match! __Y' might pick one up on the ground, but it'll cost ya!''
'Well we'll see.'
I said with a smile, turning at once to Lucia.
'Peter looks happy enough.'
She grinned.
'Sure, if he's got his burro to hold on to, tha's all he needs Honey.'
Our son was grasping tightly on to a long eared donkey, his favourite toy, the grey material of which was already showing distinct signs of wear. The boy's eyelids were already drooping and his head was laying on one side, as the movement of the taxi slowly lulled him to sleep.
'Not long now love. About forty minutes maybe.'
I murmured. Lucia's head was resting on my shoulder and I sensed that she also was slowly dozing off after the long journey from Cuba.

As we drew nearer to the region where I had once lived, I could see in the distance the wide expanse of deep green forest on the shallow hillside further to the east.
We had left the motorway now and after a short drive through the familiar suburban towns, the cab turned off into the quiet street where my parents lived, with its neat, ordered semi's and manicured gardens. In three years absolutely nothing seemed to have changed.
The cab drew up outside my parents' house and stopped.
Lucia was asleep and I shook her gently.
'Wake up love we're here!'
Peter was also sound asleep.
Drowsily she stirred and was suddenly wide-awake.
'Is this it Harry? We' here?'
'This is it love!'
With the cabbies help we carefully lifted the pushchair out onto the pavement so as not to wake the sleeping infant. The cases were removed and stood next to the pushchair. Then I paid the driver, giving him a decent tip.
He presented us both with a smile as he opened the driver's door.
'All the best guv!'
'And to you.'
Then he was gone, leaving us standing outside the front gate of the house in the deserted street.
Lucia turned to me, her deep brown eyes looking directly up into mine.

'Carino I am so nervous!'
I smiled at her at once.

'Don't be. You'll be fine and they will love you! __Not as much as I do, but__'
I shrugged and presented her with another reassuring smile.
She ran long fingers quickly through her abundant hair in an entirely unnecessary attempt to make it presentable.
'How do I look Harry?'
'Like an angel sweetheart! As beautiful as always!'

A sound from the front of the house diverted my attention suddenly. When I turned to look, my mother and father were standing in the open doorway.

THE END

Printed in Great
Britain
by Amazon